PRAISE FOR THE TOUCAN TRILOGY

Night of the Purple Moon, Colony East, and *Generation M*

Over 500 5-star reviews

"Three words: Gripping. Palpable. Well-developed." **WORD SPELUNKING blog**

"Beautifully written and youth friendly." **Reader review**

"Outrageous and completely 'out of the box.'" **MY HOME AWAY FROM HOME blog**

"Cramer creates a picture of our world that's both frightening and inspiring in this heartfelt story that both young adults and adults can enjoy." **KIRKUS REVIEWS**

"Strong recommendation!" **YA YEAH YEAH blog**

"A post-apocalyptic survival tale that has pirates, adventure, romance, suspense, betrayal, grief, evil scientists, redemption, and more." **Reader review**

"Thought provoking and thrilling." **Reader review**

GENERATION M

The Toucan Trilogy – Book 3

Scott Cramer

Generation M – Toucan Trilogy – Book 3
Copyright 2014 Scott Cramer
http://www.facebook.com/authorscottcramer

Cover artist Silviya Yordanaov
http://www.darkimaginarium.com

Editorial
Perrin Dillon: perrin.editorial@gmail.com
Laura Kinglsey: http://laurakingsley.yolasite.com
Elizabeth Darkley: http://www.elizabethdarkley.com

Formatting Polgarus Studio
http://www.polgarusstudio.com

For Team Toucan: Otto, Perrin, and Laura

CONTENTS

DAY 1

ATLANTA COLONY – EMORY CAMPUS

"I am a seed of the new society." The man had a gruff, but friendly voice.

Lisette wrinkled her nose in frustration as she carefully adjusted her headphones. They were too big and kept slipping below her ears.

"I am a seed of the new society," she repeated in her deepest tone.

"Science is the way forward," Mr. Gruff-and-Friendly said.

She stretched her arms and legs and pointed her toes upward to form a little tent under the bed covers. "Science is the way forward."

"We are the seeds of the new society." The voices that came through the headphones changed often. This woman had a stuffy nose.

Lisette pinched her nose. "We are the seeds of the new society."

In the dim light, she could see the other girls sitting up in their beds, reciting the phrases of the morning spirit drill. Unit 2A was a long room, and the beds were against the walls. Most of the girls were five years old, like she was. Lisette was glad to see that all the Emotion Meter lights were green. This meant that everyone was happy. If all the EM lights stayed green throughout a spirit drill, they would earn fifteen extra minutes of playtime at recess.

The Emotion Meter fit comfortably over her index finger, and Lisette pushed it down, making sure it was snug. Chandra, her favorite scientist, had explained how it worked.

"The EM measures your skin moisture and pulse. A racing heart indicates you are afraid or anxious. Clammy skin means you are sad. Those are times when the light turns yellow or red. Every Emotion Meter sends a signal to the central control room. If your light changes color, a scientist will turn off the recording and speak to you directly. The signal is also sent to the monitoring station, so I can tell how everyone in the unit is feeling."

Chandra was on duty at the monitoring station now.

Many of the scientists at the colony asked you to call them "Doctor," but Chandra was a little different. She had introduced herself as Doctor Ramanathan when they first met and added, "You can call me by my first name, Chandra, or even 'Mother.'"

Lisette's mom had died on the night of the purple moon, so she had decided to call her Chandra.

"The future is bright."

Lisette yawned. "The future is bright."

She gave a little wave to one of her best friends, Zoe, who was sitting up in the bed beside her. Zoe's brown hair was long and silky, and she could run like the wind. Zoe could outrun every girl in the unit and even the older boys in Unit 2B.

Lisette kept waving the EM light back and forth because it reminded her of Castine Island. Abby and Jordan would let her stay up past her bedtime so they could all go outside and watch fireflies blinking off and on. She missed home.

"The scientists care for us," a woman sang.

Lisette lifted her chin high and warbled, "The scientists care for us."

Just then, a wad of paper landed at the foot of her bed. The "Duck Game" was on. The loser was the one left holding the crumpled drawing of the duck when the spirit drill ended.

Lisette glanced left, thinking it had come from that direction. She saw Emily trying to hide a grin and knew immediately who had thrown it.

Emily was a giggler. Making sure Chandra wasn't looking, Lisette tossed the duck across the aisle to Chloe, the tallest girl in the unit. Chloe flipped it to Lydia, the shortest girl, and Lydia tossed it to Molly. Molly, who could be mean, flung it back to Emily.

"I am Generation M," the woman said in a voice swelling with pride.

M stood for Mendel. Gregor Mendel had studied genetics over a hundred years ago. That was what Doctor Perkins, the scientist in charge of the colonies, had explained on television. "Mendel's work inspires us. Our ability to effectively manage the gene pool will help us optimize society for years to come."

Doctor Perkins liked to use big words, and Lisette rarely understood him.

"I am Generation M," she said proudly.

"The epidemic killed my brother and sister," the woman said.

Lisette swallowed the lump in her throat. Images of her sister and brother tumbled through her mind: Running and jumping into Abby's outstretched arms. Jordan lifting her onto his shoulders, then splashing around in the icy ocean water as they both howled with laughter.

A new woman spoke. "Nine four four ..." Lisette's colony ID number. "... please respond." Her tone was cold and stern.

Lisette let her muscles go limp, trying to slow her heartbeat.

She fixed her eyes on her Emotion Meter light and mumbled, "The epidemic killed ...."

Abby and Jordan are alive, Lisette told herself.

She gasped in horror when she saw her EM light was yellow.

"Nine four four, pay attention!"

Lisette dragged a pajama sleeve across her damp brow, hoping the light would turn green. She buried her hand under the covers, only to remember that her Emotion Meter was sending a signal to the control room and the monitoring station. Chandra glanced over with a concerned expression.

"Abby and Jordan are dead," the woman snapped.

Lisette peeked under the covers and her stomach dropped. The light was now red.

3

"Abby and Jordan are ...." She stopped before saying something that wasn't true.

Or was it true? Shards of terror tore through her body. Lisette didn't know where her sister and brother were. Something terrible could have happened to them.

The duck landed on her bed just as Chandra rose from her seat. Lisette snatched the crumpled paper and squeezed it in her fist.

With a sympathetic look, Chandra removed Lisette's headphones and unclipped her EM.

"Come with me," she said, holding out her hand.

Lisette took Chandra's hand. Together, they moved toward the door. Lisette tossed the crumpled duck behind her back, onto Molly's bed.

As they passed the monitoring station, Lisette felt a chill. All the tracking lines were green, except one: hers. She figured the other Generation M kids had been at Atlanta Colony for so long, they no longer cared about their older brothers and sisters.

Doctor Ingard, who the girls called "Auntie," entered the unit and took a seat at the monitoring station. Auntie wore her hair parted in the middle and a perfume that Lisette liked.

After a brief word with Auntie, Chandra led Lisette down the hall to the counseling room, where they sat on a couch together. The sun was just coming up.

Lisette squirmed next to Chandra, worried about having to face her friends. Because her EM light had turned red, they would only get forty-five minutes of recess time.

"I know it's difficult to stop thinking about your loved ones, but you must," Chandra said.

Lisette folded her arms. "Abby and Jordan are alive! We caught fireflies together. They let me stay up late, and they call me Toucan. I don't like to be called 944!"

Chandra stared into space for a long moment. "You know what Doctor Perkins says, 'Happiness is the best state of mind for learning.' He wants to make sure that every member of Generation M can make an important contribution to the society of the future. If you are happy, your test scores will gradually improve."

Lisette took a test every day, it seemed. Even while she recovered from the AHA-B illness in Medical Clinic 3, the scientists had made her take tests.

"We're measuring your IQ," one scientist had told her.

Lisette looked straight at Chandra. "I want to go home. I want to be with my family again and Timmy, Danny, and Cat!"

Chandra's brow furrowed. "All families change. Children grow up and follow their own paths. We are your family now. The girls and boys in Unit 2A and 2B are your brothers and sisters."

"They are not! That's a lie!" Lisette growled through gritted teeth. "Abby is my sister. Jordan is my brother."

Chandra pulled her close and danced her fingertips across her new stubble of hair. The scientists had shaved Lisette's head many times in Medical Clinic 3 so that the sticky pads with wires coming from them would stay in place on her smooth scalp. The cold band of Chandra's gold ring slid across her scalp, and the stitching of the lab coat scratched her cheek.

"I want to tell you something, but only if you promise you won't say anything about it to anyone," Chandra whispered.

Lisette held up her pinky. She liked sharing secrets.

"Pinky swear."

She and Abby had done pinky swears all the time.

Chandra nodded and locked fingers with Lisette. "If they restore communications with Colony East, you will be evaluated today. Doctor Perkins will review your entire profile."

Lisette scrunched her eyebrows. "What's a profile?"

"Your test scores, the observations made of the way you interact with the other members of Generation M, and how you've done on the spirit drill. Doctor Perkins will decide whether you should remain in the colony."

A chill rippled down her spine. Would they put her outside the fence? Three weeks ago, they put a boy from Unit 3C outside the fence. Everyone in her unit had heard him crying. It frightened Lisette to think she might be alone, so far from home.

Just as suddenly, a thought popped into her mind that made her smile again. "If Doctor Perkins doesn't like me, will someone take me home to Castine Island?"

Chandra shook her head with sad eyes. "Our resources are limited, and the planes only fly between the colonies. Please, Lisette, if Doctor Perkins asks if the epidemic has claimed Abby and Jordan, say yes, even if you believe that it's a lie."

Lisette pressed her ear hard against Chandra's chest, which made the beats of her heart sound louder.

"Abby and Jordan are alive!" Her own heart was thudding faster.

"You can be very stubborn," Chandra said.

Lisette pushed back. "Abby says our family has a gene for stubborn."

Chandra narrowed her eyes and pressed her lips together. Creases formed in her forehead. Finally, she looked up at the ceiling and let out a small sigh. "If I let my hair down, will you promise to lie?"

Lisette's eyes shifted to Chandra's black hair tied in a bun, shining in the sunlight coming through the window.

She loved to see the long hair spill below Chandra's waist.

She folded her arms. "No."

Chandra had already removed the clips on top of her head and started to unfurl her hair.

Lisette reached out and sifted her fingers down through the thick coils, pretending that her hair would grow that long someday. She hoped her red curls would grow back enough to hide her ears by her sixth birthday. By the time she was seven, she pictured her hair coming down to her shoulders. When she was Abby's age, the curls would tumble to the middle of her back.

How she wished that Abby and Jordan were here now. She'd never forget about her sister and brother.

Never!

1.01
COLONY EAST

Doctor Perkins stepped to the fifth-floor window of the Gregor Mendel conference room in Colony East's Trump Tower. His angular face and round glasses stamped a ghostly reflection in the glass as he squinted against the early morning sunshine.

Hurricane David, now a thousand miles to the north, had brought with it the lethal bacteria, and the solution he desired was finally at hand. The surviving population outside the colonies would be eliminated by the epidemic in two-months' time. A Pacific-based hurricane would similarly introduce the bacteria from the equatorial region and address the issue in the western half of the country.

The children called the epidemic the "Pig," for the ravenous appetite the infection produced. He preferred the scientific nomenclature for the bacterial mutation, "AHA-B."

The problem had vexed him since the inception of the colonies. As the survivors outside the colonies grew older and stronger, they would become impatient with Generation M receiving all the adult resources; they would want to destroy his life's work. It was only a matter of time before he and his colleagues could no longer repel the onslaught. Allowing the epidemic to spread would nip the issue in the bud.

Hurricane David had also wrought great physical damage. From his conference room perch, Perkins could see a sample of the devastation.

Debris littered Fifth Avenue, and projectiles had smashed many of the windows in the surrounding buildings. He peered right. All that remained of the Bergdorf Goodman Building on the corner of Fifth and 58th was a large pyramid of bricks, steel girders, and office furniture. He looked left and saw a pond spreading out from the metro stop. As he had read in the damage report, the subway system was completely flooded.

His two-way radio crackled with the voice of Lieutenant Mathews.

"Report," he replied.

"Green light at the airport, sir."

Perkins sighed in relief. Clearing the runway had been critical. Now they could receive a shipment of antibiotic pills from the plant in Alpharetta. "Have you informed Atlanta?"

"That's a negative, sir. Communications are still down, but we're working on it. Estimated time for the fix is zero-eight-hundred hours."

"Make it faster," he said.

"Yes, sir."

Perkins could hear the young lieutenant's desire to climb the ranks.

"Good," he said. "Keep me informed."

He returned to his desk and flipped through a stack of damage reports. Countless skyscrapers were structurally unsound, and the storm surge had swept away every pier along the East River and the Hudson.

The energy report troubled him. The storm had destroyed nineteen of the twenty windmill stations that provided electricity to the colony. Even with diesel generators providing some electricity, the colony was operating at a mere ten percent of its capacity. They had only a five-day supply of fuel on hand to maintain even this subsistence level.

Security was equally troublesome. They could not electrify the northern perimeter fence, and they'd have to limit Zodiak patrols on the rivers, leaving them vulnerable to incursions.

When Perkins considered the totality of the problems, the conclusion was obvious. He wrote "Evacuate" on his notepad, and then underlined it twice.

Just then, Doctor Droznin, hobbling on crutches, entered his office.

Perkins marveled at how quickly the Russian epidemiologist had bounced back after being shot in the knee. She plunked her stout, short frame into a chair and set a graph on his desk.

"New data on the spectral analysis," she said. "We based our initial projections on the bacterial density at the equator. For some reason, it's far greater here."

Doctor Droznin was consumed by research data, and he figured it was best to let her proceed before briefing her on his decision to evacuate Colony East.

He knew the chart too well: a projection of the overall mortality rate outside the colonies. They understood the nature of the illness. The AHA-B bacteria attacked the hypothalamus, the gland that controls appetite. Following a three-day incubation period, a victim experienced ravenous hunger, followed by a high fever. The number of victims would increase rapidly over the first few days of exposure, and then level out. Death occurred in one to four weeks.

The spike in the death rate at Week Four was a consequence of the AHA-B symptoms. They predicted that food riots would break out, pitting the sick against the healthy, and by Week Eight, the population of survivors outside the colonies would be statistically nonexistent.

Perkins massaged his temples. "I see this in my dreams."

"Look at the X axis," Droznin said.

When his eyes fell to the horizontal scale that showed the timeframe of the lethal epidemic's rise, he sat up with a jolt. "Two weeks!"

Perkins's head was spinning. The revelation added to the emergency they faced.

He tented his fingers and informed her of his decision to evacuate Colony East. "I'll schedule a meeting with Admiral Samuels and the company leaders as soon as possible. Lieutenant Mathews will work out the logistics for transferring the cadets. Atlanta can accommodate four companies."

"What about Colony West?" she asked.

"I'm working on another plan for them, which I'll share at an appropriate time." Perkins glanced at his day calendar. "We have a meeting scheduled with Doctor Hoffer and Doctor Ramanathan today at twelve thirty to review the profile of a prospective Generation M member, ID 944. She's marginal, at best. I'll order her to be expelled, and then we can use the time to discuss the evacuation instead."

"Lisette Leigh is the candidate," Droznin said. "She participated in the early drug trials. She's part of my ongoing study on the effects of the antibiotic."

"That's right. Her older sister was ID 1002, the cadet who shot you."

Perkins feared where this conversation was heading. Droznin would argue to keep 944 for research purposes alone.

"Lisette Leigh is five years old, the youngest subject to receive the antibiotic," Droznin said.

Speaking in the patient tone he reserved for the youngest members of Generation M, Perkins leaned forward. "Svetlana, have you seen her profile? Her test scores are abysmal. When we evacuate, we'll be introducing two hundred new members of Generation M to Atlanta Colony. They won't know where to put all of us."

She insisted they conduct the evaluation.

He felt strongly that 944 would contribute absolutely nothing to the society of the future. Now was the time to weed out those who drained vital resources.

"Let's postpone our decision until later," he said, and then tried to change the subject. "How is your leg feeling?"

1.02
BROOKLYN, NEW YORK

Abby doubled over in pain, bringing her knees to her chest and hugging them as waves of cramps rolled through her stomach. She had the Pig.

Dawn light came through the window and cast shadows in the upstairs room where she had spent the night after escaping from Colony East.

The second-floor room had probably been someone's bedroom before the night of the purple moon. The hurricane had damaged the structure. One corner of the ceiling had collapsed, and water was dripping onto the heap of white chunks on the floor below. Through the window, she could see the dark buildings of Colony East across the East River.

Food might ease the cramps a little, but the small bag of cooked rice Abby had brought from the colony was the only food she had with her. She had to make it last.

She balled her fists and crossed her arms. The bag of rice was so close, and the desire to eat so powerful. How could she resist?

Her mind was playing tricks on her. The AHA-B bacteria attacked the gland that controlled appetite, and in turn, that gland sent a signal to the brain, convincing the body it was starving to death. How could she gain control of her actions when her mind was battling itself?

As the cramps intensified, Abby cried out repeatedly, bringing her hands to her mouth. When that failed to muffle her grunts and groans, she buried her face in her backpack and bit down on the strap, hoping the rough fabric pressing against her tongue would somehow mimic a mouthful of food.

As more light entered the room, she could make out the lumpy swell of tarps, blankets, and jackets that served as communal covers for the twenty other girls in the room with her.

The tribe of five and six-year-old girls had led her to this house after she had washed ashore from the East River. They had saved her life.

Abby's head pressed against some part of the girl next to her, and another girl's hand was draped over her shoulder. Everyone was snuggled close to stay warm.

Closing her eyes, Abby returned to the fantasy that had comforted her throughout the long night. She pictured herself walking down a dirt road with tall pine trees on both sides. Traces of purple dust bled into the bed of golden needles at the edges of the road. She could smell the lake in a fresh wind through the trees before she came to it. The opposite shore was two miles away, and the body of water extended to her right and left beyond her view.

The image of the cabin was clear in Abby's mind. Mandy, a girl who had saved Abby and Jordan's lives two years earlier, had described the cabin on the lake in Maine to Abby and given her directions. Mandy's grandparents had lived there.

The cabin sat thirty yards away from the water, with a chimney and a wide window that faced the lake. As Abby imagined herself stepping past the stack of firewood, Toucan burst through the door and raced to greet her, a blur of legs and curly red hair. Abby bent her knees and opened her arms wide, bracing herself for the impact.

She snatched Touk in mid-air, and while hugging her tightly, she carried her inside, where Jordan, Toby, and Jonzy were laughing and joking with each other. Jordan and Toby both had shaggy heads of hair and were lean and muscular from the day-to-day efforts to survive. Jonzy, who had spent the last two years at Colony East, wore thick glasses and looked like he had just stepped out of an exclusive prep school.

A stew of some sort was cooking on the wood stove. Inhaling the aroma, she put Touk down and went over to the pot, trying to guess the ingredients. She lifted the lid.

Abby shrieked from a painful cramp, which interrupted her fantasy. Nobody in the room stirred from the outburst. She figured the other girls, like many survivors, were used to cries in the night.

She sat up and her eyes blurred from the scent of Pink Sugar perfume mingling with the stink of dirty clothes and mildew. Grimacing, she tested her limbs and checked her fingers and toes. Nothing was broken or sprained from tumbling in the raging East River; there were only scrapes and bruises. Her wristwatch had also survived. It was 5:30.

She reached into her backpack and wrapped her fingers around the two-way radio. The rush of relief gave way to apprehension as she brought it to her ear. Were the batteries still good? She turned on the radio, heard the satisfying static in answer, turned it off, and returned it to the pack.

The walkie-talkie was the only way to communicate with Jonzy, who remained inside Colony East.

Abby stood and trembled in the chilly air. The communal blanket and collective body heat of the slumbering girls had kept her toasty throughout the night, but now her damp blue jeans pressed cold and clammy against her skin.

She slung her pack over her shoulder and made her way to the door, stepping next to heads and in between legs.

Reaching the doorway, she was about to look back at the tribe of sleeping girls, but instead continued into the hallway and down the steps. She could do nothing for them. Many would get the Pig, if they didn't have it already. She had to put the girls out of her mind. Move on.

In the kitchen, she fixed her eyes on a bounty of potatoes, dried fish, some other type of dried meat, and bottles of water on the counter. She slipped three potatoes into her pack, aware that she was stealing, yet unable to resist the pull of the food. She unscrewed a bottle cap and took a long drink of water.

On the front porch, she groaned as a fresh wave of cramps twisted her gut. No matter how hungry she was, she could not steal from the girls who had saved her life. She returned the potatoes to the counter, considering it a small victory for her willpower.

Then, unable to control her hand, she picked up a potato, brought it to her lips, and wolfed it down, completely raw.

Outside, she walked down the porch steps and stopped, feeling guilty about what she had done, yet relieved that the tiny chunks of potato sitting in her stomach were finally settling her cramps.

Under different circumstances, she would have said it was a beautiful morning. The sky was pale blue and the temperature was mild. The slight hint of a breeze carried a tang of saltiness. Beyond the broken skeletons of two bridges, Colony East rose in the distance, and The East River, thick with floating debris, moved along swiftly. She marveled at the towering hull of the freighter beached on the bank, knowing it had saved her life. Were it not for the freighter diverting a channel of water, the rapids would have swept her farther down river.

She had to make it to the Ribbentrop Fish Market today, where she planned to meet Toby. The fish market was across from the gate where she had caught her very first glimpse of Colony East in a section of Brooklyn she guessed was at least several miles away.

"Where are you going?"

Abby turned. A girl stood on the porch. She wore an oversized man's shirt and a pair of rubber boots that rose to her knees. She had ratty hair, smudged cheeks, and a bright smile. Her eyes sparkled in the sunlight.

Abby looked down. "I'm going to meet a friend."

"Are you coming back?" the girl asked.

"Sure," Abby said. It was a lie.

"What's your name?"

Abby paused, thinking that if she told her, this girl might tell her what her name was. Abby didn't want to know her name. She didn't want to know her age. She didn't want to know anything about her. Survival demanded a cold heart.

Abby turned and started to walk. "I have to hurry."

"My name is Stacy."

Abby pretended she hadn't heard.

"Do you want something to eat?" Stacy called out.

Abby's chest hitched sharply, confused by the way she was acting, but she kept walking.

1.03
CASTINE ISLAND, MAINE

Jordan paced through the dark empty house on Castine Island, clutching Abby's note and balling his fist in guilt. When his sisters had needed him the most, he had not been there for them.

He strode from the kitchen that his supposed friends had stripped bare to the memory room, where his eyes fell on the shelf of photos — loved ones who had died during the night of the purple moon — the glass catching the flickering candlelight.

He read the note again.

> Joining the crew of news gypsies was the best thing you ever did.
> We are so proud of you.
> Love,
> Abby and Touk

Neighbors had told Jordan what had happened while he was away from the island, sailing on the news gypsy vessel, *Lucky Me*. He had bartered news along the east coast. Touk had been so sick with the Pig that Abby and Toby had taken her to Colony East, where they had hoped an adult doctor would treat her. Prior to that, Toby was the only one who had helped Abby and Toucan on the island. Everyone else, including Jordan's best friend, Eddie, and Abby's friend, Mel, had avoided them, afraid of catching the Pig. From the Portland Trading Zone, Abby, Touk, and Toby had gotten a ride to Colony East from a boy, Spike, who worked for the fuel king, Martha.

Jordan had to find Spike.

At first light, he picked up his bag of supplies and stepped outside. He stopped on Melrose Street and considered which way to go. The harbor was to the left. If *Mary Queen of Scots*, the boat he had sailed to the island just before the hurricane struck, was still in one piece, he'd sail to the Portland Trading Zone. To the right lived Eddie. Jordan wanted to look Eddie in the eye and ask why he hadn't helped his sisters, but he headed for the harbor instead.

The strong winds of the storm had deposited mountains of seaweed on Front Street and damaged many of the buildings and storefronts. The big window at Sal's barbershop was broken. He prayed that *Mary Queen of Scots* had fared better.

He feared the worst at his first view of the harbor. Not one boat was moored in the half-mile stretch between the docks and the jetty.

Jordan stepped onto the dock and headed to the spot where he'd lashed the boat to two pilings, but there was no sign of her mast. What had happened? He peered over the side of the dock. She was there. Barely afloat, her hull filling with water, but she was there. The mast, though, had snapped in half. He figured he could still rig the sail in such a way as to harness the power of the wind. It might take six days to reach Portland, but it was better than being stranded on the island.

He considered another option. A small sailing skiff was moored on the eastern side of the island. He and Eddie had used the boat to teach the little kids how to sail. With some help, he'd be able to carry the skiff across the road and launch from the rocky shore. At the very least, he could take the skiff's mast and use it on *Mary Queen of Scots*.

He bailed *Mary's* hull, secured new lines, and stowed his backpack in the stern. Then, he started out on the two-hour walk to the eastern shore.

He saw a few kids along the way. All were strangers to him.

A boy who appeared to be about ten ran up to him and pleaded, "Do you have any food? My stomach is killing me." His eyes were misty from pain.

Jordan's heart demanded he help. "Sure, I have something for you."

Jordan gave him directions to *Mary Queen of Scots*. "There are potatoes and smoked fish in a canvas bag. There's a knife in the pack. Only take half a potato, okay?"

The boy sprinted away, holding his sides.

Jordan continued walking on the road that was soon matted with seaweed and shells. Farther on, he saw a large group of kids gathered at a rocky inlet. The eastern side of the island faced the open ocean, and large waves pounded the shore.

As he drew closer to the group, he saw that they were collecting clams. He had gathered shellfish along this shore many times himself, but he never ate them on the spot, raw, as these kids were doing. Kids were whacking clams on the rocks to crack the shells.

All of a sudden, a fight broke out between two girls. It seemed they had both seen a clam at the same time. Others moved in to separate them.

He arrived at the mansion thirty minutes later. The large rambling house on the hill would always hold a special place in his heart. He had lived here with Abby and Touk and others right after the night of the purple moon. After the Leighs moved out, the mansion had seen many different inhabitants come and go.

Behind the house, resting on its side against a row of rain barrels, was the skiff. The mast was still intact and it would work on *Mary Queen of Scots*, though he could have kicked himself for forgetting to bring pliers. He needed them to remove cotter pins and unbolt the chainplate.

To see if anyone inside the mansion had pliers, he stepped through the front door and came face to face with Eddie. He almost didn't recognize him. Eddie's head was shaved, and he had grown a few inches taller.

Eddie raised his hand to give Jordan a high-five. "When did you get back?"

Clenching his fists, Jordan took quick breaths to settle himself. "I need pliers."

"I'll get 'em."

When Eddie returned with the pliers, Jordan took them without uttering a word, and then turned and headed for the skiff. Eddie tagged along.

"I heard DJ Silver mention you on the radio," Eddie said. "He played *Here Comes the Sun*. That was your mom's favorite song, right?"

DJ Silver was in charge of "The Port," a kid-operated radio station in Mystic, Connecticut. Jordan, recovering nearby at Wenlan's clinic after his brush with death at the hands of the pirates who sank *Lucky Me*, had wanted to get word to Abby that he was all right. Kids on Castine Island listened to The Port at night when the signal was its clearest. DJ Silver, however, only played music. He never delivered news, but he would do song dedications. So Jordan had asked him to play the Beatles song and dedicate it to Abby and Toucan.

"It's was my dad's favorite song," Jordan said, simmering with anger.

"You need help?" Eddie asked.

Jordan walked around Eddie and yanked the cotter pin from the other stay.

"You leaving again?" Eddie asked.

"Listen, I got it, okay. You can …" Jordan's voice trailed off because he had nothing else to say to Eddie.

"I can what?" Eddie asked.

Jordan loosened the bolts that secured the chainplate, and then unscrewed each one using his fingers. That freed the mast. Next, he wrapped the stays around the mast and balanced it on his shoulder.

"Let me help you," Eddie said.

Jordan started walking. The mast was heavy and a rivet cut into his shoulder. His anger erupted, and he flung the mast. It hit the ground and bounced up. Blood pounded in his ears.

"What's your problem?" Eddie asked.

A knot in Jordan's chest threw off hot sparks. "My problem! Abby and Touk needed you."

"They needed *you*. You're the one who left them to be a news gypsy."

Breathing fast and shallow, Jordan felt his neck pulsing heavily at a different drumbeat from that in his ears.

He cocked his fist back, lunged, and struck Eddie squarely on the nose.

Following a brief moment of confusion, Eddie clenched his jaw and charged, wildly swinging his fists. One connected with Jordan's cheek.

Eddie was still coming, and Jordan met the ball of fury head on, both boys grabbing and punching, delivering just as many blows as they received.

Eddie's eye puffed up and blood streamed from his nose, splattering on both of them. Jordan felt his lip bulging fat, and when he tasted warm, salty liquid, he realized his nose was bleeding too.

He got Eddie in a headlock and squeezed him tightly, but he released the pressure, stunned at how hot Eddie felt.

Eddie wormed his way free, wrapped his arms around Jordan's waist, and drove him forward. Jordan lost his balance, and Eddie landed on top. Jordan braced for a new round of pummeling, but Eddie rolled off and lay on his back. It was over. They remained like that for a moment without speaking, both breathing hard.

"I was afraid of the Pig," Eddie said. "We all were. That's no excuse, I know. I'm sorry. I still think about it a lot. I should have helped them."

"Yeah, maybe I should have stayed here," Jordan said.

Eddie pinched his nostrils to stem the trickle of blood. "How could you have known what would happen? I wish I could have gone with you."

Jordan knew Eddie had wanted to join him on *Lucky Me*, but he had needed to go by himself. "Hey, I'm sorry."

"Jordan, I want to go with you. Abby always said that if kids work together, they're stronger, right?"

He and Eddie had proven that many times. They made a good team. "I'd really like you to come with me."

Eddie dragged his blood-splattered sleeve across his eyes. "There's something you need to know. I have the Pig."

1.04
COLONY EAST

Lieutenant Dawson moved to the window in his living quarters at the Biltmore Hotel where the morning sunlight made it a little easier to see. He unsealed the plastic bag and removed two separate photographs.

Feeling light-headed, he fixed his gaze on his wife, Lisa, and then turned her photo over to review his notes: "Five feet, four inches," "pink pajamas," "black and white bathrobe," "second floor bedroom faces west," and "elm tree outside window."

Dawson braced his forearm on the table for stability and added with a fine-tipped marker: Wedding ring with three small diamonds.

Next, the photo of Sarah. In the picture, his daughter was eleven months old, her toothless grin and chubby cheeks frozen in time. With a sob working its way up his throat, he reviewed the back of her photo: "three-years old now," "small, round birthmark on her elbow," and "light brown hair."

He swallowed the sob and unfolded the map he had drawn of Mystic. In the center was the address of the house he had shared with his family prior to the first epidemic. Twenty-three Walpole Avenue. He had traced two different routes from Colony East to the house. He added several details. One block west of his house, at the corner of Walpole and Berkley, he wrote, "International House of Pancakes." The tall IHOP sign was an excellent landmark.

He returned the map to the bag that he sealed and slipped into his rear pocket.

At 0700 hours, he started for the wing of seven-year-old girls. He knocked on doors, poking his head into each room. "Good morning. Rise and shine. Fall out to the hall."

Soon, ten girls stood at parade rest in the corridor. Since the power was out, he trailed his flashlight along the ceiling. "At ease. Have a seat."

Earlier, by radio, Admiral Samuels had ordered Dawson to inform the cadets about the evacuation and determine if any of them showed symptoms of the AHA-B illness.

The girls yawned and rubbed their sleepy eyes.

"I'm proud of how you've conducted yourselves over the past three days," Dawson said. "It's not easy being cooped up together for so long."

Cadet William's hand shot up.

"Tabby, please hold your question."

She waved her hand and blurted, "Can we go outside today, sir?"

"I'm sorry, but the answer is 'no.'"

The other cadets responded with a chorus of groans.

Tabby raised her hand again.

Dawson sighed. "What?"

"What happened to Abby?"

The cadet grapevine was alive and well. Abigail Leigh was a mystery to them. Here one day, gone the next.

"Cadet Leigh is at Medical Clinic 17," he said, hating to lie, but Job One was to keep the cadets focused and calm.

The girls traded glances and were about to ask more questions.

"No more interruptions or everyone will be confined back to quarters when the cooks bring us chow." The threat brought instant silence.

He told them about the evacuation. The first hand shot up before he had finished.

He sighed and pointed to Cadet Baker. "Let's start here."

"Where are we going?" Baker asked.

"Atlanta Colony or Colony West. However, I don't know which one yet. I'm meeting with Admiral Samuels and the other company leaders later on. I'll tell you as soon as I know."

They fired more questions at him, and Dawson realized their curiosity and pent up energy were too much to contain.

"When are we going?"

"Tomorrow, or maybe the day after," he said.

"Sir, I have a lot of friends in Sheraton Company. What if they go to a different colony?"

He nodded, knowing how important friendships were at their age. "My father was in the Navy, and when I was growing up, we'd move to a new base every two years. Each time we had to move, it made me sad, but I soon made new friends. You will too."

"Can we see our friends before we go?"

"I'll speak to the admiral about it," Dawson said.

"What should we pack?"

"I'll tell you as soon as I find out," he replied.

"Will you still be our company leader?"

He smiled. "You can't get rid of me that easily. Now I have a few questions for you. Is anyone feeling hot or feverish?"

Hands remained at sides.

"Does anyone have a tummy ache?"

Nobody spoke.

Dawson pulled his shoulders back. "Please see me if you don't feel well at any point. Chow should be here shortly. Dismissed."

He held similar meetings with the cadets on the second and third floors. After finishing with the fifteen-year-old boys on the fourth floor, he stood outside the living quarters of Jonzy Billings and barked, "Cadet Billings, is that any way for you to make a bed?"

"I can do a better job, sir," the boy announced loudly as they had arranged earlier.

Dawson stepped inside, closed the door behind him, and removed the bag containing the photo of Sarah from his pocket. He handed it over to

Jonzy. "Stow it under the mattress. After chow, study the material in the latrine."

Jonzy gave him a thumbs-up. The boy wore thick glasses and often tripped over his own feet, but Dawson was confident that if Sarah were alive, Jonzy would find her.

"Okay, let's review the plan," Dawson said. "The pills are arriving today. I'll pass them out and save the extra ones."

Jonzy outlined the next steps. "We meet on the top floor at 2300 hours. My two packs of supplies are up there already. At midnight, I will communicate with Abby. I hope she'll be with Toby. I'll tell them the fishing is good. They'll know to meet me at the fish market."

Dawson took over. "We'll leave the Biltmore and head up the west side of the colony. In the Red Zone, I'll cut the fence and return to the Biltmore."

Jonzy spoke up. "If I find Abby and Toby, I will report on the radio at 0600 hours, 'The eagle has landed.' If I'm still looking for them, I'll say, 'The fish aren't biting.'"

"Good," Dawson said. "Keep all radio transmissions short and confusing. You never know who might be listening in."

"Yes, sir. After I meet up with Abby and Toby, we'll go to Mystic and meet up with her brother, Jordan. Then, we'll look for your daughter."

Dawson felt a sob forming in his chest. "When I get to Atlanta Colony, I'll convince the scientists to make more pills at the Alpharetta plant."

"Piece of cake, Lieutenant." Jonzy went to give him a high-five and missed his hand by a good six inches.

1.05
EMORY CAMPUS

With the spirit drill over, Unit 2A was a flurry of activity as the girls straightened up and attended to personal hygiene. The countdown clock showed they had fifty-two minutes before they had to be at the dining hall for their first meal.

After tucking the sheet under the mattress and smoothing out the blanket, Lisette jumped into her blue uniform and yanked the zipper up high. She tugged at her left sleeve to make it easier to read her colony ID. The numbers 944 were stitched in yellow.

She grinned when Petty Officer Murphy entered the unit and barked, "Let's move it, ladies."

Everyone loved Murph, who took charge of them every morning while Chandra and Auntie sorted out the mobile lessons. Murph had red hair, freckles, and very pale skin. She'd said she had joined the Navy because she was sensitive to sunlight. "You don't get any sun on a submarine."

Zoe had yet to make her bed, and Murph stopped before her, placing hands on hips. "Is this any time to dilly-dally?"

Under Murph's watchful eye, Zoe got to work, while those who had finished their tasks gathered around them.

With a little smile, Murph tapped her toe. "Doctor Perkins likes us to use big words with Generation M, so this is my big word of the day. Promptitude. I'll use it in a sentence for you. I wish Zoe would show greater promptitude in the morning. Now, who can tell me what promptitude means?"

Lisette raised her hand. "Being on time?"

Murph gave her a big thumbs-up. "Five gold stars for Miss Leigh."

Lisette gushed with pride.

"This is Lisette's last day at the colony."

Everyone turned. Molly was gliding a brush through her long brown hair.

"I heard Mother talking to Auntie," Molly said, crinkling her nose. "Mother said Lisette is too stubborn to be a member of Generation M. Doctor Perkins is going to kick her out because she can't forget about her brother and sister."

Lisette shivered in the frigid blast of words.

Murph cleared her throat and narrowed her eyes at Molly. "It's not polite to spread rumors."

"Sorry," Molly mumbled.

Murph clapped. "What's everyone standing around for? Look alive! Fall in."

The girls formed two lines, one for the west wing bathroom and one for the east wing bathroom.

Murph knelt before Lisette and lowered her voice. "Here's a special word of the day just for you ... perseverant. It means never giving up. Doing what you think is right, and never giving up. Lisette Leigh is perseverant."

Still troubled by what Molly said, Lisette took her place in line waiting for the west wing bathroom.

Zoe whispered in her ear, "If they kick you out, I'll go with you."

Emily said in Lisette's other ear, "Molly's just mad that she lost at the duck game."

The kind words made her feel much better.

The line moved and she received her toothbrush, a tube of toothpaste, and a mobile lesson from Chandra. Lisette strapped the iPod to her arm, inserted the earbud, and pressed play. The voice of her Russian teacher began reviewing vocabulary words. Doctor Perkins had said that he wanted every member of Generation M to be fluent in Russian, German, and English because of all the scientific work recorded in those languages.

In the bathroom, Lisette stepped up to a sink and got up on her tiptoes to see her face in the mirror. She reached for her bottom tooth and felt the mad beating of butterfly wings in her chest when it wiggled. The tooth was much looser than last night. She put a dab of toothpaste on her brush and brushed carefully around the loose tooth.

Lydia moved to the next sink. The six-year-old always had a serious expression, as if she had just made it to the final round of the Atlanta Colony spelling bee. Knowing what was coming next, Lisette grinned at Zoe, two sinks away, who grinned back.

Lydia was the only girl in the unit who kept pace with her language lesson while brushing her teeth.

"Ya paneemayoo," Lydia said, dappling the mirror in front of her with white dots of toothpaste.

Lisette and Zoe doubled over in laughter.

A piercing whistle gained their attention, and they stopped laughing. Murph stood in the doorway with a stern expression. "Focus, ladies. The countdown clock is ticking."

They started giggling again as soon as Murph was gone.

1.06
BROOKLYN

Hugging her pack against her chest, Abby limped through the crowd streaming to the bank of the East River to pick through the assortment of items that had been washed ashore.

The kids surged forward to explore the bounty. Abby could see value in gathering boards for firewood or a soggy sleeping bag, but wondered what anyone would do with a rusty baby stroller without wheels, a broken umbrella, or a swollen paperback. Maybe the artifacts reminded kids of life before the night of the purple moon.

She kept an eye out for Toby. It would be easy to spot the dark blue Colony East coveralls among the multicolored combinations of clothing worn by the survivors. Assuming he was still wearing the uniform, of course. Had Doctor Perkins, who had kicked Toby out of the colony, allowed him to keep it? Maybe Toby had discarded the uniform, wishing to blend in with the crowd.

Despite the scrapes and bruises that hobbled her, Abby was glad to be on the move. The sights and sounds helped take her mind off her hunger. Better to focus on something louder, brighter, and more interesting than the gnawing sensation in the pit of her stomach.

Moments after she congratulated herself for this newfound approach, an aroma of roasting meat slowly crept up her nostrils. She spun around, looking for the early morning barbecue, ready to march over and ask for a bite. When she didn't see the source, she considered investigating the side streets. The odor was like a vine reaching out and lacing around her wrist, pulling her away from the river and her ultimate destination: the fish market. She had to resist the temptation.

She tried breathing through her mouth, hoping to eliminate her sense of smell, but her taste buds and pores soaked up the delicious aroma in the air. Gripped by hunger, she wandered across the road where she fell to her knees on the sidewalk and squeezed her eyes shut.

"If I have the power to stop, I have the power to avoid distractions," she said to herself. She got to her feet and stumbled back toward the river.

Farther on, kids were wading into the water to snag floating debris; some were building a raft by lashing inner tubes together. She stopped near them to rest.

She was about a mile from the Brooklyn Bridge. The fish market was another hundred meters beyond the base of the bridge. To reassure herself she still had the walkie-talkie, she reached into her pack, letting out a sigh of relief when she felt it inside, then shuddered as her fingertips brushed the bag of rice. Her mouth flooded with saliva, and she ripped her hand from the backpack to wipe the drool from her lips.

She thrust her hand back into the pack, grabbed the bag of rice and gobbled down the last morsels of her food supply. She marveled that her stomach cramps disappeared instantly.

With new energy, she pushed onward, but soon the cramps were worse than ever.

She picked her way among the carnival of scavengers to the river's edge for a drink, hoping that filling her stomach with water would ease the pain. She brought the water to her mouth in a cupped hand and gagged when she swallowed. It was salty.

Nearby, a large fish floated on its belly. She waded up to her waist into the water; careful to keep her pack high above the water, she pinched the tail between her fingers, and then pulled the fish onto the mud. She recognized it as a striped bass and guessed it weighed twenty pounds or more. They had caught stripers off the rocks at Castine Island. She poked its fleshy belly and lifted a gill. The fish was dead. She brought her nose close to the scales and sniffed. Rotting fish had a distinctive odor, but this fish didn't smell rotten at all. An alarm suddenly sounded from deep within Abby, and she looked around warily, eyeing kids in her vicinity, potential competitors for her meal, but none of them seemed particularly interested in the fact that she was hovering over a large, dead fish.

The fish presented as many problems as it solved. It could satisfy her hunger for days, and she could share it with Toby and Jonzy, but once it started to rot, it would be useless. She needed to clean and cook it soon.

She wondered if she could scrape off the scales and slice open the belly with a sharp piece of glass. Broken glass littered the ground outside most buildings. But how would she cook the fish? She could strike a deal with someone who already had a fire going, offering a portion of it in return for them cooking it.

She cradled the fish in her arms and began walking, but after a few steps, she realized it was too heavy and awkward to carry this way. She set the fish down, opened her pack, and then worked the pack over the fish's head.

Head first, only half the fish fit into the pack. She slung the pack on her back. With her arms free and the weight centered, she could take small steps.

Most kids ignored her, but a few gawked. From the desperate look in their eyes, she thought they had the Pig and wanted her fish. She met the gaze of some, trying to show she was strong, that she would fight to keep her food. She lowered her eyes at those survivors she sensed might accept the challenge and trudged onward, desperately hoping they wouldn't attack.

As frightened as she was, she counted her blessings. For those infected with AHA-B, a fever spiked in the advanced stages of the illness. She could not imagine the burden of a soaring temperature and hallucinations on top of the savage hunger she was already experiencing.

Abby stopped before a puddle. The salt from the river water she had swallowed burned the back of her parched throat. She went down on one knee and drank some of the brown water. It tasted good, so she drank more. Soon, she started coughing from the mud residue. Strangely, the grit coating her tongue and throat seemed to diminish her hunger pangs. She smiled, recalling how she had made mud pies as a little girl and served them to her dolls. Telling herself she had no time to reminisce, she took another mouthful and swished the water between her teeth to sift out the grit.

When Abby stood, a cramp exploded in her right thigh and she tumbled backward. Grimacing, she worked her arms free of the backpack straps as the muscle in her leg knotted even tighter, radiating spasms of pain. She pounded her thigh with her fist until it softened. Afraid her leg would cramp again, she thought briefly about leaving the fish behind, but in her mind, the fish had become as important to her survival as the radio.

She struggled to her feet, slung the pack over her left shoulder, stiffened her right leg, and hobbled forward.

After what seemed like hours, she spotted the fish market. The area was more crowded and lively than she remembered. She suspected the survivors were full of pent-up energy after the hurricane and were happy to be outside again. Kids were throwing a Frisbee around and playing soccer with a ball fashioned from duct tape. Skateboarders and kids on bikes flew by, missing her by mere inches.

She sadly realized the laughter and smiles would turn to cries of anguish within days, or sooner, as the epidemic gained a foothold. For many, a desperate hunt for food would replace the games they were now playing. Others would decide to fight them off to protect their food supplies. Would anyone share?

Abby finally made it to the market, staring up at the sign: *Ribbentrop Fish. The Freshest Fish in Brooklyn*. With a small smile playing on her lips, she entered the market, lugging the dead striper along.

The store now served as a shelter. Mattresses, heaped with jackets and blankets, were strewn on the floor. She stuck to the narrow pathways between them, and when a blanket moved, she realized someone was lying underneath it.

Abby felt her stomach drop. In the far corner, a leg and arm were sticking out from the bedding. She quickly recognized the Colony East uniform. It must be Toby. She choked back a sob. From the moment she learned he had been kicked out of Colony East, she had harbored a nagging feeling she would never see him again.

Her heart racing, she moved closer, but wondered if it really was him. The foot looked too small. Her hope lifted when she saw 1094 stitched in yellow on the sleeve. That was Toby's Colony East ID. Suddenly, the blanket flew back as a girl jackknifed up. Abby gasped and lurched back. The girl reached under the covers and brandished a knife.

Losing her balance, Abby tumbled backward. Sweat trickled down into her eyes, and she blinked through the sting of salt and grime. The girl appeared to be twelve or thirteen. She had spiky brown hair, a nose piercing, and a hard stare that warned, "Mess with me at your own risk."

The girl must have sensed that Abby posed no threat, because the threads of veins flaring in her neck slowly flattened, and her shallow breathing deepened.

She lowered her knife and slowly rolled up the sleeves of the Colony East uniform, revealing tattoos of purple moons and streaking comets.

Abby sucked her cheeks and mashed her tongue against the roof of her mouth to work up enough saliva to form words. "That uniform belongs to my friend."

"You're Abby Leigh, right?" the girl whispered.

Stunned, Abby nodded.

"My name is Lexi. We have to go meet Toby."

1.07
EMORY CAMPUS

The girls of Unit 2A advanced their iPods to the next mobile lesson and followed Murph outside, heading to first meal.

Doctor Martin was Lisette's History of Science professor, and his boring voice crackled through her earbud. "Darwin published his theory of evolution with compelling evidence in his book *On the Origin of Species* ...."

Lisette gaped at the devastation. The storm, which had kept them confined to their dorm for the past three days, had turned Emory Campus into a dangerous obstacle course. Ahead, the boys from Unit 2B walked inside orange cones set up to keep them away from the downed trees and power lines. Lisette caught a glimpse of her friend, Richard, and wished she could show him her loose tooth, but she'd have to wait until recess.

All around her, the cleanup was in full swing. Chainsaws whined as Navy crews cut up toppled trunks and tree branches. She shivered when she saw ensigns replacing a broken window in Medical Clinic 3.

She had spent three months in the clinic when she had first arrived at the colony and never wanted to go inside that scary place again. Scientists, trying to find an antibiotic that would cure AHA-B, had injected her with liquids that made her toes and fingers burn and tingle. Beeping machines had kept her awake at night. She had shed many tears for her friend, Lily

Meyers, another girl her age sick with AHA-B. One day, Lily's bed was empty, but nobody would tell Lisette what had happened to her friend.

Midway between the dorm and Heisenberg Hall, Lisette got a rare glimpse of survivors outside the colony. A tall fence covered in green fabric surrounded Emory Campus, but a piece of the fabric had ripped. Through the opening, Lisette saw survivors peering in with their lips moving and fingers clinging to the chain links.

She couldn't hear what any of them were saying above Doctor Martin's lecture, so she pretended to scratch her ear and removed her earbud.

"Feed us." "I'm starving." "Please, I'll eat anything." "Help us." The raspy voices crackled with fright.

Lisette reinserted the bud as a wave of panic washed over her. *Would Doctor Perkins put her outside the fence if she told the truth?*

With a chill from the desperate cries of the survivors settling deep in her bones, she paused her mobile lesson when she entered Heisenberg Hall. Today was the fourth of the month, an even number, and she took her place in the weigh-in line. The boys and girls ahead of her had even ID numbers, as did she. When it was her turn, she stepped on the scale and said, "Nine four four."

"Lisette Leigh," the ensign replied, reading from a list that matched IDs with names. "Twenty-two point eight kilograms."

He entered her weight into a computer.

She moved through the food line, where the cooks gave her scrambled eggs, an orange, and some oatmeal. After pouring a glass of soymilk, she found a seat at Zoe's table.

She let Zoe wiggle her tooth.

"Can I do it?" Molly asked.

Lisette pushed her jaw forward, and Molly wiggled it.

"I hope you stay in the colony," Molly told her.

Doctor Hoffer, Atlanta Colony's chief scientist, entered from a side door. A woman Lisette had never seen before accompanied him. Doctor Hoffer wore thick glasses, and because he had snow-white hair, Lisette thought he was the oldest adult at the colony. The woman had sandy blonde hair and carried a shoulder bag. Lisette leaned to the right to get a better view and noticed she wore a silver necklace.

Both adults stepped to the front of the cafeteria.

"Good morning," Doctor Hoffer said.

"Good morning," Lisette said in unison with the other two hundred members of Generation M.

He straightened his bowtie. "I'd like to introduce Doctor Hedrick, a physician from Colony East. She'll be in charge of our clinic. She's also starting up a new program, training ensigns to be doctors."

As Doctor Hoffer continued with the morning announcements, Lisette peeked at the boys from Unit 2B eating at the next table. Richard, whose cowlick sprung up like a rooster's tail, grinned at her and pointed to his tooth. She grinned and pointed at her tooth. He made a funny face, and she did the same. They went back and forth like this, scrunching eyes, sticking their tongues out, and seeing who could make the funniest face.

Someone tapped Lisette on the shoulder, and heat scorched her cheeks when she turned and faced the magnified eyeballs of Doctor Hoffer. Doctor Hedrick stood beside him.

"This is Lisette," he said to Doctor Hedrick. "She's having an evaluation later on. I'd appreciate it if you could send me the results of the examination before noon."

Doctor Hedrick led Lisette outside. "Please, call me Sandy."

Sandy's smile and soft tone put her at ease.

"Your necklace is pretty," Lisette said.

Sandy pinched the silver braid between her fingers and lifted a small silver heart. "My grandmother gave it to me when I graduated from high school. That was a long time ago."

She held out her hand. Lisette took it, and they started across the campus.

"I haven't had a chance to review your profile yet," Sandy said. "What's your last name?"

"Leigh." Lisette liked to spell words. "L-E-I-G-H."

Sandy stopped, removed a thick folder from her shoulder bag, and flipped through a few pages. Her eyes lit up. "I can see the resemblance. Abby calls you Toucan."

Lisette's heart thudded in her chest, and she was trembling all over. "You know Abby?"

"Abby's in Biltmore Company. All the children in Colony East are assigned to one of four companies. Would you rather I call you Lisette or Toucan?" Sandy winked. "I can always call you 944 if you'd like."

Lisette wrinkled her nose at that. "Is Abby alive?"

"Your sister is fine," Sandy replied with a frown. "Why would you ask that?"

"In the spirit drill, a woman said my brother and sister are dead."

Sandy mumbled to herself. Then, she took Lisette's hand and gave it a squeeze. "Many things here don't make sense. I don't know about your brother, but Abby is doing great."

Lisette threw her arms around Sandy and gave her a big hug.

They continued across the campus, hand in hand, until Medical Clinic 3 loomed before them. Lisette stopped. Sandy tugged her hand, but she held her ground.

"Where are we going?" Lisette asked.

Sandy gestured to the clinic. "The examination room is on the second floor."

The muscles below her cheekbones and on each side of her neck cramped, and Lisette couldn't make herself go in there.

Sandy went down on one knee and gently placed her hands on her shoulders. "You're shaking. Do you like butterscotch candy? I have a bowl of candy in my office. C'mon, let's go."

Lisette turned and ran as fast as she could.

"Toucan, come back!"

1.08
COLONY EAST

Admiral Samuels's voice crackled over Dawson's two-way radio. "I want you to demolish the ferry terminal."

"Sir?" Dawson exclaimed.

"The storm damaged it. It's ready to come down. When the survivors overrun the colony, I don't want the building collapsing on anyone."

The admiral sounded tired, almost defeated, and Dawson wondered about his mental state. An epidemic was on the verge of killing hundreds of thousands of kids outside the colonies, yet the admiral was concerned that a building might collapse.

"Will do, sir."

Do or die, never question why. Old habits were hard to break.

Fifteen minutes later, he skirted a portable generator chugging away outside Trinity Church. He pulled the handle on the massive ornate door and stepped into the high-domed cathedral — one of three supply depots at the colony.

He spotted Chief Petty Officer Thomas near the altar, on her hands and knees, with her head bowed.

Thomas had played goalie for the University of Minnesota the year the women's hockey team made it to the Frozen Four championship round, but what impressed Dawson more than her net-minding skills was her photographic memory. She always knew the location and quantity of every possible repair part stored in the colony.

As he approached her, he realized she was snoozing, not praying. He cleared his throat.

Thomas groggily rose to her feet. "No rest for the weary," she said. "Looks like you could use some shuteye too, Lieutenant."

He grinned. "No rest for the weary."

He told her what he needed, and she procured the items. Navy engineers had retrofitted the church; bins replaced pews, and tall shelving units lined the walls.

Delivering the first part of the order, she dropped the carton of waxy blocks onto the counter with little regard. The fifteen pounds of C4 had the explosive power to turn the granite church into tiny pebbles.

"My best seller today," she said with a yawn and went to fetch the wireless fuses.

He marveled at the amazing properties of C4. The plastic explosive was safe and versatile. You could slam, bang, and mold it, though you needed to handle it more gingerly once you inserted a fuse. An all-purpose explosive, you could use a little to punch free a rusty subway turnstile, and use a lot to twist steel girders and bring down a bridge. He had been part of the demolition team that blew the midsection of the Brooklyn Bridge.

Thomas returned with the fuses and a remote detonator. "What landmark are you planning to alter this time?"

"The old man wants me to blow the ferry terminal."

"You have a demolition buddy," Thomas said. "Lieutenant Mathews stopped by thirty minutes ago. Same job."

As he approached the terminal, Dawson was still scratching his head over Admiral Samuels independently assigning the same task to two officers.

He checked that his two-way radio was off. Wireless fuses operated at a unique frequency, but it was better to be safe than sorry.

The terminal building housed a machine shop, the remains of the Zodiac fleet, and a ferry that once transported cars and passengers across the East River.

He found Lieutenant Mathews lying prone on the dock, reaching her arm over the side and planting a charge on the piling.

She got to her feet and picked up her satchel of explosives. "What can I do for you, Dawson?"

Mathews had cold blue eyes that complimented her disposition. Ever since her recent promotion to Lieutenant, Junior Grade, she had started calling him Dawson. It might not have bothered him if she had said it in a friendly way, but she spit it out as if it were a bad taste in her mouth. Mathews was someone to keep an eye on. Given the chance, she'd stab anyone in the back to gain favor with the brass.

"Apparently, we received the same orders from the admiral," he told her.

"I'm here on Doctor Perkins's request." Her face remained a steely mask.

Once again, the left hand didn't know what the right was doing. "Let's divide and conquer," he offered. "I can take care of the east side of the building."

"What's that saying, Dawson? Too many cooks spoil the broth. I can handle it."

Eight years of submarine duty had taught him a valuable lesson: hit pause before you react and say something you'll later regret.

"I plan to carry out my orders from Admiral Samuels," he said in a measured tone. Then, he gestured to the east wall of the ferry terminal. "That's where I'm starting. Whatever we do, let's be safe."

Mathews shot him a death stare, and then grudgingly pointed to where she had already planted charges. Together, they mapped out where they'd place additional charges.

Standing next to the east wall, he molded the blocks of C4 in his hands, affixed them to the joists, and inserted the wireless fuses. After positioning his last cake on a joist, he met her on the dock where she was molding her last block of C4 into a ball.

She inserted a fuse, cocked her arm, and hurled the ball high onto a ledge close to the ceiling. "One for good luck."

They retreated to a safe distance. Both he and Mathews raised the antennae on their remote detonators, then powered them on. Lights blinked red then green. Each positioned a finger on the detonation button.

"On the count of three," she said. "Three, two, one. Fire in the hole."

Thirty simultaneous explosions sent out clouds of dust, and sharp thunderous booms bounced off buildings across the river and echoed back. The ferry terminal did its best to remain standing, but after several agonizing seconds, the groans and creaks began. A moment later, it seemed to surrender and collapsed in a heap of rubble that roiled the water.

As Mathews briefed Doctor Perkins on the successful demolition over her walkie-talkie, Dawson decided he'd give the news to Admiral Samuels face-to-face.

1.09
EMORY CAMPUS

In the quad, Lisette stopped running, turned, planted her feet wide, and folded her arms. She waited for Sandy to catch up.

"I'm not going to Medical Clinic 3," Lisette told her. "You can't make me."

Breathing hard from the chase, Sandy held out her hand. "That's fine. I don't like that place, either. I have another office. We'll do the exam there. It's kind of messy, though."

"Pinky swear?" Lisette held out her pinky.

Sandy gave her a serious look. "Pinky swear."

Locking pinkies with Sandy, Lisette felt much better.

Sandy was right about the mess. Her office in Heisenberg Hall was stacked tall with boxes, and fat books piled high on her desk. She cleared the books off the desk so it could serve as an examination table. Lisette hopped up.

Sandy listened to her heart, looked in her ears, pressed around her stomach with her fingertips, and took her temperature and her blood pressure.

Lisette, dangling her legs off the side of the desk, said, "Ahhh" as Sandy peered inside her mouth with a flashlight.

Sandy wiggled her tooth. "It will fall out soon. I hope you put it under your pillow when it does."

Lisette scrunched her face. "My pillow?"

"How else is the tooth fairy going to find it?"

"What's a tooth fairy?"

Sandy widened her eyes as if everyone should know about the tooth fairy.

"She takes the tooth while you're sleeping and leaves you something nice in return. When I was your age, the tooth fairy left money. I don't know what she leaves now, but I'm sure it's still something good." She glanced at Lisette's profile. "Unit 2A, bed six. I'll make sure she knows where you sleep."

"What does the tooth fairy look like?" Lisette asked.

"I've never seen her, but we talk." Sandy tapped the walkie-talkie in her coat pocket. "Tooth fairies communicate on a special frequency."

Just then, Doctor Hoffer's voice crackled over the walkie-talkie. "Doctor Hedrick, do you have the results for Lisette?"

Sandy pressed the button and spoke into the two-way radio. "I'm just finishing up. You'll have the report within thirty minutes."

Doctor Hoffer thanked her and signed off.

"That," Sandy said with a wink, "was not the tooth fairy."

1.10
BROOKLYN

"I'm supposed to meet Toby here," Abby said to the girl who, a moment earlier, had threatened her with a knife.

Lexi pointed to a lump under the covers on a nearby mattress — someone sleeping — and brought a finger to her lips. "We have to leave."

Lexi's mattress pulled on Abby like a magnet. She desperately wanted to lie down and rest after lugging the fish. If she could lie down and draw her knees to her chest, it might ease the pain in her stomach.

"I'm staying," Abby said.

Lexi strapped on a leather belt with a sheath and slipped her knife into it. "Toby said you were stubborn."

Lexi navigated the narrow pathway among the mattresses and was soon outside.

Abby decided to join the girl, but only to ask about Toby. If she didn't get a good answer, she'd return inside.

With one last look at the mattress, she struggled to heave the pack over her shoulder. A cloud of flies flew up, and then landed back on the fish to continue feasting.

Abby took a step and grunted when her right thigh muscle cramped. She took another step and her left thigh cramped just as forcefully. Gritting her teeth, she kept moving, hoping the knotted muscles would relax.

The crowd outside had grown bigger and noisier. Abby put the pack down and tried to massage her legs without being obvious about it. "Let's talk here," she said to Lexi.

Lexi glanced around and leaned in closer. "Toby has a lot of enemies."

"Enemies?"

All of a sudden, Lexi pulled out her knife, and Abby stumbled back, ready to protect herself the best she could.

"Back away," Lexi growled.

She directed the threat at a boy reaching for Abby's pack. He withdrew his hand, but otherwise stood his ground, eagerly staring at the fish. Abby recognized the look of desperation in his eyes.

Lexi, still gripping her knife, picked up Abby's pack. "We'll go meet Toby."

"I'll carry it," Abby said, concerned that Lexi might want to steal the fish too.

"You have the Pig," Lexi said.

"No," Abby blurted. But by responding so quickly, she had all but admitted she was sick.

"Let's go," Lexi said and slipped into the crowd.

Abby hobbled after her because Lexi now possessed the two most important items in her life: the walkie-talkie and the fish. She followed her down streets and driveways, and through mazes of winding alleyways until they entered the front door of a building and exited the back. The inhabitants, girls and boys around ten years old, paid little attention to them, as if strangers parading through their home happened all the time.

Abby settled into a strangely serene rhythm, skating her feet along the ground. The cramps in her stomach and aches in her joints seemed to have reached a peak.

A fight broke out between two boys on the sidewalk ahead of them. Others joined in and soon a tornado of fists blocked the path. Abby wondered if she was witnessing a consequence of the epidemic — kids fighting each other for scraps of food.

Lexi slung the pack to her chest, wrapped her arms around the fish, and reversed direction.

Later, with the sun high overhead, they came to a pool of water at an intersection, the result of a clogged storm drain. The reflection of the surrounding buildings shimmered on the brown surface. Abby's throat was dry from breathing through her mouth, but she feared that if she stopped for a drink, her muscles would seize up for good.

She watched Lexi wade up to her ankles and cup her hand to slurp water. She told herself to keep moving and plodded ahead, raising her eyes high up to the rooftops. The sound of swishing and splashing reminded her of her mom shouting, "Get ready, get set, go!" when she and Jordan would race at the beach, seeing who could reach the water first.

Still wading through the puddle, Abby stumbled and cried out as her right thigh muscle coiled into a knot. When she shifted her weight to her other leg, she felt a braid of searing pain from hip to ankle. Losing her balance, she flung her arms outward and tried whipping her right leg forward, but the limb was stiff and unresponsive. She crashed into the puddle.

Abby had a frog's view of the world, peering across the puddle. She opened her mouth to let the water soothe her tongue and the back of her throat. She swallowed and choked.

Lexi helped her to her feet and slapped her hard between the shoulder blades until Abby stopped coughing. Then, she wrapped Abby's arm around her waist and guided her forward. "We're almost there."

"Where?" Abby asked, willing her legs to keep moving.

"Toby's car."

The news gave her a boost of energy and troubled her at the same time. Why had Lexi not told her their destination before?

"Please keep the pack dry." Unable to shake her distrust of Lexi, Abby stopped short of telling her about the walkie-talkie.

She trained her eyes on the ground and focused on each step. The changing composition of the surface served as her measuring stick of progress. Patches of ash and cinders turned into a solid carpet of gray ash that thickened and made a soft crunching sound under their feet.

Lexi steered her around objects that had burned or melted. "Just a few more blocks. You can do it."

Abby lifted her eyes. Fire had gutted many of the four-story brick houses on both sides. Some buildings were nothing but heaps of broken rubble. The only cars she saw had burned. The street was a graveyard of charred cars. "Where is everyone?"

"Nobody lives here anymore," Lexi explained. "After the night of the purple moon, a factory burned, and the fumes made everyone sick. Rumor is, the air can still make you sick."

Three blocks deeper into the wasteland of ash, Lexi led her to an alley entrance and looked around. Apparently satisfied that nobody was following, Lexi tightened her grip and started down the alley. Abby panicked at the high brick walls that bowed and bulged. They appeared ready to collapse at any moment. At the end was a car covered in ash and bird poop. The tires were flat. Abby's shoulders drooped to her toes. She felt like the subject of an elaborate hoax or an evil joke. The punch line was a broken-down car.

Between the front bumper and the brick wall were two overturned buckets. Lexi took off the pack and helped Abby sit on a bucket. So many flies alighted on the fish that the scaly surface was no longer visible.

Lexi sat on the other bucket and pointed to the walls that Abby feared were about to bury them. "Toby likes this spot. No windows."

"Likes it?" Abby's raspy voice faded.

Lexi patted the hood. "This is your getaway car. The tank is full, and there's food and water in the trunk. The tires are good. Toby let the air out so the car would look unusable." She reached under the car and pulled out a bicycle tire pump. "He made lots of trades to get everything. He cheated some kids. That's why he has enemies and has to stay away from the fish market."

Lexi explained how most kids survived in Brooklyn. "Almost everyone belongs to a gang. We don't fight each other, at least not often. We share things and help each other out. When something happens, word travels fast. The word is out that Toby will cheat you.

"I met him when he showed up at the fish market. That was about three weeks ago." Lexi tugged on her sleeve. "He gave me this, and I gave him news. The more we talked, the more I liked him.

"He told me about Colony East and said that you and his friend, Jonzy, were there. He thought Jonzy would try to escape. They had planned to meet at the fish market. He didn't think you would leave the colony."

"Where's Toby now?" Abby asked.

"He'll be here. He sleeps in the car at night."

Lexi pumped the tires with the bicycle pump. It looked like hard work, and Abby offered to help, but Lexi told her she had better take it easy. "The Pig makes you weak."

"Did Toby say anything else?" Abby asked, accepting Lexi knew how sick she was.

Lexi narrowed her eyes. "Is there something else he should have told me?"

Abby paused. "Nah. That's it."

She still didn't trust Lexi. Toby knew the storm would bring AHA-B bacteria and that the adults had developed an antibiotic to defeat the Pig. For some reason, Toby chose not to share this information with Lexi.

Abby quickly added, "I'm really hungry. Can I borrow your knife to cut off a piece of fish?"

Lexi waved at the fish, scattering the flies. "You'll get sick if you eat it raw. We have to cook it, but I don't want to cook it here. The smoke might attract kids. More and more kids are getting the Pig."

After Lexi finished inflating the tires, she heaved the pack over her shoulder. "You stay here. I'll go cook it, and then come back."

Abby wanted to go with her, but she didn't think she could move yet. "Wait, there's something I need."

She removed the two-way radio from the pack and tucked it in her waistband. She offered no explanation and was glad that Lexi didn't ask for one. The less she spoke about Colony East and her plans, the better.

Lexi reached into her pocket and placed a wrapped candy in her hand. "You'll like this."

When Lexi left, Abby brought her hand to her mouth, ready to crunch the candy, wrapper and all. Practicing self-discipline, she peeled off the wrapper. Some wax paper stuck to the amber-colored candy, but she didn't care. A shiver passed through her when she placed it on her tongue and let the candy sit there. Soon, a glacier of sweet, sugary butterscotch melted into her, creeping toward her throat and spreading warmth throughout her body that dissolved her pain.

Climbing into the car, she curled up on the back seat, conflicted by feelings of sadness and exhilaration. It was incredible to think what Toby had accomplished and how far she had made it alone. If all went well, she would see Toby again soon, and, at midnight, they would contact Jonzy on the radio, and he would escape the colony, bringing antibiotic pills with him. She would take a pill, recover, and they would all travel to Mystic in the car to find Jordan. Afterward, as a team, they would figure out how to get to Toucan at Atlanta Colony.

As the butterscotch worked its magic pain relief, Abby imagined their final destination in her mind: the cabin on the shore of a lake, deep in the Maine woods, far from this horror.

1.11
CASTINE ISLAND STRAIT

Jordan moved to the bow to give Eddie a turn at the tiller. They'd switched places periodically since leaving the island three hours ago.

They were a third of the way across the strait, and if the southwest wind stayed light and steady and the mast held firm, they'd reach the Portland Trading Zone by late afternoon.

Eddie had said he was a little hungry, and his fever wasn't getting worse, but Jordan didn't know whether to believe him. Eddie hated to complain. He hoped that if Abby had found a doctor for Toucan at Colony East, maybe the doctor would treat Eddie too.

It felt good to be moving, even at a crawl. Every second spent on the water put them closer to Mystic, where they'd use Wenlan's clinic as a base of operations. Wenlan was a friend of the local fuel king, William. William would get him and Eddie a car, or they would rig a boat in Mystic Harbor and sail along the coast until they reached the East River to Colony East.

First, they had to find Spike at the Portland Trading Zone to see what he could tell them about Abby, Touk, and Toby.

Jordan gripped the mast. "Still looking good."

Not a perfect fit, but considering they had no other option, he was thrilled with how well it was holding up.

Eddie grinned. "If it snaps, we can swim."

Jordan heard the strain in his friend's voice. He dangled his fingers into the icy water. "Hey, how you doing?"

"Where do you think Abby and Touk are?"

Jordan leaned back, squinting at the sun through the haze. "All right, all right, you are fine."

"The Pig is no big deal," Eddie said. "Drop it."

The image of the mob eating raw shellfish at the water's edge was still fresh in Jordan's mind, and he'd been shocked to learn how many others on the island had the illness.

Jordan shifted around to get comfortable. Seeing how Eddie eyed the pack with the food, he moved it to the bow, and then positioned a lifejacket to serve as a pillow. "Let me know when you want to switch."

Eddie grinned. "You'll wake up in Portland."

With his head resting on the lifejacket, Jordan closed his eyes and pictured Wenlan. If the Pig was widespread on the mainland, how was she coping with all the new cases? A knot formed in his stomach. *What if Wenlan had the Pig?*

Telling himself that Wenlan was healthy and that Abby and Touk were alive and safe, he tried to relax. Sunshine covered him in a warm blanket and water lapped the hull, a sound he always found soothing. The centerboard vibrated as it kept *Mary Queen of Scots* on a true course. He listened for the repetitious shrugs of metal stays and turnbuckles as the bow lifted and dipped in the gentle swells. Erased of all thoughts of the past, his mind melted through the hull and into the dark, deep water.

1.12
COLONY EAST

With clouds of dust from the ferry terminal explosion lingering, Dawson headed off to see Admiral Samuels. The streets were eerily quiet, as if the evacuation were complete. The first sign of life he came upon was a crew of ensigns roping off a sinkhole that had opened on Fifth Avenue.

Three blocks later, he reached Trump Tower. He pushed through the revolving door, into the lobby, and sprinted up the stairs to the sixth floor. He entered Admiral Samuels's outer office, where crates were stacked on the floor and several filing cabinet drawers hung open. Ensign Parker was packing up.

The same thought flashed across Dawson's mind every time he saw the admiral's aide. How did they let a fifteen-year-old join the Navy? Dawson knew that Parker had actually enlisted after he had attended college; he just had the boyish face of a middle school student.

"You're early, Lieutenant," Parker said. "The company leaders' meeting doesn't start for two hours."

"I want to see the old man alone," Dawson said.

Parker gestured to the closed door of the admiral's office. "He doesn't want to be disturbed now." The ensign crinkled his brow. "This morning, the admiral shuffled through here like this." Parker glued his chin to his chest.

Concerned, Dawson blew out a puff of air. Admiral Samuels perennially kept his broad shoulders pinned back and strutted around with his broad chest thrust forward.

"We spoke earlier by radio, and he sounded ..." Dawson searched for a word. Depressed came to mind. "... tired."

"Maybe you should disturb him?" Parker said.

Dawson rapped on the door and pushed it open. The admiral stood by the window.

"Permission to enter?" Dawson asked.

He said it again, louder.

The admiral seemed deep in thought.

Dawson entered, saluted, and closed the door behind him. "Sir, the ferry terminal demolition was successful. Lieutenant Mathews and I worked together as a team."

The admiral turned and locked eyes with him, looking as if Mathews's involvement was news to him.

The old man lost focus. His expression went blank, and he lowered his eyes. "Good job," he said flatly.

Dawson's blood chilled. "Is everything all right, Admiral?"

Samuels turned and stared out the window.

Dawson moved beside him. "As you know, sir, I worked at the Alpharetta pharmaceutical plant. I helped maintain machinery, and I supervised the shipment of the pills to Atlanta Colony for redistribution. I understand the processes. If you speak to any of the CDC personnel who worked with me, I'm certain they'll vouch for the contributions I've made. If you assign me to the plant, I will hit the ground running." He slipped in a quick, deep breath to steady his voice. "I'm prepared to step down as leader of Biltmore Company."

The old man still stared into the distance.

"Sir, I'm making a formal request. I'd like to be assigned to the Alpharetta plant."

The admiral arched his shoulders and thrust his chest forward. The change in his demeanor and posture was both sudden and dramatic, as if someone had flicked a switch and sent electricity surging through his body. "Who gives the orders around here?"

Dawson pulled his shoulders back. "You do, sir."

As if suffering from some unseen wound, Admiral Samuels seemed to crumble. He looked away and mumbled, "Do I? Dismissed."

1.13
EMORY CAMPUS

In History of Science, Lisette looked out the classroom window at the leafy trees and thought about which boys and girls she would let wiggle her tooth at recess. *Charlie. Molly. Zoe. Tad. No, not Tad. She didn't want a nose-picking finger to wiggle her special tooth.*

Lisette squirmed in her chair. The countdown clock showed she had to wait fifteen long minutes before recess.

Doctor Martin was reading to the class. "By the start of 1856, Darwin was investigating whether eggs and seeds could survive travel across seawater ...."

He looked especially silly today, with his dark brown hair sticking up on one side of his head.

Doctor Hoffer entered the classroom. "Excuse me, Doctor Martin. I need Lisette Leigh to come with me."

Lisette drew in a sharp breath, afraid of what he wanted. The other students eyed her with jealousy, and she knew they wished Doctor Hoffer had called out their name instead so they could leave Doctor Martin's boring class.

"Remember we have a quiz tomorrow," Doctor Martin told her as she followed Doctor Hoffer out of the room.

"The communication link to Colony East is working again," he said. "Doctor Perkins would like to hold your evaluation meeting a little earlier than planned."

As they walked across the campus together, Lisette remembered the desperate cries of the survivors clinging to the fence, and trembled.

"Doctor Perkins is very busy, and I expect your evaluation will be short," Doctor Hoffer said. "Either you'll become a member of Generation M, or he will order your removal from the colony. Doctor Ramanathan mentioned that to you, right?"

Lisette nodded as her heart thumped wildly.

Doctor Hoffer led her to Mendel Hall and into a room on the first floor, which had big windows looking out on Medical Clinic 3. Chandra, who was already there, gave Lisette a huge hug and told her that Doctor Perkins and Doctor Droznin would join them soon on the television.

Lisette sat in a chair in the middle of the room, facing two televisions. One showed a live picture of a room at Colony East. The TV beside it showed a picture of her, with Chandra and Doctor Hoffer sitting at a table to her left.

A grunt came from the TV speaker, and a woman with thick, reddish-brown hair hobbled into the room at Colony East on crutches.

"Good morning, Doctor Droznin," Doctor Hoffer said.

Doctor Droznin nodded and looked at her computer.

A moment later, Doctor Perkins entered the room and sat beside Doctor Droznin.

Soon, Doctor Perkins's face filled the entire TV screen. Round glasses were perched on the bridge of a long, narrow nose, and his brow furrowed. "We have quite a mess on our hands. We are evacuating Colony East."

"What?" Doctor Hoffer exclaimed, jumping to his feet.

"We'll be sending all the Generation M children to Atlanta," Doctor Perkins said. "I'd like to propose that we cancel today's evaluation and focus on the evacuation. I've reviewed 944's profile, and she doesn't qualify as a member of Generation M."

Lisette felt like grasshoppers were hopping around in her tummy.

"I disagree," Doctor Droznin said. "We should have the evaluation."

The TV speaker went silent, and the two scientists spoke to each other. Lisette could see their lips moving. Doctor Perkins gestured with his hands.

A moment later, the sound returned.

"After deciding 944's status, we'll discuss the evacuation plan," Doctor Perkins said. "Let's begin."

The Atlanta Colony TV showed a close-up of Chandra.

"Nine four four is five years old." It sounded funny to hear Chandra use her Colony ID instead of saying her name. "She arrived March sixth...."

"Yes, yes, yes, we all know her background," Doctor Perkins interrupted. "Please display her aptitude scores."

A colorful picture with numbers appeared on the screen. "As you can see, her test results in math and science are somewhat poor," Chandra said.

"Extremely poor," Doctor Perkins said.

"Lisette started her coursework three weeks ago," Doctor Droznin interjected. "We should consider these results as a benchmark. We can retest her again in three months."

Doctor Perkins tapped his fingertips together. "Nine four four's intellect ranks in the lowest percentile. Additional testing will not change that."

"How do Lisette's scores compare to the pre-comet population?" Doctor Droznin asked.

"She has an IQ of 134," Chandra said. "That would have put her in the top two percentiles of the general population."

Doctor Perkins cleared his throat. "The pre-comet population is irrelevant now. The society of the future demands we nurture only the best and brightest. The average IQ for Generation M at Atlanta Colony is 155."

"May I see the Torrance results?" Doctor Droznin asked.

Lisette did not understand what the scientists were talking about, so she kept an eye on Chandra. If Chandra looked afraid, Lisette would think the evaluation was not going well, and she would become even more afraid.

A new screen appeared with a line shaped like a mountain. The mountain had a green dot placed near the peak. "Nine four four is one of the most creative children in the colony," Chandra said.

Lisette understood that, and she felt proud for a split second before her fear returned.

Doctor Perkins spoke up. "We need to develop engineers, mathematicians, physicists. The arts and humanities are a lesser priority."

"Creativity is essential in science," Doctor Droznin said. "Einstein played the violin. Leonardo da Vinci, the greatest scientist of his time, was also the greatest artist of the day."

"Albert Einstein had an IQ of one-hundred sixty," Doctor Perkins said. "Creativity, combined with an average IQ, is worthless."

Doctor Hoffer raised a finger. "We believe 944 has other promising attributes."

"Can we please expedite the evaluation?" Doctor Perkins said. "Show us 944's mating profile."

The faces of three boys, along with their ID number and location, flashed on the screen one at a time. The first boy from Colony East wore thick glasses. The second one from Colony East had a devilish grin that made Lisette think of her friend, Timmy, on Castine Island, and the last boy from Colony West had freckles and a spiky cowlick.

"There are three optimal pairings, two from Colony East, and one from Colony West," Chandra said.

"Only three?" Doctor Perkins leaned forward. "Future generations are as critical as the present one. It's the reason we set a benchmark of *five* potential pairings."

The speaker went silent again. Doctor Perkins and Doctor Droznin seemed to argue. Doctor Droznin's face reddened. As Lisette watched the two scientists, she placed her tongue against her tooth and pushed it forward. It was so close to falling out.

The sound returned and Doctor Perkins said, "Please continue."

"We made the following field observation during a free-association period," Chandra said.

Lisette's jaw dropped when she saw herself with a bright red dot above her head. A blue dot hovered above a group of kids standing close to her. They were in the free-association yard where recess was held.

The scene came to life. Ernie, from Unit 2B, pushed Molly to the ground. Lisette remembered that happening. Ernie had tripped Molly to be mean. Lisette watched herself approach Ernie and wag a finger in his face. Ernie lowered his head and went over to Molly.

"From post-incident interviews, we know that 944 made 912 apologize to 468," Chandra added.

"Lisette Leigh has leadership potential," Doctor Droznin declared.

Doctor Perkins let out a long sigh. "Nine four four, you've been sitting there so quietly. It's my job to determine who will remain part of Generation M. Despite having only an average intellect, you have made quite an impression on my colleagues. Of course, I understand Doctor Droznin's motivation for having you remain in the colony. You are an important test subject. Frankly, I find myself on the fence." He took off his glasses and looked at a sheet of paper. "Several references are made to your stubbornness."

Lisette flushed with excitement. "My family has a stubborn gene. Abby told me that."

"I'm glad you mentioned family. There was an incident at the morning spirit drill. Tell me, 944, do you believe that your brother and sister are dead?"

The words washed over Lisette like ice water. Chandra stared intently at her, nodding. Doctor Hoffer also nodded. They both wanted her to tell a white lie. Because if she lied, she could stay at Atlanta Colony and she could see her friends again.

Lisette, her heart beating so fast she heard a humming sound inside her head, looked directly at the TV and shouted, "Abby and Jordan are alive!"

Doctor Hoffer dropped his chin to his chest, and Chandra covered her mouth with her hand.

Doctor Perkins nodded. "Nine four four, you leave me no choice but to expel you from the colony. I can also tell you without a doubt that your sister is dead. She drowned in the Hudson River while trying to escape the colony."

Lisette ignored the sob rumbling in her chest and jumped to her feet.

"That's a lie! Abby knows how to swim. She's alive!" She marched up to the TV and put her hands on her hips. "Abby is alive! Abby is alive! Jordan is alive. Abby and Jordan are alive." She shouted until her throat became too raw to make noise.

"Will someone please escort 944 to the processing center?" Doctor Perkins said.

Lisette felt an arm around her shoulder. Chandra kneeled beside her, and Lisette buried her face in her white lab coat.

"Let's not be hasty," Doctor Hoffer said. "I have a procedure that will help Lisette forget about her brother and sister."

"I don't want to forget them," Lisette said in Chandra's ear.

Chandra pulled her closer, and a long moment of silence followed. Lisette twisted her head and saw that Doctor Droznin's and Doctor Perkins's lips were moving at the same time.

Lisette did what she always did to feel less afraid. She pressed her ear against Chandra's chest and counted the beats of her heart.

The TV speaker came to life with Doctor Perkins's voice.

"Doctor Hoffer, your procedure is still in the experimental phase."

"Yes, but I believe it's safe," Hoffer replied.

"Fine," Perkins said. "Go ahead, perform your procedure. I'll look forward to seeing the results. In the meantime, 944 will remain a provisional member of Generation M. We'll conduct another evaluation in three months. Now, let's discuss the evacuation."

"Please take Lisette to Medical Clinic 3," Doctor Hoffer said to Chandra.

Lisette dropped to her knees and curled into a tiny ball, which made her feel safer. Every muscle was twisting tight with fear. Tears blurred her vision, and she took tiny sips of air, which was the only way she could breathe with her chest frozen. Chandra draped an arm over her back and said, "You won't feel a thing, I promise. Come with me."

Chandra's voice sounded far away.

Suddenly, Lisette felt something hard between her lip and gum. The tip of her tongue found an open gap. Her tooth had fallen out.

1.14
BROOKLYN

The butterscotch candy had dissolved on Abby's tongue a lifetime ago.

In the back seat of the getaway car, she hugged her knees to her chest. The stabbing pain in the pit of her stomach faded and a new ache flared across her back. The pain was like gooey putty. By twisting and bending her torso, or tightening her stomach muscles, she could squeeze it to a new location, but it never went away. The good news was that she was running out of body parts that could hurt.

She checked the time. Lexi had been gone for nearly two hours, and Abby feared the worst: the girl had disappeared with the fish.

She remembered Lexi saying that Toby had stockpiled food and gasoline in the trunk. Abby lifted her head above the seat to peer out the back window. With nobody in sight, she crawled into the front seat and pulled the lever on the driver's side door to pop the trunk. She stepped out of the car and quietly closed the door behind her.

Before opening the trunk, she hobbled to the alley entrance and discovered the street was clear in both directions. Getting their food stolen by some kid infected with the Pig was the last thing she wanted.

Picturing in her mind a trunk packed with a variety of tasty treats, Abby's mouth watered as she limped back to the car. She lifted the trunk lid and discovered the trunk was empty, except for a balled-up tarp.

Crushed with despair, she grabbed the tarp and flung it, sending a hail of mouse droppings to the ground, and then slammed the trunk shut. She buried her face in her hands.

A cold ache swirled in Abby's heart as she realized she was on her own. Lexi had lied to her about the food and gas, and probably about everything else too.

She had to make it back to the fish market. Could she find her way? Did she have enough strength to make it that far? The only way to find out was to start walking. She put her hand on the walkie-talkie tucked in her waistband for reassurance.

Suddenly, fingers pinched her shoulder, and her hair stood on end as her adrenaline surged. She shouted and wheeled around, ready to defend herself. The boy had a shaved head and was shorter than her. He wore a hooded sweatshirt. Diamonds studded the outside of one ear.

"Stop it," he said in a hushed but forceful voice.

His calloused hands gripped her wrists hard, but she pulled her right arm free. She flailed and kicked, and he seemed shocked that someone so sick was fighting back.

He took several steps back and raised his hands as if to surrender. "Abby. Stop it."

How did he know her name?

She stared at the boy. "Oh my God," she cried. "Toby."

1.15
COLONY EAST

Dawson noted the unusual seating arrangement for the emergency meeting of company leaders and command staff. Ordinarily, Navy personnel clustered together in one quadrant of the big round table in the Gregor Mendel conference room, while the scientists sat on the opposite side of the table. Now, Lieutenant Mathews and Doctor Perkins were elbow to elbow, while Doctor Droznin and Doctor Levine perched closer to Dawson, Lieutenant Marks, Lieutenant Masters, and Admiral Samuels.

Dawson worried more than ever about the old man. The parts of his personality that commanded respect were missing. He seemed hollow.

Doctor Perkins glanced at his gold watch and began the meeting at precisely the top of the hour. "Doctor Levine, will you give us a status update on the antibiotic shipment?"

Doctor Levine, a soft-spoken scientist with graying hair, said the jet from Atlanta Colony had landed an hour ago. "The pills will be delivered to Medical Clinic 17."

"That's wonderful news," Doctor Perkins said. "Lieutenant Mathews, will you coordinate the distribution of pills to the companies?"

"Yes, sir," she said.

Perkins reviewed the antibiotic's effectiveness. "One dose is typically all that's required for protection against the bacteria. If someone has contracted AHA-B, they should feel better within a few hours of taking a pill. For others, a second dose will be needed to provide a full cure. We requested enough pills for Generation M to take multiple doses."

Dawson's spirits lifted. With the colony having received more doses than it needed, he could skim pills and obtain at least two each for his daughter, Sarah, Abigail Leigh, her brother Jordan, and Toby Jones. Beyond them, every additional pill he acquired for Jonzy to take with him could save the life of a survivor outside the colony.

"Do you wish to add anything Doctor Droznin?" Perkins asked.

Droznin kept her nose buried in her laptop.

Perkins cleared his throat. "Doctor Droznin?"

"Nothing to add," she replied curtly.

Dawson wondered if the chilly exchange and seating arrangement signaled friction between the two. He disliked the Russian scientist, but he could not deny her toughness. She'd been shot in the knee less than forty-eight hours ago by Cadet Leigh, yet Droznin had hobbled to the meeting on her own steam.

"Are there other questions?" Doctor Perkins asked.

Dawson waved his hand. "Can you share any updates on the plan to distribute pills outside the colonies?"

Dawson had asked the question many times before.

"Generation M is, and will remain, our top priority," Perkins said. "But I remain deeply concerned about the children who fall outside of our direct care. We're doing the very best we can in light of the available resources."

Dawson waded deeper into the quicksand of Doctor Perkins's lies. "If the plant in Alpharetta is operational, we can manufacture and distribute pills and care for Generation M at the same time."

Perkins cast his eyes around the table. "Once we've completed the evacuation, we can turn our attention to other matters. Lieutenant Mathews will brief you on the next steps of the evacuation plan."

Mathews smirked at Dawson, a subtle dig that nobody else would have picked it up.

"All companies are moving to Atlanta Colony," she began. "The evacuation flights will leave tomorrow. Armed convoys will escort the cadets to the airport, one company at a time. The only thing the cadets should bring is the clothes they have on their backs."

Dawson was relieved to learn that Biltmore was going to Atlanta where he could join forces with Sandy.

"Thank you, Lieutenant," Perkins said. "Our final agenda item deals with several reassignments. Lieutenant Dawson, you will go to Colony West for special projects. Lieutenant Mathews will assume command of Biltmore Company."

An invisible fist slammed into Dawson's chest and flattened his lungs, leaving him lightheaded and gasping for air. Special projects was code for "twiddle your thumbs behind a desk." He could have cared less what they wanted him to do. He'd stand on his head and blow bubbles through his nose, so as long as he went to Atlanta. In the rush of chaotic thoughts tumbling through his brain, he focused on the single goal of keeping his tone measured.

"May I ask why you are reassigning me?" he asked calmly.

"Change is healthy," Perkins replied.

"If Lieutenant Mathews takes over Biltmore Company, there will be an opening at Sheraton," Dawson said. "I can fill that."

Perkins impatiently glanced at his Omega. "Doctor Levine will assume command of Sheraton Company."

Dawson snapped his head to the mild-mannered Levine. "You're putting a scientist in charge of a company?" he blurted.

"A growth opportunity for Doctor Levine," Perkins said, pushing his chair back, ready to stand.

Mathews chimed in, "Dawson, I need you to update the cadet profiles. I'll stop by Biltmore at sixteen hundred hours to meet with my cadets."

Dawson focused on Admiral Samuels. "The cadets need continuity. I can accompany them to Atlanta. I'll transfer to Colony West once they've adjusted."

"Your cadets will be in capable hands." Perkins smiled, now on his feet.

"Sir, do you support my transfer?" Dawson asked the admiral.

The old man lifted his chin and his barrel chest rose and fell visibly. He rested his large hands on the table and swiveled his head.

"Yes, Lieutenant Dawson, I support the transfer."

With that, the meeting adjourned.

1.16
CASTINE ISLAND STRAIT

Jordan couldn't form words or even move. Wenlan, wearing a white doctor's jacket, stood beside the bed, stitching together an open wound on his lower leg. Her silky black hair fell just above her waist.

Cries came from outside of the room. He must be in the clinic in Mystic, and the kids screaming were suffering from the Pig.

Jordan blinked and squinted into a bright haze glowing overhead. The air had a damp, briny bite. He was relieved to see he was on *Mary Queen of Scots* about a mile from the mainland. Eddie had made excellent progress.

"My turn," Jordan said, stretching his arms.

With his hand on the tiller, Eddie lowered his eyes. "I'm sorry, dude."

"Sorry? Look how far we've gone!" Jordan startled when he saw the food pack at the stern next to Eddie's feet. "You got into the food?"

"All I think about is food," Eddie said without looking up. "My stomach hurts so bad. I'm so hungry. I just snapped."

Jordan was about to ask if any food was left in the pack, but he stopped himself. He knew the answer. He had one sweet potato in his pocket that would have to last them until they reached Mystic.

1.17
BROOKLYN

Abby tilted the can to her lips and let the sweet drops of pear juice sparkle on her tongue.

She and Toby were in the alley behind the car, sitting next to each other on the overturned buckets, close enough for their legs to brush.

She had told him about her escape from Colony East, and he had described what he had done after Doctor Perkins kicked him out of the colony.

Abby willed herself to pass the can of pears back to Toby before she drained it. "Please keep this out of my sight."

"I can get you something else."

Hidden in the trunk, where the spare tire normally went, was a bounty of canned fruits and vegetables, fresh beets and turnips, and plastic bottles filled with gasoline.

Abby shook her head. "Once I start eating, I won't be able to stop."

Toby cursed and said, "I hope you killed Doctor Droznin."

"Don't say that!"

The scientist had surprised Abby while she was searching Doctor Droznin's lab, looking for pills, and she had shot her by accident. Abby had meant to fire the gun to frighten Doctor Droznin so she wouldn't call for help.

"She infected you with the bacteria, like some kind of lab rat," Toby said.

Abby lowered her eyes. It was hard to argue against the truth.

Toby kept cursing, directing his wrath at adults everywhere for conceiving of the colonies. When his venom ran out, he covered the can of pears with a piece of cloth cut from the tarp, secured it in place with fishing line, and dashed to the back of the car where he returned the can to the trunk.

Abby folded over. It felt like a hand with sharp claws had tunneled into her stomach, slicing and squeezing her insides.

"Abby. Abby," Toby called out and rubbed her back, but she could only grit her teeth.

The pain finally lessened, and she took several deep breaths.

"I've gone without food before, perhaps a week or longer," she said in a shaky voice. "After a few days, I stopped feeling hungry. This time is different. I've had the Pig for five days, and the cramps keep on getting worse. I think about food constantly."

Frowning, Toby said, "That's what Touk went through."

"Toby, we need to get her."

He placed his hand on the top of hers. "Jonzy will bring us pills. I'm sure of that. We'll find Jordan in Mystic, and then we'll go to Atlanta and get Toucan."

Abby's heart melted. She had always noticed Toby's eyes. Even when she had hated him in the seventh grade, she felt his eyes revealed his real character. He would act like a jerk, but his eyes showed flashes of compassion. Now, they were swirling with kindness.

She rested her head on his shoulder. "Thank you."

"I have to make one more trade," he said. "The price of food is sky high, and we need a little more gas to make it to Mystic."

"You're leaving?" she asked with dread.

His shaved head magnified his sheepish expression. "I have to. Lexi will be back soon."

"I don't trust her," Abby said.

Toby chuckled. "I never thought I'd hear you say that about anybody."

Abby winced. "There's something about her I don't like. I just feel it."

"Lexi introduced me to her friends. She shaved my head so I'd fit in with the local kids. And she brought you here. You can trust her."

Lexi had apparently tricked Toby, which meant Abby would have to keep a close eye on the girl. "Hurry back," she said.

1.18
PORTLAND TRADING ZONE, MAINE

Jordan navigated *Mary Queen of Scots* around the overturned hull of a fishing trawler in Portland Harbor, one of many boats damaged or sunk by the storm. The graveyard of sailboats blown from their moorings that stretched along the seawall dashed his hopes of finding a bigger, better boat to sail to Mystic.

At the bow, Eddie spliced a piece of line he'd been working on for the past hour. He'd splice the strands together, sort them apart, and then start over. Jordan thought Eddie kept busy to focus on something other than his ravenous hunger.

Jordan called out when they were close to the pier. Eddie shifted to the port side and grabbed the ladder as Jordan let go of the mainsheet and the boat glided to a stop. Eddie dragged himself up the ladder and secured the bowline to a cleat.

The boys left the boat rigged because they were in a hurry. Jordan caught a last look at *Mary Queen of Scots*. She'd done her job well, safely delivering them to the mainland.

They headed straight to the fuel depot, which was two miles to the north. Huge fuel tanks rose above the houses and trees. The depot seemed the most likely place to find the fuel king, Martha, and the driver who worked for her who had taken his sisters and Toby to Colony East.

Normally, in the middle of the afternoon, kids looking to trade, or just hanging out, crowded the Portland Trading Zone. Today, only a girl with a rag wrapped around her nose and mouth rolled by on a skateboard, and a small group of kids milled around a park bench.

Jordan and Eddie thought the Pig explained the absence of activity; kids were afraid of catching it.

The streets were as empty as the trading zone, though Jordan noticed they were being watched. Curtains and shades moved in windows as they passed.

Jordan spun around when a branch snapped behind them. He saw nothing, but he sensed danger. Certain someone was following them, he eyed driveways and the narrow spaces between houses, considering each path as a possible escape route. He steered Eddie to the center of the street so if kids chased them, they'd have more directions to run in.

Jordan slipped his hand into the pack and gripped the knife handle. If it were true that the Pig was spreading, the potato he had moved to his pack was a prized possession.

Out of the corner of his eye, he watched Eddie grimace as he clutched his sides. He bent forward, but kept trudging ahead anyway.

"Hey, how are you doing?" Jordan asked.

"Great," Eddie said.

Eddie was tough, but he was far from feeling great. Jordan wondered how much longer his sick friend would last on grit and determination.

A Jimi Hendrix song played in a nearby house. "The first time I met DJ Silver, he was playing Hendrix," Jordan said.

"What's Silvy like?"

Jordan whistled. "Full of himself, but he's pretty cool. The Port is right off the highway in Mystic. We'll stop there to see what he knows."

"I want him to dedicate a song to Mel," Eddie said.

Mel and Abby had been best friends. Jordan always thought Eddie liked Mel, but his friend was too shy to approach her.

He nudged Eddie. "Is she your girlfriend?"

Eddie's eyes softened. "I like her a lot."

"What song are you going to dedicate?" Jordan asked.

"*Purple Rain.* You talked about Wenlan in your sleep."

Jordan's jaw dropped. "What did I say?"

Cans rattled behind them, and Jordan pulled his hand from the pack with a firm grip on the knife. Two dogs were rooting through a pile of trash.

"What did I say about Wenlan?" Jordan asked again, his heart racing from the surge of adrenaline.

"Something about missing her. You like her?"

Jordan shrugged. "She's okay, I guess."

Eddie cocked an eyebrow. "She's more than okay."

"Did I say anything else?"

"What's it worth to you?" Eddie had a teasing gleam in his eyes.

Jordan pointed his finger. "Just wait. I'll get you."

"I'm shaking," Eddie said.

Horsing around the way they used to was having a positive effect on them. Eddie walked taller and grimaced less, and Jordan's paranoia about their perilous situation eased, his mind less troubled by the hundreds of frightening "what if" scenarios.

A block ahead on the right, the front yard of a house had a smoldering fire pit. Wispy smoke rose from the pit like steam off the street after a hard summer rain.

"I got a bad feeling about that place," Jordan said and steered Eddie to the left side of the street.

When they were opposite the house, both boys doubled over and gagged from a sickening odor. Jordan felt as if two oily fingers had been jammed up his nose. The stench left a rancid, metallic taste in the back of his throat.

He grabbed Eddie's arm and dragged him until they were away from horrible smell.

"Oh my God," Eddie cried. "What was that?"

"I don't know," Jordan said, spitting to rid the taste from his mouth. The air was fresher, but he feared the odor would linger in his memory for a long time. "I don't want to know."

1.19
COLONY EAST

Lieutenant Dawson had fifteen minutes to himself before Lieutenant Mathews came to deliver antibiotic pills for him to pass out, and to meet the cadets of Biltmore Company. His cadets would soon fall under her command.

Seated at his desk, he reread the note he had penned.

> Being assigned to Colony West. Perkins claims the CDC is working to develop and distribute the antibiotic outside the colonies. We have to take action ourselves. We need to increase production at the Alpharetta plant. Who has the expertise to operate the plant? Who can you trust? Find them. Talk to them. Situation at Colony East is volatile.

Dawson folded the note and tucked it carefully inside the stack of cadet medical profiles on his desk. Presenting the profiles to the new leader of Biltmore Company was a routine matter. Lieutenant Mathews would pay little, if any, attention to the package before she delivered the profiles to the medical team at Atlanta Colony. Sandy, on the other hand, would review every profile in detail once the cadets arrived.

Next, he found the profile for Tabatha Williams, knowing Sandy would pay extra attention to it. He'd spoken to Sandy many times about Tabby's reoccurring nightmares.

In Tabby's Issues and Strengths section, he wrote: Monitor channel 17.

Channel 17 was a seldom-used frequency and part of his contingency plan. If he found himself operating outside the system, he needed a way to contact Sandy inside Atlanta Colony.

He returned Tabby's profile to the pile and then sealed all of the profiles in a pouch.

Mathews knocked on the door as though she were punching a speed bag.

Dawson left the pouch on the table and opened the door. "Is that necessary, Lieutenant?" he asked, gesturing to the gun strapped to her hip. "You'll be meeting many of my cadets for the first time. First impressions are very important. You don't want to frighten them."

Mathews narrowed her eyes. "We're fully exposed on the northern perimeter. The fence is no longer electrified, and every security resource has been assigned to secure the route leading to the airport." She gave a little, snippy sniff. "You tell me, Dawson, is carrying a weapon a smart precaution to take?"

"You're right. A rag-tag army of twelve-year-olds is about to invade the colony. It's a good idea to arm yourself."

His dose of sarcasm brought her to a boil, and her cheeks reddened.

Mathews rested her hand on the Navy-issue Colt 45. "Look, I don't have all day."

"We'll start on the first floor and work our way up," Dawson told her. "Where are the pills?"

She produced an amber bottle from her shoulder pack. "I'll pass them out. Are any of your cadets experiencing symptoms?"

Dawson's heart rate spiked, and he curled the corners of his lips slightly upward to hide his concern.

"Leave some with me in case I need to administer any second dosages." He relied on every ounce of discipline and control he possessed to speak in a calm, steady tone.

"Radio Doctor Levine if you need more pills," she replied sharply. "The pills are being stored in Doctor Perkin's lab in Medical Clinic 17. Levine will administer the dosages."

He nodded, trying to appear thoughtful. "That's a good option, but a cadet might need to take a pill in the middle of the night when Doctor Levine isn't available."

"Levine will handle it. He's your only option." Mathews glanced at her watch. "Can I meet my cadets?"

With his head spinning, he led her down the hallway and into the wing of seven-year-old cadets.

"Fall out," he shouted.

Soon, ten cadets had formed a neat line outside of their living quarters.

"Good afternoon," Dawson said.

Mathews stepped in front of him. "I've got it, Dawson."

He bit his tongue hard. His petty issues with Mathews were minor compared to the larger goal of producing and distributing pills to the kids outside the colonies.

She marched down the line of girls. "I'm Lieutenant Mathews. I want to get to know you all better. Michelle. Who's Michelle?"

Michelle Timilty, who was easy to spot with her red hair and freckles, raised her hand.

Mathews kneeled. "Hmmm. This could become confusing. I'm Michelle, too. I have an idea. My older brother called me Meesh. Would you ladies rather call me Lieutenant Mathews, Michelle, or Meesh?"

"Meesh," they shouted in unison.

Mathews smiled. "Meesh it is. When we get to Atlanta Colony, I'd like for all of us to do some fun things. Any ideas?"

"Stay up late," Cadet Barnes said.

"Lieutenant Dawson makes us turn the lights out at eight," Tabby said.

"Yeah, no talking either," Cadet Francona chimed in.

Mathews swiveled her head Dawson's way and said with a grin, "No talking after eight, huh? What kind of company leader are you?"

He clenched his jaw as rage-induced perspiration trickled into his eyes.

Mathews joked around some more with the cadets and then gave each one a pill.

"Crunch it up or swallow, your choice." She finished off by saying, "I'll see you tomorrow, ladies. Bright and early."

The introductory meeting scene repeated itself on the second, third, and fourth floors with the rest of the Biltmore Company cadets. Mathews won them over with an abundance of smiles, jokes, and the promise of doing fun things together. She told them facts about herself that seemed to grab their interest. She was shy growing up. She played on a championship Frisbee team in college. Her mom had taught her that playing fair and square was important, but it was also important to win.

"Winners shine," she had told them.

After Mathews had passed out the last pill, Dawson escorted her to the Biltmore's front door.

"Forgetting something, Dawson?" she asked.

"What? You expect a salute?"

"The medical profiles."

Dawson nodded and soon returned with the pouch. "Take good care of my cadets."

Mathews snatched the pouch and walked away without a word. He watched as she climbed into a Humvee and raced off.

Dawson hadn't forgotten a thing. Having shown so little regard for the profiles, he hoped she'd see no reason to study them. That accomplished, he now needed to formulate a plan for him and Jonzy to steal pills from Medical Clinic 17.

Winners shine.

1.20
BROOKLYN

Abby gripped the banister and waved her other arm through the air to clear away spider webs as she climbed the stairs.

Survivors had once occupied the dwelling next to the alley, evidenced by the heaps of trash on the floor. Now it was silent as a tomb and dark with shadows.

She reached the second floor, then the third, her fingertips plowing up dust on the banister. The shadows darkened, and silence pressed in on her as if she were deep underwater.

On the fourth floor, she turned right and crashed face first into a sticky veil of spider webs. She licked her lips and sucked on the strands that stuck to her tongue, wishing they had taste. She continued down the hall to the second room on the left, dragging her left hand along the wall for guidance.

She entered the room, and wading through crumpled paper, empty cans and plastic bottles, and blankets, she moved to the wall, expecting to find a door. Panic bubbled up her throat when her hands discovered only a boarded window.

Toby had told her how to get to the roof. Had she remembered his directions correctly?

Retracing her steps, she breathed easier when she discovered she had overshot a bedroom door. Soon, she was standing outside on the flat roof.

The rooftop told the story of the kids who had once lived in the building. A pillow stuffed inside a plastic garbage bag, along with empty cans and food wrappers scattered about, suggested some had camped here, maybe sleeping outside to stay cool on summer nights. When Abby saw a spear made from a flagpole and tipped with a razor blade, she wondered if the roof had served as a guard post. An arsenal of bricks and rocks piled close to the edge confirmed that suspicion. Rocks and crude spears raining down from high above would have given any potential intruders second thoughts.

Colony East rose in the distance about three miles away. The vista gave her a good sense of where she had come from and where she and Toby must go to meet Jonzy.

Toby had said the rooftop would be the best place for radio communications with Jonzy, and he was right. Nothing stood in her line of sight between her and the tops of the tall buildings. The hairs stood on the back of her neck in anticipation of speaking with Jonzy at midnight, less than eight hours from now.

She removed the two-way radio from her waistband and clicked the button, murmuring in relief upon hearing the hiss of white noise. She turned the radio off and set it on the roof.

Sensing her stomach was about to experience a fresh tsunami of cramps, Abby gathered the lumpy pillow and lay on her side. The surface of the roof was a layer of pebbles stuck in tar. As the pain in her gut intensified, she removed the pillow from under her head to let the sharp bite of pebbles against her scalp create a diversion.

After several minutes, the cramping lessened, and she rolled onto her back. Looking up, she wondered when, or if, Lexi would return to the alley. That started dark thoughts snowballing. Lexi had tricked her.

Unable to do anything about the betrayal, Abby closed her eyes and took a journey in her mind, picturing herself at the cabin on the lake in Maine. Touk and Jordan and Toby were all on the dock with her. She dove in and swam underwater until her lungs ached, and when she broke the surface, ripples spread out in every direction.

Abby forced her eyes open, trading the comfort of her fantasy for the bitter reality of her ravaging hunger. She had to stay awake and alert.

A car engine fired up. Thinking Toby had returned, she shot to her feet and raced toward the side of the roof that looked over the alley. Her legs wobbled from weakness, and she teetered from the dizzying height. She dropped to her knees and stretched out flat on her belly, hanging her head over the edge. Someone was backing the car out of the alley.

Abby crawled along the edge as the car outpaced her. For an instant, looking straight down, she saw the driver had on a blue Colony East uniform. It was Lexi. Lexi was stealing the car.

By the time Abby reached the corner of the building, Lexi had backed into the street. Abby picked up a brick and hurled it in frustration. The car was driving forward when the brick struck the rear window, cracks in the glass webbed out from the point of impact. Lexi sped off and was soon out of sight.

Abby rested her cheek on the roof and grabbed a handful of pebbles. Her intuition about Lexi had proven correct, and she had exercised extremely poor judgment in coming up to the roof.

How would she and Jonzy and Toby reach Mystic now?

She balled her fist tighter. They'd sail, bike, walk, and even crawl if necessary. Despite her rising fever and savage hunger, Abby's drive to find Jordan and Touk grew stronger by the minute.

The reality of them requiring a car sunk in, and with despair enveloping her like fog off the water, Abby opened her hand and let the pebbles rain down.

1.21
EMORY CAMPUS – MEDICAL CLINIC 3

Lisette drifted in a blur of orange and gray. The sky was sometimes this color when Generation M walked to Jung Auditorium in the evening.

She tried to open her eyes, but her eyelids weighed a thousand pounds, so she gave up trying.

Beep, beep, beep ....

Lisette had no idea what was making that steady, nearby sound. Her nose crinkled from a familiar odor, providing the first clue. Only one place smelled like chemicals: Medical Clinic 3.

Lisette was about to call out to ask a scientist what she was doing here, but she decided to remain still and quiet. The scientists moved the girls and boys who shouted too much into a separate room. It was more fun to be in the ward with others.

Something stretched the skin on her head, and she slid her fingertips through her stubbly hair to see what it was. A round pad with wires coming from it was stuck to her scalp. Four more pads were stuck on the back and sides of her head.

Lisette was trying to think of reasons she might be in Medical Clinic 3 when a door opened, and she heard voices.

"What gives him the right?" a woman asked.

"Before the comet, Doctor Hoffer was a leading researcher in the field of memory." That was Chandra. "He published several very influential papers on Alzheimer's disease. He came to the CDC to work on a grant from the Veterans Administration. He was researching a cure for Post-Traumatic Stress Disorder, because so many war veterans had experienced traumatic events in battle. He wanted to find a way to ease their anxiety."

"Experimenting on rats, I imagine," the woman said angrily.

"Doctor Hoffer started with rats and then moved to primates," Chandra confirmed. "He was conducting the first human trials when the epidemic hit. The early results were very promising."

"I'm a doctor," the woman said. "I understand the risks associated with human trials."

Lisette stayed very still, worried she was overhearing a private conversation. She didn't want to get caught.

"Her health and well-being are Doctor Hoffer's number one priority," Chandra said. "The procedure is completely safe. When we remember an object or event, the brain releases a unique chemical. Think of that chemical as a neural fingerprint. By initiating a memory and then targeting the chemical with a drug, Doctor Hoffer neutralized any unwanted memories."

The woman muttered, "Neutralize? I think erase is a more accurate description."

"Erasing memories implies the memories are gone forever. Lisette has retained all of her memories, but some are buried deep in her subconscious. She may dream about them," Chandra replied.

Lisette gulped. They were talking about her.

"That is cruel," the women hissed.

"Doctor Hedrick, you have to consider the options we had. Doctor Perkins would have expelled her from the colony if Doctor Hoffer hadn't performed the procedure."

Lisette didn't know Doctor Hedrick or why she seemed so angry.

"Can you explain the procedure to me?" Doctor Hedrick asked.

"She had strong neural fingerprints of her brother and sister, and of her home as well. Those were the primary memories that Doctor Hoffer initially targeted. He also tried to reduce her anxiety about Medical Clinic 3."

Lisette sighed in relief. They were talking about another girl named Lisette. She didn't have a brother or sister.

"What about other memories?" Doctor Hedrick asked.

"She will remember very little about the past two days, which is just as well." From Chandra's soft tone, Lisette pictured her crinkling her eyes. "She'll be much happier. She'll have a better chance of keeping up with her peers. Her test scores will improve."

"What about her ability to be human? Pain, sorrow, and longing are all part of life. They make us stronger." Doctor Hedrick now sounded more tired than angry.

"She can still experience those emotions," Chandra said.

"You sound like Doctor Perkins."

"Did you have children?"

"No," Doctor Hedrick quickly replied.

"Were you married?"

After a long pause, Doctor Hedrick replied in a voice that was barely a whisper, "I was engaged."

"I was married for fifteen years," Chandra said. "We had two children. Do you know how much it hurts to think about my family?" Chandra sniffled. "I asked Doctor Hoffer if he could help me forget my husband and children."

Doctor Hedrick gave a little gasp. "I'm sorry."

"I thought about it long and hard before I made my request. I knew exactly what I was asking him to do. I wanted to make it as if they had never existed. He told me to think about it for a while." Chandra started to cry.

After a few minutes, Lisette heard footsteps, followed by the door opening and closing. Either Chandra or Doctor Hedrick had left the room. She sensed the closeness of the adult who had remained behind, and soon a hand touched her arm.

"Lisette," Dr. Hedrick said.

Harsh light came through the cracks as her eyelids lifted. When she blinked, it felt like someone was pushing needles through her eyes. Gradually, the pain stopped as her eyes adjusted.

She was in bed, and a woman she had never seen before sat beside her. She had sandy blonde hair and sad eyes. Lisette thought she was pretty.

"Who are you?" Lisette asked.

"I'm Doctor Hedrick. But I want you to call me Sandy."

"What am I doing here?"

Sandy's eyes misted. "We wanted to run a few tests on you, that's all. How are you feeling?"

"Sleepy. When can I see my friends?"

Sandy pressed something into her hand and folded her fingers around it. Lisette had no idea what it was, but it felt cold and slippery.

"Look," Sandy said.

Lisette gasped at the silver necklace. "It's so beautiful."

She looked at it more closely and saw it had a small silver heart dangling from the chain.

"It's yours," Sandy said. "The tooth fairy left it for you."

"The tooth fairy!" Lisette exclaimed.

"Smile," Sandy said.

When Lisette smiled, Sandy reached forward and gently pressed her finger against her lip. "Yep, the tooth fairy made a trade. Your tooth for the necklace."

Lisette pushed her tongue forward, exploring the gap where her tooth had been. When had it fallen out? The tooth barely wiggled the last time she touched it.

Sandy pinched one end of the necklace and lifted it. "Want me to put it on for you?"

Lisette nodded and giggled. She liked the tooth fairy and liked Sandy even more.

1.22
PORTLAND TRADING ZONE

Jordan, with Eddie by his side, watched a boy crawl out from inside a rusting SUV. The tires were flat and the passenger-side door was missing. Clothes spilled out like an upturned laundry bag from the passenger's seat. They were close to the fuel depot, the tall fence that surrounded Martha's compound only twenty meters away. Beyond the fence, massive fuel tanks and generators hummed like beehives. Floodlights on tall poles shined over a fleet of fuel trucks and several trailers. A girl wearing a baseball cap and rubber boots paced back and forth inside the fence.

"You got food?" the boy from the SUV asked in a deep, demanding tone. He had broad shoulders, and a fleshy scar split his forehead horizontally. His arms hung loosely by his sides, and he hunched forward.

"No," Eddie said.

"We've come to see Martha," Jordan said.

"F-O-O-D" Scar Boy said, spelling it out.

A glint of red light caught Jordan's attention. Scar Boy held a knife in his hand and the blade reflected the sunrays.

"Where are you from?" Scar Boy asked, twisting the knife.

"None of your business," Eddie snapped.

"Castine Island," Jordan said, thinking it was best to be friendly.

"Do kids there have the Pig?"

"Why do you care?" Eddie asked.

"Some do," Jordan replied.

Scar Boy gestured to Eddie. "You've got it. You know what it's like to eat and eat and eat, but never feel full."

He made a show of inserting the knife into a sheath that hung from his belt and then held his hands out in a gesture of peace. "Anything you got, please. Just a bite."

Jordan reached into his pack and took out the potato. "You can have a piece."

Scar Boy pounced and grabbed Jordan's wrist. Jordan focused all his attention on the knife the boy wielded in his other hand. Eddie cocked his fist, but Scar Boy threw a roundhouse kick that smashed Eddie in the face. A knee came out of nowhere and landed in Jordan's midsection, knocking the wind out of him. He doubled over, still clutching the potato. Scar Boy bowled him over and pinned him to the ground. Eddie was on his back a few feet away.

"Take it," Jordan said, feeling Scar Boy's pounding heart. "It's all we have."

Scar Boy grabbed the potato. "Give me your shoes, too," he growled.

Jordan, using his fingertips, swept the dirt and gritty pebbles from the parking lot surface into a pile under his palm. Greeting Scar Boy with a face full of dirt might buy them a few seconds to deflect the knife and strike back.

Chung chung.

The sound was unmistakable, and Jordan's rapid heartbeat shifted into an even higher gear. Someone had cocked a shotgun.

The boy gripping the gun towered over them. Purple tattoos adorned his ripped, muscled arms, and above his lip was a scar or a mustache. The guard with the baseball cap stood next to him.

Purple Tats gestured to her, and she took the potato from Scar Boy and handed it to Jordan.

Then Purple Tats swiveled the barrel at Jordan. "What do you want Martha for?"

"I'm looking for someone who works for her. His name is Spike. He drove my sisters and a friend to Colony East."

Keeping the gun aimed at Jordan, Purple Tats said, "Martha went to Canada. She thinks nobody has the Pig there." He gestured to Eddie. "Who's that?"

"My friend," Jordan said. "We're on our way to Colony East. I want to find my sisters."

Purple Tats pointed the gun at Scar Boy. "Get lost."

Scar Boy cursed bitterly. "We're all going to die soon." His tone was fearless.

Jordan gulped, wondering if Scar Boy was daring Purple Tats to shoot him. Purple Tats braced the butt of the gun against his shoulder.

Scar Boy had just tried to harm Jordan, but burning deep in his gut was disgust toward the senseless violence he feared he was about to witness.

"He's hungry, that's all." Jordan took a bite of the potato, spit the piece into his hand and passed it to Scar Boy, who scarfed it.

Scar Boy and Purple Tats locked eyes. Then Scar Boy slowly stood and skulked into the SUV.

"That was a waste of food," Purple Tats said, resting the gun on his shoulder. "Lisette, right?"

Jordan's heart stopped. "Yes, she's my kid sister."

"Abby called her Toucan. I'm Spike."

1.23
BROOKLYN

Abby paced across the roof's pebbled surface. Imagining something terrible had happened to Toby, she clenched her jaw to keep her teeth from chattering. It was eleven forty; he should have returned by now.

He had every right to be angry with her. If she had remained in the alley, she might have been able to stop Lexi from stealing the car.

She glanced to the south. The Colony East skyline was barely visible under a dome of stars and a half moon. Jonzy would soon head up to the top floor of the Biltmore Hotel, if he weren't already there. They'd be speaking to each other in less than fifteen minutes.

Abby turned on her walkie-talkie and celebrated a few seconds of white noise before flicking it off again. Then she sat cross-legged and placed the radio beside her.

The temperature had dropped a few degrees since the sun had set, but her fever gave her chills. She ripped a hole in the garbage bag, pulled it over her head, and then hugged a ratty pillow to her chest to generate warmth. Looking up, she identified the North Star, her lucky star. She made three wishes: for Toby to hurry up and join her, for Jonzy to safely escape the colony with antibiotic pills, and that they'd find a way to Mystic to meet up with Jordan. Pressing her luck, Abby made two more wishes: that they'd get Touk from Atlanta Colony and all go to the lake in Maine where they'd live in peaceful seclusion.

Hearing voices from the street, Abby listened intently. Ignoring the persistent cramps in her stomach, she crawled to the edge of the roof and peered down. Someone swept the end of the alley with a flashlight. The beam lit up the corners and then zigzagged on the ground where the car had been. *Toby?*

The light flared in her eyes, and she inched back, fearing she had been spotted. Toby would have called out to her.

The only way on to the roof was through the door. She thought about blocking the entrance with piles of bricks and stones, but then she couldn't remember whether the door pulled or pushed open. Instead of wasting precious seconds lugging bricks, she decided to arm herself with the flagpole spear.

Before she took a step, the door opened and a figure stepped out, concealed in dark shadows. Starlight revealed the walkie-talkie lying on the roof. The flagpole spear was somewhere beyond it.

Abby crept toward the weapon as the roof's surface announced each step with a loud *crunch, crunch, crunch ….*

"There you are!"

Abby drew in a sharp breath as Toby rushed to the edge of the roof. "Lexi, we're up here," he said in a hushed tone.

Ten minutes later, with Lexi and Toby huddled next to her, Abby trembled for a different reason. She was sky-high with relief.

Lexi explained why she had taken the car. "Kids saw me with the fish, and they followed me back here. Toby and I had always figured that kids might find the car, so we came up with a second hiding place, just in case. Abby, I was worried when I couldn't find you in the alley. Then I was really worried when the brick struck the car."

Abby turned on the radio three minutes before midnight. The crackling hiss of white noise reminded her of the sound a wave makes after it crashes on shore and the sheet of water slides back down the sand, churning up air bubbles from buried clams.

Two minutes before midnight, Jonzy's voice crackled over the radio. "Bossy, this is Lemon. Do you copy? Bossy, this is Lemon. Do you copy?"

Toby pumped his fist. "Yes!"

Abby's spirit soared as she pressed the button. "Lemon, I copy. I'm with the Trader."

"You and the Trader are together. I'm fishing at dawn. Do you copy?"

She choked back tears. "Lemon, I copy."

"Fishing in six hours. Over and out."

Toby put his arm around her, and Lexi was grinning. Abby glanced up at the night sky and thanked her lucky star for granting one of her wishes.

DAY 2

COLONY EAST

Ten minutes past midnight, Lieutenant Dawson gazed north from the top floor of the Biltmore. He and Jonzy would venture outside soon, and he was on the lookout for any vehicles or foot patrols. A half-moon outlined the buildings all the way to the Red Zone. The buildings were dark, and he saw no nearby movement. He raised the binoculars and scanned Eighth Avenue. The avenue was empty.

He moved beside Jonzy, who scanned the area east of the Biltmore. A large fire burned in the distance, about ten miles away in Connecticut, and a few barrel fires dotted the Brooklyn side of the East River.

Jonzy lowered the binoculars. "It's too quiet. Shouldn't there be patrols out there?"

Dawson shrugged. "The evacuation is a big operation. I guess everyone is consumed with getting ready for it."

"What will happen after everyone leaves, Lieutenant?"

Dawson had imagined the scenario. The survivors would see four or five jets lift off from the airport and know something was up. They'd discover the rivers were free of patrol boats and the colony was without lights. Then they'd invade.

"We're leaving a lot of useful items behind," he said. "Tools. Clothing. Food at Grand Central Station. Potable water. The chickens at the United Nations Coop. The kale crop at the Central Park Farm. I hope the kids can find the leftover food."

"They need antibiotic pills, Lieutenant, not tools and clothing."

He clenched his jaw and gave the cadet a quick nod. In approximately twelve hours, he'd be making his case to Admiral Thomas at Colony West, but first he had to make sure Jonzy escaped the colony with a handful of pills.

They moved to a table where they had piled the two backpacks holding supplies and sat on the floor. Dawson unfolded the checklist, cupped his hand over the flashlight, and turned it on to read the list.

"You should come with me, Lieutenant," Jonzy said.

"Wire cutters?"

"Check," Jonzy replied.

"Knife?"

"What can you do from Colony West?"

"We have a plan," Dawson said. "Knife?"

"*You* have a plan."

Dawson looked at the boy. "Listen, you have to trust me. I understand how the Navy works. From Colony West, I can operate within the system and get a lot more done. Admiral Thomas will support me. I know it. He'll send resources to Atlanta Colony."

Jonzy held out his hands in frustration. "What if he doesn't? What if you get stuck out there? If we all go to Atlanta, you can contact Doctor Hedrick. We can go to the pharmaceutical plant in Alpharetta and help them to start it up."

Dawson absentmindedly pinched the hem of the tablecloth. The silk cloth had been on the restaurant table, collecting dust since the comet had streaked by Earth three years earlier. Every fiber of his being wanted to go with Jonzy and search for his daughter, then to Atlanta, but he had weighed the pros and cons. The right thing to do was go to Colony West, where he had the best odds of saving hundreds of thousands, perhaps millions, of lives.

"Cadet, I assume you have a knife?"

Jonzy persisted. "Tomorrow, Doctor Perkins will find out that the pills were stolen, and I'll be gone. Biltmore Company will have lost two cadets. They're going to blame you for it."

"Everyone will be focused on the evacuation," Dawson said. "When they notice you're gone, it will be too late."

Before Jonzy could argue with him, Dawson quickly ran through the remainder of the checklist. Knife. Maps. Rope. MREs. Two-way radios. Flashlight. Hammer. Blanket. And finally, the map of Mystic with Dawson's home address.

"What's my address?" Dawson asked.

"Twenty-three Walpole Ave," Jonzy said. "It's near the intersection of Freemont Ave and Berkley Street. Your house is green. It's the only green house on the entire street. There's a pancake restaurant on the corner."

"IHOP," Dawson interjected. "International House of Pancakes."

"Sarah is three and a half years old," Jonzy continued. "She has a birthmark on her right elbow. We'll find her."

Dawson stood and picked up his pack. "Thank you."

Jonzy popped up and slung a pack over his shoulder. Together, they entered the stairwell and started down the forty-three flights in the dark.

"Hold on to the rail." Dawson kept his voice low. The stairwell was like an echo chamber.

Jonzy chuckled. "You know how many times I've gone down these stairs in the middle of the night?"

"More than I want to know?"

"Way more."

A rollercoaster of emotions interrupted Dawson's concentration, and he quickly lost count of the landings. Jonzy was right. He should go to Mystic. No, a sense of duty and logic told him to go to Colony West. *What about the duty of fatherhood?*

Telling himself to stick to his plan, Dawson cupped the flashlight and turned it on. They were halfway down. Jonzy took the lead.

On the ground floor, they exited the stairwell, slipped through the dark lobby, and were soon outside the Biltmore.

Dawson looked left, right and listened. The drumbeat of his heart sent ripples into a sea of silence. Moving on, they hugged the edges of the buildings where the shadows were the darkest. Moonlight revealed most obstacles, but they occasionally stubbed their toes on hunks of concrete, bricks, and other debris.

At intersections, one of them would creep to the corner and peer in all directions, while the other stayed twenty or thirty meters back, keeping an eye on the flank. The lead scout would dash across street. The other would wait to receive an all-clear hand signal before making his dash.

Two blocks from Medical Clinic 17, they heard a vehicle approaching. Jonzy dashed behind a building column and plastered himself on the ground. Dawson dove into an alcove. A quarantine van drove by, heading north, with its headlights out. Dawson couldn't see the driver.

After the van was out of sight, he crawled up to Jonzy. "It's heading toward the Red Zone."

"It came from the direction of Medical Clinic 17," Jonzy said.

Dawson chided himself for not considering a second escape route. The idea of passing through the Red Zone had appealed to him because Jonzy couldn't swim.

"If we come across a patrol in the Red Zone, you can disappear into one of the apartment buildings and wait until the colony has been evacuated," he told the cadet.

"Abby expects me to meet her at dawn."

"Better to be safe than sorry, Cadet."

"Why was the van driving without lights?" Jonzy's eyes widened. "What if someone else is escaping too?"

He gave Jonzy a friendly cuff. "'What ifs.'"

He checked the time. They were still ahead of schedule, but he had to get back to the Biltmore no later than zero-four-hundred hours, when he was supposed to rouse the cadets so they would be ready for the convoy to the airport.

On the move again, Jonzy's comment burned in his mind: was someone else escaping the colony?

Five minutes later, they huddled in an alley across the street from Medical Clinic 17. The clinic was dark, but the hum of a nearby diesel generator informed Dawson that the building had power. One or more scientists were possibly working inside their labs, wrapping up experiments and preparing for the evacuation. Doctor Levine might be camped out in Doctor Perkins's office, ready to deliver antibiotics to any cadet who needed an emergency second dose.

The thick artery in Dawson's neck throbbed against the collar of his Colony East uniform. He was about to pass the point of no return. Once he and Jonzy broke into the clinic, he had to be prepared to subdue anyone who stood in the way.

On hyper alert from the adrenaline pumping into his bloodstream, he sprinted across the street in a crouching position and took shelter behind a row of shrubs next to the base of the clinic. The scent of pine rising from the bed of wood chips spread around the bushes took his mind far from the colony. He shook his head and focused on the task at hand. He scanned the area and waved to Jonzy, signaling it was safe for him to cross the street. He removed the hammer and blanket from his pack. Jonzy crawled up next to him.

The video camera trained a cold, dead eye on them from the front door. The lobby, as seen through the glass door, was dark. Dawson handed the blanket to Jonzy and gripped the hammer in his right hand, ready to smash the glass. Jonzy pulled the door handle. To their surprise, it opened.

Dawson returned the blanket to the pack and kept hold of the hammer as they entered the lobby. Swimming through the pungent odors of alcohol and lab chemicals, they headed for the stairwell door. In pure blackness, Dawson pinched Jonzy's uniform to make sure they stayed together and held his other arm straight out as a probe. He made contact with the wall and followed it left until he came to the stairwell door.

When they were both inside the stairwell, he turned on the flashlight. If Jonzy were nervous or frightened, he wasn't showing it. They climbed to the third floor, heading for Perkins's lab.

Dawson had visited the lab once, in the early days of the colony when Perkins had wanted to show the company leaders the proper way to jab an Epipen in case a member of Generation M experienced an allergic reaction.

Before they stepped out of the stairwell, Dawson wiped his sweaty hand across his uniform and adjusted his grip on the hammer, ready to bring it down on someone's head.

"Hold on," he whispered as he turned out the flashlight and quietly opened the door.

Dawson made sure the door closed behind them without making a sound and moved to the opposite wall, tugging Jonzy behind him as he felt his way down the hallway. He stopped when he came to the third door, Perkins's lab. No light leaked out under the jamb, but that told him nothing. The labs had been securely built to contain fumes and biological agents. Right now, someone could be inside the lab with every light on, and they wouldn't know it.

Dawson thought the best approach was for him to go in alone and fast.

"Stand here," he whispered in Jonzy's ear.

Dawson turned the knob with a hand slick with fresh sweat. He pushed open the door one millimeter at a time. The lab was dark. He slipped all the way in, closed the door, and flicked on the flashlight. Seeing he was alone in the lab, he guided Jonzy inside and turned on the overhead light.

On a desk in the middle of the lab were three metal canisters, each the size and shape of a tall thermos bottle. They carried a warning: DANGER - CONTENTS UNDER PRESSURE. He instructed Jonzy to begin searching for the pills in the drawers.

"Look for an amber-colored bottle," he said. "The pills are blue or white."

Dawson searched a shelving unit along the wall.

After Jonzy had gone through every drawer, he sorted through bottles of chemicals and glassware on a bench. Continuing his own search, Dawson inspected every nook and cranny that might hold bottles of tiny pills, including the pockets of two lab coats hanging on hooks.

Five minutes later, they met up at the desk.

"Nothing," Jonzy whispered. "Now what?"

"Maybe Doctor Levine took them with him. I don't know where his lab is. Droznin's office is on the second floor. There might be some in there." Dawson checked the time. They were ten minutes behind the schedule he had set for them.

"Go to Doctor Droznin's office," Jonzy said. "I'll keep looking here."

"We should stick together."

Jonzy grinned. "Sure, Lieutenant. We'll stick together all the way to Mystic and then to Atlanta."

Dawson grabbed the flashlight. "We'll go to Droznin's office first."

Ignoring him, Jonzy picked up one of the silver canisters from the desk and started to unscrew the cap.

"Hey, hold it away from your face," Dawson sputtered, thinking it held liquid nitrogen or some other gas.

Jonzy followed his advice and removed the cap. He poured tiny blue pills into his hand.

Dawson inspected a pill up close. "It's the antibiotic. Perkins tried to hide them right under our noses."

Jonzy checked the other canisters; they also held pills. "Something's not right, Lieutenant. This is too easy."

Dawson was grateful it was easy. He shivered at the magnitude of their find. They had hundreds of pills. Each one could save a life. A ticking clock and an awareness of the dangers Jonzy would face quickly put him back on task. He placed two of the canisters in Jonzy's pack.

"We'll leave one just in case any cadets need a second dose."

Once they exited the clinic, they slipped behind the bushes. They were still a few minutes behind schedule, but Dawson's spirits soared nonetheless. The mission had gone flawlessly. They'd make up the time.

"I'm worried," Jonzy said.

"Everything is fine, Cadet. Let's hope getting you through the Red Zone is just as easy. Keep your eye out for that Q-van."

Jonzy persisted. "I have a bad feeling, Lieutenant. The door was unlocked. Someone wanted us to find the pills."

Dawson cuffed Jonzy's arm. "If you're worried, you can find a place to hide. By noon tomorrow, the colony will be a deserted ghost town. I'm sure Abigail and Toby will stay at the fish market."

"I'm just saying, Lieutenant. Something is not right."

They scurried across the street and followed the route they had plotted beforehand that took them along the west side of the colony. The shadowy silhouettes of windmills stood silent in the Hudson River, and a few campfires burned on the opposite bank. Farther on, the George Washington Bridge, both ends blocked with cement, looked like a monstrous etching against the starry sky.

Feeling safer, they crossed streets and intersections faster than before.

They were back on schedule when they entered the five-block buffer zone at the colony's northern perimeter. The few times Dawson had been to the Red Zone, he had always thought of Arlington National Cemetery in Washington DC, where the sacrifices of soldiers were on display in row after row of white crosses, stretching almost as far as you could see. Here, the horrors of the first epidemic were on display. Only recently had Navy teams begun the grim task of clearing remains, car by car, building by building, room by room.

He and Jonzy took a left onto Columbus Avenue, which led to the perimeter fence. Months earlier, a bulldozer had cleared the avenue of rusting vehicles, allowing security patrols to drive all the way up to the fence.

Dawson, realizing he was too comfortable, which made him less cautious and sloppy, suggested they resume the practice of splitting up and watching out for each other as they crossed streets and intersections. Continuing on, they moved more deliberately.

The fence came into view. He pointed it out to Jonzy and both took cover behind the rear wheel of a bus. He was surprised to see that no survivors were loitering on the other side of the fence. He'd heard stories of kids hanging laundry to dry on the fence surrounding Emory Campus, the main section of Atlanta Colony. Of course, there was a significant difference between that fence and this one. This fence delivered seventeen thousand volts.

"If you want to hide and wait until the colony has evacuated, now's the time," Dawson whispered, eyeing the buildings along Columbus Ave. There were hundreds of safe spots to pick from.

Jonzy looked all around. After a long pause, he shook his head. "I'm good. I'll go."

"Okay, wait here."

Dawson darted closer to the fence, stopped, and removed a pad of steel wool from his pocket. He teased it wider until the metallic threads stretched to about a foot long. He approached the fence and tossed the steel wool forward. It came in contact with two strands of the fence without sparking. The power was off.

He hurried back to Jonzy and gave him a big thumbs-up. Dawson's excitement, however, was short lived. Even in the prison of shadows, he saw Jonzy had narrowed his eyes in concern.

"I heard something," Jonzy whispered.

He cupped his hands around Jonzy's ear. "What?

Jonzy cupped his hands around Dawson's ear. "A car door."

The ropy muscles in Dawson's neck twisted tighter as he listened intently for several minutes. He heard nothing but the torrent of blood coursing through his arteries and veins.

Dawson's tension ratcheted higher. They were so close to the fence, and with this latest delay, time shifted from friend back to foe.

"We should find you a place to hide."

Jonzy's face brightened. "I'll make it through the fence. I'm sure."

The boy's beaming smile and confidence almost knocked Dawson off balance, and he found himself nodding in agreement.

They reached the fence without incident. Dawson used the wire cutters to snip three horizontal wires, making an opening just wide enough for

Jonzy to escape through. He dropped the pack he was carrying on the other side of the fence, and Jonzy did the same with his pack.

"See you in Atlanta," Jonzy whispered and crawled through.

Dawson saluted. "Good luck, cadet."

Jonzy slipped one strap over his shoulder and hooked the other pack in the crook of his arm. "Don't worry, I'll find Sarah."

A metallic click put every hair on Dawson's head on end. He'd know that sound anywhere. Someone had just taken the safety off a gun.

"Run," he shouted to Jonzy.

In no time, Jonzy had disappeared into the night on the other side of the fence.

Dawson, with his heart thundering, wheeled around as a flashlight burst to life, the beam drilling directly into his optic nerves. Someone stood only fifteen meters away. Squinting, he made out the silhouette of the automatic weapon, but he could not see a face. He had nowhere to run, so he raised his hands, hoping to stall long enough for Jonzy to get away safely.

"Going somewhere, Lieutenant?"

Dawson dropped his hands to his sides in shock. Lieutenant Mathews. She raised the barrel of the M-16 rifle and stepped closer, keeping the light trained on his face. He shifted his eyes left and right, looking for any place he could dive for cover. This close to an automatic weapon, only a sudden, unpredictable move would give him even a small chance of escape.

"Hands up," she barked as if she could read his mind.

He wondered how long she'd been watching them from the shadows. She must have seen him cut the fence and seen Jonzy crawl through. Why did she let Jonzy go?

"This ought to get you a promotion," he grimaced.

"Shut up and turn around."

He faced forward, pulled his shoulders back, and maintained eye contact. The old Westerns he used to read always said that even a cold-blooded killer wouldn't shoot someone while looking them in the eye. Mathews would need a heart of ice to shoot him now.

Fearing that her heart *was* that cold, he realized he was cornered. His mind whirred. Trashcans sat five meters to her right, but they offered no protection from automatic weapon fire. If he could make it to them and kick or hurl one at her, it might buy him a few precious seconds to sprint away. At the Naval Academy's target range, he had learned that hitting a moving target was much harder than it looked.

She brought a two-way radio to her lips. "Doctor Perkins, this is Lieutenant Mathews, over."

"Perkins. Over."

The scientist had responded immediately, as if he had been waiting for Mathews to radio him.

"I've got Dawson."

"What about the cadet?"

"Escaped," Mathews said.

"With the pills?"

"Yes, sir."

Hearing each new piece of data mystified Dawson as much as it troubled him. How did they know so much? Had he and Jonzy been seen on a security camera? Had Perkins or Mathews monitored the radio communications between Jonzy and Abigail? He was certain of one thing: Mathews could not have seen the pills that were inside the canisters buried inside the packs. His blood turned cold when he thought Mathews might have found the secret note he had written to Sandy.

"You know what to do," Perkins's voice crackled.

"Yes, sir."

"Perkins out."

Dawson gulped. Was Lieutenant Mathews supposed to execute him on the spot?

"I need to get back to Biltmore," he told her. "Get the cadets ready for the evacuation."

"We'll tell them you were chasing a cadet who tried to escape and you both fell into a sinkhole."

What struck him was her matter-of-fact tone. Mathews was going to kill him in cold blood and had already worked out a story to tell his cadets.

A vehicle approached on Columbus Avenue. The headlights were out. Dawson saw it was a quarantine van. Was it the same Q-van he and Jonzy had seen? It drove straight for them but at quite a slow speed. The headlights switched on, lighting them up.

"Don't move," she hissed at him, seeming to be just as surprised as he was by the mysterious van.

The van stopped and Admiral Samuels climbed out. "What's going on?"

"Lieutenant Dawson aided a cadet in escaping. The situation is now under control."

"I can explain," Dawson said.

The admiral cast a hulking figure before the headlights.

"Stand down, Lieutenant Mathews, I've got this." Samuels started toward them.

"Admiral, the situation is under control," she repeated.

The admiral stopped and planted his hands on his hips.

"Under control?" From his tone, Dawson knew the admiral was about to unload a full broadside verbal attack. "I said, stand down." His voice boomed, like the admiral of old.

Mathews's eyes darted from him to the admiral and back.

"Mark, there's something you need to know," the admiral said.

Flames burst from the M-16's muzzle and the admiral stumbled backward before he could say another word. Fighting to stay on his feet, the old man glared at Mathews.

Dawson leaped at her just as she squeezed the trigger again. As he was stretching out, in mid-air, he watched the admiral take several jerky steps sideways and crumple to the ground.

Enraged, Dawson clubbed his fist on Mathews's forearm and the weapon dropped. She fell to the ground too. He reached for the gun, but she spun around and caught him in the windpipe with her elbow. He gasped and grabbed his neck, expecting to find something ruptured.

Sitting on the ground, she gripped the gunstock and twisted her upper torso to take aim at him. Dawson lunged and managed to get hold of the barrel, pushing it away as bullets whizzed by his ear. The deafening cracks of gunfire followed a split second later. He held on, despite the hot metal searing his hand. She squeezed off fresh rounds that obliterated the van's headlights, plunging them all into darkness. A blunt object struck his head and stunned him. He received another blow. She was kicking him. He was still holding on to the gun, knowing that whoever held on the longest would most likely win this fight to the death.

Dawson's head snapped back from another blow, and he had to let go of the gun. He fought to maintain consciousness. Mathews grabbed the gun, scrambled back a few feet, and went on one knee. He groped the ground, feeling around for a rock, a brick, anything heavy and hard to hurl at her. His fingers curled around the rim of the garbage can lid.

Mathews cursed at him and connected the butt of the M-16 to her shoulder.

"Lieutenant Dawson, I got your back." Jonzy stood on the other side of the fence.

When Mathews turned her head, Dawson hurled the lid at her and raced for the opening in the fence. He heard it strike her and rattle on the ground. She cursed once again. He rolled through to the other side and hit the ground. Bullets tore through the air and some of them kicked up bits of pavement.

He felt strangely calm, as if he had punched through the inner wall of a hurricane to find himself in the eye of the storm. His mind was clear and time seemed to slow. He saw Jonzy up ahead, within range of the weapon but relatively safe, peering out from behind an old rusting vehicle.

He ran toward him, zigzagging, keeping the pattern random. Not until he reached Jonzy did he realize that Mathews had stopped firing. He made sure Jonzy was fully shielded by the car, and then he peered around the front. She was banging the gun with her palm. It had jammed.

He clenched his fists as sour bile burned the back of his throat. Admiral Samuels wasn't visible in the dark shadows, but Dawson knew the approximate location of the body. He trembled from the rising waves of anger, ready to charge Mathews.

"We have to go, Lieutenant. We have to meet Abby and Toby."

Every hot fiber of his being wanted to kill Mathews with his bare hands, but cold military logic kept him rooted in place. The goal was to save hundreds of thousands of lives. The goal was to find Sarah. Dawson slung a pack over his shoulder and nodded to Jonzy. Next stop was a fish market in Brooklyn, then Mystic, and then his house at 23 Walpole Ave.

2.01
PORTLAND

Jordan, Eddie, and Spike left the fuel depot in Spike's red Mini, heading to a place outside of Portland where Jordan hoped to steal a motorcycle. Spike had told them that getting a motorcycle would give them their best chance of reaching Mystic, some two hundred miles away. "The storm caused a lot of road damage," he'd said. "A car would never make it."

From the passenger seat, Jordan turned to check on Eddie, who had started running a fever. Curled in a ball, he clutched his sides and groaned, his face buried against the seat.

"You good?" Jordan asked.

"Great," Eddie said. A tortured cry followed his absurd reply.

Feeling helpless that he couldn't do anything for his friend, Jordan faced forward as the headlights lit up the eyes of a pack of feral dogs. The pack bolted away into the night.

Spike kept one hand on the wheel and the other hand resting on the shotgun cradled in his lap. Jordan had mixed feelings about the gun. Abby had it right, he thought. Better to talk and reason rather than threaten. Sometimes, that approach backfired, but she had proved it worked most of the time.

A log fire burned ahead of them, and they drove by a group of kids who were digging in the soil by the side of the road.

"They're looking for worms and grubs to eat," Spike said. None of the diggers paid attention to the passing Mini.

The scene repeated itself again and again.

"What was Toucan like growing up?" Spike asked.

Spike had asked all sorts of questions about his sisters and Toby, obviously concerned for them, but something about Touk, in particular, had touched him.

"Our dad was a librarian, so there were always books lying around the house. Abby read to her a lot, and that made her smart. I liked to horse around with her, and that made her tough."

Spike smiled sadly. "Well, I sure hope you find her."

"Come with us to Colony East. Help us find her."

Spike stared straight ahead for a long moment before he shook his head. "I'm sorry. I can't."

It was the second time Jordan had invited Spike to join them. Earlier, Spike had immediately declined, saying Martha had entrusted him with the fuel depot while she was in Canada. This time, he had hesitated. Was Spike having second thoughts?

As they neared their destination, Jordan's stomach twisted as memories of two years ago flooded his mind. He and Abby, both deathly sick from the illness that claimed kids when they hit puberty, had sailed to Portland from Castine Island, on their way to Boston where the CDC was passing out antibiotic pills. Their greeting party in Portland had been a motorcycle gang led by Kenny. Mandy, a tough member of the gang, had tried to rob them.

Jordan recognized a landmark in the headlights. A gas station sign had melted into a cone of black, hard plastic. Two years of rain and snow, deep freezes, and the blistering heat of summer had not changed the fiery sculpture.

"That way," he said, pointing out the road that led to Kenny's compound.

Spike turned down the road, carefully squeaked around a toppled tree, and took the first right. The Mini lurched as a front wheel dipped into a pothole, eliciting a tortured cry from Eddie. Thirty meters down the road, Spike parked at a street barricade constructed of washing machines, refrigerators, and televisions with a gap just wide enough for a motorcycle to pass through. A similar barricade prevented cars from entering the other end of the street. The gang's compound, a three-story house, was halfway between the two makeshift appliance barriers on the right side of the street.

Jordan didn't know what to make of the fact that no kids were guarding either entrance, but he felt a measure of relief when he spotted five motorcycles parked in front of the compound.

Spike handed Jordan a flashlight, killed the headlights, and climbed out. Gripping the shotgun, Spike raised the Mini's hatch and grabbed a gas can. Jordan told Eddie to wait for him in the car. Eddie mumbled something in response.

Jordan took the pack of food with him, worried Eddie would eat everything while he and Spike were away. From here on, he'd treat the food as medicine, doling out tiny bites to his friend in the same way you spooned out cough syrup.

Navigating by moonlight, Jordan and Spike slipped through the barricade and approached the compound. Speaking in hushed voices, they pointed out fat oaks and a rusty washing machine that could serve as a hiding place if they came under attack.

They reached the motorcycles without seeing anyone. Each bike had a key in the ignition, which made sense. Anyone would be crazy to walk up and steal a motorcycle within spitting distance of the compound like they were about to do.

Spike popped a tank cap. Bone dry inside. He checked two more motorcycles with the same results.

"Take your pick," Spike whispered.

If Eddie were stronger, Jordan would have preferred to take two bikes.

"Whichever one starts," he said and set his pack on the ground. "I'm going inside."

Spike held out the gun, offering to let him take it. Jordan's brain said yes, but he listened to his heart.

"No thanks." His brain informed him that listening to his heart was risky business.

"Shout if you need help," Spike said. Then he started dribbling gas into a tank.

Jordan stopped before the steps and looked up at the house, which was perched against a field of stars. Two years had passed since he was here last, but it felt like a hundred. Maybe survivor years were like dog years. Multiply the dog's age by seven to get its real age. Multiply every year after the night of the purple moon by fifty for all the horrors and tragedies the survivors had endured.

The glass in the front door was broken and a rank odor greeted him. The air inside was a swamp of decay and urine, sweat and body odor, and mold and mildew.

The flashlight lit up spider webs that crisscrossed the hallway and draped the doorway to the kitchen. It appeared as if Kenny's gang had evacuated the compound. He figured they had been unable to find any fuel and had simply left their motorcycles behind. Were they out digging worms? Maybe they had fallen prey to a bigger, more ruthless gang? That's how things often worked on the mainland.

On one hand, Jordan was relieved to find the house empty. For two years, he had harbored a thousand fantasies of coming face to face with Kenny. In the majority of those fantasies, he had seriously hurt Kenny.

Jordan knew the best course of action was to focus all of his energy on reaching Mystic, but something deep inside pushed for a confrontation with the boy who had left him and Abby on the side of the road to die, and who had indirectly been responsible for Mandy's death.

Jordan entered Kenny's lair and headed for the stairs, tiptoeing around piles of trash and trying to be quiet to preserve the element of surprise in case gang members were sleeping upstairs.

He remembered little of the compound's interior, mostly because he had been delirious with fever his last time here.

He recalled one incident in detail: Abby struggling to get him up the stairs. Nobody offered to help her. Weak and feverish herself, she had cajoled, poked, prodded, and half dragged him to the second floor where she had found a ratty mattress for him to collapse on.

Jordan started up the stairs but froze on the first step when he heard rustling in the shadows. His heart sent thumps into the darkness like sonar pings. Wishing he had accepted Spike's offer of the gun, he turned on the flashlight and swept the area where the sound had come from.

A small, pale face came into focus. A boy, sitting on his haunches, stared back at him.

The boy followed Jordan's every step with his eyes as he approached him. Jordan guessed he was eight or nine years old. The boy wore jeans that were free from rips or stains, and his collared shirt had a price tag on it. The tag triggered a memory. After the night of the purple moon, Kenny's gang had raided a nearby Target department store, squirreling away thousands of articles of clothing.

Jordan kneeled and aimed the light beside the boy. "I'm Jordan. What's your name?"

The boy stared through him.

"Are you alone?"

The boy kept his lips sealed, remaining as motionless as an owl.

Jordan moved closer. "Is Kenny here?"

Fear curdled the boy's brow.

Jordan tensed. The boy's body language had shouted, "Yes, Kenny is here." Blood rushed to his head as his heart pounded in his throat.

"Where is he? Upstairs?" The boy's eyes remained wide with fear. "Is anyone else here?"

The boy shook his head.

"Just you and Kenny?"

"I'm taking care of him," the boy whispered. "He's got the Pig."

Jordan inhaled sharply. The fact the person he hated most in the world was suffering from the Pig saddened him. He thought it a strange response.

"Are you hungry?" Jordan asked.

The boy nodded vigorously.

Worried the boy might also have the Pig, Jordan slowly reached out and rested his hand on boy's shoulder, startled by the sharpness of the bone, and then he moved his hand to the boy's head. Under the tangled matt of hair, his scalp felt cool to Jordan's touch. If the boy did have the Pig, he was in the very early stage.

"My friend is outside. His name is Spike. Go see him and tell him I want you to have some of our food."

"Henry."

Jordan smiled. "Your name is Henry?"

The boy nodded.

"Hurry up, Henry."

As Jordan shined the light, Henry skipped through the room, vaulted over a trash pile, and was soon out the door in search of food. The pattering of feet down the front steps and Spike trying to kick-start the motorcycle broke the heavy silence.

Jordan climbed to the second floor and opened a bedroom door. A bombshell of chills exploded in his chest, and he jumped back as a branch whipped out and smacked the floor by his feet. He danced the light across the oak tree that had crashed through the roof, crowding the room with leafy branches.

The hunt continued, and three doors down, Jordan found the monster lying in bed with his eyes closed and a blanket pulled up to his bare chest. Were it not for the long, stringy blonde hair, he might not have recognized him. Kenny had gained thirty or forty pounds.

Fearing Kenny might pose a threat regardless of his condition, Jordan looked for weapons, scanning the floor and the two tabletops beside the bed. Seeing none, he walked over and stood beside the bed.

Kenny's pale, puffy cheeks drooped, and folds of skin formed an accordion under his chin. Dark rings cradled his eyes. They were the telltale shadows of death. Kenny did not have long to live.

A motorcycle fired up. The engine revved several times before settling into a low-throated purr.

Kenny's eyes shot open. He stared straight up as confusion flashed across spidery blood vessels on the surface of his eyes.

"Who's on my bike? Who has gas?" His voice was raspy. "We traded all of our gas for food. What I'd give to ride one more time."

He shifted his head side to side.

Kenny spotted Jordan and blinked in disbelief.

Then his look deepened and he parted his lips. "You. You. Jordan, right? Abby and Jordan. That's it. The sailors from Castine Island."

A second motorcycle fired up, and the two engines burbled harmoniously.

Kenny coughed and coughed. "If you're not going to kill me, get me some water."

A bottle of greenish liquid sat on the table beside the bed.

Jordan pointed the flashlight to the table and slipped his hand under Kenny's head. The pillow was wet from perspiration. Jordan's fingers sunk into hot, sweaty folds of flesh as he gently lifted Kenny's head and brought the bottle to his lips.

Kenny slurped. "More."

Jordan gave him a second drink.

"That was good," Kenny said with a sigh.

Another motorcycle fired up. Jordan felt the throbbing vibration of the three bikes surging through his bones.

"Do you want to know what happened to Mandy?" Jordan asked. The words blurted out. All of a sudden, he realized this was what had driven him to enter the house. He had never intended to harm Kenny. He wanted Kenny to know that Mandy had sacrificed her life to save others.

Kenny looked up through two slits. "I bet she's at her grandparents' cabin. We were supposed to go there together someday. A lake in northern Maine. That's where she went. She always said it was so peaceful and beautiful there. I know Mandy better than anyone else."

"She died." Watching Kenny's expression closely, Jordan told him the story of how Mandy had fought off a gang at the water's edge so that he,

Abby, and Timmy could escape and safely sail to Castine Island. "Timmy was the boy you almost shot at Logan Airport. Mandy was his protector."

Kenny clenched and unclenched his fist. "Did she put up a good fight?"

Jordan nodded as the violent grunts and shouts of that fight echoed in his memory and sadness solidified in his chest like cement. "She fought four of them."

A small smile played on Kenny's lips, and the tears pooling in the corners of his eyes glistened in the light.

"Mandy was special. I miss her." His expression turned somber. "After the night of the purple moon, we had little kids living with us who couldn't pull their own weight. One of them was Mandy's little brother, Sammy."

He paused, staring up at the ceiling, as if watching a movie.

Jordan knew the story, knew how the movie ended; bitter anger flooded his heart.

"I told her she had to leave Sammy in the woods," Kenny continued. "Mandy was as tough as they came, but that broke her up. She was never the same again. I'm so sorry I made her do that."

Jordan swirled the green liquid in the bottle as his anger morphed to despair. "Do you want another drink?"

Kenny's eyes fluttered as he struggled to keep them open, finally surrendering to the weight of the lids. "One more ride on my bike. That's all I want."

Jordan dribbled a few drops onto Kenny's lips and gently dabbed the corners of his mouth with the blanket.

Spike charged into the room. "I've decided to go with you. I want to help find Toucan."

In the swirling sadness, Jordan felt a tiny flicker of hope. The odds of them finding Abby, Touk, and Toby, however slim, had just increased a thousand fold by Spike joining them. Spike knew how to survive.

"One more ride," Kenny mumbled to himself as the boys left the room.

Outside, Jordan let the fresh air wash over him and scrub his lungs clean of the foul odors festering inside the house.

Henry stood by the motorcycles, munching on a piece of potato.

Jordan stepped closer to Spike and lowered his voice. "Can we take him to your fuel depot?"

"Yeah, they'll look after him there."

"Eddie can ride with me," Jordan said.

"I got the little man," Spike said. "Henry, hop on a bike."

Something stopped Jordan from following Spike down the steps.

"I'll be right there," he said and reentered the house to give Kenny a small slice of potato to ease his pain during his final hours.

Abby would be proud.

2.02
BROOKLYN

Abby leaned forward and pressed her forehead against the steering wheel. She and Lexi were alone in the car, parked in an alley five blocks from where Lexi had first taken Abby to meet Toby. They waited for Toby and Jonzy to arrive.

Imagining the car could conduct pain the way copper wire conducted electricity, Abby willed the terrible cramps in her stomach to travel up to her head and then enter the steering wheel where the pain would spread out and disappear through the tires.

The cramps resisted the power of her mind and remained anchored in her gut. Frustrated, she sunk her teeth into the steering wheel, biting down until her jaw muscles burned. She lifted her eyes and searched the sky overhead for the North Star, but she would need more than a lucky star to survive. Where were the boys?

Lexi kept an eye on the street through the back window. Abby remained suspicious of her, so much so she wondered if the bacteria had infected the part of her that generated trust and belief in others. AHA-B had killed her old self, leaving in its place someone who was untrusting and paranoid. *Paranoia can be a lifesaver*, Abby thought. Lexi wanted something from them. Sooner or later, the girl from Brooklyn would make her intentions known.

She turned the key in the ignition one click to power the radio and tabbed to FM 101, The Port, which returned only static. She tried FM 98.5 next. The CDC station was also off-the-air.

"We could pick up The Port from Castine Island at night," Abby whispered.

"What makes you so sure that your brother's at the station?" Lexi asked.

"DJ Silver played a Beatle's song, *Here Comes the Sun*, and dedicated it to Abby and Toucan. Jordan knows that was our dad's favorite song. How many Toucan's are out there?"

"What's Jordan like?"

Why did Lexi care? Would that information give her an edge when she finally made her move? The less Lexi knew about her family, the better. "You'll meet him soon enough," Abby said.

"I'm not going with you to Mystic."

For a second, Abby forgot about the ten thousand spinning saw blades chopping up her insides. "Where are you going?"

Lexi took a deep breath. "Nowhere. This is my home. All of my friends are here. I'll miss Toby, and you. We could have become good friends, but I belong here."

Abby's intestines exploded in flames, and she flung herself to the side, cracking her head against the cup holder.

"Hang in there," Lexi whispered, gently stroking Abby's head.

After several minutes, Abby sat up. Maybe Lexi actually wanted nothing from them.

"When I escaped from Colony East, some girls saved my life," Abby began. "I might not be here if it weren't for them. They found me on the bank of the East River and took me to their house to recover. There are fifty or more girls living there. I don't think anyone is older than seven."

Lexi periodically looked out of the back window, but now, Abby could tell she was facing her.

"I'm worried about them," she continued. "Since you're staying here, could you check on them?"

Abby knew it was a lot to ask, but she had to try and repay the girls' kindness.

"Yeah, I'll do that," Lexi said. "Tell me where the tribe of munchkins lives."

Abby described the house and its proximity to the freighter in the East River that had run aground. When she finished, Abby realized she had narrowed down the location to hundreds of homes.

"A girl named Stacy lives there," she said, immediately thinking there were probably lots of survivors named Stacy.

Lexi seemed to sense her frustration and quietly asked, "Were you wearing your Colony East uniform?"

"Yes."

"Kids talk," Lexi said. "It's big news when a girl washes ashore in a blue uniform. I'll find them. I promise. So what's Jordan like?"

"Caring," Abby said. "And stubborn. He's a great brother."

When a long silence followed, Abby wondered if Lexi had a brother or sister. She wanted to reach out and comfort her in the darkness, but that nagging distrust held her back.

Abby reached instead for a bottle of water in front of the passenger seat and found that putting her head lower than her stomach kept the cramps at bay, at least temporarily. She stayed in this position.

In between scanning for threats, Lexi told her snippets of what life was like in Brooklyn. Her voice sounded more and more distant to Abby, and she knew she was drifting to sleep. Sleep promised momentary relief from the pain.

Abby walked down a path through the woods. Golden pine needles crackled and snapped underfoot, and dirt, silky and fine as powder, worked its way between her toes.

Up ahead was a cabin on a lake that stretched around the bend and maybe went on forever. Touk and Jordan stepped onto the porch and waved for her to hurry up. Touk couldn't wait any longer, so she leaped off the porch and ran toward Abby through the spears of sunlight. Abby opened her arms wide, ready to catch the giggling bundle of energy approaching her.

Abby grunted and her eyes shot open. Under a pale sky in a confined space of shadows, someone jiggled her shoulder. Several seconds passed before she remembered the bald boy with the diamond-studded ear was Toby.

"Sit up," he said, carefully lifting her.

The passenger door was open. Toby, with Lexi behind him, unscrewed the cap of a silver thermos and poured small pills into his palm. They formed a little cone, like a pyramid of marbles.

"Jonzy brought hundreds of pills. Maybe thousands," he said. "Take one. You'll start to feel better in four hours or so."

Toby then gave a handful to Lexi.

Abby pinched a pill between her fingers and felt better already, just knowing the antibiotic would soon go to work. She swallowed it. "Where is Jonzy?"

Toby pointed to the street. "Over there." He sneered. "You'll never believe who came with him. Lieutenant Dawson."

In spite of Toby's feelings toward the lieutenant, their plan was falling into place. Jonzy had made it safely here. The antibiotic was going to work in her system, killing off the AHA-B bacteria. They had a car, gas, food, and an adult.

Lexi made eye contact with her, reading Abby's mind. "Don't worry. I'll give pills to the kids who saved your life," she said.

Abby blinked back tears. "Thank you."

"Good luck finding your brother and sister," Lexi said. Then she gave Toby a kiss on the cheek and jogged out of the alley.

Distrust, like a chilly fog, settled over Abby as she had a sudden, certain sense that Lexi would sell the pills.

2.03
BROOKLYN – MYSTIC, CONNECTICUT

Jonzy whistled a block away. "Lieutenant, hurry up."

Dawson waved back, signaling he noted his urgency.

Then he reached down and gently gripped the wrists of the little boy wrapped around his leg and pried his arms back. The boy's skin felt piping hot, and he assumed AHA-B bacteria were the root cause. Before the boy could clamp onto his leg again, Dawson went on one knee and produced an MRE from his pack. The kid had already torn into the food pack by the time Dawson held the tiny blue pill in his hand.

"Chew it," Dawson told him.

The boy stared back warily.

"Go on. It will make you feel better."

The boy shook his head.

"It's candy," Dawson tried, and the boy gobbled it down.

Seeing that more kids were coming for handouts, Dawson sprinted to Jonzy.

"Hop in," Jonzy said, gesturing to the car that idled just around the corner of the alley.

Dawson opened the driver's side door and saw Toby behind the wheel. "Move over. I'll drive."

Toby looked straight ahead. "Get in the back."

Dawson froze, stunned. "Hurry up, Cadet!"

"Let's get one thing straight," Toby fired back. "I'm not a cadet. I'm not in Biltmore Company, and we're not in Colony East. We don't take orders from you."

"But I know the way to Mystic," Dawson said.

"Feel free to walk then," Toby said.

From across the street, kids spotted him and ran toward the car. Dawson hopped in back.

"Get down," Toby ordered.

Dawson obeyed, realizing he had entered a different world, a place where adults like him had consistently ignored the plight of survivors. He would have to earn Toby's trust.

The car lurched forward, and they were soon moving through the streets of Brooklyn.

Resting his head on the back seat, Dawson watched as a dizzying panorama of building tops, many gutted by fire, glided by against the blood-red sky of dawn.

Abigail sat in the front seat, not looking at all well, her face contorting from the constant state of pain, eyes half closed.

"Abigail, did you take a pill?" he asked

"It's Abby," Toby corrected.

"Yes," she said. "I'm feeling better."

"Oh, my God!"

They all turned to Jonzy, who was pressing his nose against the side window.

"Why are those kids fighting each other?" Jonzy exclaimed.

"Probably fighting over food," Toby said. "We have the adults to thank for that."

"We have to tell kids what's causing the epidemic," Jonzy said.

"Let's get to Mystic first." Abby grunted and doubled over.

"I thought you were getting better," Toby said in a concerned tone.

"I'm fine," Abby said. "It just takes time."

Toby sped up and slowed repeatedly, and rarely drove in a straight line. Dawson felt vibrations coming from the car's undercarriage. The axle or driveshaft was out of kilter.

"Will this car make it to Mystic?"

"Have you got a better plan, Lieutenant?" Toby asked.

"Call me Mark. No, I don't have a better plan."

"We'll make it to Mystic, Lieutenant," Toby replied.

Miraculously, the car kept running. The faster they went, the smoother the ride became. The kids spoke to each other in snippets, and Dawson knew when they had crossed the Whitestone Bridge, and when they hit Route 95. If they maintained their current speed, he thought they should arrive in Mystic within the hour.

"Mark, tell them about Atlanta Colony," Jonzy said.

"There are three primary locations in Atlanta," Dawson began. "The underground bunkers at CDC headquarters, the campus of Emory University, where most everyone lives, and the pill plant five miles outside the city, in Alpharetta.

"When we get to Atlanta, I need to contact Doctor Hedrick. She'll help us." He told them about the message he had left in Tabatha Williams's medical profile.

"How will we get to Atlanta?" Jonzy asked.

"We'll trade for gas," Toby said. "We have food and pills. We'll find the local fuel king in Mystic, or go to the closest trading zone."

"Fuel king?" Dawson asked. "Trading zone?"

"Before the Pig came, we found lots of ways to work together," Toby said. "Kids are smarter than you think."

Dawson bit his tongue, realizing it was senseless to argue with Toby. They rode in silence for a few minutes.

"Let's see if we can get The Port." Abby turned on the radio.

Toby shrugged when they couldn't pick up the station. "Maybe the antenna blew down in the storm."

"Maybe DJ Silver has the Pig," Abby offered.

"The station is a good way to tell kids about the Pig," Jonzy said.

Toby shouted, "Jonzy, lie on top of the lieutenant, look dead. There's a gang behind us. Cover him up."

Jonzy sprawled on top of Dawson as a roar of motorcycles grew louder until it reached a peak, and then it remained at that decibel. Dawson guessed the bikers were cruising on both sides of the car.

"Stay still," Toby commanded. "They're looking in. A big dude with an axe is checking us out. Abby, look sick."

The roar spiked as the bikers accelerated.

Jonzy sat up when the sound had faded. Dawson raised his head to peek out the window. The riders were speeding off, far ahead of them.

Dawson lay back on the seat, thinking about the potential for violence outside the colony and that which he had experienced in the Red Zone. A corrosive stream of questions ate away at him. What had Admiral Samuels wanted to tell him? What was the old man even doing in the Red Zone? How had Mathews known he would be there?

"A sign for Mystic," Jonzy cried.

Dawson felt an icicle pierce his heart. For the past two years, Sarah had lived in his imagination, happy and safe. Now, he was about to learn what had happened to his daughter.

2.04
MAINE - CONNECTICUT

Keeping their speed under twenty miles per hour to save fuel, Jordan, Spike, and Eddie headed south on Route 95. The highway ran the entire length of the east coast, from Maine to the tip of Florida, and passed within a mile of Mystic, Connecticut.

Jordan carried a shoulder pack and a full can of gas on the seat in front of him. Spike had his gun and a pack and also carried a gas can. They hadn't given Eddie anything to carry, so he could focus all his energy on riding.

Assuming Eddie found the strength to survive the rigors of the trip, Jordan thought they could reach Mystic by sundown.

They crossed the border into New Hampshire and passed through the state without incident. The three-lane highway was as deserted as the majority of streets in Portland. They saw a few kids on foot, several pedaling around on bicycles, and four on motorcycles that roared by on the opposite side of the highway. The lead rider had an axe slung across his back.

Approaching the bridge that separated Massachusetts from New Hampshire, Jordan shook his head at the irony. He was riding a motorcycle that belonged to Kenny's gang, passing by the spot where, three years earlier, Kenny had left him and Abby stranded.

When they were halfway through Massachusetts, still making steady progress, he realized they might arrive in Mystic several hours earlier than he had estimated.

Jordan kept his mind busy by focusing on the objects in his path, including the occasional sinkhole.

During brief stretches of smooth, unobstructed road, Jordan turned his thoughts to Abby and Touk. When that made him too anxious, he calmed himself with daydreams of Wenlan.

They stopped to gas up and take leaks within sight of the Rhode Island border, which was announced by a graffiti-covered sign. They chose to keep the empty gas cans with them, thinking they might come in handy later. The boys caught grasshoppers. Jordan and Spike stomped the insects with their feet before eating them. Eddie scarfed his down live.

About to roll on, Jordan held up his hand to stop them when he heard a horn blasting in the distance. Two trucks zoomed by on their side of the road, kicking up dust. Blinking in the gritty wind, Jordan guessed the trucks were going seventy or eighty miles per hour. The white pickup truck in the lead had a large, dead animal in the bed, evidenced by four bony legs with hooves sticking up. The boys continued on, and when the city of Providence first came into view, Jordan pointed out a crowd about a mile ahead of them. Kids were blocking all three of the southbound lanes.

They slowed and came to a stop about a quarter mile away. The crowd swelled as kids raced toward its center.

They crossed the median strip, revving their engines to power through the tall grass. On the wrong side of the highway, they traveled in single file down the breakdown lane, wary of vehicles that might come in the opposite direction. Jordan's eyes widened as they neared the mob. The white pickup truck seen earlier had flipped on its side. The other truck had flipped over too; its nose poked over the embankment. Kids were tearing into the animal carcass.

A quarter mile farther, the boys returned to the southbound side of the highway. The gruesome sight of the feeding frenzy stayed with Jordan.

About halfway between Providence and the Connecticut border, kids appeared from the tree line and raced to the edge of the road. Fearing they might collide with him, Jordan veered left, but the kids stopped at the last second. In his mirror, he saw them form a line. Were they playing a game?

The locals played "scare the biker" twice more in Rhode Island. Each time, Jordan swerved and experienced the same heart-pounding surge of adrenaline.

A mile into Connecticut, what appeared like a solid black carpet rippled across the road. They were crows. Jordan had hated crows ever since the night of the purple moon. The birds feasted on remains, and to see the birds gathered around an object on the ground always filled him with dread.

The throb of the approaching motorcycles triggered an explosion of flapping wings as the birds lifted off in a hurry. He breathed a sigh of relief to see the road was empty.

They stopped, congratulated themselves for making it to Connecticut, caught a few more grasshoppers, and consulted the map. Mystic was off Exit 90, seven miles away.

"Stay alert," Jordan told them. "We're tired. The final leg of a journey is always the most dangerous."

Just beyond Exit 87, Jordan noticed something amiss out of the corner of his eye. Spike had disappeared from view. When he looked back, Spike was sliding on the ground, separated from his bike.

Following two loud pops, Jordan's handlebars wobbled violently. He braked and held on for all he was worth, realizing his tires had been blown. Ahead of him, Eddie suddenly toppled to the right and bounced on the road, hard.

Jordan managed to keep the bike upright and came to a stop approximately twenty meters beyond Eddie. Eddie, pinned under the bike, shouted for help. Spike, thirty meters back, limped slowly toward Eddie.

Jordan headed for Eddie. Halfway to him, he saw nails scattered on the road. It was an ambush.

By the time he reached Eddie, the ambushers had come over the embankment, three girls and four boys all around fifteen years old. They took big strides. Each kid held one or more weapons: knives, lengths of heavy chain, bats. Eddie continued to scream as if his leg were clamped in the steel jaws of a trap.

The armed gang stopped when Spike cocked the shotgun.

Jordan lifted the bike and pushed it away from Eddie.

From skidding on the road, Eddie had nails hanging at odd angles from his pants and shirt, and some had punctured his skin. Eddie's ankle had swollen to twice its normal size, and Jordan feared it was broken.

"That's close enough," Spike said to a boy with chipmunk cheeks who was swinging a chain and inching closer.

Tears streamed down Eddie's cheeks. "Leave me," he said when Jordan started pulling nails.

"Yeah, leave him," a girl holding a brick said.

"I'll count to three," Spike said in a calm tone.

Chipmunk kept coming.

"One, two …." The gun was an inch from Chipmunk's nose.

"Three," Chipmunk said. "I dare you."

Spike held his arm rock-steady and began squeezing the trigger. The blast of silence tore into Jordan's heart. The slightest pressure on the trigger would decapitate the boy.

Maybe Chipmunk finally realized Spike wasn't bluffing. Fear clouded the boy's face and his cheeks jiggled as he swallowed hard. He cursed and turned. Within a minute, the gang had disappeared over the embankment.

Jordan and Spike both went to work on Eddie to patch him up the best they could. Eddie kept saying they should leave him. They told him to shut up and used Jordan's belt and the shaft of the motorcycle mirror to splint his ankle. Spike went to collect what gas he could salvage from the tanks, dribbling it into the can, as Jordan inspected Eddie's puncture wounds. The blood had clotted, but he worried about infection. Wenlan might be able to get Eddie some penicillin.

Jordan and Spike got Eddie to his feet, and then each hooked an arm over their shoulder.

Eddie cried out when they took their first step.

"Three miles," Jordan said. "You can do it. I believe in you."

Mystic was more like eight miles away, but Jordan knew if your mind believed something enough, you could make your body believe it too.

2.05
MYSTIC

Abby swallowed the last bite of the MRE Jonzy had given her and let her head flop back on the car seat. She had taken the antibiotic pill two hours ago, and it finally seemed to be working. Although she still ran a fever, she only had a mild stomachache, the kind she used to get in the seventh grade when she'd eat a peanut butter and jelly sandwich too fast.

Her brief sense of relief ended when they turned off the highway and entered Mystic. They'd reach The Port soon, and she worried about Jordan. What if they couldn't find him right away? How long could they look for him before they had to leave for Atlanta?

"Where are we?" Mark asked.

"We're passing a school," Abby said. "I think it was a school, anyway. There's a burned out school bus in the grass by a flagpole."

"Can I take a look?" he asked.

Abby, Toby, and Jonzy all scanned the immediate vicinity. On the right side of the road, a pack of survivors seemed preoccupied with catching bugs.

"All clear," Toby said. "Make it fast."

Mark briefly sat up and ducked down once he got his bearings. "That's the McCarthy Middle School. We're about three miles away from The Port. We should arrive at a Shell Gas Station in half a mile."

127

Abby turned the car radio on again, but the only thing coming from the speaker was a loud hiss.

They reached the site of the gas station, which was now a huge crater in the ground.

"We're at the station," Abby told Mark.

He peeked out the window. "Take the next right. Go about a mile. You'll see a water tower. Take your second left."

"What message should we broadcast?" Jonzy asked.

Abby thought that Jonzy was as keen to spread the news about the epidemic as she was to find Jordan.

Toby chimed in. "Go to Atlanta and attack the adults."

"Tell them to listen to the CDC channel," Mark said. "When we get to Atlanta and get the Alpharetta plant running, we'll broadcast instructions on the pill distribution. Until then, everyone should remain calm and orderly."

Toby banged the wheel with his palm. "The Pig will kill everyone while they're trying to stay calm and orderly."

Abby cast her eyes out the window. The flecks of glittering purple space dust imbedded in the sand that streamed by at the edge of the road hypnotized her.

"We should tell them how the bacteria attacks your body," she said. "Your mind makes you think you're hungry."

Toby placed the back of his hand on her forehead, his expression pinching with concern. "You're burning up."

"You can take a second pill four hours after the first," Mark said.

"I'm really feeling much better," Abby said, wanting everyone to concentrate on finding Jordan and Mark's daughter and restarting The Port.

"For real?" Toby asked.

"Watch the road," Abby told him.

After they took the second left from the water tower, Mark informed them that the radio station was about a mile ahead, on the left-hand side of the road, at the bottom of a big hill.

"The antenna," Jonzy cried, pointing to it.

Abby did a sweep of the area. Route 95 was now about a mile away. Plenty of vehicles clogged the highway, none of them moving.

"Mark, it's safe to sit up," she said.

Toby turned into the station parking lot. It had a few cars in it, but all of their tires were flat. A bicycle on its side offered a glimmer of hope that someone was inside the squat building. The car radio delivered an uninterrupted torrent of white noise.

With her stomach on fire, Abby wondered when the four hours would be up so she could take a second pill. She wanted to ask Jonzy for another MRE, but instead bit her tongue, knowing it would alarm Toby.

They exited the car. Fuel drums and a generation were to the right of the building. Jonzy used a screwdriver lying on top of a drum to pry off the cap. He put one eye close to the opening to peer inside, then sniffed. He waved his hand across the opening, wafting the odor.

"Diesel fuel," he said.

Mark pulled the starter cord to a generator. The engine fired up on the fourth try. He turned it off right away to preserve the fuel.

With a broad grin, Jonzy skipped to the station door.

The others followed him, feeling less enthusiastic.

"Hello," Jonzy called into the shadows.

A sleeping bag was bunched on the floor next to a couch. That lifted Abby's spirit a bit. Someone had been here recently. Soggy material covered half of the couch. The roof above had leaked, and the ceiling was partially collapsed. Empty peanut shells covered the floor.

Abby scanned for whole shells, consumed with the thought of crunching a salty peanut.

In the wall opposite the front door, a window looked into another room filled with equipment and a microphone. There was a door next to the window.

"That's the control room," Mark said and turned on his flashlight.

Through the window, he trained the beam on the ceiling of the control room; it, too, had sustained a lot of water damage.

The door opened and a boy stepped out. He had on a baseball cap, and gold chains around his neck tangled like strands of spaghetti. Despite the dark room, he wore sunglasses.

His jaw dropped when he spotted Mark. "Whoa, a big dude!"

"Who are you?" Abby asked.

"Who are you?" the boy asked, removing his sunglasses to stare at Mark.

"I'm Mark Dawson."

"Unreal," the boy said.

Abby stepped forward. "I'm Abby Leigh, and I'm looking for DJ Silver."

"That would be me."

"*You* are DJ Silver?" Toby said.

"True is the word. Sorry, I'm not taking any song requests. Water leaked on the soundboard, and it got fried."

"I'll get The Port on the air again," Jonzy said.

"And who are you?" DJ Silver asked.

"He's a genius," Toby said.

DJ Silver rubbed his chin and once again stared at Mark. "A freaking adult. Amazing."

Abby stepped between them. "I'm looking for my brother. Jordan Leigh."

DJ Silver scrunched his eyes. "Sounds familiar."

"We're from Castine Island," Abby said.

The DJ's eyes popped wide. "Hey, that is so cool! I got a lot of fans there."

Abby traded glances with Toby, then Jonzy. They had stumbled into another universe and were meeting one of its inhabitants.

"You dedicated a song to me and my sister," she said. "*Here Comes the Sun.* To Abby and Toucan."

DJ Silver snapped his fingers. "Yeah, yeah, yeah, Abby and Toucan. That's it. Your bro walks with a limp. He took a bullet in the leg from pirates." The DJ held his hand up when he saw Abby's jaw drop in fear. "He's fine. Wenlan is taking good care of him."

"Wenlan?" Abby blurted.

"Yeah, his girlfriend. How many fans would you say I have on Castine Island?"

2.06
CONNECTICUT

Jordan kept his right arm around Eddie's waist, hooking two fingers through Eddie's belt loop for a better grip. His arm crossed beneath Spike's. Spike served as a human crutch on Eddie's right side. Eddie had an arm draped over each of their shoulders. They inched ever closer to their destination — Wenlan's clinic — at a rate Jordan estimated would take them a long three days to reach.

"Step," Jordan said.

Eddie yelped as he slid his good foot forward.

His ankle had swelled to three times its normal size, and his skin felt hot as tar baking in the sun. Splotches of blood had soaked through his shirt and pants, though the bleeding from the puncture wounds and road rash seemed to be under control.

Jordan battled his own pain, his left hand cramping from carrying the can of gasoline. "Step."

"I can't," Eddie said. "The vibration goes up one leg and down the other leg to my ankle."

"Step," Jordan repeated. "We'll be at Wenlan's in no time."

Eddie went limp, forcing Jordan to shift his feet to brace himself while holding up the dead weight.

"Put him down," Spike said. He was also contending with his shotgun and a can of gasoline.

The two human crutches bent their knees, and soon, Eddie lay sprawled at the side of the road. They sat beside him.

A car approached, and Jordan jumped to his feet, holding up the gas can, pointing to it.

"Trade a ride for gas," he shouted as the car sped by.

Dejected, he sat back down. "Who would turn down gasoline?"

Spike shrugged. "How does the driver know there's gas in the can?"

Jordan picked up Spike's shotgun. "This is what scared them. Nobody would pick up someone carrying a loaded shotgun."

Spike cracked the gun open. "Who says it's loaded?"

Jordan's jaw dropped as he peered into the empty chambers. "All this time …."

"Yep," Spike said. "All you need to survive on the mainland is confidence. If you believe you are powerful, people will respect you."

"Trust me, Spike, your gun makes a difference."

"Confidence makes the difference," he replied, tapping his head.

Glancing at Eddie, Jordan knew his friend couldn't go any farther, and he and Spike were not strong enough to carry him outright. They had discussed splitting up, but Jordan had been against it. Now, they were out of options.

"I'll go to Wenlan's," Jordan said. "She'll talk to William, the local fuel king, and get a car for me."

Spike gave a nod. Jordan went to tell Eddie to stay strong, but his friend had passed out.

"Confidence," Spike said.

Luck, too, Jordan thought as he headed off.

2.07
MYSTIC

DJ Silver had given them directions, and Abby identified Wenlan's clinic immediately when Toby turned onto Shattuck Avenue. A line of survivors extended out the front door and into the street.

She scanned the crowd, keeping an eye out for Jordan. He might be hard to recognize. Toby had undergone a drastic change, shaving his head and piercing his ear to fit in. Her brother might have done something similar.

Jonzy was back at The Port, trying to put the station on the air, and Mark was curled in the backseat, hidden from view.

Abby shoved a fistful of pills into her pocket. "You guys go look for Sarah."

"Forget it. I'm staying with you," Toby said.

Abby took his hand. "Mark needs you. We'll all meet back here."

Toby narrowed his eyes, but before he could argue with her, she leaned over and kissed him on the cheek. "Hurry."

Mark sat up. "I can drive. I know the way."

"Tell me the way," Toby said.

"It's easier if I drive."

Toby made a face. "If kids see you, we'll never get there."

Abby stepped out of the car and headed off. Glancing back, she felt encouraged to see Toby slide over to the passenger seat.

After a few steps, she gripped her sides and doubled over as spasms erupted throughout her midsection. When she straightened, she fished a pill from her pocket, desperate for some relief from the pain, and swallowed it.

Many of the kids waiting in line were clutching their sides and crying out, obviously suffering from the Pig. A few hung their heads lethargically. Several kids held bloody rags up to their faces. Abby wondered if they had been involved in fights over food.

She couldn't decide what to do. One part of her wanted to help the kids in line, especially those who looked the sickest, by giving each one an antibiotic pill. Another part wanted to enter the clinic straightaway and see Jordan. She headed for the door.

Kids directed loud, angry shouts at her.

"Hey, wait like everyone else!"

"Who do you think you are?"

"Go to the end!"

Abby withered under the hard glares. "I'm not sick. I'm looking for my brother."

"Liar," a girl screamed. "I have the Pig too."

About the same age as Touk, the girl had toothpicks for arms and legs, and she had as much dirt smudged on her face as on her bare feet.

Abby slipped her hand into her pocket and pinched a pill, as if the muscles in her arm somehow remembered she used to care about others.

She gave the pill to the girl. "Swallow it if you can. You'll feel better soon."

"She's got candy," a boy shouted.

Out of the corner of her eye, Abby saw a flash of movement, and as she was turning her head, a girl drove a shoulder into her ribcage. Abby stumbled sideways. A boy with wild eyes wrapped his arms around her legs, and a second boy bowled into her, knocking her to the ground. A cloud of desperate faces blotted out the sun as kids descended like vultures, grabbing at her and pelting her with grunts and curses and raspy pleas for candy.

Helpless, she felt hands pushing into her pockets. Kids started to fight each other, and she became the recipient of their wayward kicks and punches.

Patches of blue finally appeared overhead and the sky brightened. The sun shone in her eyes as she lay, sprawled on the ground alone. Her sleeve had been ripped off and her pants were torn. A front pocket hung by a thread. She patted the pocket that had held the pills. It was empty.

"I told you no fighting!" a girl said sternly from the porch, addressing the kids waiting to enter the clinic.

The girl had on a white jacket, the type that doctors wore before the night of the purple moon, and her straight black hair fell below her shoulders.

Abby gulped, wondering if it was Wenlan. DJ Silver had never said what she looked like.

The girl came over and knelt beside Abby. "Are you okay?"

"Are you Wenlan?"

She nodded and lightly pressed her fingertips on a lump that had risen on Abby's cheek. "Does that hurt?"

Abby had just survived a mob of kids mauling her, and it hurt a lot, but it had been worth it to meet Wenlan.

"I'm looking for my brother. His name is Jordan Leigh."

Wenlan gasped and brought her hands to her mouth. "Jordan left a week ago."

2.08
MYSTIC

Dawson sat taller behind the wheel, craning his neck to thread the car between a downed tree and a minivan. The streets were an obstacle course of potholes, rusting vehicles, and the occasional crude barrier constructed of oil drums, cinderblocks, and other heavy objects.

In the mirror, he saw the number of survivors following them had increased. He reminded himself he was the first adult they had seen in over three years.

"There were two babies on Castine Island," Toby said. "Clive and Chloe. After the night of the purple moon, the older kids looked after them, thanks to Abby. You just have to hope that someone like Abby lived in your neighborhood."

Dawson squeezed the wheel tighter. Many kids had lived in his neighborhood, but he never knew their ages or names.

A girl, bearing her teeth like an animal, slapped her hand hard on the trunk. The crowd had caught up.

Ahead of them was a straightaway free of debris, and Dawson accelerated. Some kids broke into a run to keep up.

He steered around two young boys standing in the middle of the road with vacant stares. "Ever since Colony East opened, I wanted to look for Sarah, but in the Navy, you have to ask for permission from your superior officer. I asked three times. Three times my request was denied."

"I would have asked a hundred times," Toby said. "Then I would have just gone."

A rock struck the rear window, and they both jolted. Looking back, Dawson saw that one of the boys he had just driven around had a rock in his hand, and he sped up.

"That's what I should have done," Dawson said. "Listened to my heart, not Admiral Samuels and Doctor Perkins."

A mile from the home he had shared with his wife and daughter, he spotted familiar sights: the library, the town garage where snowplows were stored, and the car dealership where they had bought their Honda. All the buildings were gutted, burned, or covered in purple graffiti.

A quarter mile from his house, the IHOP sign still stood tall and proud — a witness to a Dawson family tradition. Before every tour of duty, he and Lisa, and Sarah after she was born, would go to the International House of Pancakes for a large breakfast. Afterward, Lisa would drive him to the submarine base in nearby Groton. They had always treated these farewells unceremoniously, as if he were going to a normal day job, not out to sea for five months. He would give Sarah a peck on the cheek, a slightly longer kiss to Lisa, and then tell them he'd see them "soon."

Soon had turned into forever.

He took a right on Walpole Avenue, ready to shatter into tiny particles, and slowed to a stop in front of his house. He struggled to catch his breath, as if he were inside a sealed bowl with the oxygen running out. The house looked empty, abandoned. Meanwhile, an army of kids filled up the street behind them.

"Nobody's there," Toby said. "Let's ask around the neighborhood."

"I need to go inside," Dawson said.

Toby stuffed a fistful of antibiotic pills into his pocket along with some MREs. "I'll meet you back here, Lieutenant."

Dawson inhaled sharply, trying to pull himself from the darkest part of his mind. "Yeah. See what you can learn."

Toby was already outside and talking to a husky boy when Dawson stepped out of the car with his pack. Toby gave the boy an MRE, and they both walked over to the car as the survivors surged forward.

"Get back!" the husky boy shouted, brandishing a knife.

The survivors stopped behind an invisible line. When a young girl crossed the line, the boy lunged at her. Before Dawson could react, the boy picked her up with one hand and threw her backward. She landed hard on the ground but seemed unharmed.

Toby stepped closer to Dawson. "If he protects the car, I'll give him more food, but we have to hurry. Someone meaner and nastier will come along, and then we won't have a car."

About to learn the fate of his daughter, Dawson lifted his chin and headed for the front door, floating through the tall grass as much as walking. Survivors tagged after him. Some of the braver kids reached out to touch him.

He stood on the porch and waved his arms. "Everybody back. Back!"

They held their ground. With the force of the crowd building behind them, he wondered if it were even possible for them to back up.

He entered his home and closed the door behind him. The silence confirmed his worst fear. He glanced in the kitchen. Cabinet doors open, shelves bare. The fridge was open and empty.

He stepped to the door that led to the back porch and faced a carpet of white and yellow daisies in the backyard. He had kept all of his gardening tools in the basement. His eyes misted over. He could get a shovel and lay Lisa and Sarah to rest in this beautiful spot. That was his purpose for coming here: to keep his wife and daughter together.

He moved to the base of the stairs, took a deep breath, pulled his shoulders back, climbed up the stairs, and soon stood outside the master bedroom on the second floor. He stepped inside.

The room was empty.

All of a sudden, he imagined a scenario that he had never considered. What if Lisa had taken Sarah to a friend's house so they could put the babies to bed and watch the moon turn purple together? The wife of a submariner, Lisa had an extensive support network.

Had he come here from Colony East during the past year, this is what he would have found: an empty house.

He moved to Sarah's bedroom and stopped cold.

Sarah's crib was in the room, along with two others. He wondered why there were more cribs. Toys littered the floor: teething rings, rattles, a slinky, a yo-yo. A heap of crusty diapers lay in the corner.

A mobile of circus animals hung above his daughter's crib. Spiders had woven a tent of silk that stretched from the cutouts to the crib's rails. He gently parted the strands, looked down at her, then dropped his chin to his chest and wept.

Sobs wracked his body as he relived the decisions he had made. If only he had come here the moment he had arrived at Colony East, made the one-hour trip, spoken up to Admiral Samuels.

In the darkest moment of his life, he straightened and clenched his jaw. Hundreds of thousands of children depended on him. He wiped a sleeve across his eyes and rested his hand gently on the blanket, praying that Sarah's soul was at peace, somewhere far from this terrible planet. He could only guess at what had happened to his wife in the hours leading to her death.

Deciding to let Sarah rest in peace, he stepped outside her room, where survivors filled the hallway. He stepped among them and closed the door behind him. A head taller than the tallest kid, he saw that they packed the length of the hallway and stood on the stairs. They had come through the front door and risen like the tide.

Dawson estimated he had around three hundred antibiotic pills in his pack. He could save three hundred lives. "Everyone out," he barked. "Now. Out. Move it. I want you to line up outside. Fall out."

The tide receded, and then he found himself on the front porch. The husky boy was still duly guarding the car, and there was no sign of Toby.

"If you have the Pig, raise your hand," he shouted.

He faced a forest of arms.

140

He ordered the line to move and started to give out pills. "Chew it, move on."

He felt alone and overwhelmed as the number of pills in his pack dwindled.

Toby pushed through the crowd and climbed the steps. "I found Sarah. She's been living in a commune down the street. A girl named Bettina has been looking after her. Sarah has the Pig, so I gave her a pill. They're in the car."

Dawson grabbed Toby's arm. "Are you sure it's her?"

"Yeah, I'm sure. Birthmark on her elbow. She sorta looks like you, Lieutenant."

"But in Sarah's room, I saw ...." Dawson couldn't finish his thought, suddenly dizzy and sick from the unknown child lying beneath the circus animals and spider webs.

"After the night of the purple moon, they used your house as a nursery for all the babies in the area," Toby explained.

Dawson took a deep breath. The typhoon of emotions raging inside of him had already left him battered and bruised, but they weren't about to subside anytime soon.

He handed Toby the remaining pills to pass out and stepped into the crowd. The tortured cries of "daddy" and "I'm hungry" rising from the ranks of feverish children sobered him as he made his way toward the car, expecting to experience the most intensely bittersweet reunion of his life.

2.09
MYSTIC

"Jordan talked about you and Toucan all the time," Wenlan said. "He told me you were the First Medical Responder on Castine Island. He wanted to talk you and your sister into moving to Mystic."

Abby and Wenlan were inside the clinic, alone in a room with teddy bear wallpaper. Abby had told her she'd come from Colony East, but little else. She wanted to hear more about Jordan first.

Abby listened with a combination of horror, sadness, and gratitude as Wenlan told her about the circumstances of Jordan's arrival and his four-month stay at Mystic.

In the back of her mind, Abby debated whether she should go to Atlanta and get Touk, or go straight to Castine Island and take an antibiotic pill to Jordan. She leaned toward going home, but she knew her brother too well. The minute he saw the note she had left for him, explaining she and Touk had gone to Colony East, he would come for them. It was possible he might even stop at Wenlan's on the way.

Tears streamed down Wenlan's cheeks. "The Pig is spreading. The only thing we can do is pass out slices of boiled turnips and potatoes. That takes away the pain, but only for a short while." She started sobbing. "My sister, Cee Cee, has the Pig."

Abby draped an arm across Wenlan's shoulder. The slight movement impaled her with a spear of searing pain, and she gritted her teeth to keep from crying out. "We have pills that cure the Pig." She told Wenlan about Jonzy, Toby, and Mark, and their plan to go to Atlanta.

Wenlan sniffled and leaned back with a look of disbelief. "You're burning up. How come you haven't taken a pill?"

"I have. A scientist at the colony infected me with a very strong strain of the bacteria. I'll feel better soon."

Wenlan peppered Abby with questions, which Abby did her best to answer. Then Wenlan said the local fuel king, William, could get them whatever they needed.

Wenlan left the room to send someone for the fuel king, and Abby curled up on one of the beds and stared at the teddy bear wallpaper. She closed her eyes and let out a string of grunts and groans, thinking about potatoes and turnips.

"Hey, Miss Bossy!"

Toby stood beside the bed.

Abby swallowed hard. "Did you find Sarah?"

"Yup, we found her. So, where's your ugly brother?"

2.10
MYSTIC

Amazed to be in a clinic started and run by kids, Dawson moved to a corner of the room, making sure to stay out of Sarah's sight. Bettina, who had cared for his daughter since the night of the purple moon, carried Sarah to the bed.

The other bed held a girl who was very sick with AHA-B. She had long black hair. Groaning softly, she lolled her head back and forth on the pillow. He expected the condition of both this girl and Sarah to improve now that they had received a pill.

Dawson tiptoed across the room to get a better view of his daughter, but she screeched in fear when she spotted him, and he backed out of sight again.

Bettina stroked Sarah's head and his daughter eventually quieted. "Mark's your daddy."

Sarah mumbled something, and Bettina put her ear close to her lips.

Bettina smiled sadly, shaking her head. "Not every daddy died during the night of the purple moon. Mark was on a submarine. After that he lived in a special place for adults."

Guilt turned Dawson's muscles to butter, and his shoulders sunk forward.

"I was on duty when Sarah was born," he said and paused to see if his voice would create an outburst. His daughter looked his way, seeming less frightened. "The commander sent me to the communications center where they had set up a live video link to the hospital."

Dawson smiled at the memory of Sarah's first, red-faced cry in the world. "My wife told me to sing to her. The first song that came to mind was the Marines' Hymn. My father used to hum it to me when I was a baby. So, I started humming. Under the ocean, ten thousand miles away, I serenaded my wife and baby daughter.

"When I finally arrived home, Sarah wanted no part of me at first. She was *very* attached to her mom. Who was this strange man? I'd pick her up, and she'd practically break my eardrums with her screams.

"So at night, I'd sit by her crib and hum the tune. One day, she pointed her finger at me. A lot of people have told me that a two-month old baby can't point. It's just some random movement of their arm and index finger, but I know that Sarah was pointing at me, because I pointed back, and she giggled. It was the first time she smiled when my wife wasn't around. After about two weeks of humming and pointing, guess what happened? She squeezed my finger. She wouldn't let go, and I wasn't about to leave. That night, my wife found me asleep on the floor with my hand between the rails of the crib."

"Hum to her," Bettina said.

Dawson tapped his foot and began to hum, voicing the words in his mind. *From the Halls of Montezuma to the shores of Tripoli. We fight our country's battles in the air, on land, and sea.*

Dawson took a step forward as he hummed, then another step. *First to fight for right and freedom and to keep our honor clean.*

He moved next to the bed. *We are proud to claim the title of United States Marine.*

Bettina gestured for him to have a seat. He wasn't about to press his luck, so he remained standing. Still humming, he started over.

Sarah had tucked one hand under her leg, but her other one was open beside her face, palm facing up. She gazed up with wide eyes, and the corners of her lips curled slightly up. He held up his index finger, and she slowly reached out, and he gently pressed it against her palm. She curled her fingers around his. Dawson hung his head, trembling in the heat of his melting heart.

2.11
MYSTIC

Abby gripped her sides and tried to keep from crying out in pain as the fuel king, William, pondered the question of how they could reach Atlanta. Pacing back and forth by the window, the boy reminded her of a slender, shy, fifth grader.

Toby, Mark, Jonzy, and Wenlan were also in the teddy bear wallpaper room. True to Wenlan's word, William had so far pledged to get everything they had asked for.

Abby was happy with William's proposal to deliver pills to Castine Island, in case Jordan was there. William had said he'd done a lot of trading with Martha, the fuel king in Portland. In the morning, he would send one of his gang members to Portland on a motorcycle with a supply of antibiotic pills. "Martha can keep half the pills if she agrees to deliver the other half to the island."

The pills, of course, would come from their dwindling supply. Wenlan had been passing them out as quickly as those infected with the Pig entered the clinic.

In case Jordan had already left the island, Toby was working on a map for her brother, showing the location of the Alpharetta pill plant. They'd leave the map with Wenlan.

Jonzy was still beaming from his conversation with the fuel king.

"Water leaked into The Port's transmitter and it short-circuited," Jonzy had explained. "I tried to reset the circuit breaker, but it's fried. I need a five-amp circuit breaker, wire cutters, solder, and a soldering iron."

"My gang controls an electrical supply house in Groton," William had said, adding with a shy smile that the demand for electrical parts had been low since the night of the purple moon.

William stopped pacing. "There are two ways to get to Atlanta: fast or slow."

The door swung open, and one of Wenlan's assistants barged in with wide eyes. "Wenlan, come here. You'll never believe who just came in."

Wenlan followed her assistant out of the room.

"Because of all the wrecks, only a motorcycle can navigate the roads," William continued. "I can get you motorcycles and enough fuel to make it to Newark, New Jersey. I know the leader of the Ponytail Gang in Newark. Leo owes me a favor. He'll give you gas and food, but then you're on your own. You'll have to deal with the White House Gang, and even if you make it past them, there are the Grits in Georgia. Have you heard about the Grits?"

"You eat them for breakfast," Toby said.

"The Grits will eat you for breakfast," William said. "They're a super gang. The leader rides a green Harley Davidson. From the stories I've heard, she's pure evil."

The Grits and a girl on a green motorcycle were of little concern to Abby as the cramping intensified. She worried more about her ability to ride a mile on a motorcycle, let alone a thousand miles. She hardly had the strength to stand. Even sitting on the back of a bike would be difficult. They'd have to lash her to the rider.

She imagined the slow way was to sail down the east coast. The idea of being stuck in a boat for three-to-five days was not very appealing either. How many kids would fall victim to the Pig while they were on the way? What if the wind died?

"Are sailing and riding the only options?" she asked William.

Wenlan returned.

147

"Who mentioned sailing?" the fuel king asked.

"That's the slow way, right?" Abby said.

"Going by motorcycle is the slow way. Your other choice is to fly, but there's only room for three of you in the plane."

2.12
MYSTIC

Even though Jordan had lugged Eddie for two hours and he had no sleep and little to eat over the past two days, he felt energized. His legs felt strong and fresh. Figuring he was about four miles from Wenlan's clinic, he broke into an easy jog.

Jordan wondered if the Pig was only widespread on the island and in Portland, but that hope deflated when he came across more survivors catching insects in a meadow, while other kids, armed with bats and rocks, guarded the field. They eyed him warily as he passed by.

Jordan spotted The Port's antennae a mile away. He remembered his last visit to the station. DJ Silver owned a bicycle. The Port was half a mile out of his way, but he decided the time he could save on a bike would make it worth checking out.

He reached the station in less than an hour and pumped his fist when he saw a bicycle. One tire was flat, but most bike owners had repair kits. The generator next to the building was running, leading him to believe that DJ Silver was inside.

He stepped inside, greeted by DJ Silver's voice crackling over the speaker mounted in the reception area. He stopped to listen.

"For real, dudes and dudettes. Call it what you want, the Pig or AHA-B, the germs are everywhere. The adults have known about it for months. They've developed an antibiotic and are only giving it to their precious seeds for a new society. You heard me, seeds for a new society. Those are the kids who live in the colonies. What about us? I'm afraid we're out of luck, big time."

Jordan shook his head to make sure he was awake. DJ Silver only dedicated songs. The Port only played music. Now, the DJ was talking about the Pig?

Jordan moved to the window to look into the control room. DJ Silver, kicked back in a chair with his feet propped up on the desk, had the mic to his lips.

"We can do something about it. They can make pills in Atlanta. I want every single one of you to go to Atlanta. Tell your family and friends to go there. Demand that the adults make pills for us."

A boy, fourteen or fifteen years old, stood next to him, scribbling on a piece of paper. He handed the paper to DJ Silver.

"Late breaking news," DJ Silver said into the microphone. "The Pig doesn't kill everyone, but if everyone riots, everyone will be killed. Share your food."

Jordan stepped inside the control room. Immediately, DJ Silver sat forward and put the mic down. He stared at Jordan. The other boy also stared, giving him a funny look.

DJ Silver grinned and shook his head. "Cool. We're having a Leigh family reunion here."

2.13
EMORY CAMPUS

An ember of agitation burned in Doctor Perkins's chest as he peered out his second-story office window, surveying the grounds of what was once part of Emory University.

Perkins could not pull his eyes from the perimeter fence. Some type of green material was affixed to it. A section had ripped, and he could see ragged-looking survivors gawking at them. Did guards even patrol the area along the colony perimeter? Under normal circumstances, a six-foot high fence topped with razor wire would serve as a deterrent, but the desperation of the survivors increased by the day.

Lieutenant Mathews's voice crackled on his walkie-talkie. "Doctor Perkins."

Perkins brought the radio to his lips. "I was about to contact you."

"There's something you should see, sir. A communication we picked up from a radio station in Mystic."

After signing off, Perkins retreated to his desk and reminded himself that compared to the day's biggest event, all these problems were minor. Earlier, four planes had safely transported the seeds of the new society to Atlanta from Colony East.

Mathews entered his office five minutes later and passed him a transcript.

DJ Silver says be cool. Dudes, the adults are giving us the shaft. They have a cure for the Pig, but they don't want you to know it. They want us to die or kill each other over food. Are we gonna let that happen? No way. Dudes, listen to Silvy. The adults have gone to Atlanta.

Perkins crumpled the paper and dropped it into the trash. "Dawson?"

"It has to be," Mathews said.

"What's the range of the station?"

Mathews maintained a steely expression. "About a sixty-mile radius during the day. At night, someone could pick it up from several hundred miles away."

Perkins drummed his fingers, pleased with the idea that popped into his mind. "Start up the CDC station. Inform the survivors that we are making progress on the development of an antibiotic, and we expect to begin distribution soon. Tell them to stay indoors and wait for further updates."

"Yes, sir."

"Don't call it the Pig. It's the AHA-B mutation syndrome. I abhor sloppy scientific terminology."

Mathews nodded. "Don't worry about Dawson."

Perkins tented his fingers. "He's a thousand miles away, and he has three thousand useless sugar pills, but he's proven he can still be a thorn in our sides. It's prudent to remain wary."

She narrowed her eyes. "I can handle him."

"Yes, I'm sure. Now, for more important matters. The security here is appalling. I want you to prepare the bunker to house everyone on campus. We should plan to stay there for up to two months."

"When do you want to make the move?"

"ASAP."

Mathews saluted and headed for the door.

"Lieutenant," he called before she exited. "I told Doctor Hoffer to inform the staff that Admiral Samuels had a massive heart attack. Hoffer asked if I was planning to hold a memorial service. I thought you should know."

"A memorial service is an excellent idea, sir."

Perkins studied her face. It was a mask of pure composure. Less than twenty-four hours ago, she had gunned down her commanding officer, and she seemed pleased to hold a memorial service for him.

"Have a seat," he said, wanting to find out what made Mathews tick. "I bet you didn't know I had an identical twin brother? His name was Donald. We were inseparable. We played chess together. Our parents gave us an ant farm."

In the chair, Mathews sat ramrod straight with the cold eyes of an assassin.

"Sadly, we were born with a heart condition known as Wolff-Parkinson-White Syndrome. Our hearts had an extra circuit. For those with the syndrome, electrical signals sometimes travel down an abnormal pathway that stimulates the ventricles to contract prematurely. The heart races, pumping less and less blood. Three hundred beats per minute are not uncommon.

"Donald went into cardiac arrest and died at the age of ten. The year after his death, medical researchers at Princeton developed a procedure to burn the extra circuit. I had the procedure performed on me, and my heart has beaten steadily ever since. My grief has never left me. It ages like wine.

"I came away from that experience with a revelation. Science can end suffering. The greatest crime of humanity would be to sit idly by as we lose the foundation of our knowledge. That's what drives me to ensure the success of Generation M. Lieutenant, do you believe in God?"

"Yes, I do believe in God."

"I'm afraid I don't," Perkins said, "but if there is a higher power, I've fancied that He created the Perkins twins for a reason. If one of us failed, the other could carry on and complete the mission. We were a redundant system, so to speak. What about you, Lieutenant? Has a life event shaped your direction? What motivates you?"

"I like to win."

Perkins waited for more, but her stare unnerved him. "Very well, then. Both Generation M and I are counting on your winning ways, *Captain Mathews.*"

That got a grin out of the assassin.

2.14
MYSTIC

Abby trembled in fear as she stood before the red and white airplane. The wing was above the cockpit. There were two seats up front and two in the back.

As much as her stomach hurt, it seemed risky to fly to Atlanta at any time, but with only one hour of daylight left, it seemed suicidal.

The plane's pilot was Maggie, a fourteen-year-old girl with blonde pigtails. William had introduced her as his best pilot.

"How far have you flown before?" Mark asked the pilot.

"I've gone to Providence," Maggie replied.

Providence was north. The round trip there and back was around a hundred miles. Atlanta was a thousand miles south.

Maggie flipped through the pages of a road atlas. "We'll fly low and follow the major highways. We'll need to land once to refuel."

"At night?" Toby asked in a tone of concern.

"The moon's out," Maggie replied.

"What if it gets cloudy?" Mark asked.

Maggie shrugged. "We turn around and land where we can."

Her tone of confidence put Abby a little more at ease.

"The plane cruises at a hundred and thirty miles per hour and has a range of seven hundred miles," Mark said, reading from a manual he had found in the cockpit. "We could land at Ronald Reagan airport in Washington DC. After refueling, we can fly all the way to Atlanta."

"No problem," Maggie said with a gleam in her eye.

"It says you need fifty meters of runway to take off," Mark went on. "We're carrying a lot of extra weight. How long is this runway?"

Abby looked down the straight stretch of Route 1 that had been cleared of trucks and cars. There was an overpass at the end. Imagining the plane slamming into the bridge, the shred of calmness she had evaporated.

"Sixty meters," William chimed.

The color drained from Maggie's cheeks. "We're not going to let a little bridge stop us, are we?" After a long beat of silence, she added, "Good. Let's hit the sky."

"Help me get in, please," Abby said to Toby, feeling her legs were about to give out.

He furrowed his brow. "Abby, I think we should wait until morning."

She didn't have the energy to argue. "Fine, I'll get in myself."

Scrunching his brow at her stubbornness, he hooked his arm around her waist, and just in time, because Abby felt her knees buckle. Soon, she was sitting in the back, fastening her seatbelt.

Mark, Maggie, and Toby loaded the supplies into the plane's cargo bay. William had provided them with thirty gallons of aviation gasoline in five separate cans, as well as drinking water, a few potatoes, a fully charged car battery, flashlights, and a tool kit. If they made it to Atlanta, they could use any leftover aviation gas in an automobile.

Abby saw William give a handgun to Mark. Toby saw the gun, too. Without saying a word, Mark slipped it into his pack and climbed into the co-pilot's seat.

"Who says you're sitting up front?" Toby said.

"Do you know how to fly?" Mark asked.

"No, do you?" Toby challenged.

Mark shook his head.

"Toby, sit next to me," Abby said. Every second they argued delayed them.

Keeping his eye on Mark, Toby said, "Just so you know, I'm letting you sit up front."

He buckled in next to Abby and held her hand.

"Look after Sarah, please," Mark said to William. "I think she'll start to improve soon. Make sure she drinks plenty of water. Bettina should stay with Sarah. As soon as we start manufacturing pills, I'll come back to get her."

"Bring lots of pills with you," William said.

After the fuel king had moved back from the plane, Maggie pushed a silver button on the console in front of her and the engine coughed to life. Through the spinning propeller, Abby saw the overpass ahead of them.

Maggie coaxed a knob forward, revving the engine. The whole plane vibrated and then started to roll. Maggie eased the knob back. The plane turned, and she taxied to the end of the runway. She was going to need every available inch of runway to clear the bridge.

Toby squeezed Abby's hand so hard it hurt, and Mark stared straight ahead with a clenched jaw.

"I have a confession," Maggie said. "William has better pilots, but none of them would take you. I volunteered because I believe in what you are doing."

She pushed the knob all the way forward. Shuddering and shaking, aching to fly, the plane didn't budge. When Maggie released the brakes, they lurched forward.

Wishing to keep her eyes open, but not wanting to look at the approaching bridge, Abby focused on what had once been a Jiffy Lube shop. When it passed by, she knew the bridge was getting close. The wheels were still rumbling along the ground.

Abby's heart hammered in her chest as the milliseconds ticked by. They were going fast, and she figured they were now past the point of no return, and it was too late to brake.

The wheels lifted off the ground, and the nose of the plane reared back, pushing Abby against her seat. All she saw was sky straight ahead. Looking out the side window, she realized they were climbing almost vertically. The bridge passed beneath her, then a horn started blaring, sounding like an alarm clock.

"We're going to stall," Mark shouted.

The nose dropped, and Abby felt weightless. The horn silenced and the plane leveled off. They started climbing gradually.

"I've known a lot of aircraft carrier jet pilots, and very few of them could have flown like that," Mark said.

"You are the best pilot and the bravest," Abby added.

The coastline came into view, and she settled back in her seat as they sped toward Atlanta at a hundred and thirty miles per hour. All that separated her from Touk was a brave pilot flying them a thousand miles through the night.

2.15
MYSTIC

In The Port's parking lot, Jordan pumped up the tires of DJ Silver's bike.

The story Jonzy Billings had told him had stirred up every emotion imaginable, but rage and hope seemed to float to the top.

Finished pumping the tires, Jordan took a spin around the parking lot and pulled up to Jonzy.

"After I get help for my friend, Eddie, want to come to Atlanta with me and Spike?" Jordan asked.

The way Spike felt about Toucan, Jordan was sure he would join him.

Jonzy grinned. "You bet. We can start up radio stations along the way."

The boys agreed to meet at Wenlan's later on.

Jordan pedaled away, still in shock that he had come so close to seeing Abby.

Gravity was his friend on the first leg of the ride to the clinic. Praying the tires held up, he cruised down the hill fast enough to feel the tug on his scalp as the wind blew his hair back.

Gravity exacted its toll as he struggled to climb up a steep incline. With the hill amplifying his fatigue, he hopped off the bike and pushed it, slowly trudging up the hill. When he reached the crest, he pedaled his brains out, all the way to Wenlan's.

A crowd had formed two blocks from the clinic. Kids, sick with the Pig, filled the street and formed a bottleneck at the clinic's front door.

Jordan ditched the bike and went to the back door. It was locked. Eddie's life was more important than the glass in the door, but just as Jordan was about to smash it with a rock, he saw a window on the first floor slightly ajar.

He piled cinder blocks on the ground beneath the window, stood on them, opened the window wider, and launched himself inside. Halfway in, with the sill digging into his stomach, he saw two beds with patients in them. It took him a moment to recognize the girl with dark hair: Cee Cee, Wenlan's twelve-year-old sister. The other girl was a toddler.

Jordan wormed his way into the room and tiptoed over to Cee Cee. Not wanting to frighten her, he whispered, "Cee Cee, it's me, Jordan."

Cee Cee's lids barely lifted, revealing watery, bloodshot eyes. His stomach dropped when he rested his hand on hers. Cee Cee was burning up with fever. She looked as bad as Kenny had.

Cee Cee closed her eyes. If she had recognized him, she hadn't shown it in any way.

Jordan rested his hand on the toddler's forehead. She, too, was suffering from a high fever.

His heart pounded as he stepped into the hallway, figuring he'd find Wenlan taking care of patients and passing out the pills that Abby, Toby, Jonzy, and the adult had given her.

He opened the door to the examination room, and his knees buckled. Wenlan had her back to him. She was using her fingertips to probe the neck of a boy who had his shirt off, revealing a lattice of bony ribs.

Jordan cleared his throat.

Wenlan turned, and her jaw dropped in shock. They stared at each other for what felt like an eternity. Jordan's mind was as frozen as his limbs.

They met halfway and embraced. As he held her trembling body, he closed his eyes to block out all other distractions. When he opened them again, the boy on the examination table stared back listlessly.

He could have held Wenlan for hours, but an image of Eddie flashed across his mind, and he pushed back, still keeping his hands on Wenlan's upper arms. He drew in a sharp breath, horrified at how exhausted she looked. He must have looked equally as tired, as well as dirty and weather-beaten. What mattered most was that Wenlan's skin felt cool to the touch. Thank God she didn't have the Pig.

"My friend is sick. I need to get a pill for him," Jordan babbled. "Can William get me a car? We need to go to Atlanta. I don't mean by car. We need motorcycles. I met Jonzy at The Port. I know where Abby went."

Words tumbled from Wenlan too. "Cee Cee has the Pig, but she will get better soon. William will get you a car. Abby was very sick, but she took two pills. She'll get better. You should take a pill. We're passing out pills, but the number of sick kids showing up keeps increasing. Everyone wants food. Fights keep breaking out. And Jordan? I love you."

He embraced her, pulling her closer and closer. The beating of Wenlan's heart anchored him in the turbulence that surrounded them. "I love you, too."

DAY 3

WASHINGTON DC - GEORGIA

Abby was grateful for the steady, loud noise of the propeller and engine because it allowed her to grunt freely as endless waves of cramps steamrolled her midsection. She wanted Mark and Toby to concentrate on navigating, not on her condition.

Delirious with fever, Abby rested her head against Toby's shoulder, slipping back and forth between the blur of dreams and an awareness of the moment. One minute, she'd know it was the moon out the window; the next minute, she'd ask herself why someone was shining a light in her face.

Maggie flew low, just above the treetops. The moonlight painted the highway pavement a lighter shade of gray, and the shadowy hulks of eighteen-wheelers were like buoys marking a channel.

Earlier, Abby had tried to help navigate, but her mind turned the highway into a twisting river and the sporadic fires burning below into stars in a black sky.

They were on the second leg of the journey to Atlanta. After flying over the White House, they had landed at an airport in Washington DC where Mark had hopped out, removed the gas cans from the storage area, and poured gas into the wing tanks. After taking off, they had flown for about two hours.

"Route 385 should be coming up soon," Mark said. "Follow it to the right. It goes southeast."

By knowing their air speed and the time aloft, he could plot their course on a road atlas.

"Shield your eyes," he said before turning on the flashlight to read the atlas.

Bright light damaged night vision. Heeding Mark's instruction, Maggie held up her right hand as a shade, and Toby dropped his chin to his chest and covered his eyes with his hand. Cupping the flashlight, Mark turned it on and consulted the map. Abby fixed her eyes on the lines between his fingers glowing bright red. When he flicked off the light, she saw a haze of gold and green.

"I'm giving Abby another pill," Toby said.

She felt his fingers walk across her face, pry apart her lips, and push an antibiotic pill into her mouth. It was her third one. It crumbled and sat under her tongue like a pinch of chalk. She didn't have enough saliva for it to dissolve.

Bomb blasts of cramps exploding in her stomach got her attention, and she forgot about the pill.

Toby cried out excitedly that he spotted Atlanta ahead, but Mark said the tall buildings were in the city of Charlotte, North Carolina. The wings suddenly dipped hard left, then right. Each change of direction coincided with a force that pushed Abby into her seat and made her head spin.

"That was close," Mark said. "Good job, Maggie."

Abby's fingers hurt from how hard Toby had squeezed them. He, too, must have feared they would crash into a building.

Sometime later, she became aware of the plane tilting one way, then the other. They were making long sweeping turns, maybe even flying in a circle. She listened to the chatter of voices and learned they were low on fuel, and the moon had gone behind the clouds.

"Let's look for a place to land," Mark said.

"How far are we from Atlanta?" Maggie asked.

Mark warned them he was going to turn on the flashlight. "Maybe twenty miles," he said while looking at the map.

"I can climb above the clouds," Maggie said. "There might be a break ahead. We'll keep heading southeast."

Maggie, Toby, and Mark engaged in a debate. Should they look for a place to land or forge ahead? In the feverish landscape of her mind, it was hard for Abby to make sense of what they were saying. She understood it was risky to land in the pitch dark and just as it was risky to fly above the clouds. Descending through the clouds, they would be blind to trees, buildings, and the contours of the land. Mark wanted to land sooner rather than later. Maggie wanted to climb higher and hunt for a break in the clouds closer to Atlanta. Toby kept changing his mind.

"We should land now," Mark interjected.

"Abby, what do you want to do?" Toby asked.

Mark shook his head. "She's still recovering from the Pig. She doesn't even know where we are."

Abby lifted her head. "Go to Atlanta."

Toucan was in Atlanta, and Abby wanted to get as close to her as possible.

"If that's what she wants," Toby said, "then so do I. Let's do it!"

Mark remained silent, the engine roar grew louder, and Abby felt herself pushed deeper into the seat. Soon, her ears were popping.

Maggie called out their altitude in increments of five-hundred feet. "One thousand. Fifteen hundred. Two thousand."

The plane buffeted when they entered the clouds. "Twenty-five hundred. Three thousand."

Still in the clouds at four-thousand feet, Abby tightened her seatbelt and cried out from the increase of pressure on her stomach. She unbuckled the belt, fearing she would pass out from the pain.

After climbing another five-hundred feet, they burst into the clear with a starry sky above. From moonlight reflecting off the tops of clouds, a brilliant sea of white stretched out before them in all directions. The ride was so smooth, it felt as if they had stopped and were suspended.

Maggie climbed to ten-thousand feet, and Mark spotted it first. Up ahead, what started as a tiny rip in the clouds spread wider, and in the dark gap, skyscrapers poked up like little matchsticks.

Abby's optimism shattered into shards of dread as the whistle of wind replaced the growling vibration.

The engine had quit.

Nobody spoke for a long moment.

"We can make it," Maggie said. "I think."

"What's the glide ratio of this plane?" Mark asked in a shaky voice.

"Five to one," Maggie said.

"So, if our altitude is one mile, we can glide about five miles?" Mark said.

"That's right," the pilot replied. "We're at nine thousand five hundred now. We can go almost ten miles."

"That might do it," Mark said.

Abby loosely buckled her seat belt and pressed closer to Toby. His arm was around her shoulder, and he pulled her even closer. She started to speak, but her voice choked.

She took a breath to settle herself and said, "If something happens to me, find Touk and Jordan. Then all of you should go to Mandy's cabin in Maine. You'll be safe there."

Toby leaned back with a scowl. "Are you giving up?"

She was not giving up. She was being realistic. "Please, promise me."

Toby's scowl deepened, and he muttered angrily. "Stop it. Nothing is going to happen to you."

His scowl and angry tone were the result of his fear, Abby realized. Toby was as fearful of losing her as she was of losing him and never seeing Touk and Jordan again.

"Four thousand," Maggie said.

Abby sat up and saw the skyscrapers had quadrupled in height. The plane was skimming the creamy cloud tops, taking aim for the break in the clouds ahead.

Toby joined Mark in peering out the window, looking for a place to touch down.

"Three thousand five hundred. Three thousand. Two thousand five hundred ..."

Abby felt that her heart was going that many beats per minute.

"Emory Campus," Mark called, pointing to the right. "That's Atlanta Colony."

The site glowed with electric lights. Toucan was there, unaware her sister was soaring silently through the night sky right above her.

"Two thousand. Fifteen hundred. A thousand feet."

With every foot they dropped in altitude, it seemed like time sped up. Moonlight revealed that every major road was clogged with trucks and cars.

"Can you land in water?" Toby asked, nose pressed against the window.

"That's the Chattahoochee River," Mark said. "It has rapids and rocks."

They flew past the inviting, but deadly river.

"Five hundred feet," Maggie called out in a strained voice.

"Let's shoot for Olympic Park," Mark shouted. "It's near the center of the city. There's lots of open space. It's right up ahead."

"We're too high," Maggie said. "Hold on."

The left wing tip dipped violently, and the plane seemed to drop straight down. Just as suddenly, Maggie leveled the wings, ending the rapid descent.

Ahead, Olympic Park had trees growing on the right and left, and miraculously, the open field before them appeared to be free of kids and obstacles.

"It doesn't look level," Maggie said.

"Piece of cake," Mark said in a shaky voice.

Abby gripped Toby's hand, and he gripped harder. A blur of buildings out the side window indicated how fast they were going.

Maggie came in for a perfect landing in an open field of tall grass in the middle of Atlanta. What sounded like a cloud of bugs striking the windshield were the wheels grazing the tall grass.

The plane cartwheeled. There was a loud bang and crunch of metal as the nose struck the ground. A flash of pain from the vicious pull of the belt against her lap blinded Abby for a moment.

The ripping of metal and tumbling lessened, and the shouting ended as soon as the plane came to rest. Abby realized that in the stillness, she alone was crying out.

3.01
EMORY CAMPUS

In Unit 2A, Lisette waited in line for Mother to inspect the contents of her backpack. Molly, Lydia, and Zoe were ahead of her in line, holding their packs.

Excitement crackled in the air as all the girls were scrambling to collect their belongings. This morning, they were going on a trip to the CDC bunker. Mother had said that Generation M would stay there for a while. More exciting to Lisette, she would get to ride on a bus.

"On the double, ladies," Murph barked. The Petty Officer stood by the monitoring station with hands on hips. "Remember, just two uniforms. If I find anyone has three, I will be very distressed. That is the word of the day. D-I-S-T-R-E-S-S-E-D. Does anyone know what it means?"

Zoe raised her hand. "You'll wear a dress?"

"Nope. Anyone else?"

"You will be unhappy," Lisette shouted.

"Very good," Murph said. "I will be quite unhappy if you pack more than two uniforms. Thank you, Miss Leigh."

Lisette grinned.

Ahead of her in line, Mother inspected Molly's pack, removing the items one by one. A toothbrush, a hairbrush, underwear, iPod, and two uniforms.

"What's this?" Mother asked, crinkling her forehead. She held up a crumpled piece of paper.

Molly looked down. "The duck."

"I'm sorry, Molly, but Captain Mathews said everyone must bring essential items only. Then Mother cracked a small smile. "I know how fun the Duck Game is. I'll bring it in my pack."

Mother repacked the bag and sent Molly to the other line of girls eagerly waiting to go out to the bus.

Mother peered into Lisette's pack and took out a hairbrush. "Do you need a brush?" she asked.

Lisette ran her hand over the stubble on her scalp. "All the girls are bringing brushes."

Mother smiled with sad eyes and returned the brush to her pack. "You can keep it. Hurry up and get in line."

In the new line, Lisette received five offers from girls wanting to sit with her on the bus, but she felt sorry for Tabby, one of the girls who had just arrived from Colony East. Tabby didn't have any good friends yet.

Lisette walked up to her. "Can I sit with you?"

Tabby's face lit up.

When the line moved, Lisette took Tabby's hand, and they stepped outside together. The boys from Unit 2B were already climbing into their blue bus.

Black material covered the bus's windows and half the windshield. When the girls around Lisette started complaining that they wouldn't be able to look out the windows, she announced loudly, "I bet the bunker has a big play area. The scientists want it to be a surprise."

Grumbles turned into giggles.

3.02
ATLANTA, GEORGIA

The plane was upside down, and Abby was stuck, unable to unbuckle her seatbelt. She had to pull herself up to lessen the pressure on the strap, but she was too weak and had given up after several futile attempts.

Only she and Maggie were conscious. Maggie had managed to unbuckle her belt, but she couldn't move from the pilot's seat; she was pinned in place by the crumpled instrument panel.

"Toby," Abby called and squeezed his hand.

Even though Toby was unconscious, she prayed he could hear her voice. Earlier, he had lightly squeezed her hand, though Abby wondered if she had imagined it.

The warmth of his hand and the steadiness of his pulse, which she felt by pressing her fingertips against his neck, kept her hope alive.

"How's Mark?" Abby asked.

Since Maggie had regained consciousness, the two of them kept speaking to each other, mostly about the condition of Mark and Toby.

Maggie's voice came out of the darkness. "His skin is cold."

"Can you hear him breathing?"

A long pause. "No."

Abby shuddered from a frigid ache in her chest. Her heart already fluttered from fighting gravity, as it struggled to pump the blood pooling in her head, and Mark's death was a crushing blow. He had found his daughter, Sarah, saving her from the Pig, and now she would be twice orphaned. Abby also wondered how she, Maggie, and Toby, should he recover, would find Atlanta Colony or the pill plant. How would they even get out of the plane? Abby swallowed a sob. There would time for crying later. Still, tears blurred her vision and dribbled through her eyebrows and down her forehead.

Mark grunted.

Abby lurched in shock and then flushed with relief.

"Mark," Maggie cried. "Mark."

He didn't respond.

"I can hear him breathing."

"Keep talking to him," Abby said and did the same for Toby. She had to let him know she was there for him.

As the sky lightened, Abby saw they were upside down in a forest of grass. Enough light filtered through the grassy curtain to inspect the injured.

"Is there any blood on Mark?" Abby asked.

From her position in the backseat of the plane, she could not see any open wounds or blood on him.

Abby was checking Toby's legs for wounds when Maggie reported that she didn't see or feel any blood on Mark.

A face appeared in the window. Abby had expected kids to be curious about a flipped-over airplane in Olympic Park, but the hollow-cheeked boy startled her nevertheless. He was on his hands and knees, looking at her sideways.

"One of them is dead," the boy said.

"No," Abby croaked. "Everyone is alive. We need help."

She heard other voices nearby.

"Do you have food?" the boy asked.

Loud banging startled her. It sounded like a rock striking metal. The fuselage shifted slightly with each bang, and she realized the kids were breaking into the cargo area.

"Yes, we have food. We'll give you some. Open the door and help us out."

The banging stopped, and the boy stood. Abby saw his knobby knees in the tall grass for only a second before he walked out of sight. After a period of silence, she knew the kids had taken their food and left.

She and Maggie resumed their efforts to resuscitate Toby and Mark with words and hand squeezes.

A thought crawled into Abby's mind, which she brushed aside, but it popped back, sharper and more detailed, and she forcefully expelled it again with a jagged grunt, but it quickly consumed her, filling her head the way the rising sun was flooding the interior of the plane with light. Abby would outlive Toby and Mark and then die from the Pig, the three of them hanging upside down, leaving Maggie as the sole survivor, pinned in her pilot's seat.

The persistent image spread throughout Abby like poison, withering her vocal cords, but she kept squeezing Toby's hand.

Sometime later, he groaned and shook violently. The spasm passed quickly, and he blinked and groaned more.

Abby mumbled, "Toby."

He opened his eyes. "Where are we? What happened?" His brow crinkled. "Oh. We're in Atlanta. We crashed."

Maggie explained that she and Abby were stuck, and Mark was seriously injured.

"My head is pounding," Toby said with confusion in his eyes. "I got to get out. I'll get all of us out."

He unbuckled his belt and fell from his seat.

"My head!" he cried.

When he couldn't open the door, he elbowed the window until the plastic popped out. Then, grunting and groaning, he wriggled his body inch by inch through the opening. He stood, and Abby saw him immediately topple into the tall grass.

A moment later, he opened the door on Abby's side, undid her buckle, and tried his best to cushion her fall.

Abby had entered a new realm of pain. It was a constant. Breathing hurt. Doing nothing hurt. Toby dragging her from the plane hurt. The blades of grass where she lay hurt her skin. Her body was nothing but pain.

She slowly got to her feet. Toby stared into the distance.

"Open your eyes and look at me," she told him, gripping his arm to remain upright. One of Toby's pupils was a black pinpoint, the other a saucer with a larger diameter. "You have a concussion."

She looked around. They were in the middle of the park with a cluster of tall buildings, many of them burned-out shells, on the right. No one was around to help them.

"We have to get Maggie out," she said.

Toby managed to yank the pilot's door open, and Abby stepped in to help him, but he waved her off, so she went to Mark's side of the plane. That door opened easily. Mark's head lolled to one side, and his forehead felt cold, but Abby figured she couldn't correctly gauge his temperature because of her own fever. She pried open an eyelid and saw only the white of his eye.

Toby had pulled Maggie out of the cockpit, and the two of them joined Abby. They discussed the risk of moving Mark. If he had a spinal cord injury, they might paralyze him, but they quickly agreed that not moving him would result in his eventual death anyway.

Mark weighed a ton, and they pulled and tugged him as gently as they could until he was mostly on the ground. They grabbed his wrist and pulled him away from the plane.

"There's an adult over there," someone shouted.

Kids appeared from around the perimeter of the park, leading Abby to believe they had been watching them all this time. About thirty feet away, a small group swelled into a crowd, with more approaching as word of the adult sighting spread.

Toby removed Mark's pack from the cockpit and then retrieved the gun that William had given him.

Abby gasped. "What are you doing?"

"We need a car," Toby said.

She watched in dread as he stumbled dizzily toward the crowd.

"Abby, help me." Maggie held Mark's head up. "He needs something under his head."

Right after she had positioned the pouch as a pillow, Abby jumped from the loud crack of a gun ripping through the air. She turned just as Toby fired a second shot at the sky.

"Now do you believe it's loaded?" she heard him say.

"Abby," Maggie cried.

Mark had opened his eyes.

3.03
CONNECTICUT – NEWARK, NEW JERSEY

On motorcycles that William had provided, the boys left Mystic on Route 95. Jordan, riding alongside Spike, frequently checked his mirror to keep an eye on Jonzy, who was twenty meters behind them. It was Jonzy's first time on a motorcycle, and he was prone to wobbling.

Jordan wished Eddie could have joined them, but that was not possible. He felt good about Eddie's chances of making a full recovery. Wenlan had set his broken ankle, cleaned all his puncture wounds, and most importantly, given Eddie a pill to cure the Pig.

Jordan hoped they'd arrive in Newark and meet with Leo, the leader of the Ponytail Gang, before dark. Each boy carried a spare can of gas, water, a small ration of food, and antibiotic pills for trading. Jordan had Toby's map, showing the way to the pill plant in Georgia.

They kept their speed around twenty miles per hour, and at midmorning, crossed the New York state border. The plan was to continue until Exit 19, where they'd turn onto Route 44.

They had to find a way to cross the Hudson River. Jonzy had reported the shortest route to Newark, The George Washington Bridge, spanning from Colony East to the New Jersey side of the Hudson River, was impassable, blocked at both ends with cement that the adults had poured.

Consequently, they were headed toward the Tappan Zee Bridge, forty miles upriver. At Exit 19, they turned onto Route 44. Wary of an ambush, Jordan constantly looked for nails in their path.

A few kids on bicycles were the only signs of life. The absence of kids gave him the same uneasy feeling he had experienced in the empty streets of Portland.

Jordan breathed a sigh of relief when the Tappan Zee Bridge came into view. A steel cable dangled from its midsection, reminding him of a giant guitar string that had snapped.

They pulled into a rest area about a mile from the entrance and filled their tanks. Continuing, they crossed the bridge and headed south on Route 9, hugging the Hudson River. About two hours later, Spike pointed excitedly when Colony East appeared on their left. Jordan reacted quite differently to the sight of the tall, dark buildings. The first and only time he had set his eyes on the colony's skyline was when he had sailed by on *Lucky Me*, three miles out at sea, only hours before the pirates had attacked. The colony was a reminder of lost friends.

They turned onto Route 107, heading west, and after five miles, approached a "Welcome to Newark" sign covered with purple graffiti.

Jordan's motorcycle sputtered, and he turned into a gas station. The gas needle had been bouncing on empty for the past five miles. The boys followed him, and they all killed their engines.

To get out of sight, they pushed their bikes into a mechanic's bay, where plastic forks and fine, needle-thin bones on the floor informed them that kids had sought shelter here at one point.

"I'll take the gas in Jonzy's tank and look for Leo," Spike said.

"I can go," Jordan said.

Spike shook his head. "You're not ready."

Jordan smirked. "Says who?"

"The look in your eyes, that's who."

Rather than waste time arguing, Jordan used a rubber tube he was carrying to siphon what remained in Jonzy's tank into Spike's, about a liter or two.

When the throb of Spike's motorcycle faded into silence, he and Jonzy split up to investigate the rest of the gas station. Around back, Jordan stepped into a small bathroom. He pumped the soap dispenser above the sink and ants crawled out. He pinched some between his fingers and ate them as though they were chocolate sprinkles.

In the mechanic's bay, he and Jonzy settled in to share ants, water, and stories.

"What did you think of Abby when you first met her?" Jordan asked.

"Bossy," Jonzy said with a smile. "But after I got to know her, I thought she was really nice, not bossy, just *very stubborn*."

"That's her, all right. Abby is bossy and stubborn, but she's also the most caring person you'll ever meet, and she's *way* too trusting."

"I don't know about that," Jonzy said. "Maybe she's changed since you saw her last."

Jordan chuckled. "Impossible. Abby trusts everyone. She taught me to be more trusting."

"Lemon taught me a lot of things," Jonzy said.

"Lemon? Who's that?"

"My grandfather." Jonzy had a big smile on his face as he spoke about his grandfather, Lemon Billings, who had lived with Jonzy and his mother before the night of the purple moon.

Lemon had taught physics at Brooklyn College, the first African-American to head the department.

"Lemon taught me how to build a radio from spare parts we bought at Radio Shack," Jonzy said.

"How did he get his nickname?"

Jonzy laughed. "Lemon is his real name. When he was born, his head was the shape of a lemon."

"When my sister, Lisette, was born, she had a really big nose. Abby said she looked like a toucan. After that, everyone called her Toucan."

The frequency of their yawning increased, and they decided to alternate catnaps. Jonzy went first, and despite sporadic bursts of gunfire in the distance, he fell asleep within seconds of resting his head on a big truck tire.

About thirty minutes later, an ambulance pulled into the gas station. Jordan jostled Jonzy to wake him. The boys peered around the corner and were relieved to see Spike hop out the passenger side.

Spike entered the bay, carrying a full can of gas. As he filled their tanks, he described his meeting with Leo.

"I told him everything. I gave him a few pills. We listened to DJ Silver. Leo couldn't believe The Port was back on the air." That got a grin from Jonzy. "Then Leo talked about himself for an hour straight. A lot of fuel kings have big egos, and trust me, Leo wins the prize for having the biggest."

"Is he going to help us?" Jordan asked.

Spike shrugged. "He's thinking it over. He's worried about the White House Gang and the Grits. He said it would be a bloody battle to get past both gangs."

"Did you tell him I know the White House Gang leaders?" Jordan asked.

Spike nodded. "He's more worried about the Grits."

"We'll talk the Grits into joining us," Jordan said.

Finished gassing up the bikes, Spike popped the top on Jonzy's tank. "Like I said, Leo's thinking it over."

Spike told them to follow the ambulance to Leo's compound before climbing into the passenger seat.

Jordan and Jonzy fired up their bikes and pulled up behind the ambulance. The driver squealed the tires as she drove onto the street

The boys barely managed to keep the ambulance in their sight as it swerved left and right, and sped up and slowed down repeatedly, as if taking evasive maneuvers. The driver would creep down one road, then make a sharp U-turn and accelerate past Jordan and Jonzy.

The ambulance stopped before a brown, package delivery truck blocking a street. A girl with a long ponytail poked her head out the door, and a moment later, she backed up the truck so they could drive pass.

On the next block, the ambulance stopped and parked, and the boys parked beside it and dismounted their bikes. They followed Spike up steep steps to the front porch of a three-story house. A lanky boy, hair tied in a ponytail, patted them down for weapons before they entered. The boy confiscated Jordan's Swiss Army knife.

They entered the house and climbed the stairs to the third floor where Leo required no introduction. Tall and muscular, he wore thick gold chains around his neck, and his purple ponytail fell below his waste.

Crushed pokeberries made rich, long-lasting hair dye.

Leo wasted no time in showing his support for their mission. "I want to go to Georgia with you. We'll bring an army. If my gang members are healthy, they're coming. We'll need an army to make it past Pale Rider."

"Who's Pale Rider?" Jordan asked.

"The leader of the Grits. Her three lieutenants are just as ruthless. There's only one thing I want from you."

Sure of what Leo was about to demand, Jordan prepared to give him the rest of their pills. His secret fantasy was to roll into Atlanta with an army of kids; giving up the rest of their pills was a small price to pay for Leo's support.

"What do you want?" Jordan asked.

Leo ran his hand through his ponytail. "My own radio station."

3.04
CDC BUNKER, ATLANTA

Doctor Perkins eyed the unfolding scene with concern. Security monitor number four showed survivors amassing outside the front gate of the CDC bunker.

Clearly, the word of the exodus from Emory Campus had spread, and children arrived with the false hope that the CDC would provide care.

All four monitors affixed to Perkins's office wall were streaming live feeds from outside the bunker. The mob featured on number four swelled by the minute. Half the children sprawled over the ground and most had blank, vacant stares. Curses directed at adults mixed with desperate cries of pain. Perkins muted the microphone.

What troubled him most was not the growing number of children, but rather a specific boy who stood out in the crowd. He appeared to be ten or eleven years old, though the nutritional deficiencies outside the colonies made it difficult to judge ages. The boy stared at Perkins right through the camera. His eyes were wide and brimming with sadness, absent of all hope.

Doctor Droznin hobbled into his office and placed a report on his desk.

"The latest analysis of AHA-B concentrations," she said in her typical, cold tone.

He gestured to the chair before his desk. "Please, have a seat."

She remained standing.

He glanced at the sheet of data. *More statistics.* "Anything I should be aware of?"

She glared at him. "The aggregate mean is what we expected."

Perkins studied her. Were Svetlana's feelings hurt because he relied more and more on Captain Mathews? No, that couldn't be it; Droznin didn't have feelings for anything other than the mountains of data she produced. They had disagreed sharply over how to handle ID 944, but she'd won that argument, at least for the time being. Of course, everyone's patience suffered from confinement in the bunker.

Not wishing to play nursemaid to the Russian scientist, Perkins concluded that he didn't care what was bothering her.

He stood and walked to Monitor number four. "I'm reminded of a saying attributed to one of your comrades, Joseph Stalin. It goes something like this: 'The death of thousands is a statistic, the death of one man is a tragedy.'"

He pointed out the boy with the sad eyes. "See that face. It jumps out, right? "That ratty, unkempt survivor puts a face on the epidemic. He makes it a tragedy. People respond to tragedies in spontaneous, irrational ways. It's best we nip it in the bud."

Perkins returned to his desk, and in a few keystrokes, killed the video feed to monitor number four. A few more keystrokes switched the monitor to an internal feed that showed a chess tournament underway in the Generation M living quarters.

Doctor Droznin gave him a long, hard stare that unnerved him. "My great-grandfather lived in Moscow. He was not a scientist or a professor. He was a baker. He wore glasses so he could read recipes. Joseph Stalin thought that anyone who wore glasses was an intellectual, an enemy of the state. One day, Stalin's henchmen murdered my great-grandfather."

She hobbled away.

Murdering someone just because he wore glasses was tragic, and Perkins decided he would be smart to no longer reference Stalin in his lectures. Settling back in his chair, he returned his attention to the chess tournament, happy that in this environment intellectuals received accolades and an opportunity to flourish, not the axe.

3.05
ATLANTA

In Olympic Park, Abby had found that by lying on her side and drawing one knee to her chin, the pain in her midsection eased to excruciating from unbearable.

Over the past five hours, she had thought a lot about her family and closest friends living at the cabin on the lake in Maine, and that provided a few moments of relief.

Toby lay next to her in the tall grass, gripping the gun he hoped to trade for a car. He kept sitting up to see if the girl he had negotiated with had returned.

A crowd of gawkers had swelled to nearly a hundred, though the crumpled airplane was not the source of their curiosity. Mark was. Abby worried their anger toward adults in general might boil over, leading them to attack Mark.

Maggie jostled Mark, as she had been doing every fifteen minutes. Because of the concussion he had suffered, Abby knew it was best to keep him awake, but that had proved impossible. So Maggie would agitate him just enough to make him open his eyes. Mark would groan, curse, and roll onto his stomach in response. He seemed to be growing stronger by the fact his groans grew louder and his curses more varied.

In the late afternoon, a car horn beeped twice, and Toby sat up. "It's her."

He and Maggie helped Abby to her feet, and then prodded and cajoled Mark until he stood. Abby thought he looked half descent for someone, who a few hours ago, she feared would die.

Toby huddled them and said in a low voice, "I'm the lead negotiator. Nobody should say anything, okay?"

Mark clutched his head. "We shouldn't trade the gun. Let's give her something else."

Toby narrowed his eyes. "Like what, Lieutenant? Antibiotic pills? What good have they done Abby? The radio is too important. We have a hammer and two flashlights, but nobody would want them. You can't eat a hammer. The gun is valuable because someone can use it to take food. We need a car to get to Atlanta Colony."

"I'll talk to her," Mark said.

Abby started to say that Toby knew what he was doing, but a violent cramp stole her breath.

"No, you won't," Toby told him. "Keep your mouth shut. Let's move before the trader changes her mind."

They all headed toward the graffiti-covered red Toyota. The trader was a girl with spiky blonde hair.

Toby ran the negotiation, but the deal almost imploded when he saw how little gas was in the tank.

"Take it or leave it," the girl said.

Toby removed three of the six bullets in the gun and replied, "You can take it or leave it."

They struck a compromise: the girl dribbled in some more gas and Toby loaded one more bullet into the chamber.

Deciding they had to hide Mark, Abby climbed into the back seat with him. Toby drove with Maggie as his copilot.

Mark gave directions to a spot about half a mile from Emory Campus, the site of Atlanta Colony. "They have cameras everywhere. It's safer if we stay away from the colony. The radio has a range of two miles."

He explained he had instructed Sandy in his note to monitor channel 17 and then turned on the walkie-talkie. He brought his lips close.

"Alpha Zulu, do you copy?" He released the button. After a moment, he tried again. "Alpha Zulu, do you copy?"

Though Abby's thundering heart made her cramps unbearable, hearing Sandy's voice crackle back would be better than a shot of morphine.

"Alpha Zulu, do you copy? Alpha Zulu, do you copy?"

Half an hour passed.

"What if she never saw your note?" Abby asked.

The color drained from Mark's face. "Alpha Zulu, do you copy?"

3.06
NEWARK

Jordan traced his finger on the roadmap, showing Spike the route they would take from Newark, New Jersey to Washington DC. "We take Route 95 to Route 195, which takes us straight into DC. Should the Ponytails wait outside the city?"

Spike studied the map. "It depends how many kids Leo brings. If it's an army, it might be better for you to talk to the White House Gang leaders first. Otherwise, they might think they're being attacked."

"I hope it's an army," Jordan said.

"I hope the White House Gang leaders remember you."

Jordan nodded. "They will. We traded with them when I was on *Lucky Me*. They'll definitely remember Captain Jenny."

It was dawn, and the two boys were waiting for Jonzy, who was inside the building of the small radio station — AM 1030, Northern New Jersey's Home of Country Music. Jonzy had put the station on the air earlier and was teaching a Ponytail Gang member how to use the control panel.

Leo had ordered gang members to pass out batteries to kids outside his compound, so they could listen to the station. He wanted them to learn about the Pig, and more importantly, understand what he, Leo, the supreme leader of the Ponytail Gang, was doing for them.

Jonzy emerged from the building and gave them the thumbs up.

"'Leo Central' is on the air," he said with a smile. "His ego will love it."

The three boys headed for what they hoped was an army amassing on a highway entrance ramp, half a mile away.

Jordan's eyes widened when he spotted them. He started counting motorcycles, but quit at thirty-five. There was more than twice that number. Ponytail boys outnumbered girls, but not by much, and everyone appeared to be over the age of twelve. A few Ponytails gripped their sides. Apparently, the antibiotic pills they had taken last night had yet to take effect.

Leo seemed to be well aware that every army needed food and fuel to fight and had provided them with a fuel truck and an ambulance stocked with raw vegetables — potatoes, carrots, and cabbages — as well as bottled water.

Jordan took a moment to imagine their trip south. The Ponytail army was just the beginning — a snowball ready to roll downhill, picking up riders along the way and gaining mass and momentum. The army might soon triple or quadruple in size with the addition of the White House Gang members, if he could convince them to join the fight. After that, Pale Rider and all her healthy Grits would add to their ranks.

Leo, his purple ponytail flowing long and silky from his helmet, straddled the biggest, shiniest Harley Davidson motorcycle Jordan had ever seen.

Jonzy handed Leo a radio so he could hear the station for himself. With a satisfied smile, Leo turned on the radio and raised the antennae. He thumbed the wheel and frowned.

Immediately, Jordan recognized the robotic voice. The CDC station must have returned to the air.

"Emergency bulletin one point zero. The pathogen, introduced into the atmosphere three years ago by Comet Rudenko-Kasparov has undergone a lethal mutation. Symptoms of the fast-spreading AHA-B mutation syndrome include fever and intense hunger. CDC personnel have begun distributing antibiotics to the populations most affected. New distribution locations will be announced shortly. Stay indoors, avoid contact with those infected, and expend as little energy as possible. Stay tuned for additional updates."

Leo turned off the radio and tossed it to Jonzy.

"Do you believe that?" Jordan snorted.

"What a bunch of crap," Spike said.

"They want you to go home and die," Jonzy said. "Don't cause trouble. Just curl up and die."

Leo fired up his bike. "The adults have finally decided to help us."

"What do you mean help?" Jordan blurted. "They're bullshitting us."

"You're the one who's bullshitting us," Leo said. "Look at them." He pointed to the sick kids who had taken pills. Jordan had to admit that each one looked even sicker. Leo spat. "Your pills are bullshit. They don't work."

The leader of the Ponytail Gang waved his arm in a circle. "Everyone back to the compound. The adults are working on a real cure for the Pig."

He clicked his bike in gear and rode off.

The throb of motorcycle engines soon faded. The fuel truck and ambulance were the last vehicles to drive away.

3.07
ATLANTA

"Alpha Zulu, do you copy?" Maggie's voice sounded hoarse. "Alpha Zulu do you copy?"

Hugging her knees, Abby leaned her head against the door handle in the back of the car. She pressed harder, scrunching her eyes and baring her teeth as the metal dug into her scalp. This new pain offered something to focus on, other than the endless waves of cramps.

"Alpha Zulu, come in," Toby said.

Maggie's shift had ended. Throughout the night, Mark, Toby, and Maggie had taken turns trying to reach Sandy. Abby had been in too much pain to help.

Abby heard a front door open.

"Where are you going?" Mark asked.

"Atlanta Colony," Toby replied. "Maybe I can learn something if I see the place."

From the way his voice sounded, Abby could tell that Toby was outside the car.

"Keep trying to contact Sandy," Mark said.

Toby chuckled coldly. "Until when? Next week?" The car door closed.

"Hey, come back," Mark shouted.

"Wait," Abby said in barely a whisper.

"Abby has something to say," Mark shouted louder.

That brought Toby, back and the door opened. She thought Toby's idea was good, but he shouldn't go alone.

"Maggie should go too."

Mark repeated what she said.

Soon, it was just Abby and Mark in the car.

"Toby's a good kid, but I don't understand him," Mark said. Abby bristled. "If it weren't for Toby, my sister and I would have never made it to Colony East. He also got the car that got us to Mystic. And he found your daughter. And he got this car."

"Yes, I know all that, but it would be easier if he would work with me, instead of fighting me."

"You're like a lot of adults. You give orders, but you never listen. Maybe …." Abby stopped, because in many ways, Mark was different. He was one of the few adults in the world who were trying to help.

"You might be right," Mark agreed, ending their conversation.

Several minutes later, both front doors opened, and Toby and Maggie hopped in. They reported that Atlanta Colony was empty of adults.

"Kids have taken over the place," Toby said, out of breath. "They're burning buildings, looting, looking for food."

"They must have taken Generation M to the bunker," Mark said. "It's an underground facility in the city."

They drove to a location near the bunker, and for an hour, tried without success to contact Sandy.

"We should go to the Alpharetta pill plant," Mark suggested. "I have no idea what to expect. Sandy might already be there, although I doubt it. I can scout it out and maybe get the generators running."

"How far is the plant?" Maggie asked.

"Six miles," Mark said.

"We don't have enough gas to get there and back," Toby said. "Abby is too sick to walk. Maggie can drive you. I'll stay with Abby."

Abby understood a thing or two about giving orders; Mark wasn't the only one who ordered people around. Jordan often accused her of being bossy, and quite often, he was right. But as the older sister of a stubborn brother and stubborn sister, giving orders was sometimes the only way to make sure things got done right, as she needed to do here.

"Toby, you should go with Mark," she said. "You two worked well together while searching for his daughter. After you help him, come back here. Maggie and I will stay and keep trying to contact Sandy. Please give me the radio."

Nobody argued.

3.08
CDC BUNKER

Deep in the bunker, Doctor Perkins removed his headphones and stepped back from the communications console. He was troubled, but not panicked, by the recording that Ensign Ryan had played for him.

The bunker's communication center was a small, claustrophobic space, jam-packed with radio and video equipment. The presence of Captain Mathews and the ensign in the room, both invading his personal space, added to his discomfort.

"The signal went off the air?" Perkins asked.

"Yes, sir," Ryan replied. "The broadcast ended five minutes after I found it."

Perkins detected a trace of a southern drawl. The "sir" from Ryan's lips dripped with respect. Southern parents seemed to have discovered the recipe for instilling manners in their children, something Perkins made a mental note to explore later on for Generation M.

"How long was the station broadcasting?" Perkins asked.

"Sorry, I don't know that."

"Do you know the location in New Jersey?"

"The northern half of the state is my best guess," Ryan replied. "Maybe Newark."

"Play it again, please."

Through his headphones, Perkins listened to what he thought was a twelve-year-old male.

"If you have the Pig," the crackly voice said, "Leo is going to take care of you. The adults have pills to cure the Pig, but they are not sharing them. Leo is going to Atlanta to get the pills for you. Every member of the Ponytail Gang will receive pills. Leo wants you to share your food. Leo doesn't want anyone to fight. Leo is going to take care of you."

Perkins removed the headphones. "Captain Mathews, come with me."

He led her to the bunker's library, and convinced they were alone, he said, "Shut the door."

He stepped to a whiteboard on the wall and sketched a bird's-eye schematic of the Alpharetta facility. "What I have to tell you is highly confidential."

"You can trust Ensign Ryan," she said.

"That's good to know, but this is something we must keep to ourselves. We know Dawson went to Mystic and started up a station. Now, he's started up a new station in New Jersey. We have no idea how he's traveling or where he is, but we know his intended destination is the Alpharetta pill facility. It's prudent to develop a contingency plan. Redundant systems, Captain. One part fails, you fall back on a replacement part."

"Yes, sir."

He gestured to the whiteboard. "Every component in the plant is critical, but this is how we can make certain that no pills are produced."

He tapped the cluster of circles he'd drawn, putting a black dot in the center of each circle, twelve dots in total. "The fermentation vats hold live cultures. We can start up the antibiotic process immediately using those cultures. I'd like you to prepare to destroy the vats, but only if it becomes necessary."

"Sir, I can take down the whole plant."

Perkins shook his head. "The plant is crucial to Generation M. We plan to make vaccines, vitamins, and a whole host of pharmaceuticals there. With Dawson posing a remote threat, a strategic placement of explosives is what's called for. If we only take out the vats, repairs to the plant will take weeks versus months."

"Should I assign guards to the plant?" Mathews asked.

"That won't be necessary. The scientists who can operate the plant are inside the bunker. It's much easier to keep an eye on them here. Keep me informed."

3.09
ATLANTA

Abby and Maggie waded into the trash piled at the back end of the alley. Toby and Mark, who had just dropped them off, were on their way to the pill plant.

The alley was uninhabited, but whoever had once lived here had used the back part as a dumping ground for paper goods, plastics, cans, and the like. Ants had gnawed the gristle from the dried bones of pigeons.

The alley supplied them with a perfect place to hide in plain sight, two blocks from the CDC bunker.

Abby sat and Maggie pushed trash around her. Maggie then plunked down and covered herself until just her head poked out.

A nearby scream sent chills crawling over Abby's skin. It sounded like a boy, and the fading voice echoed in the alley, or it might have been bouncing off the walls of her mind. She felt the boy's fear as he used up the air in his lungs, took a gasping breath, and screamed again.

Maggie put her arm around Abby's shoulder. Human touch was the best medicine for fear.

When the screams ended, Maggie turned on the two-way radio. The girls agreed to take turns trying to contact Sandy every half hour.

"Alpha Zulu, do you copy?" Maggie said. "Alpha Zulu, do you copy?" She gave up after ten minutes.

"How did you become a pilot?" Abby asked.

Maggie rolled her eyes. "William has a theory. If your mom or dad could do something, you can do it too. Wenlan's mother was a doctor, so he put her in charge of the clinic. My mom was a pilot for Delta Airlines."

"Did you know anything about flying?"

"Nothing," Maggie said. "William sent three of us to the airport in Providence to learn how to fly. Rex's dad had been a helicopter pilot, and Frank's older brother had flown fighter jets in the Air Force. We read books on flying and studied the instrument panel and taxied around the runway. One day, I just took off, flew around the airport a few times, and landed."

"That was brave," Abby said.

"Looking back, I'd say it was kind of dumb, but when I'm really afraid of something, I pretend I'm brave. I tell myself to face the fear. Every time I take off in Mystic, I think I'm going to crash into the bridge at the end of the runway."

"Every time?"

Maggie gave a big nod. "I pretend I'm brave, and then I go for it. What do you when something frightens you?"

Abby pressed closer. "I hate fog, and in the summer before seventh grade, we moved to Castine Island, the foggiest place in the world. When the fog rolled in, I'd pull the shades down and stay in my room until it lifted."

The conversation was dredging up other frightening episodes from the past two years, and Abby had to change the topic. "Do you know my brother?"

"I've heard about him," Maggie replied. "My best friend is the fisherman who found him when his boat got blown up. Your brother had tied himself to an empty gas can. He was barely alive."

The girls tensed when a group of kids raced by the alley.

Maggie suggested that they take turns sleeping. "You first."

Abby closed her eyes, but the combination of her cramps, her concern for Jordan, and the lingering adrenaline from the kids running by kept her awake. She gave herself the mental exercise of planning how she, along with friends and family, would prepare for the winter once they reached the cabin in Maine.

Abby described the cabin to Maggie and told her, "You can come live with us. We'll be a million miles away from all this."

"I can fly a float plane," Maggie said with a smile.

When it was Maggie's turn to nap, she fell asleep instantly, and her head flopped on Abby's shoulder. One of her pigtails rested on a crumpled can of purple beer.

Careful not to disturb Maggie, Abby whispered into the radio, "Alpha Zulu, do you copy? Alpha Zulu, do you copy?"

After about ten minutes, she turned off the radio.

She heard someone approaching the alley, grunting, cursing, and scuffing their feet. Labored breathing grew louder. Abby thought about waking Maggie, but instead shifted so they settled deeper in the trash pile. A shirtless boy with long stringy hair dragged something past the alley entrance. Abby shuddered when she got a good look. He was pulling a body by its arm.

3.10
ALPHARETTA, GEORGIA

To provide relief from the pounding headache that had dogged him since he had regained consciousness, Dawson pressed against his temples. He was under a blanket in the back seat. He expected they would arrive at the pill plant within fifteen minutes.

"We're getting low on gas," Toby said from behind the wheel.

"Is it safe for me to come out?" Dawson asked.

"Hold on, Lieutenant," Toby said. The car swerved, sped up, and then swerved again. A crescendo of shouts from outside the car rose and faded. "All good."

Dawson sat up and peered through the front and side windows, recognizing a former fitness center. At one point, kids had probably used it as a shelter, but the windows were now broken, and it was empty.

"We're almost there. Another two miles. Keep your eye out for the water tower. It should be that way." After pointing, he concealed himself under the blanket again.

"Why did the scientist use a brewery?" Toby asked.

"Apparently, brewing beer and making antibiotics both require a fermentation process," he explained. "During the first epidemic, the scientists needed to make tens of millions of pills. The brewery offered many advantages. It was nearby and had large copper fermentation vats, but it's misleading to still think of it as a brewery. They brought in very sophisticated pharmaceutical equipment."

Toby sped up, slowed down, and sometimes drove off the road to get around obstacles. He reported threats, mostly roving gangs of kids.

"The gas light came on," Toby warned.

Dawson took that as good news. Most cars could travel another ten to fifteen miles once the light came on. After dropping him off at the pill plant, Toby could make it back to Abby and Maggie.

Dawson tried to concentrate on the mission, but he had trouble focusing. *Check the perimeter fence to see if it's electrified. Check for video cameras and infrared sensors.* He gave up, too mentally exhausted to think about it.

"The water tower," Toby said. "You can look."

Peering above the seat, Dawson directed Toby through the side streets and into an industrial park. They parked behind a cupcake factory next door to the pill plant and set out on foot.

Dawson had brought his burglary tool, a hammer to smash the brewery window, and his digging tools, a knife and two empty soup cans. If the fence were electrified, they'd dig under it.

The plant came into view. The huge building, surrounded by a large parking area, stretched for nearly half a mile. Tall weeds grew between the parking lot and the perimeter fence. A section of the fence opposite them appeared to be missing. A forest of tall Georgia Pines was beyond the gap.

Dawson's blood turned cold. Though a Humvee was parked near the door, a far bigger problem loomed. Last time he was here, the entrance to the plant was through the brewery lobby, which had wall-to-wall windows. Now, a door stood at the base of a windowless, towering, cement wall, and all the windows had been sealed. The plant was a fortress.

He and Toby crawled up to the fence on their bellies. Dawson gripped his head, unsure of what to do next. His throbbing headache seemed to bludgeon his thoughts into senseless fragments. *Test the fence*, Dawson somehow remembered.

He tossed the metal hammer against the wires and no sparks erupted. No sparks. *Good.* "The fence is safe to touch," he said.

"If there's no electricity, that means the cameras probably aren't working," Toby said.

"You're right," Dawson replied.

The door opened and Lieutenant Mathews exited the building. Carrying an assault rifle, she climbed into the Humvee. Dawson couldn't escape her.

"Who's that?" Toby asked.

"Our worst nightmare. Lieutenant Mathews."

Mathews drove to the gate, got out, unlocked the padlock, and swung it open. After driving through, she closed and locked the gate, and then drove off.

Head throbbing, Dawson stared into space as a cocktail of rage further jumbled his thoughts. The walls of the plant seemed to grow thicker and taller. Befuddled, he was at a loss about what to do next.

3.11
NEW JERSEY – WASHINGTON DC

The boys, riding abreast, continued their hard push south. They were an army of three. The only kids Jordan spotted were those guarding fields of corn, potatoes, and kale, armed with baseball bats and crowbars.

The river of tar streaming under his handlebars was hypnotic, and he wondered if they were doing the right thing. Maybe it was all a misunderstanding. Maybe the adults were planning to help the survivors. The robotic voice on the CDC station was telling the truth.

Lurking danger snapped him back to the present. They had entered a stretch of swampland with tall elephant grass growing next to the road, an ideal spot for an ambush.

They made it through ambush alley without incident, and soon crossed into Delaware, a vast, deserted wasteland of concrete and abandoned factories.

An hour later, they stopped outside Baltimore. They had made it one hundred and eighty miles.

Jordan shared his concerns. "Maybe the adults are telling the truth for once."

"Are you kidding me?" Jonzy blurted. "The CDC doesn't want to help us. There's only one reason the scientists put their station back on the air: they feel threatened."

"By the three of us?" Jordan said with a chuckle.

"Lieutenant Dawson, Toby, and your sister," Jonzy said. "They've probably already taken over the pill plant. They still need our help. We have to fight back." A small smile played on Jonzy's lips. "We have to take over the CDC radio frequency. We'll own the airwaves. We'll tell the truth."

He pursed his lips, brooding. "The only way to do that is to either get a more powerful transmitter, or a bigger antenna, but the CDC probably has the biggest transmitter made and a very tall antenna. There has to be something we can do."

With Jonzy racking his brain and Spike appearing his usual calm self, the three boys gassed up their bikes and headed off for their unannounced rendezvous with the White House Gang.

Five miles outside of Washington DC, the boys cut pine saplings, stripped off the branches, and tied short lengths of gauze bandages to the ends. They lashed these poles to their backs with rope.

Flying white flags, they exited Route 195, entered a neighborhood of brick houses, and stopped twenty yards from a barricade made of tires and refrigerators.

Two guards, both wearing germ masks, were on duty, a boy with dreadlocks, and a girl, who despite the heat and humidity, wore a leather jacket.

Jordan and Spike dismounted and leaned their white flags against the bikes. Jonzy stayed on his bike, deep in thought. He seemed completely focused on finding a way to broadcast his own message over the CDC radio frequency.

The girl produced a long, curved sword, which Jordan thought had probably come from a museum, perhaps once the property of a Civil War general or a Samurai.

"That's close enough," she warned.

"We want to see Bombie, Single Cell, and Low," Jordan said. "I know them."

The girl scoffed. "Get lost."

Jordan took a step forward. "I have news about the Pig and about what the adults are doing to us."

The girl waved the sword. "Single Cell and Bombie don't care about your news. They died from the Pig."

Jordan's blood chilled. He remembered Low as being the toughest of the three leaders.

"Then I want to talk to Low." His voice trembled.

The girl pulled a gun from behind her back and aimed it at him. "I said get lost."

Spike stepped next to Jordan.

"Wait 'til she finds out you didn't let us through." Spike cracked a smile and kept walking. "We'll sell our information to someone else."

His tone was calm as the girl held the gun at arm's length, aiming it at his chest. Spike shrugged, turned, and headed for his bike.

"Wait," the girl barked. To Dreadlocks, she said, "Contact Low."

"Low hates being bothered."

"Do it," she snapped. "What's your name?"

"We're friends of Captain Jenny," Jordan said.

Dreadlocks stepped away and spoke into a walkie-talkie, listened, spoke again, and then listened some more. He walked over to the girl and whispered in her ear.

She returned the pistol to her waistband behind her back, and Dreadlocks approached them. "Follow me."

The boys rode behind Dreadlocks, who pedaled a BMX bike. They passed massive government buildings made of marble and granite, and then arrived at The White House. In front of the mansion, what had once been a great expanse of manicured lawns and rose gardens was now a field of tall grass and weeds.

Dreadlocks led them through a heavily guarded gate and down a long driveway. They parked by the white columns and followed Dreadlocks inside.

Incredibly, the White House had air-conditioning. Boxes lined the walls, two and three deep. Every box had the same logo: USDA FOOD.

They walked down a corridor, dodging kids on skateboards who all wore germ masks, and they passed paintings of former presidents. Jordan wondered what had become of the President and her husband right after the night of the purple moon.

At the end of the corridor, Dreadlocks swung open a door and said, "The Oval Office."

Jordan recognized Low from the red dreads that fell well below her shoulders. She and an opponent, both wearing germ masks, played Ping-Pong on a shiny wooden desk, with a row of food cans serving as the net.

Low set down her paddle and walked up to them. She studied Jordan. "Yeah, I remember you. How's Jenny?"

Jordan told her what had happened to *Lucky Me* — the pirate attack and the ship catching fire and sinking. "I was the only survivor," he told her.

"I hope you got the pirates and made 'em suffer." Low's eyes, uncovered by her mask, burned with rage.

Jordan had tracked the pirates and come within seconds of cutting the throat of the twelve-year-old boy who had murdered his crewmates, but he had let the boy live, learning something important in that moment: he was not a cold-blooded killer.

"Yeah, I got 'em," he told Low and then launched into the story of the adults, Jonzy's escape from Colony East, the epidemic, and the reason they were going to Atlanta. Something about the trip to Atlanta rattled the hardened gang leader. He gave her a pill.

"What do you want from me?" Low asked.

"Food, fuel, and healthy kids to ride with us." Jordan's voice was steady, his tone firm.

Low chuckled coldly. "The Grits will never let you pass through their turf. Because you were a friend of Captain Jenny, I'll give you food, gas, and weapons, but I'm not sacrificing any of my gang."

"I need something else!" Jonzy interrupted. His eyes widened and his face glowed through the grit and grime of the road. "I need a radio station that's near railroad tracks."

3.12
ALPHARETTA

Drowning in doubt, Dawson got to his knees and gazed at the pill plant through the fence.

"What should we do?" he asked in a shaky voice.

Toby jerked his head and stared at him in shock.

Dawson, unable to meet the boy's gaze, dropped his chin to his chest.

"First, we should get our asses on the other side of the fence," Toby said and started up the fence. He stopped at the top. "C'mon, Lieutenant. Move it!"

Dawson stood and looked up. The fence appeared too high to climb. *What a time for a dizzy spell.* He positioned his left foot on the lowest strand of wire and then grabbed a strand higher up with his right hand. He stepped on the next lowest strand with his right foot and pulled himself up. *One step at a time.* He could handle that. When he reached the top, he swung one leg over, then the other, and slowly worked his way down.

"Jump," Toby said.

Dawson let go and landed beside the boy.

Toby jogged toward the plant, and Dawson followed him.

Toby pulled the handle of the door, and not surprisingly, discovered it was locked.

He stared up. "It would take a long piece of rope to reach the roof."

Dawson nodded in agreement.

"If we had dynamite," Toby continued, "we could blow the door, but we don't have dynamite."

Dawson lamented that they had no explosives.

The boy walked in a circle, thinking. "We could smash into the door with the car. That might work! But we'd never make it through the gate."

Dawson eyed the gate, which was secured with a padlock. Toby was right. A Humvee could smash through it, but not the car that had brought them here.

"Follow me," Toby said.

They walked around the perimeter of the building. Impenetrable steel doors blocked entry from the opposite end, and all the walls were high and windowless. Dawson had no idea what to do.

"We could wait here, hope that an adult comes, and ambush them," Toby said. "But we might be waiting a long time."

"That's right," Dawson said, knowing the situation was urgent. They couldn't afford to wait.

Toby rubbed his chin and exclaimed, "That's it." He pointed to the water tower. "What's in there?"

Dawson shrugged. "At one point, water, though it's probably empty."

"What's beer made out of?"

"Hops."

Toby threw up his hands, frustrated that his student was failing the quiz. "Water! Lieutenant, this was a brewery before it was a pill plant. They must have made bad batches of beer. I'm guessing they didn't flush thousands of gallons down the toilet. There must be underground pipes. Big pipes."

"Yes, there must be a connection to the local sewage system!"

"Mark, look at me!" Toby grabbed his arm. "We can do this! You worked here, right? Do you remember anything?"

Dawson nodded. "There are floor grates inside the plant. We should look for a manhole cover, or a storm grate."

"Where would it be?"

Dawson paced. "I bet it would be on the property."

Toby nodded. "Let's split up and look for it. I'll take this side, you go over there."

Dawson's head was still throbbing as he jogged along the perimeter of the property, looking for a metal plate or grate hidden in the tall weeds, but his headache was nothing, a mild annoyance. More and more, he was feeling like himself. Losing confidence had been terrifying. He thought his head injury in the plane crash could be the cause, but he knew that paralyzing doubt could strike anyone down. He remembered his father describing a panic attack he had experienced during a drill on the battleship he'd commanded.

"I was lucky to have a strong second-in-command," his father had said, asking him never to repeat the story to anyone because it would have ended his father's career in the Navy.

Dawson was lucky to have Toby.

A hundred meters away, Toby waved his arms and shouted that he had found something. Five minutes later, they were standing beside a circular, steel cover. Dawson pried the heavy lid up with the claw of his hammer, and together, they flipped it aside.

A ladder descended into the darkness. Dawson gave Toby a flashlight and gestured for him to go first, shining his light as Toby climbed down the ladder.

A cylindrical pipe, twice Dawson's height, extended both directions from the base of the ladder. His pulse quickened, seeing that the pipe led to the plant.

"The beautiful smell of beer," Dawson said. "It reminds me of shore leave."

The odor permeated the tunnel.

"My father used to make me cook dinner for him," Toby said as they headed toward the plant, dancing their flashlights on the pipe walls. "I'd have to go get him at the tavern. That's what it reminds me of. Walking home with him, drunk and angry, wondering if he'd throw a punch."

The light cast on Toby's face showed him reliving the pain and anger.

Dawson reached out and rested his hand on Toby's shoulder, keeping it there as they continued.

When they were clearly below the plant, they came to a ladder that ascended to a steel grate.

"After you, Lieutenant," Toby said.

Dawson scaled the rungs and tried to push aside the grate, but it only moved a fraction of an inch.

Toby climbed up the opposite side of the ladder, and they pushed together, raising it about half an inch.

The grate thudded back in place.

"Are we going to let this thing stand in our way?" Toby asked.

"Hell no, Cadet."

Toby grinned and asked for the hammer. "When you raise it, I'll insert the hammer. Then we'll use the hammer as a lever."

Dawson pushed up for all he was worth, and Toby inserted the claw.

"When I jack it up, put your fist in the gap," Toby barked.

"Aye aye," Dawson said.

Toby pulled down on the hammer's handle. When the grate rose, Dawson inserted his fist, thumb side up, into the gap. Toby released the hammer and Dawson's hand bones held firm.

After discussing the next step together, Toby inserted the hammer sideways into the gap and hung from the handle, allowing Dawson to insert a second fist on top of the first.

"Do or die time," Toby said. "I'm going up a rung to push with my back. As soon as it moves, you have to do the same."

Toby positioned his shoulder against the metal plate and grunted as he drove upward with his legs. The pressure lessened on Dawson's double-fist tower, and the moment his hands were free, he climbed a rung and applied his shoulder to the effort. He drove upward with his legs until his thigh and lower back muscles trembled and were on the verge of exploding in spasms. Both he and Toby grunted and cried out. Muscles in his back seized, shooting an icy bolt of paralysis between his shoulder blades. Dawson willed his quads, calf muscles, and toes to contract and push harder. The grate started to rise, and he gripped the ledge with both hands and pulled, hoisting himself up another rung.

"Go," Dawson shouted when the gap had widened enough for Toby to slip through.

Dawson screamed from the increased load as Toby scrambled from the ladder and into the plant. If he let go now, the grate would cut the boy in half.

Once Toby could stand, he braced his feet against something and leaned forward, arms extended, and pushed the grate. Dawson felt the slow release of pressure, and when he saw Toby visibly shaking, he called on his leg muscles to complete one more task. He stepped up and propelled himself forward through the gap as Toby started to collapse. Dawson pulled his foot out of the way just as the grate crashed back into place.

With "what if" scenarios snaking through his brain, Dawson put his arm around Toby as they both trembled and caught their breath.

"Why did you say Mathews was our worst nightmare?" Toby asked.

"She's a cold-blooded killer. When Jonzy and I were about to leave the colony, she surprised us in the Red Zone. Admiral Samuels showed up, and she shot and killed him."

"You never told us that," Toby said.

"I didn't want to think about it, I guess."

Toby hung his head. "Hey, I'm sorry."

Dawson's jaw dropped. "For what?"

"Acting like a jerk. I guess I've never liked adults, or trusted them."

"I always knew you had to earn someone's trust, but I guess I never realized how hard it was to do," Dawson replied. "Barking orders is easy."

They sat in the stillness. The plant felt like a living entity that held them in her palm of silence.

"You're all right, as far as adults go," Toby offered.

The boy said it jokingly, but Dawson heard the undertone of hurt. He stood, gripped Toby's hand, and helped him to his feet. "If you were my son, I'd be the proudest father in the world."

Toby shifted uncomfortably, and then he dragged his sleeve across his eyes. A small smile played on his lips, brightening his mask of determination.

"Lieutenant, are you ready to kick some scientist butt?"

Dawson pulled his shoulders back. "I can't wait."

He led Toby toward a room that housed the plant's generators. While the outside of the building had undergone serious renovations, the interior was as he remembered it. The flashlight's beams revealed gleaming, high-tech machinery, robotic arms, and miles of piping and wires. The large copper fermentation vats were at the other end of the plant.

In the generator room, Dawson checked a fuel gauge.

"We have plenty of diesel," he said and then punched a start button.

Four massive generators roared to life. Dawson threw on five light switches, illuminating the plant. It was a high-ceilinged cathedral of science, the walls and floors white and spotless, the equipment shiny and bright.

"I want to get back to Abby and Maggie," Toby said.

They walked the length of the plant. Close to the door, something caught Dawson's eye – a white substance fixed to the side of a fermentation vat. There were twelve vats in total, each as wide as an elephant, rising three quarters of the way to the ceiling. Sweeping his eyes across the other vats, he saw each one had a similar substance affixed to it.

"Toby, get back," he barked, his heart contracting into his throat.

Dawson was certain it was C4. The reason for Mathews's visit was now evident. She had wired the plant with plastic explosives, knowing exactly how to stop the production of antibiotics.

Mathews's other motivations remained a mystery, though. Why hadn't she detonated the C4? Given the limited range of a remote, she should have done so before leaving the grounds, unless she had set up a repeater, which would allow her to detonate the explosives remotely from inside the bunker.

With that as a possibility, Dawson wanted Toby out of the building as quickly as possible. He explained the situation, omitting the terrifying fact that the C4 could go off any second. He played up the fact that it was safe to handle, as long as you left the wireless fuse intact.

"I'll help you get it," Toby said.

"There are twelve vats. It will only take me a few minutes to clear them. Sandy needs to know about this. You need to get back to Abby and Maggie."

Toby argued briefly, but eventually gave in and raced out the door.

As Dawson peeled off the first wad of C4, he wondered if the scientists knew he was in the area. No, that was impossible. Kids had seen him, "the adult," but they would not have communicated with scientists in the bunker.

Convinced he still enjoyed the element of surprise, he got to work on ridding the plant of explosives.

3.13
ATLANTA

When Maggie awoke, Abby told her about the boy she'd seen dragging a body.

"Don't be afraid," Maggie said and took hold of her hand. "We have each other."

Maggie brought the radio to her lips and tried to contact Sandy. "Alpha Zulu, do you copy? Alpha Zulu, do you copy?"

Dusk had fallen, and Abby wondered how long they should keep trying. With no other options, the answer was obvious: for as long as they had voices.

"If something happens to me, you have to keep trying to contact Sandy," Abby said.

"I will," Maggie replied with sadness filling her eyes.

Abby's heart contracted from the swiftness of Maggie's response.

After a long pause, Maggie added, "You're going to make it. Hang in there."

Abby realized she must look as sick as she felt. She was dying. Exhausted, she rested her head on Maggie's shoulder and closed her eyes, thinking about Touk and Jordan, then Toby and Mark. Had they safely reached the pill plant? She hoped Toby would return before dark and press against her, but quickly a sense of dread cuddled up next to her when she wondered if she would ever see him again.

"Alpha Zulu, do you copy? Alpha Zulu ...."

Maggie's voice grew fainter as Abby felt herself approaching sleep, sinking deeper into a quicksand of strange, fever-induced images and disconnected thoughts.

"Wake up! Abby, wake up! Abby!" Maggie said in an urgent tone, tugging her arm. "Abby, wake up."

Abby blinked and the night pressed against her eyeballs like sandpaper. It was completely dark. She glanced at the glowing hands on her watch and realized she'd been asleep for hours. "What's wrong?"

"Shhhh." Maggie was inches away, but Abby couldn't see her. "Some kids are just outside the alley," she whispered. "They know we're here. I heard them talking."

Abby heard only the thudding of her heart, but a voice screamed a warning in her mind, and she squeezed Maggie's hand harder when she felt her pulling away.

"Stay," Abby pleaded. "We're safe here."

Maggie easily broke the grip and placed the radio in Abby's hand. "Keep trying to get Sandy."

Maggie started a little avalanche of cans when she stood and shuffled toward the front of the alley.

Maybe the kids had moved on, Abby thought, or maybe Maggie had been mistaken, or they were just a bunch of survivors sick with the Pig, trying to endure the pain, not wanting to cause any trouble.

"Oh my God," Maggie cried out. "The smell is so awful."

A bloom of icy shivers started down Abby's neck, and before they had reached the base of her spine, Maggie screamed. The jagged grunts and cries of a violent struggle followed, Maggie's voice mixing with those of strangers, both boys and girls. To help her friend, Abby tried to stand, but she immediately folded over from a cramp.

Frantic footsteps informed her that Maggie had broken free. She was running and her attackers were chasing her. The sounds faded into the night.

A startling truth struck Abby. Maggie had wanted to engage the strangers to lure them away from the alley, giving Abby a chance to contact Sandy.

With tears trickling down her cheeks, she anchored the radio against her lips. "Alpha Zulu, do you copy?"

She hung her head and wept, too choked with sadness to go on.

The brave pilot would lose her attackers and return to the alley. Toby, too, would arrive at any minute. Her positive thoughts did little to flush the despair from her heart.

An hour later, Abby turned on the radio and pressed the button. "Alpha Zulu. Please, do you copy?"

A voice crackled in the heavy silence. "This is Alpha Zulu. Who are you?"

"Abby Leigh."

Abby waited for a response. None came. Had she lost the connection? She had forgotten to release the button. "I'm Abby Leigh," she said and took her finger off the button.

"Abby, thank God. This is Sandy. Where are you?"

"I'm near the bunker. Mark and Toby are at the pill plant."

"I discovered Mark's message," Sandy said. "I have several colleagues who I can trust. We're preparing to go to Alpharetta. Can you meet us there?"

Abby slumped into the trash pile. "My friend disappeared. Someone chased her, but I'm too sick to look for her. I can't go very far. I have the Pig."

"You have AHA-B?"

"I took three antibiotic pills, but they aren't working. I'm dying."

"Abby, listen to me very closely, I want you to die."

Abby's heart stopped. Then, with the shockwaves of Sandy's words echoing in her mind, she put the walkie-talkie close to her ear and learned how she was going to die.

3.14
WASHINGTON DC

"I lived there for about a year after the night of the purple moon," Low said, pointing her mass of red dreadlocks toward Union Station, a huge granite building that was once the district's train station. "That's where I met Bombie and Single Cell." With a smile, she added, "Two months later, I was sleeping in Abraham Lincoln's bed in the White House."

Jordan and Low were parked in a Jeep Cherokee a hundred meters from Union Station. Two trucks of White House Gang guards were parked nearby.

Thousands of kids were milling around the station, and Jordan's attention was drawn to a fight that had broken out, likely over food.

Inside Union Station, Jonzy, Spike, and a contingent of other White House Gang members were splicing copper wire onto the tracks. Earlier, Low had arranged for her gang members to strip the wire off telephone poles.

Low scrunched her brow. "Do you really think Jonzy can broadcast over the CDC station frequency?"

"Honestly, no," Jordan said. "But he's already started up two stations, and when he was at Colony East, he built a radio to eavesdrop on the scientists. Jonzy was born a genius. When he was little, his grandfather taught him how to build a radio using spare parts, so I could be wrong."

Jonzy's plan was to start up a local station and set the transmitter's frequency to the CDC's channel. To compensate for whatever transmitter he used being weaker than what the government was using, he would make his antennae longer than anything the CDC had — hundreds of miles longer.

He had explained his theory, saying that when he first learned about Doctor Perkins's secret plan to let the epidemic finish off the survivors, he wanted to find a way to spread the news outside Colony East. At the colony library, Jonzy found an article that described what a small college station in Massachusetts had done. They had connected their transmitter to train tracks, and for the next twenty-four hours, the only station playing in Montreal, Canada — two-hundred miles north — was the college's station.

Inspired, Jonzy wanted to hook up a radio station inside Colony East to the subway tracks. Train tracks were out of the question because Grand Central Station was being used as the mess hall. In the end, he had faced too many obstacles and had abandoned the idea.

When Jonzy and Spike piled back into the Jeep, Jonzy was bubbling with mad energy.

"We wired it up to tracks that go straight through Atlanta," he said. "Doctor Perkins will turn on the radio in Atlanta Colony and hear 'Pig Central.'"

The three-vehicle convoy drove two blocks to M Street, pulling up to a building that housed Radio Free Asia. Jonzy grabbed his tool bag, which Low had obtained for him, and together with Spike, entered the dark lobby, crunching over broken glass.

They quickly returned outside, reporting that survivors had stripped all the knobs from the soundboard.

The convoy made a U-turn, drove a block, and turned left on North Capital Street. The next stop was immediately on the right, National Public Radio. The windows were still intact in the three-story building. Spike used the butt of his shotgun to smash one, and then he and Jonzy entered the building.

Jordan turned on Jeep's radio, tuning into the CDC station.

"Distribution of the antibiotic to the areas hardest hit has begun," the robotic voice droned. "We expect to broaden the distribution to other areas as soon as possible. Until then, everyone should seek shelter and stay put. The AHA-B mutation syndrome is lethal, but we fully expect to eradicate it."

Rather than drive his fist through the windshield in anger at the CDC's lies, Jordan exercised discipline and lowered the volume.

Several minutes later, Spike raced from the building and reported that Jonzy had everything he needed, which started a chain of events. Low chatted on her walkie-talkie, organizing the move of a generator. It was on a flatbed truck, and she told her team where to bring it. Then she instructed her other team where to string the wire that was connected to the tracks.

Jordan remained with Low because he still held out a sliver of hope that he could convince her to send gang members to Atlanta with them.

"Why are you so afraid of the Grits?" he asked.

"They're ruthless."

"A lot of kids say the White House Gang is ruthless," Jordan said.

Above her germ mask, Jordan could tell Low was blushing.

"Thank you," she said, "but we don't ride over our enemies. You know about Pale Rider?"

Jordan nodded. "I heard she's the leader. She rides a green Harley."

"Her eyes glow," Low warned. "Her gang took over all of Georgia, and they're moving north. Before the Pig hit us, the Grits were our biggest concern."

"They're not immune to the Pig," Jordan said.

Nodding slowly, Low replied, "The Grits don't care if they die."

Jordan understood how a rumor started and took on a life of its own. Pale Rider's eyes did not glow, and the members of the Grits wanted to live as much as the other survivors did. Rumor or not, though, he realized he would never change Low's mind about Pale Rider and the Grits. Then he had an idea.

He found a pencil and envelope in the glove compartment and wrote a message to the Grits. If Jonzy's crazy, railroad-track idea worked and the signal traveled all the way to Atlanta, he would ask the White House Gang DJ to read it on the air. It might give them a chance.

Jordan showed the note to Low. "What if Pale Rider hears this on the radio?"

Low chuckled coldly. "When Pale Rider puts her front wheel on your chest, I hope you die quickly so you won't suffer much."

As Jordan entertained that image, Jonzy's voice came over the radio. "Test, test, test. Hello, Washington DC."

Jonzy Billings, boy genius, had commandeered the CDC station frequency. "Test, test test. Lemon, I'm dedicating Pig Central to you."

Lemon Billings had shown his grandson how to build a radio, and now his grandson hoped to hook up the world's longest antennae and broadcast the truth all the way to Atlanta Colony. Lemon must be smiling down on them from above.

In honor of Lemon, Jordan slightly altered his message to the Grits.

3.15
ATLANTA

Shivering, Abby shuffled through the dark alley. The night swept through her the way icy fog sifts through bare tree branches.

"Maggie," she called in a raspy voice, fearful of giving herself away.

An odor slithered up her nostrils and left an oily, metallic taste in the back of her throat. She covered her nose with her hand, fighting the urge to gag, and stumbled out of the alley.

A half-moon provided some light in the street. The horrible stench was stronger here, and she doubled over, choking and spitting. Taking tiny sips of air through her mouth, she headed right, the direction to the CDC bunker, and the way she thought Maggie had run.

Two blocks farther on, she came to a corner. The bunker was to the right, and halfway down the street, in the middle of the road, a bonfire blazed. Black smoke billowed up from the flames, blotting out the moon.

Abby crept forward and stopped cold when four kids appeared. They seemed to step out of the fire. From thirty meters away, their stares sent chills rippling down her spine.

She had nothing of value. No pills, no food, and no weapon. The two-way radio was back in the alley. With Sandy's instructions swimming in her head, Abby had forgotten to bring it. She was just another sick kid.

Sensing someone behind her, Abby spun around. The fire's glow was putting on a freakish show of giant shadow puppets. Seeing no one, she turned back and shuddered. A boy had moved within ten feet of her. She rocked back on her heels when she identified him as the shirtless boy with long, straggly hair she'd seen earlier.

Feverish and on the verge of dry heaving from the stench, her insides churning with pain, Abby retreated to a tiny outpost in her mind and concluded the situation was dire. She was too weak to fight and too sick to run away.

With an expression blank as stone, Bare-chested Boy took a step toward her. Her eyes fell to his hand, and to the charred human foot he held.

Revulsion filled her and fueled her rage. She charged the boy, flailing her arms and shouting. His eyes widened in shock as her hand scraped his face.

Abby took aim at the others, and when they stood their ground, she had no choice but to veer and run through the perimeter of the flames. Blistering heat scorched her as she willed a heavy right leg forward, a heavy left leg forward, right leg, left leg, right, left and she broke through to cool air.

She plodded on for what felt like hours, but was probably less than thirty seconds. Ahead of her were the lights of the CDC bunker.

Survivors had gathered out front, and Abby wondered if Maggie was among them. She tapped into her last ounce of energy to keep on her feet until she reached the crowd. She pitched forward and caught a face-full of weeds between the sidewalk and street.

Abby clenched fistfuls of dirt. The adults were doing more than withholding a cure for the Pig. They were responsible for turning kids against each other, for killing the human spirit. She had to stop the scientists from inflicting more evil. She was not ready to die.

DAY 4
CDC BUNKER

As Doctor Hedrick stood before him, Doctor Perkins noted her bloodshot eyes and sallow skin and recalled how much more vibrant she'd been at Colony East. He must look just as worn out to her.

She had entered his office unannounced, saying she wanted to discuss an urgent matter relating to Generation M.

Mulling another thought, Perkins considered the mutual fondness that Lieutenant Dawson and Hedrick had for one another. A conspiracy between those two was not out of the question.

"What is the issue, Doctor?" he asked.

"Ensign Royce and I conducted an autopsy on an AHA-B victim and discovered extreme kidney damage," she said.

This concerned him. "The victim died of renal failure?"

Hedrick pondered the question. "It's possible. My concern is a secondary infection. Even those of us who've taken the antibiotic might be at risk."

"Have you heard from Lieutenant Dawson?" he asked, focusing on her eyes, watching for a flicker of fear, a split second of mental calculation.

"Excuse me?"

"The lieutenant is a dear friend, is he not?"

She crinkled her tired eyes and smiled sadly. "Yes, I have a great deal of respect for Lieutenant Dawson. I miss him as a colleague and a friend."

"Has he contacted you?"

Doctor Hedrick appeared confused.

"Last time I checked," she said, "Ensign Ryan couldn't establish communications with Colony West." She brightened. "Do you have an update?"

"I'll look into it," he said, sensing her optimism was genuine. Satisfied that Hedrick was here with a legitimate concern, he added, "How would you like to proceed?"

"We need to conduct more autopsies."

"Indeed." He nodded. "I suggest a minimum of five corpses."

"Perhaps we can collect victims in the city?"

Perkins typed a command on his keyboard and Monitor number four came to life, showing the mob of children outside the front gate.

"Low hanging fruit right at our doorstep," he said. "See Captain Mathews. She'll arrange security for your team."

Her brow crinkled. "Captain?"

"Mathews received her promotion for outstanding service to the colony."

"I'll contact her immediately," Hedrick said.

"Sandra," he called as she was heading for the door. He reserved first names for moments of paternalistic advice. "You could use some rest. We all need some."

"Sorry, Doctor Perkins, but now is not the time to rest."

"Generation M thanks you," he trilled in a tone that spoke of his delight. Such dedication brightened his morning.

4.01
ATLANTA

Abby let herself go limp, yet remained on her feet, propped up by the crush of surrounding survivors. Hundreds crowded the area in front of the CDC bunker. Most had the Pig, evidenced by the nonstop groans and cries for food. Abby added her voice to the chorus.

She was within twenty meters of the perimeter fence. Another fifty meters beyond the fence, four doors, each large enough to drive a big truck through, were built into a concrete wall.

It had taken her hours to reach this position so close to the fence. Using her hand as a crowbar, she had wedged it between kids to pry them apart, quickly moving into the gap she had created.

"The adults have tacos," a girl shouted.

The crowd surged toward the fence, producing an enormous force that squeezed Abby's chest. She took rapid, tiny sips of air, praying she would not pass out. As the taco rumor slowly died out, the pressure released and she could breathe again normally.

About thirty minutes later, the large door on the right lifted and a truck drove out. The taller kids in the crowd shouted out what was happening.

"Six adults wearing hazmat suits."

"They have food."

"They're coming to help us."

An adult voice boomed from a speaker on top of the truck. "Move back from the gate. Everyone move back. Back up immediately."

Just the opposite happened. The predominant force of the crowd took aim at the gate. With her ribcage near its breaking point from the crush of bodies around her, Abby started to black out from the lack of oxygen. Colors leeched from her vision, and soon the world was cast in shades of gray. She tried to breathe with the rapidity of a hummingbird.

The adults fired a water cannon, hosing the kids with a jet of icy water. The spray cooled Abby's fever and seemed to do the same for the other survivors.

Cries of "more" and "over here" changed the adults' tactics. Something exploded high over Abby's head, leaving a puff of white gas that slowly descended on the crowd. Her eyes and throat burned as more explosions followed and the little white clouds settled over the kids.

Like a sudden shift of the wind, the crowd reversed direction, pushing away from the gate. Maybe the kids finally understood that the adults were not coming out to help them.

The shades of grey darkened, a sign that Abby was seconds away from passing out. Believing the risk of suffocation was greater than the risk of kids trampling her to death, she raised one shoulder and pressed her arm flat against her side and wiggled her hips, shifting back and forth, moving with the crowd while at the same time sinking lower.

Finally sprawled on the ground, eye level with a forest of legs and feet, the air was hot and stale, but at least she could breathe. Knees repeatedly knocked against her head. To protect herself, she curled into a tight ball and covered her head with her arms. The battering eased as the crowd dispersed.

Eventually, the sky reappeared. She stretched out and lay motionless. Others were also on the ground, claimed by the Pig or by the same forces that had come close to making her a victim. The area looked like a battlefield after the armies had retreated.

She closed her eyes until they were two, thin slits, and she watched the adults in hazmat suits climb out of the truck and fan out among the bodies.

One of the adults had to be Sandy, but Abby couldn't see the faces behind the bubble masks.

Two adults came straight for her and knelt beside her. One of them carried a large black bag.

"Don't move."

Abby recognized Sandy's voice.

"If you can hear me, give a small nod," Sandy said.

Abby nodded.

"Good. Doctor Perkins may be watching us on a monitor, so you have to remain perfectly still. Nod if you understand me."

Abby gave a little nod.

Sandy and her partner rolled Abby to her side, positioned the long bag beneath her, and then carefully maneuvered her inside.

The body bag blocked out all light and was smooth, but the zipper hurt where it pressed against her nose and forehead. In the chaos of the past minutes, Abby had completely forgotten about her desperate hunger and fever, but her senses were magnified inside the dark cocoon. As waves of painful cramps rolled through her stomach, she wanted to bring her knees to her stomach and hug them, but the bag constricted her.

Abby heard voices — two men — and then felt herself being lifted by the handles above her head and below her feet. The men carried her the way they would a rolled up rug.

The bag pressed against her face, forming a seal against her nose and mouth. She drew in a sharp breath that tightened the seal. A trillion bubbles of panic coursed through her blood stream. She was suffocating.

Trying to create a little pocket of air, she tensed her stomach and chest muscles and blew out through her nose, emptying her lungs. Immediately, she tried to take a breath but only sucked the plastic against her mouth and nostrils, tight as tape. With her lungs depleted of oxygen, a burning sensation flared in her throat and down her legs.

The voices of the two men sounded distant, and she tumbled into her mind.

Sunshine splashed the tops of tall pines across the lake as they swayed in the breeze, and Abby followed the ribbons of air as they unfurled and picked up the scent of the forest floor. Standing on the dock, she could almost taste the perfume of moss and dirt as the fresh air blew across the lake. Added to it was the honey flavor of the green pollen floating on the surface. Filled with serene peacefulness, she closed her eyes and inhaled.

She jerked her head and gasped, forcing hot, stale air down the constricted pipe of her throat. The bag lay against the side of her face, and she felt the warmth of the material on her ear. The men were still carrying her, and her heart thundered in fear.

They finally set her down on a hard, flat surface, and a moment later, a truck engine started, the vibrations spreading throughout her body. The truck lurched forward.

When the truck stopped and the engine turned off, she figured she was inside the bunker.

She was lifted and placed on a new, flat surface. Soon, she sensed motion. They must be wheeling her on a gurney.

"We'll begin the first autopsy at zero one hundred," Sandy said loudly.

Again, Abby felt herself being lifted, and this time, her face was in a better position. She was placed on a smooth surface that moved and then stopped. Something clicked. It was dark, silent, still, and the temperature dropped.

She felt as if she were buried alive, headfirst in a coffin-like enclosure. Her scream came without warning and was quickly absorbed in the heavy silence the way water soaks into sand. She screamed a second time and then a third. She kept screaming until her raw vocal cords gave out.

4.02
WASHINGTON DC - GEORGIA

In Jordan's motorcycle mirror, the Washington Monument faded in the early morning haze. Spike and Jonzy flanked him.

Low had given them extra gas, drinking water, cheese, and words of advice:"Go through Georgia at night. Maybe you'll get lucky, and the Grits won't see you."

The boys made steady progress and turned onto Route 85, the road that made a beeline for Atlanta

At ten o'clock, after they'd gone one-hundred-and-seventy miles, Jordan signaled for them to stop, needing to stretch and take a leak.

Jonzy raised the radio antennae and held the speaker close to his ear, aiming the antennae in a number of different directions.

Jordan heard the robotic voice on the CDC station, urging survivors to stay indoors, keep listening to the station, and wait for help to arrive.

Jonzy shrugged. "We're too far from the tracks to pick up Pig Central."

Jordan bit his tongue to keep himself from blurting out that it had been a good but crazy idea.

After filling their stomachs with cheese and grasshoppers, they got back on the road. Route 85 had only a few obstacles, allowing them to increase their speed to fifty miles per hour. They stopped next a few miles north of Charlotte, North Carolina. The Georgia border was about an hour away.

Jonzy tried the radio again and reported he only picked up the adult station. If Jonzy was discouraged, he didn't show it. Just the opposite. He beamed like someone who had found a freezer filled with ice cream.

Jonzy kept trying to pick up Pig Central while Jordan and Spike debated Low's idea of holing up until nightfall.

"I think we should keep going," Jordan said.

"Nighttime is safer," Spike countered.

"Time is not on our side," Jordan countered back. "Abby, Touk, and Toby might need us."

"They might need us, but we wouldn't be good to anyone if the Grits kill us."

Jordan swallowed hard. "I'm ready to take on Pale Rider."

The corner of Spike's lip curled. "Okay, let's roll," he said and hopped on his bike.

Jordan drew in a sharp breath, wondering if he had spoken too soon.

Jonzy whooped, and they raced over to him. He was holding the antenna against a minivan. The burned-out hulk of metal allowed the radio to pick up a weaker signal.

"Pig Central," he exclaimed. "Listen!"

The robotic voice of the CDC and the voice of the White House Gang DJ wove together in a garbled mess. They could clearly identify each source from a word here and a word there, but it was impossible to understand anything.

Jonzy turned off the radio, thrilled that his experiment had worked, while Spike had a puzzled expression, likely thinking the same as Jordan. *The Grits wouldn't understand gibberish.*

They made their first contact with the gang members just south of Charlotte. Three bikers on Harley Davidsons, carrying rifles, approached them and then made U-turns and sped off. Jordan thought they were scouts.

The boys slowed to twenty-five miles per hour, and Jordan resumed his habit of constantly looking right, then left, wary of ambushes.

After ten miles, they stopped at the top of a long rise. Jordan squeezed the grips, fearing a puff of wind might topple him off his bike. He turned to Spike, who for the first time ever seemed speechless. On Jordan's left, Jonzy stared in wonder or terror, or maybe both.

A river of motorcycles stretched before them, filling the southbound lanes of the highway for as far as he could see. Not a single engine was running.

"You told me you were ready," Spike said.

Jordan was ready for his heart to jump up through his throat, out his mouth, and flop around on the pavement.

"Jonzy and I will wait here," Spike added.

Jordan revved his engine. Between him and Atlanta stood a super gang whose reputation of evil had spread far and wide. Gunning the engine, he felt his mind, and then his heart, fill with the belief that he could do anything.

He put the bike in gear and powered forward, but his confidence evaporated when he got a good look at the four Grits at the head of the pack.

He killed his engine and rolled to within five feet of them. There were three boys and a girl, all on different colored Harleys. The eerie silence gave Jordan the sense of having entered a tomb.

Pus dribbled from sores on the face of the boy on the white motorcycle. Another boy had a shotgun slung over his back. The third boy, straddling a black Harley, was skinny as a skeleton.

The girl on the green motorcycle wore a red bandana over a shaved head. She had to be Pale Rider. Her eyes terrified and captivated him at once. The irises were translucent orbs that pulled him into them.

She glared at Jordan, turning his blood into icy slurry, but he managed to meet her stare.

"We're going to Atlanta to fight the adults," he said, grateful his voice worked.

"You have to get by us first." Pale Rider's low, raspy voice triggered a fresh wave of shivers.

Suddenly, Jordan's shivers vanished, and he laughed to himself. He didn't care what happened next. Either he had lost his fear of death, or more likely, he had grown numb in the face of overwhelming odds. His spirit soared.

"Join us or get the hell out of the way," he shouted and fired up his bike.

Pale Rider remained motionless, drilling him with her ghostly stare. With a small smile playing on his lips, he stared back.

"What's your name?" she asked.

Pale Rider's voice chilled his heart to the core.

"Jordan Leigh."

She nodded. "We heard about you on the radio. I wanted to see what you were made of. We'll ride together."

Pale Rider raised her fist and hundreds of Harleys rumbled to life. The Grits, as if reenacting the parting of the Red Sea, backed up their bikes.

Pale Rider gestured to the open lane down the middle of the highway. "There's a fuel truck ahead. Gas up your Lemon Gang."

Jordan raised his eyes. Lemon Billings was most certainly smiling down on them now.

4.03
CDC BUNKER

Touk pressed against Abby, using her shoulder as a pillow. The night was so dark that Abby couldn't see her sister lying beside her on the dock. Not a star was out, nor a blade of moonlight between the clouds, and not even the blink of a firefly. They had snuggled like this for hours.

Touk vanished, and Abby worried she had fallen asleep and Touk had slipped into the water. When she tried rolling on her side, something pinned her shoulders and arms down, preventing her from moving.

Abby cried out and lifted her head, but immediately the tip of her nose bumped into something. Recent events flooded her mind. Toucan was not drowning. Abby was. She was inside a body bag, inside the CDC bunker, in a soundproof vault.

Gasping, she sucked in stale air. She needed more oxygen, but it was almost too much of a chore to breathe. Her lungs burned, signaling something was terribly wrong, but she found the spreading warmth strangely comforting.

Abby startled at the river of light flowing beneath her, growing brighter, and rising ever higher. It washed over her and carried away her fear and pain. All she had to do was go limp, submit, and let the brilliant light sweep her away.

Never give up! The words tore through her brain. She might suffocate in this plastic cocoon, or maybe the AHA-B bacteria would kill her first, but she would never willingly quit living. She'd fight the blissful calling one strained breath at a time.

She inhaled and then exhaled. Breathed in and then breathed out.

It felt as if someone were piling bricks on her chest. Her muscles, starved of oxygen, fatigued, and each breath she took satisfied her lungs less and less. Jagged huffs of air turned into sips, and exhalations became feeble puffs that would not have made a candle flame flicker.

Never never never give up!

Light from above exploded and unleashed a silent waterfall of cold, fresh air. Sandy, who had just unzipped the body bag, peered down with concern.

"I'm sorry I couldn't get you out sooner, but I had to block the camera." She pointed to a corner of the room where a wall-mounted camera had silver tape covering its lens. "Doctor Perkins likes to keep tabs on what's going on inside the clinic. We have to move you before he sends someone here to investigate."

Sandy helped her sit up, and Abby gulped air until her head spun from a rich abundance of oxygen. She started to fall back, but Sandy caught her.

"How long have I been here?" Abby croaked.

"Only a few minutes," Sandy said.

How was that possible?

Abby felt a pinch in her arm. Sandy was giving her an injection.

"The antibiotic," Sandy said. "You'll recover from AHA-B, but you'll feel very weak for several days."

"I took three pills already," Abby said. "Why didn't they work?"

Sandy shook her head. "One pill should have worked."

"We handed out hundreds of pills. What if they were all bad?"

"All we can do is start making pills and distribute them as quickly as possible," Sandy said.

"How are you going to do that?"

"I'm working on that. First, we need to get you to my living quarters and hook you up to an IV to hydrate you."

"Where's my sister?" Abby asked.

Sandy crinkled her brow. "Lisette is doing well. She's here with the other children." She looked over Abby's shoulder. "Ensign?"

"This is becoming a habit," a deep voice said.

Abby turned to see Ensign Royce. She had liked him when she was at Colony East. He, along with Sandy, had cared for her right after she had attempted to swim across the East River to reach the colony.

Ensign Royce reminded her of a gentle bear. He was tall, broad, and had enormous hands. He gripped Abby's shoulders with his paws and lifted her as Sandy tugged the body bag in the other direction.

He carried Abby across the room and gently placed her into a large laundry bin on wheels.

"We're going for a little ride," the ensign said as he covered her with several hospital gowns.

She briefly tried to claw them away until she realized she had plenty of fresh air, and it wasn't completely dark under the gowns.

Ensign Royce pushed her at an easy pace. Along the route, he exchanged greetings with several other adults. The ride ended in Sandy's room, where he put Abby on the bed.

"Do you know my sister, Lisette?"

"Yes, I believe I have had the pleasure of meeting her." He smiled and spoke in a warm, joking tone, but the eyes of the big gentle bear filled with sadness.

A chill rippled down Abby's spine. "What's wrong?"

The ensign walked over to a TV mounted in the corner. The screen was divided into four equal sections. Three of the sections showed areas outside the compound. In the remaining quadrant, children were playing inside. He pointed to them. "This is the Generation M quarters. Keep your eye out. Maybe you'll see Lisette."

The ensign went to work on hooking Abby up to an IV.

"Don't open the door for anyone," he said when he finished, and then he turned off the light, stepped outside, and Abby heard the click of the lock engaging.

She focused on the monitor. Some of the children in blue uniforms were playing tag. Others were playing chess. A few were reading books.

Betting that Touk was playing tag, she scanned the Generation M kids, trying to spot a head of red, curly hair. Abby's drooped from exhaustion.

Toucan raced out of the cabin. Abby, standing at the end of the dock, bent her knees and braced herself, ready to catch her sister. But Touk ran right by her as if Abby didn't exist, jumping into the water and making a big splash.

4.04
ALPHARETTA

Dawson paced by the plant's door that he had left open a crack so he could hear if a vehicle approached. While he hoped it would be Sandy and a team of scientists accompanied by Abby, Toby, and Maggie coming to fire up the pill manufacturing process, he knew it could just as easily be Mathews, returning to detonate the C4.

He had placed all twelve charges outside. A massive explosion one-hundred meters from the plant ought to give Lieutenant Mathews pause.

After that little surprise, how long could he fight her off? *Not long.*

The only weapons he had managed to procure were seven fire extinguishers: three for chemical fires, three for electrical fires, and one all-purpose.

He had built a barricade with fifty-five-gallon drums of a chemical reagent. All he had to do was roll the last one in place.

For Dawson, one battle had already begun. He fought the urge to sprint to the CDC bunker to help Sandy.

He had figured out how the scientists knew he was in the area. Perkins and Mathews had intercepted the note he'd placed in the cadet's medical records.

Knowing he could do nothing for Sandy, he told himself he belonged at the plant, where he could make a stand, possibly his last.

He unfolded the photocopy of Sarah's picture and swallowed the lump in his throat as he gazed at his daughter. After failing to search for her when he was at Colony East, he had been given a second chance, and now Sarah was recovering from AHA-B in the care of responsible kids.

But what kind of life would she have if they failed to make and distribute pills to the hundreds of thousands of other sick kids?

Dawson hefted a fire extinguisher. If Mathews wanted a fight, he would give her one.

DAY 5
CDC BUNKER

Abby heard hushed voices, but when she tried to open her eyes, it felt like her eyelids were glued shut. She went to rub her eyes for relief, but one arm seemed to be tied to something, and the other weighed a thousand pounds.

"Can we trust Doctor Ramanathan?"

"Yes."

Ensign Royce had asked the question and Sandy had answered.

Abby opened her eyes a crack. She was in Sandy's living quarters. Her right wrist was secured to a bedrail with a belt, and an IV needle was taped to the top of her hand. Five adults, including Sandy and Ensign Royce, were seated at a table in the corner. She recognized Doctor Levine from Colony East. The other two wore jumpsuits, the type worn by the Navy. One was a woman with red hair and a freckled face, and the other a man who looked to be in his late teens.

A whiteboard on the wall had the names: PERKINS, DROZNIN, MATHEWS, RYAN, BEECHAM.

A digital clock gave the time as 02:58. Was it day or night? Abby realized it was nighttime when she saw the TV monitor. Spotlights illuminated the external views, and the quadrant where the Generation M kids had been playing was deserted. The kids must be sleeping.

"Miss Sleepy is awake," Ensign Royce said.

Sandy approached the bed and placed her hand on Abby's forehead. "How are you feeling?"

"Better," Abby said, though it came out as a croak. Her mind was still a little foggy, and her stomach rumbled, but the cramps were gone.

Sandy removed the IV needle, undid the belt, and helped her sit up. She introduced the two Navy personnel. The young-looking man was Ensign Parker, and the freckly-faced woman was Petty Officer Murphy. Sandy told Abby to stay in bed and rest. She returned to the table, and the adults continued their discussion.

"We can make antibiotics, but we have no way of distributing them," Ensign Royce said.

"Let's worry about making the pills first," Sandy said. "When we're at the plant, we need to protect ourselves. Mathews has locked up all the weapons."

Levine pointed to the white board. "We can't trust them, but we need the support of everyone else inside the bunker."

Ensign Parker pointed to the TV. "We can send everyone a message over the monitors. Tell them what we're trying to do. Ask for help."

"Ensign Ryan will stop you," Sandy said.

"I can get access to the communications center." Parker rapped the table with his knuckles and grinned. "I'll worry about Ryan."

"The minute Perkins sees one of us on a monitor, he'll order a lockdown," Doctor Levine said.

Parker nodded. "That's true, but it will also create a diversion. There will be a small window of time for you to leave in a vehicle. I can pre-record the message here. When I play it, that's when you go."

"If you're in the communications center, how will you get out?" Ensign Royce asked Parker.

"He won't," Murphy answered.

"Hey, someone has to do it," Parker said, grinning and acting as though it were no big deal. He turned serious. "I worked for Admiral Samuels at

Colony East. I don't know what happened to him, but he didn't die of a heart attack." His voice choked. "I'm doing this for the old man."

There was a long moment of silence.

Ensign Royce turned to Sandy. "You should give the message. Everyone respects you."

Sandy was nodding when Abby spoke up. "I know what the epidemic is doing to kids, and I've had the Pig. I'll do it."

The adults faced her with blank expressions, leading her to wonder if they had forgotten she was in the room with them.

"They might respond to her," Ensign Royce said. "How many of the scientists have actually seen a survivor?"

"I'd listen to her," Murphy said.

"What do we do with her afterward?" Doctor Levine asked the others.

"Take her with you to the plant," Ensign Parker said.

"It won't be safe there," Sandy said. "Perkins and Mathews will come for us."

Abby stood and steadied herself. The absence of cramps was a strange sensation. "My friend, Toby, went to the plant. That's where I want to go."

"I suppose it's safer than anyplace else," Levine said.

"All right. Does everyone agree that Abby should be the one to give our message?" Sandy asked.

All the adults nodded.

Abby's blood turned cold at a sudden thought. "Will my sister be safe?"

"Now that you mention it, Doctor Perkins will know right away that you are Lisette's sister," Sandy said. "He's unpredictable. I can't say what he'll do. I really think one of us should deliver the message."

Abby's mind went blank, but a debate raged in her blood and bones. How could she put Touk's life at risk? Couldn't one of the adults deliver the message just as well as she could? She knew in her heart they couldn't.

"I'm ready to tell the truth about what's happening out there." Wobbly knees told her she wasn't ready, but she would speak up anyway.

Ensign Parker stood. "I'll get a video camera."

A knock on the door froze everyone in place. The adults glanced at each other with terrified expressions. Sandy crept to the door and looked through the peephole.

"It's Droznin," she whispered and turned off the light. The glow from the digital clock dappled them in faint red light.

Abby's adrenaline surged, knowing that the scientist who had infected her with the Pig stood on the other side of the door, the person Abby had shot.

The knocking continued.

They spoke in whispers.

"What does she want?"

"Invite her in. We'll grab her."

"Just wait. She'll leave."

When it was evident the Russian scientist wasn't going away, Sandy opened the door a crack. "Doctor Droznin?"

"I'm sorry to bother you at this hour, Doctor Hedrick, but it's important. I'd like to discuss your autopsy results. I'm concerned about the efficacy of the antibiotic."

Sandy yawned. "I can write up a report for you."

"It will just take a minute."

Another yawn. "Doctor Droznin, I've had a really long day."

Sandy closed the door. Droznin knocked again.

"She'll go to Perkins if you don't let her in," Levine whispered. "He'll send Mathews to kick down the door."

Sandy held up her hands. "Get ready."

Ensign Parker and Ensign Murphy got into position, one behind the door, one to the right of it.

Sandy opened the door. "Please, come in."

In a flash, the lights were on and the door shut. Ensign Parker wrapped his arms around the scientist, and Murphy held her hand against Droznin's mouth. Sandy picked up the crutches that had crashed to the floor.

Droznin's eyes widened when she saw Abby.

"I'll take my hand away if you promise to stay quiet," Murphy said.

Droznin nodded.

Ensign Parker maneuvered the scientist into a chair and secured her hands behind her back with the belt that had secured Abby's hand to the bedrail.

Staring at Abby, Droznin whispered, "Remarkable. They said you drowned."

"Does she look like she drowned?" Murphy said, stripping the pillowcase. "One more peep out of you and this is going in your mouth."

Ensign Parker slipped out of the room to get the video camera. When he returned, he instructed Abby to stand against a blank wall, and then he aimed the video camera directly at her. A tiny red light on the casing blinked on.

"Any time," he said.

Butterflies fluttered in her empty stomach, and then she remembered the words Mark had spoken to her over the radio after she had escaped Colony East. *"Keep your shoulders back."*

Abby did just that. "My name is Abby Leigh. I'm fifteen years old. I was living on an island off the coast of Maine during the night of the purple moon. My parents died that night, and I had to care for my brother and sister ...."

The words tumbled out as she explained what it had been like to survive the first epidemic, and how kids had learned to work and live together. She spoke about setting up schools, medical clinics, and trading zones. She told them how the Pig struck, and instead of kids working together, they were fighting each other and suffering horrible deaths.

"We need your help to make the antibiotic pills. Kids will help with the distribution. I'm sure of it. It's time to start over. Please."

The room remained completely silent.

"I'll help," Doctor Droznin said. "I designed the Alpharetta facility. I can get it running."

Murphy shot to her feet, ready to gag the scientist.

Sandy intervened. "Wait. She can save us a lot of time."

Doctor Levine narrowed his eyes. "She's known Perkins for twenty-five years. She'll sabotage what we're trying to do."

They debated what to do with Doctor Droznin. Sandy wanted to give her a chance. Ensign Royce and Doctor Levine were against the idea.

Abby walked up to the scientist. "Why should we believe you?"

"I agree with what the colonies stand for," Doctor Droznin said. "Every piece of data I've seen informs me that focusing a finite number of resources on a controlled population is the best way to establish a society of highly-educated citizens.

"But I have also started to question some of my assumptions after seeing what's happening outside the bunker. I believe we should help the survivors. We need time to reassess our strategy."

Abby looked for clues in Doctor Droznin's eyes and her facial expression. Could they trust her? She saw nothing that helped her decide either way.

Something stirred deep inside of Abby, a faint voice, a feeling, and a memory of the way she used to think. *People are good. They want to help one another.*

Doctor Droznin maintained a serious, cold expression, and the voice inside Abby grew fainter, sputtering like a candle consuming the last bit of wax.

"I trust her," Abby said before the flame died out. "I believe Doctor Droznin will help save lives."

5.01
CDC BUNKER

Lisette giggled so hard her sides ached. Charlie was chasing Zoe around the big room, and he reached out to tag Zoe as she would zig or zag to avoid his hand.

Lisette, and practically every other girl from Unit 2A, stood off to the side and cheered for Zoe. The boys from Unit 2B stood on the opposite side of the room, naturally rooting for Charlie.

Mother raised her hands. "Please slow down."

The shouting and laughing almost drowned out her voice.

Zoe suddenly stopped, and Charlie almost crashed into her.

"Got you," he cried, eliciting a loud cheer from the boys.

Zoe didn't seem to care that Charlie had caught her. She was staring at something else. When Lisette turned to see what Zoe looked at, she smiled in wonder.

A girl with red curly hair and freckles was on the TV monitor. Usually, that TV showed pictures of Generation M kids playing.

When the room quieted, they could hear her.

"We call it the Pig," the girl said. "I had it. I know how awful the illness is, and I've seen what it does to other kids. It makes them desperate for food. They'll do anything. Two months ago, those same kids were working together and forging lives for themselves. Now they are dying and fighting with each other."

Lisette liked the girl's voice, but she loved the girl's hair even more.

5.02
CDC BUNKER

Doctor Perkins jolted forward in his chair. All four monitors featured a ratty-looking teen talking about the epidemic. He punched in the intercom code for the communications center. "Ensign Ryan, what is going on?"

Perkins recognized the child. It was ID 1002 from Colony East. Abigail Leigh had supposedly drowned in the Hudson River while attempting to escape the colony.

He put his lips almost in contact with the intercom's microphone. "Ryan, respond!"

Perkins balled his fist. Dawson was behind this. He had lied about the girl drowning in the Hudson River. Now the lieutenant and 1002 had infiltrated the bunker. Dawson needed to be stopped.

To kill the video feeds and black out every monitor throughout the bunker, Perkins danced his fingers across his keyboard, but the command failed to execute. He frantically repeated the sequence.

"All of you can help by making and distributing pills. Kids will help with the distribution. I'm sure of it …."

Someone in the communications room had taken control of the system. Unable to shut the girl up, he drowned out her voice by tapping a key to sound the general alarm. The emergency light in his office flashed red, accompanied by a piercing wail.

The alarm, designed to warn of a wide range of threats from biological agent contamination to radiation exposure, started a chain of events. Lab doors were sealed. Teams of scientists jumped into hazmat suits, and Generation M went into lockdown in their living quarters.

He grabbed his two-way radio. "Captain Mathews."

Her voice crackled back immediately, "I'm on my way to the communications center."

"It's Dawson," he said, seething. "We have to stop him."

"We're ready for all threats," she replied in such an angry growl that Perkins wondered if Mathews relished the thought of having a showdown between her and Dawson.

"I'll meet you there," he said and signed off.

He paused to collect himself before stepping outside his office. As a leader, it was important to project quiet confidence and wisdom.

He moved through the hallways at an unhurried pace, smiling and giving reassuring nods to those who jogged past him. The look in their eyes deeply concerned him. He sensed their fears and their doubt in his strategy to create the colonies. The Leigh girl had put both a face and voice to the tragedy.

Approaching the communications center, he heard a loud pounding above the screaming alarm. When he rounded the corner, he saw Captain Mathews banging on the door with the butt of her assault rifle.

He moved to her side. "Report."

"Whoever's in there has locked the door."

"Dawson and the girl?" he asked.

Mathews flashed him the steely look of an assassin. "I'm ready for all threats. Please back away."

Perkins stepped back, using his hand to shield his eyes from the flashing red beacon on the opposite wall.

Mathews attacked the door with powerful kicks, striking a spot next to the knob with her heel. Lab doors could survive the punishment, but the communications' door was less secure, and it started to budge.

Someone on the other side pushed back, though. Mathews's strikes would budge the door forward an inch, but then it would shut again.

She brought the M-16 level with her hip and squeezed the trigger. Bullets ripped through the door in a circular pattern. Perkins, formulating how he would explain this event to his colleagues, was glad the alarm had muted the gunfire. Keeping the barrel aimed at the door, Mathews gave it one more heel thrust and then rammed it with her shoulder. She charged through the narrow opening. Perkins, expecting more gunfire, took another step back and covered his ears.

Mathews poked her head out. "All clear."

Ensign Parker lay crumpled on the floor, dead. Mathews was freeing Ensign Ryan, who sat in a chair with duct tape covering his mouth, his ankles and wrists secured with more tape.

Mathews's radio crackled to life. "Captain, come in."

"It's Ensign Beecham," she told Perkins and brought the radio to her lips. "Go ahead."

"A vehicle just left the facility," Beecham said. "Doctor Hedrick was driving. There were others in the vehicle, but I couldn't identify them."

Perkins massaged his temples. Hedrick and Dawson had obviously communicated with each other prior to this to coordinate the breakout. He couldn't speculate who else was with her, other than Dawson and the Leigh child.

Mathews barked commands to Ensign Beecham. "Get assault rifles. Ryan and I will meet you in the garage."

Perkins raised an index finger.

"Beecham, hold on," Mathews said.

"We know they're going to Alpharetta," Perkins said. "First, let's mop up this mess and patch the door."

As Mathews conveyed new orders to Beecham, Perkins sat before the communications room computer and typed in a command that ended the alarm and flashing red lights. He turned on the video camera and looked into it. Behind him, he could see blood splatters on the wall, so he shifted his position until the background was clean.

"Everyone quiet," he said and tapped a command that put him on every monitor throughout the bunker.

"Thank you for participating in the drill." He smiled and paused, allowing his confidence to shine through the screens. "Everyone performed admirably, including our young actress from Unit 4T. If ID 121 were not such a genius in mathematics, I might suggest she pursue a stage career. Please write up summaries of the drill and send me your reports."

He ended by saying, "The future is bright," and switched the video feed to the Generation M living quarters.

By the time his colleagues realized it was not a drill and there was no ID 121, the crisis at large would be over. Dawson and the Leigh girl would be dead, and the renegades who'd left the bunker would be back in the fold.

5.03
CDC BUNKER – ALPHARETTA

"Ensign Parker will be okay. I know it," Murphy said from the passenger seat of the Humvee that rumbled toward the pill plant. "I've only known him a few days, but I can tell you he is one tough S.O.B. He can handle Mathews."

Sandy drove and Abby sat in the backseat, wedged between Doctor Levine and Doctor Droznin. Ensign Royce rode in the cargo section.

"Petty Officer Murphy, do you know my sister, Lisette?" Abby asked.

"Call me Murph. Yeah, I know Lisette. Great kid."

"Lisette's fine," Sandy said.

Something struck the front windshield and everyone jumped. Kids were throwing rocks. More rocks pelted the side of the vehicle.

"Can you blame them?" Levine asked.

The rock throwers, along with the fights, the corpses, and the desperate survivors they'd all seen since exiting the bunker, were normal sights to Abby.

"What is wrong with Toucan?" Abby asked. "Please, will someone tell me?"

"She's in excellent health," Sandy said, making eye contact with her in the mirror.

A chill rippled down Abby's spine at Sandy's troubled expression.

"There it is." Doctor Levine pointed to a water tower rising above the charred buildings about a quarter mile away.

Abby did her best to put Touk out of her mind. Knowing they were close to the plant, she wondered if Mark and Toby had ever made it there, having seen first-hand how kids reacted to an adult. She reminded herself that Toby was one of the most resourceful boys she knew. Toby would have made sure that Mark reached the plant safely.

Due to cars and trees in the road, it took them an hour to reach the front gate of the plant. The gate was closed, secured with a heavy chain and padlock. Sandy stepped on the gas pedal and rammed the gate, bursting through it as if it were tissue paper. She stopped the vehicle near the building and blasted the horn.

The door opened a crack, and Mark stuck his head out. The release of tension did wonders for Abby's weak legs, and she jumped out of the Humvee and rushed over to him. "Where's Toby?"

Mark's brow crinkled. "Looking for you."

5.04
CDC BUNKER

Doctor Perkins wished the commando team would hurry, because it was crucial to tamp down the mutiny in a timely manner.

With blood throbbing in his temples, he climbed into the front seat of the Humvee that would take them to the Alpharetta facility, and turned on the radio. To his shock, the voice of a child came over the CDC channel.

"This is a message for Pale Rider and the Grits. The adults know how to cure the Pig, but they want everyone outside the colonies to die. The Lemon Gang is ready to fight them. Jordan, Spike, and Jonzy are on their way to Atlanta. They're taking Route 85, and while they are small in number, they'll fight anyone who stands in their way ...."

Perkins angrily clicked off the radio. How many more tricks did Dawson have up his sleeve? And how could Ryan have missed another party broadcasting over the CDC channel?

A moment later, Captain Mathews, Ensign Beecham, and Ensign Ryan entered the bunker's garage, all carrying weapons and wearing helmets and bulletproof vests.

Perkins climbed out and stood beside the vehicle, eager to hear Mathews's report.

"Sir, we've taken an inventory of personnel. Doctor Droznin, Doctor Levine, Petty Officer Murphy, Ensign Royce, and 1002 went with Doctor Hedrick."

He rocked back on his heels, caught off-guard by the news that Droznin and Levine had joined the renegades. Why couldn't they see that the colonies offered the only path to a bright future?

More unsettling, those two possessed enough knowledge to train a pack of monkeys to make antibiotic pills.

"What about Dawson?" Perkins asked.

Mathews shook her head. "He never breached the bunker. Ensign Beecham reviewed the video logs."

"So how did 1002 get inside?"

Mathews narrowed her eyes. "We have a theory. You remember that Doctor Hedrick and her team collected corpses? We believe they placed the Leigh girl inside a body bag. Immediately after Hedrick's team returned inside, the clinic's camera went dark for five minutes."

Perkins nodded. "For that level of coordination, Dawson must have communicated with Doctor Hedrick. It appears he's outsmarting all of us."

Mathews's neck muscles tensed like steel bands. "We'll have the situation under control soon."

"Will you?"

"Dawson is mine."

"And what if your plan fails?" Perkins asked.

Mathews unclipped the remote detonator from her belt. "We decommission the plant."

"Twelve charges?"

"Thirteen, sir. I added one more for good luck."

She held out the detonator for him to take, but he waved her off. They piled into the Humvee, and Mathews, behind the wheel, raised the steel reinforced doors using a remote. They drove outside the facility where a sickening odor came through the vents, and Perkins punched the button to recycle the air inside the vehicle.

The mob of unruly children from earlier had vanished, and Mathews drove in a straight line across the plaza. The Humvee leaned left, then right, back and forth again and again as the tires rolled over objects in their path.

Ahead of them was a group of survivors who stood in the middle of the intersection, and Perkins cringed when it appeared that Mathews was about to drive right through the crowd.

"Stop," he cried, squinting out the side window. A face caught his attention, a boy with a shaved head and earrings. He looked familiar.

The revelation stole Doctor Perkins's breath. Months ago, the boy had entered Colony East with Abigail Leigh. Perkins would bet he had come to Atlanta with the Leigh girl and Dawson. "That boy in the green shirt," he said, pointing him out. "Get him."

5.05
ALPHARETTA

The presence of Doctor Droznin troubled Dawson. He hadn't liked or trusted the Russian scientist at Colony East, and he worried about the tricks she might try to play now that she was inside the plant.

Sandy must have seen the look in his eyes, because she whispered, "Give Doctor Droznin a chance."

He gathered everyone together and briefed them on the explosives and the likelihood that Perkins would mount an assault.

Dawson described the white, waxy look and feel of C4 and said, "I found twelve charges inside the plant. Perkins wanted to take this plant offline for a long time. The explosives are outside now, a safe distance away. I combed the plant twice, and I believe I found everything. If you find something that resembles C4, get me right away. It's safe to handle as long as the fuse remains imbedded."

Then he raised his security concerns. "Perkins will send a team after us. You can bet Lieutenant Mathews will lead it."

"*Captain* Mathews," Murphy corrected bitterly.

A sour pit formed in Dawson's stomach. "We have no weapons, unless you count fire extinguishers. All we can do is barricade ourselves and wait for the cavalry to arrive."

"Who's the cavalry?" Murphy asked.

"I thought you might know," Dawson said grimly. "If it looks like we can't hold the plant, I'll show you a way out through an outfall pipe. It leads to a storm drain near the perimeter."

Sandy shook her head in determination. "I'm ready to do whatever it takes to give the kids outside the colonies a chance. No matter what happens, I'm staying."

"Count me in," Ensign Royce said.

Doctor Levine raised a finger. "Make pills or bust."

"I'm not going anywhere," Murphy said.

"We're wasting time," Droznin said. "Let's get started."

Abby, hanging her head, looked dejected. Dawson understood that Toby's absence and Maggie's disappearance was on her mind. If a silver lining existed, it was that Abby looked a hundred times better than the last time he had seen her. The pills were finally working.

He put his hand on Abby's shoulder and jostled her. "Hey, Toby's a survivor, and Maggie's the bravest pilot ever."

Abby stared through him, saying nothing.

"Abigail, I need you to help me," Droznin said.

The huddle of scientists had broken, and Sandy, Doctor Levine, and Ensign Royce started to assess the equipment near the end of the plant.

Abby and Droznin, the most unlikely of pairs, headed toward the opposite end of the plant.

That left Dawson alone with Petty Officer Murphy.

"Looks like we're the defense team," he said. "How well do you know Mathews?"

Murphy shook her head. "Hardly at all. When we moved to the bunker, she confiscated our weapons."

"Does she have anyone on her side?" Dawson asked.

"Maybe Ensign Beecham and Ensign Ryan. I've seen them eating together and speaking in low voices."

"What can you tell me about the ensigns? They might be the weak links."

"I served with Ryan on the *Alabama*. He's a communications specialist. Beecham handles security and video surveillance at Atlanta Colony."

Dawson pointed out their arsenal. "A fire extinguisher isn't much of a weapon against assault rifles, but it's all we have."

"What about the Humvee?" Murphy asked. "We can pack it with all the C4 you found. If Mathews shows up, I can drive at her. If she detonates the C4, maybe I'll be lucky enough to be close to her. Otherwise, I'll run them all down."

What the Petty Office described was a suicide mission, one that had a very small chance of success.

"I'll be the driver," he said.

"It was my idea, Lieutenant."

"Give me the key. That's an order."

"Mark," Sandy called. She waved frantically and pointed to her two-way radio.

He rushed to her side.

"Doctor Hedrick." Perkins's voice crackled over the radio. "Doctor Hedrick."

"Ignore him," Dawson said.

"We know you are inside," Perkins said. "Let's talk. We've all been under a great deal of stress. It's time to return to the bunker and focus on Generation M to end this foolishness. Is Lieutenant Dawson with you? How about the Leigh girl? I will personally guarantee the safety of every scientist and medical officer. Doctor Hedrick, I'm a patient man. You know that. Do you remember Toby Jones from Colony East? He entered the colony under false pretenses. We have him."

Dawson's blood turned cold.

"You're probably thinking this is a ruse," Doctor Perkins said. "Young man, say something."

They heard Toby cursing.

Dawson grabbed the radio. "Perkins, this is Dawson."

"Welcome to Atlanta, Lieutenant. I'll turn things over to your fellow officer, Captain Mathews."

"Dawson, I want you outside. Alone. Thirty seconds, or the boy is dead."

5.06
ALPHARETTA

Abby noticed a commotion at the other end of the plant. Mark and Murph were taking apart the barricade by the door. Then Mark stepped outside, and Murph closed the door behind him and began reconstructing the barricade.

Sandy, Doctor Levine, and Ensign Royce continued to work on the plant's equipment as Doctor Droznin had told them to do. Seeing the adults so focused on their tasks eased Abby's fears for Mark. If there were trouble outside, they would be acting differently.

Abby craned her neck, looking all around. Studying the building and equipment helped take her mind off Toby. The plant, a place where purple beer had been brewed in honor of the approaching comet, was as big as a football stadium.

"Abigail, press the green button," Doctor Droznin said. The scientist stood nearby at a console with hundreds of buttons and knobs.

Abby stepped up to the large robotic arm twice her height and pressed the green button at its base.

"Back up," the scientist told her.

Abby moved out of harm's way as the robotic arm straightened, bent, swiveled, and twisted, as if doing warm-up exercises.

Doctor Droznin tested the equipment, making sure that everything worked.

Abby's mind wandered to Toby and feelings of fear and helplessness twisted her stomach into knots. She could only think about him.

"What does that big arm do?" she asked.

The scientist kept her eyes on the console. "Mixes live bacteria with an emulsifier powder."

"That thing is a giant mixer?"

Doctor Droznin, annoyed by the interruption, looked up. "I need to concentrate."

One of her crutches, leaning against the console, fell to the floor, and Abby jumped to pick it up.

When she bent down, something caught her eye. About thirty meters away, resting on top of a pipe along the wall, was a small, round, white object. Abby set the crutch next to its mate and moved to the robotic arm for a closer look. She got on her hands and knees and placed her cheek inches from the floor. Between her and the object was a rat maze of pipes and wires, but through a sliver of open space, she saw that the object resembled Mark's description of the explosive, C4. "Doctor Droznin, come here."

"Press the green button again," Droznin said in an agitated tone.

"You have to see this," Abby cried.

Droznin's brow crinkled. "Is it important?"

"Hurry, please."

When the scientist was beside her, Abby pointed. "That white thing against the wall, what is it?"

Doctor Droznin took off her glasses and squinted. "I don't see anything."

Abby kept pointing, but Doctor Droznin's eyesight was poor. "It sort of looks like C4," Abby said.

Droznin shook her head. "Way back there? Impossible. How would Mathews have put it there?"

Abby shrugged. It was a good question. It was unlikely Mathews had lowered herself from the ceiling, and it would have been impossible for her to crawl beneath the equipment; she was too big. The space between the floor and the equipment measured less than two feet. Even if Mathews had tried to worm through on her stomach, a forest of vertical steel posts, all part of the equipment, would have blocked her. The robotic arm was about ten feet tall, and the rest of the equipment was that height or higher, making it very unlikely that she had climbed over the equipment.

Abby's blood turned cold. "What if she threw it, like a ball?"

Droznin nodded slowly. "Dawson should check it out."

"He left the building," Abby said.

The scientist frowned. "When?"

"A few minutes ago."

"All right. Get Petty Officer Murphy."

Abby dropped to her stomach and started worming her way beneath the equipment. None of the adults could make it all the way to the far wall, so Abby would retrieve the object for them.

"What are you doing?" Doctor Droznin asked.

Abby kept going. "Murph can't squeeze through here."

The scientist awkwardly lowered herself to the floor, laid on her side, and tried to grab Abby's foot. Abby wiggled beyond her reach just in time. Doctor Droznin spoke in Russian, in a tone that led Abby to believe she was extremely upset.

Abby used her elbows to inch her way forward. "Whatever it is, we need to get it. I'm the smallest one."

"Doctor Hedrick and Doctor Levine might have a better idea. Abigail, come back," Doctor Droznin snapped.

Navigating the maze was difficult, and with Doctor Droznin yelling at her, it was even harder. "Please be quiet," Abby said. "I'm going to get it."

Doctor Droznin sighed in resignation.

"Keep talking to me. I want to know that you are all right." Her tone was one of concern with a dash of fear.

Abby groaned in frustration when the back of her shirt caught on something. She reversed direction until she was free.

If she were on her back, she could avoid such hang-ups. As she rolled over, her hipbone scraped against the bottom of a machine and almost got stuck, but she completed the turn.

That solved the problem of snagged clothing — her hands were free in case she got caught up again — but it meant she moved more slowly, and she couldn't see where she was going.

She kept bumping her head and shoulders against vertical pipes. The only way to go around them was to bend her arms and legs and contort her body. She pretended she was playing Twister, a game where someone spun a needle and a player had to put a hand or foot on the color the needle stopped on. If you tumbled over, you lost. The longer the game lasted, the more contorted the players became. She was the Leigh-family champ, beating Jordan nine times out of ten.

After making good progress, she paused to catch her breath. Layer and layer of intricate piping and wires ran straight above her. She ended her rest when she imagined the destruction an explosion would cause to the delicate equipment.

"How are you doing?" Doctor Droznin called.

"I'm almost there."

It was true. She must have been within ten feet of the object, but she didn't tell Doctor Droznin that it could take her another thirty minutes.

5.07
ALPHARETTA

Mathews stood forty meters from the plant, gripping Toby by the scruff of his neck. With her were Doctor Perkins and two ensigns. As Dawson approached the group, Mathews leveled her M-16 assault rifle at him and barked, "Lift your pant legs."

Dawson did as she requested, lifting them one at a time. He noted she and the ensigns wore bulletproof vests, and he spotted a remote detonator and walkie-talkie clipped to Mathews's belt.

"Pockets." She waved the rifle's barrel.

Dawson turned his pockets inside out.

"Hands up. Turn around."

Dawson raised his hands and slowly turned around.

"Pat him down."

An ensign patted Dawson's legs, his backside, and his chest.

"Beecham or Ryan?" Dawson asked.

"Shut up," Mathews commanded.

"He's clean," the ensign told her.

Knowing that Toby had a defiant streak, Dawson was especially concerned for his safety. Toby glared at Mathews.

"You have me," Dawson said. "Let the boy go."

"Two birds in the hand are better than one," Doctor Perkins said in a singsong tone.

The scientist appeared to be his unflappable self. Under his lab coat, he wore a pink shirt and green bowtie. He could have passed for a college professor on his way to deliver a lecture.

"I'm impressed with your ingenuity, Lieutenant," Perkins continued. "How were you able to override the CDC's station signal?"

What was Perkins talking about? Dawson stared back at the scientist, hoping he'd learn more.

"Very well, I love mysteries," Perkins said.

Toby muttered a curse at Mathews.

In response, quick as a lizard, Mathews swung the butt of the gun around, stopping just short of Toby's ear, and then smiled.

She was sending both Toby and Dawson a message. She could crack Toby's skull like an eggshell in the blink of an eye.

Dawson shifted his weight to the balls of his feet, ready to leap if any harm came to Toby.

Toby cursed again, and Mathews's cheeks flushed red.

"Captain," Perkins said, "let's see if Lieutenant Dawson can talk some sense into Doctor Hedrick and the others. Hand him the radio."

With a sneer, Mathews unclipped the radio from her belt and placed it on the ground. Then she grabbed Toby's ear and yanked him back several steps.

Having his ear almost ripped off must have hurt, but Toby remained silent.

Dawson picked up the radio and brought it to his lips. Pretending to push the button, he said, "Doctor Hedrick, this is Lieutenant Dawson, over. Doctor Hedrick, come in."

After a moment, he held the radio by his side and pressed the button that would allow Sandy to hear what he was saying. "Doctor Hedrick, Doctor Droznin, Doctor Levine, and others are apparently choosing to stay inside the plant. They've decided they no longer want to follow the warped ideas of Doctor Perkins, who is about to become the greatest mass murderer in human history. It's not too late to help the hundreds of thousands of survivors." Dawson eyed the ensigns, who he believed might crack under pressure first.

Mathews trained her weapon at Dawson's chest. "Doctor Perkins, do I have your permission to fire?"

5.08
ALPHARETTA

On her back, slick with sweat of her own making, Abby inched along the polished cement floor. Perspiration soaked her clothing and plastered her hair to her face. She'd given up trying to spit the strands out of her mouth.

"Are you close?" Doctor Droznin called.

"Yes."

"How close?"

Even with her head tilted back as far as it would go and her eyes rolled back, Abby couldn't see the wall.

Above her, coils and loops and lengths of silver-colored and copper tubing, all intermingled with wiring, connected to more of the same.

A wave of claustrophobia washed through her and panicking, she felt her throat close up, which made her panic more.

"Abigail, are you there yet?"

Abby gritted her teeth and resumed her snail's journey.

"Abigail, answer me."

After a few inches of progress, Abby again arched her neck and rolled her eyes back in their sockets. Seeing the wall for the first time gave her a burst of courage.

"I'm almost there," she cried.

She lengthened her right side, then the left, using her shoulder blades for purchase, and moved in a rhythm similar to rowing.

She groaned when the crown of her head struck another a metal post. Wrapping her right hand around the post, she pulled and guided her head past it, protecting her ear. To search for other posts, she stretched out her other arm and finally touched the wall.

Maneuvering herself until her body pressed against the wall lengthwise, she reached up and felt around for the object.

Her blood turned cold when her fingertips brushed against a waxy surface. Doctor Droznin asked for updates, but Abby remained silent, focusing all her thoughts and energy on the task of getting the bomb into her hand. She nudged it right and left, but couldn't reach up high enough to grasp it.

By lightly pressing against it and dragging her fingers down, she managed to roll it up and onto a pipe. She held her breath as it balanced there. One more gentle swipe down was all it took before she was cradling the C4 in her palm.

"I have it," she called.

"Describe it for me," Doctor Droznin said.

"It's shaped like a ball, and it has a little thing sticking out of it."

"Roll it to me," Doctor Droznin said.

That was a terrible idea. It would surely strike one of the numerous metal posts in the way. Then what? Even if it didn't blow up, Abby might never find it, or reach it. She had to carry it out herself.

"Abigail, roll it."

Abby had no intention of rolling it, and now she faced her greatest challenge yet — turning around.

5.09
ALPHARETTA

Planted as firm as a rock, Mathews trained her weapon on Dawson. From four feet away, the odds of her cutting him to shreds were one hundred percent, if that's what she decided to do.

She gripped Toby by the ear and held his head at an awkward angle. Dawson sensed the boy's rage building.

In his peripheral vision, he saw Perkins deep in thought. The ensigns, standing beside Perkins, looked every bit as mean and nasty as Mathews, but he discounted their appearance. Beecham and Ryan, he thought, wished they were a million miles away.

Dawson inhaled and exhaled through his nose, trying to slow his racing heart. "You killed Admiral Samuels in cold blood. Are you going to kill me too?"

Mathews didn't flinch. "Shut up."

The ensigns exchanged worried glances. Apparently, the admiral's murder was news to them.

Toby balled a fist, and Dawson feared the boy would try something stupid.

Mathews seemed to read Dawson's mind and jerked Toby's ear hard. "Easy does it, mister."

Toby yelped and cursed at her.

"Lieutenant, I'm afraid I'm responsible for Admiral Samuels's demise," Perkins said in a strangely courteous tone. "Captain Mathews was simply following orders. You see, I suspected your disloyalty since the early days of Colony East. How many times did you ask permission to search for your daughter? I always worried you might just leave."

"She shot the admiral in cold blood," Dawson repeated.

Perkins let out a long sigh, as if Dawson was a petulant child acting up.

"Hurricane David broke the camel's back," he said. "I never believed that it was a coincidence that one of your cadets tried to escape. Abigail Leigh never jumped in the Hudson River as you reported, did she?"

"It's treason to murder an officer," Dawson said.

Perkins ignored his comment.

"My opportunity to neutralize you happened as a result of the evacuation. I assigned you to Colony West, but suspecting you might have some trick up your sleeve, I asked Captain Mathews to share some misinformation with you."

Dawson swallowed the lump in his throat, wondering if they had some unknown advantage over him.

"You took the bait," Perkins continued. "You and 761 broke into my lab at Medical Clinic 17 and found what you believed were antibiotic pills. You stole three thousand sugar pills."

Dawson's knees wobbled as he conjured up the memory of holding Sarah's warm, tiny hand. Having taken a useless sugar pill, his daughter might be dead now. Multiple explosions of rage detonated at once, and he had to exercise every ounce of his willpower to keep from leaping forward and snapping Perkins's neck like a twig.

Perkins cocked his head with a quizzical expression. "Lieutenant, are you learning about the placebos for the first time? If you passed them out, you must have realized that nobody got better."

Dawson lifted his chin. There was a fleeting chance Sarah was still alive; he needed to bring her the real antibiotic. And hundreds of thousands of desperately ill survivors needed the pills just as urgently, including those he had given the fake pills to.

"Mathews gunned down the admiral," Dawson said, trying to break through to Ensign Ryan and Ensign Beecham.

Perkins gave a dismissive shrug. "We knew you would head to the Red Zone. It was the most logical exit point with the electric fence down. Looking back, my mistake was sharing my plan with the admiral. I believe he experienced a pang of guilt. He wanted to save you. Mathews had no idea the admiral would turn up."

All of a sudden, Perkins frowned and craned his neck. Mathews and the two ensigns did the same.

Dawson became aware of a rumbling in the distance. He felt the vibrations in his ears and bones. The harmonic throbbing grew louder and louder. He didn't have a clue what, or who, was approaching.

5.10
ALPHARETTA

From his motorcycle, Jordan saw a tall water tower rising beyond a factory ahead of them. Even with a few mislabeled roads, Toby's map had delivered them to the Alpharetta industrial park. The tower was supposedly next to the antibiotic pill plant.

Jordan goosed his throttle. The roads were relatively clear, so it was safe to increase his speed. His growing anxiety and surging exhilaration demanded he go faster.

Spike and Jonzy rode on his left and right, respectively, and immediately behind them were Pale Rider and her three lieutenants.

Farther back were hundreds, maybe thousands, of kids on motorcycles. During the nonstop ride, Jordan had seen kids drop out of their column, running out of gas or weakening from the Pig, but it seemed that more joined the ranks all the time for a net gain. On one straight stretch of highway, the riders had extended as far back as he could see.

Jordan revved his engine, shifting up a gear, ready to fight the adults, but hoping they might find a peaceful solution.

As they approached the pill plant, Spike pointed to a small group of people standing fifty yards from an enormous building. One vehicle was parked near the building, another close to the people. Jordan recognized the vehicles were Humvees, the type of vehicle that soldiers used to drive.

From this distance, the people looked like adults. They were the first individuals over the age of fifteen that Jordan had seen in three years. As he neared them, he became certain they were adults, and then he spotted what he thought was a kid among them.

Two of the adults sprinted to the Humvee closest to them, jumped in, and squealed the tires, heading toward the gate. Jordan worried they would collide with him and the other bikers at the head of the column. Pale Rider roared ahead — straight for the vehicle. If she had a weapon, Jordan didn't see it. He expected they would flatten her, but then the vehicle swerved and accelerated in the opposite direction. The Humvee drove to the left of the building and was soon out of sight.

"It's Toby!" Jonzy cried.

Jordan realized the boy with the shaved head was indeed Toby Jones. Closer, it appeared the woman next to Toby was aiming a gun at him.

Jordan rolled to a stop twenty yards from the group and dismounted. Jonzy and Spike did the same.

"The guy in blue is Lieutenant Dawson," Jonzy told them. "The guy in the white coat is Doctor Perkins. The one with the gun is Lieutenant Mathews."

"What's her problem?" Spike muttered.

The boys approached the group.

"Toby, are you all right?" Jordan asked.

"It's about time you showed up," Toby replied.

"Shut up," Mathews said jerked Toby's ear.

"You are screwed," Toby told her.

She cuffed the side of his head. He shook off the blow and cursed at her. She cuffed him again, harder.

Asking for a third smack, Toby spit on Mathews's boots, but this time, she jammed the gun barrel against his forehead. "Try me. One more word."

Showing no fear, Toby glared back, and Jordan feared Toby would call her bluff. He doubted she was bluffing.

"Where's Abby?" Jordan asked.

"Abby's inside the plant," Lieutenant Dawson said. "She's safe." Holding up his hands, he took a step toward Mathews. "Let's talk."

"Keep coming if you want to talk about a dead boy," Mathews fired back.

Jordan drew in a sharp breath when Dawson advanced another step.

5.11
ALPHARETTA

The situation was ready to explode, the dynamics shifting by the second, and Dawson realized that his next move could determine the fate of Toby and untold numbers of survivors.

The blood had drained from Mathews's face, and blossoms of perspiration spread from under her arms, darkening her uniform. Her eyes darted from him to the growing number of kids arriving on motorcycles. Ensigns Beecham and Ryan had driven off in the Humvee, leaving her stranded with the mad man.

A cornered animal was the most dangerous kind.

"Mathews, why don't you just leave," Dawson told her. "I won't try to stop you."

"What about them?" She nodded to the bikers.

The riders were fanning out in a slack noose around them. "You have a weapon," he said. "They'll let you go."

Perkins adjusted his bowtie. "Captain, may I remind you of our mission?"

"Shut up," Mathews said, unclipping the remote detonator from her belt. She held it high. "I have something far deadlier than an M-16. I can cripple the plant. Without antibiotic pills, everyone here will die."

"Don't listen to her," Toby shouted. "Mark removed the explosives from the plant."

Mathews's easy smile sent a chill down Dawson's spine. "How many charges did you find, Lieutenant? I bet twelve. They were relatively easy to find, right? Well, you must give me more credit than that. Did you find lucky charge thirteen? One strategically placed charge of C4 is all it takes."

Toby elbowed her in the gut.

Mathews didn't flinch. The blow seemed to have the force of a gnat. Fire belched from her weapon, and Toby jerked back as the bullets tore into him. He stumbled and sprawled on the ground.

Dawson sprung forward, flying through the sound waves of Toby's blood-curdling screams. His fingertips grazed the gun barrel as Mathews began firing indiscriminately.

He thudded to the ground and grabbed her ankle, yanking it toward him. She toppled backward, continuing to fire the weapon, raining hot lead into the sky.

When Mathews landed on her back, he lurched, trying desperately to push the gun away and get a hand on her throat at the same time.

He threw himself to the ground and grabbed her jaw, but somehow she spun away, got to her knees, and chopped the gun butt down on his shoulder. His right arm went numb.

Mathews had dropped the detonator, but Dawson didn't see it anywhere.

She was lowering the barrel at him when he lunged at her. Dawson expected the lights to go out at any second, expecting to be dead before he hit the ground. Instead, his shoulder slammed into her midsection, and she discharged the weapon with the muzzle next to his ear.

Deafened by the loud blast, he watched Jonzy and Jordan land on top of Mathews. Jordan pinned the gun to the ground with his body, and Jonzy wrapped his arms around her legs. Mathews easily broke free of Jonzy and kicked him in the face, smashing Jonzy's eyeglasses.

Mathews leaped to her feet, ready to pounce and keep fighting. Time seemed to stop for everyone. Jordan was aiming the gun at her, his finger firmly on the trigger. Blood streamed from Jonzy's nose, and Toby, grunting and groaning, lay on the ground, bleeding.

Dawson spotted the remote close to Toby. Mathews saw it, too. He was closer. He was about to leap for it, when Mathews bolted. She ran toward the spot with the fewest motorcycles, beyond which was a field of weeds, and then woods.

Dawson grabbed the M-16 from Jordan and went down on one knee, planting the stock against his shoulder. He filled his lungs to the bursting point and then slowly exhaled to steady his hands. He put his eye to the scope, placing the crosshairs between Mathews's shoulder blades. He raised it slightly to the back of her head when he remembered she was wearing a bulletproof vest. For someone who had received advanced survival training, she was committing a cardinal sin by running away in a straight line.

She breached the ring of riders and was now in the weeds. Dawson saw the bikers to the right and left, and Mathews beyond them. He had a clean shot. He felt the resistance of the trigger on his fingertip.

He applied more pressure to the trigger, recalling how Admiral Samuels had stumbled backward before he made a final stand like a proud bull, eventually crumpling. Tributaries of rage combined into a forceful river that rushed down his right arm and streamed into his index finger.

He raised the rifle as he pulled the trigger, screaming the bullet above Mathews's head. The time for killing had ended. It was now time to save lives.

Dawson rushed to Toby's side and choked out a grunt of relief. Miraculously, the boy was sitting. Jonzy had removed his shirt and was using it as a tourniquet, applying it to Toby's upper arm. The bullet had gone through the fleshy part of the arm near his shoulder. Dawson checked Toby all over, just to make sure he had no other wounds.

The loud roar of motorcycles captured his attention. He turned and watched three riders accelerate into the field, parting the tall weeds like speedboats powering through water. Mathews was about twenty yards from the woods. The bikers closed in on their prey, and Dawson knew she would never reach the trees.

He picked up the remote detonator, cracked the back of it off, and popped out the small battery. Then he hurled the battery and stomped the remote under his boot.

"I suppose I will have to ensure the future of Generation M." Doctor Perkins reached into his lab coat pocket.

Dawson's heart nearly exploded when he saw what Perkins had in his hand.

Perkins positioned his thumb on the remote detonator's button. "Redundant systems," the scientist said. "If one part fails, you should always have a backup." From his other pocket, he took out a two-way radio and brought it to his lips. "Doctor Hedrick, you and your colleagues have one minute to leave the plant."

5.12
ALPHARETTA

From the faint footsteps slapping the cement floor, Abby knew that several adults were racing toward her end of the plant. *Sandy, Doctor Levine, and Ensign Royce? Murph and Sandy? Two of them? All three? Maybe Mark had returned. Maybe they had news. Good news? Maybe ...* She snipped the wild, loose threads of speculation and focused on the job of squirming another inch.

Abby's head struck a steel pipe. Every few feet, it seemed, she encountered an obstacle: another steel leg, or another piece of metal that snagged her clothing.

"Doctor Hedrick and Doctor Levine are coming," Doctor Droznin said.

Wriggle, squirm, wriggle. Abby kept moving.

When Sandy and Doctor Levine arrived, Doctor Droznin cried, "She's under there."

The ball of C4 on Abby's belly lit up in the beam of a flashlight.

"Oh my God, Abby, listen to me," Sandy said. "Doctor Perkins is going to detonate the explosive in forty seconds."

The beats of Abby's heart boomed with such force that she feared her chest would crack apart. Breathing hard and fast, she glanced upward through a new set of eyes. The pipes and wires were as fragile as veins and arteries.

"You now have thirty-seven seconds to get rid of it," Sandy shouted.

Abby chided herself for wasting three precious seconds and resumed squirming, telling herself she could reach the adults in time for one of them to hurl the bomb to the opposite side of the plant, away from the machinery.

Thirty-six, thirty-five, thirty-four ... Abby counted in her head as she maneuvered herself beneath the delicate labyrinth.

The adults shined flashlights. They shouted encouragement and directed her on how to avoid obstacles. They were frightened cheerleaders.

"Hurry."

"Roll it."

"Stop, go left."

"Thirty seconds."

The words flew past her and faded in the dark maze.

Abby tuned out the adults the best she could, choosing to trust her body to find the way out, advancing by trial and error. Her unrelenting stubbornness, tempered by patience, helped her cope with the bruises and repeated setbacks.

Twenty-seven, twenty-six ....

Her pocket caught on a piece of metal jutting from a steel post. Summoning every bit of strength, she surged ahead and the pocket ripped.

Twenty-three, twenty-two, twenty-one ....

Abby whacked her head hard on a post. She inched back, aimed to the right and whacked it again. A warm gush of blood streamed down her scalp. Undeterred, she inched back again, aimed left and found an opening.

Nineteen, eighteen, seventeen ....

Using her shoulder blades like a lizard uses its front legs, she clawed her way toward the adults, increasing her speed. In a race with a turtle, the turtle might have won, but this was the fastest she'd been able to go. The Twister champ was flying.

Sweat trickled into her eyes, but she couldn't wipe them with either arm, so she squeezed them shut, trying to wring the salt out.

Fifteen, fourteen ....

Abby could tell she was getting close to the adults from their voices, and when she opened her eyes, the light beam glinted off the web of shiny silver and copper metal above her. She arched her head back and the brilliant eyes of two flashlights ruptured into splashes of blinding light. The shadowy figures of Sandy, Doctor Droznin, and Doctor Levine were so close. If she stretched, she might reach their outstretched hands.

Thirteen, twelve ....

Abby went to grab the C4 to hand off to them, but her heart exploded into a million particles of despair instead. The ball of plastic explosives was gone; it had rolled off her belly.

Ten, nine ....

She reversed direction, sweeping her hands back and forth, patting her palms over the cement. A fire hose of adrenaline coursed through her body and drove her to go faster while a single thought convinced her that she should search in a slow, methodical manner. She could not risk hitting the C4 with her hand and having it roll out of reach.

Eight, seven ....

"Got it!" she cried.

Gripping the bomb tightly, Abby started back but instantly realized she could not make it. The C4 would explode in her hand, or go off as she tried to pass it to the adults. She could not let that happen. A direct blast would gut the delicate machinery.

Abby imagined all her muscles were steel bands and her skin was made of bomb-proof material.

Five, four ....

Pressing the ball against her stomach, she rolled on top of it and pictured her brother and sister in her mind. Abby wanted her final memory to be of her family together and happy.

Three, two ....

The three of them were on the dock at the lake in Maine. It was dusk, the sky a pastel of pale blue with red streaks from the setting sun. Abby pulled Touk and Jordan close to her. Feeling their beating hearts and the warmth of their bodies, she drew in a long, slow breath of the sweet, piney wind.

One.

5.13
ALPHARETTA

Doctor Perkins pulled back the sleeve of his lab coat to check the time. Sunlight flashed off the crystal face of his Omega watch. One minute was up.

Sadly, Doctor Hedrick and his other colleagues had not heeded his warning, but his mind was clear, and he felt at ease.

He glanced at the remote cradled in his palm. The green light indicated a strong battery. He repositioned his thumb squarely on the button.

The ugly sounds of survivors finishing off Mathews subsided. He had kept his eyes averted from the grisly scene, realizing he would soon suffer the same fate.

Perkins recalled the brief flashes of doubt he had experienced over the past three years, questioning if there might have been a better way to do things. Could the adults have organized the survivors in such a way as to provide limited educational opportunities for all children? Could they have done something, anything, to help the children outside the colonies?

The behavior of these savages flushed all doubts away. They would have relished the chance to destroy the colonies and Generation M.

The colonies, once a germ of an idea, had blossomed into a dream that had exceeded his wildest expectations. Imagining their continued growth and success, Perkins closed his eyes and pushed the button.

The sharp boom of an enormous explosion shook the ground. A cloud of dust rose near the area of the security fence on the perimeter of the plant's grounds. Dawson had obviously removed many of the explosives, but as Mathews had intimated, he had not found them all. Perkins's dream of Generation M would live on.

They were coming after him now. A horde of vicious, dirty children closed in, some on foot, most on motorcycles, and in the lead was a leather-clad girl on a green motorcycle.

Perkins felt fear like never before as he fixed his gaze on her ghostly eyes. She revved her engine and reared back, raising the front wheel high off the ground. The bike struck him in the face, knocking his glasses off as he fell into a black void and kept falling.

5.14
ALPHARETTA

Jordan took off running toward the plant. He had a dreadful sixth sense that Abby was in trouble.

Propelled by this fear, he pumped his arms and lifted his knees high. He sucked air into his lungs until they were about to burst. He blew out repeatedly.

Debris from the explosion rained down, and he squinted from particles of dirt peppering his face. Dawson came up beside him, his arms and legs a blur, and they ran together, stride for stride.

He tried to stop as he neared the door, but his legs disobeyed his mind's command to slow down, and he rammed up against the building with his shoulder. He thumbed the lever and swung the door open.

Cursing the cloud of acrid smoke that wafted out, Dawson bolted inside. With Dawson in the lead, they sprinted toward a small group of people gathered at the other end of the plant.

As he got closer, Jordan saw that several adults were on their knees, huddled around a body on the floor. Jordan's gut told him it was his big sister.

"Abby," he cried.

Dawson reached the group first. Jordan slowed his pace and stopped ten feet away, choking on the sickly odor of fresh blood that mingled in the haze.

"Tighten the tourniquet," a woman shouted.

"Stay with us. Stay with us." That was Dawson.

"Begin compressions," the same woman said. "Breathe, breathe, breathe."

Jordan sank deeper into a quicksand of grief, barely able to move, but he forced himself forward. He needed to see Abby before....

A violent sob completed his thought.

Chest heaving, he clenched his fists and shuffled his feet, skating an inch, then another, approaching a scene that would forever haunt him. Icy fingers wrapped around his throat, squeezing tighter and tighter the closer he got.

"Open your eyes," Dawson shouted. "Keep them open. That's an order, damn it."

"Breathe, breathe, breathe."

The adults frantically tried to save her life, but the desperation in their voices told Jordan that their efforts were in vain.

Realizing that any second could be Abby's last, he had to be at her side and had to hold her hand. His knees buckled, and he dropped to the floor, where he started crawling.

"Jordan."

He stopped. That was Abby calling out. From the intense, ongoing struggle of the adults, Jordan must have imagined his sister's voice. Trembling, he planted one hand on the floor and slid his knee forward.

Movement caught his eye and Jordan looked right, drawing in a sharp breath. Abby was not the person adults surrounded. His sister was lying on her side in a narrow space between the floor and lots of pipes and equipment.

Gasping in relief, Jordan lay flat on his belly and wormed his way toward her. "Abby. Abby."

When she didn't respond to his shouts, he feared she had been hurt in the blast.

He reached out and gripped her arm. "Abby, are you okay?"

She looked at him with a blank stare. He patted a hand up and down her legs and then scooted closer to her to check her backside for wounds or broken bones. The only thing he found was some sticky blood on top of her head, but the cut seemed small.

He gripped her hand. "Talk to me. Are you okay?"

She nodded and squeezed his hand. Those were good signs.

Jordan realized the adults were no longer shouting. The silence was bone chilling. They had moved back from the person they had been trying to save. He could see it was an adult, a woman, her white jacket in tatters.

Jordan had no idea how Abby had survived the blast while the one scientist had not, but all that mattered was that his sister was alive.

"Toucan," Abby said in a raspy voice.

He squeezed her hand, too choked up to speak. Where was Touk? Was she safe? How would they get her?

"We'll get her, Abby. We'll get her."

Abby gave a little nod and closed her eyes. "Toucan," she whispered.

DAY 6

CDC BUNKER

Abby shook her head and rubbed her eyes, freeing herself from the sticky web of sleep. She squinted in the bright light of an overhead fixture and sat up in bed. Where was she? The small room had a single window that looked out to the incredible scenery of wildflowers and snowcapped mountains. Then she realized it was a poster. The room had no windows. Another poster hung next to the door, issuing a warning."Emergency Protocols" was written in bright-red letters. She scanned the list of items: radiation exposure, nuclear blast, contamination. By the time she got to "electrical fire," the events of last night drifted through her mind, and she knew she was in the CDC bunker.

The events were fuzzy with gaps in the sequence. Someone had cradled her in their arms and carried her from inside the pill plant to a truck. It might have been Jordan, but she couldn't say for certain. Outside the plant, a mob of kids had formed. Angry shouts and the roar of motorcycles had filled the air. She remembered a bumpy truck ride and entering the underground bunker where a medic who spoke with a Southern accent had checked her blood pressure and temperature.

The medic had held out a little, yellow pill. "Take this, it will help you sleep."

Then the medic had helped her into a wheelchair, and that's where her recollection of events ended. Abby supposed she had fallen asleep, and someone had pushed her here.

The room had a table next to the bed and a dresser. A door led to a bathroom. *The scientist who lived here, must have put the wildflower poster on the wall to stop from going crazy.*

The cold fingers of claustrophobia wrapped around her throat, and she closed her eyes, pretending she was at the lake in Maine, drawing in fresh air with each and every breath.

A medic interrupted Abby's daydream when she entered the room with a tray of MREs.

"Good morning. How are you feeling?" The medic had dark circles under her eyes.

"Who are you?" Abby asked.

"Ensign Rossi. I work with Doctor Hedrick."

One look at the MREs turned Abby's stomach. "I'm tired and my ears are ringing."

"The ringing should stop in a few days," Rossi said. "You were very close to the blast."

Abby shivered as a vivid memory bubbled to the surface of her mind. She was covering the bomb with her body when something poked her shoulder; Doctor Droznin jabbed her with a crutch. She told Abby to place the C4 in the space at the top of the crutch, which Abby did. The scientist then pulled the crutch back.

"What happened to Doctor Droznin?" Abby asked.

Rossi shook her head sadly. "She died in the blast. She protected the equipment. Thanks to you and her, we resumed the antibiotic manufacturing process last night."

Abby had trusted Doctor Droznin to help them, and the scientist had sacrificed her life to save the survivors. The news had little effect on Abby. Before the night of the purple moon, a dentist had given her a shot to numb a tooth before filling a cavity. Now, it felt as if she had received that numbing shot to her heart.

Ensign Rossi picked up a MRE and held it out to her.

Abby waved it off. "I'm not hungry." It felt strange to decline an offer of food.

"You're still in shock," the ensign said with a knowing nod. She flashed a light into each of Abby's eyes to check for signs of a concussion. "You'll probably feel tired for a few more days, and you will find it difficult to concentrate. I predict your appetite will return in a hurry. You've lost quite a bit of weight. Doctor Hedrick will be here soon."

"Can I see my sister now?" Abby asked.

Ensign Rossi headed for the door. "Wait to speak to Doctor Hedrick first."

"Why? Where's Toucan?"

"Doctor Hedrick wants to speak with you first."

Abby's blood turned cold. "What's wrong with my sister?"

"Doctor Hedrick will explain everything."

"Is my brother, Jordan, here? Where's Toby? I want to see Toby."

Ensign Rossi left the room and closed the door behind her.

Abby slid her feet to the floor, but her head rode a wave of dizziness back to the pillow. What had happened to Touk? And where was Toby? Had she really seen her brother? The questions slithered through the muck in her brain, leaving her with a hard knot in her stomach.

"I understand you have a few questions."

Abby opened her eyes, and immediately felt at ease seeing Sandy's warm smile. "I'd like to see Touk."

"Tomorrow," Sandy said.

"Why not now?" Abby blurted.

Sandy sighed. "The Generation M kids have been through a lot, and their lives are about to change dramatically. We'll be deciding how to run the colonies from now on, and it will be different. We're speaking to them as a group today. It's best if they have their friends around them for support."

"Toucan is my sister," Abby pleaded. "She'll be happy to see me. Is my brother here?"

"Yes, Jordan is here." Sandy's brow furrowed. "Please, this is best for everyone. You and Jordan can see Lisette tomorrow."

Abby shuddered. Knowing Toucan was safe, she decided she could wait to see her, but she had to see her brother. She could not wait for that.

"Where's Jordan?"

Sandy took a seat on the bed. "Let me tell you what's happening. That may help answer many of your questions."

"Where's Toby?" Abby asked.

"He's recovering."

Abby drew in a sharp breath. "From the Pig?"

"He was shot."

Abby hugged herself and cried, "No!"

Sandy reached out and took her hand. "Toby is fine. The bullet grazed his arm. We've started the manufacturing process. The first batch of pills will be ready in five days, but we found a stockpile of fifty thousand pills. That is nowhere near enough, but it will allow us to start saving lives. Mark and Jonzy went to Mystic last night."

Abby sat forward. "How did they get there?"

"They flew to Colony East in one of the reconnaissance planes. The pilot left them at the airport. I haven't heard from them since they landed." Sandy nervously rubbed a corner of the blanket between her fingers. "Mark told me his daughter is very sick. He said he couldn't wait."

"Cee Cee has the Pig, too," Abby said. "That's Wenlan's sister. Wenlan runs the clinic."

Sandy stared blankly at the wall. After a long pause, Sandy nodded. "I'll feel better after I hear from Mark."

Sandy's radio crackled to life with a man's voice. "Doctor Hedrick."

Sandy spoke into the radio. "Go ahead."

"We need you in the medical bay ASAP."

"Be right there."

Sandy stood and headed for the door. "I'll have someone let Jordan know he can see you. Try to eat something."

Abby took a nibble of a protein bar, putting it firmly in the category of gourmet sawdust. Although she didn't want any more, she couldn't bear to waste even the tiniest grain. She carefully wrapped up the bar and returned it to the box.

She used the toilet, and then splashed cold water on her face, which relieved some of her dizziness. She opened the door and peered down the corridor, but thought it best to remain inside her windowless cell; the minute she left, Jordan would probably show up. She read about emergency protocols and studied the scenic poster in detail, counting the petals of the wildflowers.

Her heart fluttered when someone knocked on the door. Jordan poked his head inside, and that's when Abby's heart stopped. She rushed at him as he rushed to her. They crashed and threw their arms around each other, barely managing to stay on their feet after the impact. Just by hugging him, she could tell he had grown taller and stronger since she had last seen him six months ago.

He finally leaned back, tears dribbling down his cheeks. This told her he had changed in other ways. Jordan never used to cry in front of other people.

He stared at her with a big grin and gave her another hug.

For the next two hours, they chattered nearly non-stop, telling stories of what they had seen and done. They interrupted each other, gasping, asking questions, and crying. When Jordan described how pirates had attacked *Lucky Me*, a long period of silence descended. Abby pictured every member of the news gypsy crew in her mind. Another shock came when Jordan told her that he had seen Kenny in Portland and had spoken to him about Mandy, and that Kenny had been sorry for what had happened to Mandy's little brother. In barely a whisper, Abby told Jordan what she had witnessed in the streets of Atlanta. In a voice choked with sadness, he described evidence of identical behavior in Portland. They quickly moved on to a new topic.

"I can't wait to see Touk," Abby said.

Jordan nodded. "Sandy told me that Toucan is healthy, but we have to wait to see her."

"Think we'll recognize her?" she asked. "I bet she's grown a lot."

"I hope she recognizes us," he said. "We've changed. Nothing personal, Abby, but you look terrible."

"I've never felt better," she said, and actually meant it.

"I'm sure one thing about Touk hasn't changed," Jordan said. "She's stubborn."

Abby winked. "Not as stubborn as you."

"Look who's talking!"

Abby felt her strength returning just by being with Jordan, joking around with him, and acting like brother and sister.

The topic of Eddie, however, put a swift end to the joking.

"He has the Pig," Jordan said. "He was in bad shape when we left him at Wenlan's. Cee Cee has the Pig, too. I almost asked Mark if I could go with him last night, but I wanted to see you and Touk first."

"If you hear anything about them, let me know right away," Abby said.

"I will. And if you hear anything, tell me."

"Wenlan seems nice," Abby said slyly.

Jordan blushed. "You, me, Touk, and Toby can live at the clinic. Wenlan could use your help."

Abby had her mind set on going to the cabin in Maine, but she would be willing to tend to routine injuries for a few months in Mystic. Compared to tending to kids dying of a lethal epidemic, she bet that setting a broken leg would be fun.

"Do you remember where Mandy and Timmy were going before…?" Her voice trailed off.

Clearly reliving the moment when Mandy had fought to her death against Brad and his gang, Jordan nodded sadly. "Yeah. Some lake where her grandparents lived."

Abby leaned forward. "I know how to get there. Wenlan and Cee Cee can come with us. Eddie, too. Toby's going, for sure. We'll invite our friends. It will be like Castine Island right after the night of the purple moon. We all worked together. We'll live that way again."

Abby studied her brother's face, waiting for his eyes to widen and brighten and expecting a big grin to develop. Instead, he looked confused.

"How are we going to help anyone?" he asked. "The epidemic is tearing everything apart. Kids will need food and shelter. Some have lost all their friends. Many of them will be orphaned just like after the night of the purple moon."

"Jordan, haven't we helped enough people already? We need to help ourselves. I want to go far away and be around my family and friends."

He looked over her shoulder, staring at the wall. "I can't believe these colonies."

Abby sighed. Jordan must be in a mild state of shock, and she had given him too much information to process, so he had changed the subject.

"I need to get back to the staging area," he said.

"We're putting pills in packages, and members of the Grits gang are taking them to survivors. It's amazing what we're doing. Adults and kids are working together to figure out the fastest way to distribute pills. Want to join me?"

Abby smiled. "Jordan, I'm so proud of you."

He rolled his eyes. "Don't be weird."

"I'm too tired to work," she said, "but I have a favor to ask. The girl who flew us here, her name is Maggie. She's about my height, and she has blond pigtails. We got separated in the night. Kids entered the alley where we were hiding, and Maggie made sure they chased her. She did that so I could contact Sandy. Can you ask the kids on motorcycles to look for her? They should give her a pill."

Jordan nodded grimly. "Maggie with blonde pig tails."

"Ask them to bring her to the bunker," Abby added. "She saved my life, maybe everyone's life."

Jordan gave her a hug. "If you change your mind and you want to help, ask anyone how to get to the staging area."

Then he left and closed the door.

A moment later, the door opened, and he stuck his head in. "Abby, thank you."

"For what?"

"What you said about being proud of me. That means a lot." Then he was gone again.

Abby sighed happily, realizing it was incredible that the family was almost together again; all they needed was Touk.

She forced herself to finish off the awful protein bar and then set off in search of Toby. On a hunch, she headed for the medical bay where Ensign Rossi had treated her the night before.

She passed through the self-serve cafeteria where several adults ate, all appearing exhausted, with their heads slumped over their bowls. One scientist snored loudly, cheek pressed against the tabletop.

Abby saw a sign with an arrow for the medical bay, and she headed down that hallway. Halfway to the next intersection, Toby rounded the corner, his arm in a sling.

Abby broke into a run, arms wide open, and Toby raced toward her. She tried to brake, but they crashed into each other. Toby yelped in pain and pulled her closer to him with his good arm. She squeezed him tightly, careful to avoid pulling on his bandaged arm. Words stuck in her throat as she held the boy who had sacrificed so much for her.

They visited the cafeteria, where they sat at a table and Abby learned how lucky Toby was to be alive. She reached out and took his hand as tears filled her eyes. She took a deep breath and told him about Jordan and Toucan. He already knew about Mark and Jonzy.

"I'll go with you to Mystic," Toby said. "I'll go with you to the cabin in Maine, too. Heck, I'll even go with you to Castine Island if you want."

She squeezed his hand, and while looking him in the eye, she smiled and slowly nodded. "Thank you."

Toby told her he would help in the staging area, using his good arm.

"Jordan's there," he said. "You want to come with me?"

Abby shook her head. "All I can think about is Touk."

"Let's go see her," he said, jumping to his feet. "C'mon, she's your sister. We'll get her together."

Toby was ready to charge into the Generation M living quarters and snatch Toucan, all because he thought it would make her happy. Time after time, his actions showed how much he cared for her.

"No, I told Sandy I'd wait," she said after a long pause. "I'm going to my room to rest," she added, knowing that if she stayed with Toby any longer, she would accept his offer to rescue Toucan.

DAY 7
CDC BUNKER

In the morning, Abby, who had slept for fifteen hours, was already dressed and waiting for Sandy to arrive.

Sandy entered the room, looking exhausted, but her eyes, while bloodshot, were bright and sparkling. "We heard from Mark last night. He reached Mystic just in time. Sarah is getting better. The other two kids who have AHA-B, Cee Cee and Eddie, will also improve over time."

Abby's eyes blurred with tears of joy. The part of her that had been numbed slowly came back to life. Feeling again was both a blessing and a curse. As the fog lifted from her mind, she recalled the events from inside the pill factory. She couldn't shake the image of Doctor Droznin placing the C4 on the floor and covering it with her body. The happiness from Sandy's news mingled with the shadows of her darker memories.

Sandy explained that Mark and Jonzy planned to remain in Mystic and use Wenlan's clinic as one of the major distribution centers for the antibiotic. "The submarine base in Groton is nearby. That can serve as a base of operations."

"Where's Jordan?" Abby asked. "We want to see Toucan."

Sandy's expression turned somber. "I need to talk to you and your brother first."

Abby's blood turned cold. "What's wrong?" she blurted.

Sandy took a deep breath. "Both of you need to hear what I have to say."

As they walked to the cafeteria to meet Jordan, Abby held off asking any more questions because Sandy seemed entrenched in thought.

They faced off in a quiet corner of the cafeteria. Abby and Jordan were on one side of the table, Sandy on the other. Abby gripped Jordan's hand.

"When your sister arrived," Sandy began, "she was very sick. She participated in an experimental drug trial and was one of the first children to recover from AHA-B. After that, they integrated her into the colony."

"Integrated?" Jordan asked.

"She moved into a unit and started attending classes," Sandy said. "There are some things you need to understand about Atlanta Colony. In some ways, it was similar to Colony East. But Doctor Perkins wanted Atlanta Colony to stand out. He wanted only the most brilliant children to reside here. He wanted to create an ideal environment for learning. Your sister was somewhat different."

Jordan objected. "Toucan is really smart."

Sandy raised her eyebrows. "Yes, that's true. She is smart, and has many incredible talents, but every child originally selected for Atlanta Colony is a genius. Doctor Perkins conducted periodic evaluations to make sure the children were performing at the highest academic level. If they weren't, he expelled them."

Abby released Jordan's hand and dragged her palm across her leg to dry off the sweat. "Touk is here, right? Doctor Perkins didn't kick her out?"

Sandy pursed her lips and nodded. "Your sister is here."

Jordan fidgeted. "So let us see her."

"Doctor Perkins believed that happiness promoted learning. Twice a day, the children participated in a spirit drill. They repeated phrases designed to keep them happy or identify things that were making them sad. They clipped sensors to their fingers that measured their varying emotional states."

"This place is weird," Jordan said.

Sandy nodded in agreement. "On the morning of her evaluation, Lisette refused to repeat the phrase that everyone in her family had died in the first epidemic."

Abby shot forward. "Why would they make her say that?"

Sandy grimaced, and Abby understood why. It wasn't Sandy's idea to run the colony this way, but she had played a role in it.

"Everyone's parents had died, and many of the children had lost older siblings and relatives. Doctor Perkins wanted every member of Generation M to focus on the future. He wanted them to bury their pasts."

Abby shrugged. "Jordan and I are here. Touk will see that we're alive."

It was hard to believe they were having this conversation. They should have seen Touk already.

Sandy looked away for a long moment.

When she turned back, Abby drew in a sharp breath. Sandy's narrowed eyes were glistening, seeming to burn with rage and smolder with despair. Abby's heart stopped. What awful thing had happened to Toucan that would elicit such anger and sadness?

"Your sister won't know you," Sandy said in a quiet voice. "They performed a medical procedure on her brain that essentially erased all her memories of her family. If they hadn't done that, Doctor Perkins would have expelled her. You, your parents, your home, your sister's former friends, those memories only exist deep in her subconscious."

A moment passed before Sandy's words fully sunk in. Then Abby chuckled in disbelief. "Toucan will know us. We've lived with her all her life."

Jordan made a face and nodded. "Trust me, she'll know us."

Sandy sighed. "I don't want you to get your hopes up. Many of Lisette's memories were erased. You have to prepare yourself. I'm going to have you speak with Doctor Ramanathan. She's been taking care of your sister since they released her from Medical Clinic 3."

Sandy led them to an area of the underground bunker that housed the kids of Generation M and then into an office that Doctor Ramanathan shared with other scientists. Sandy wanted to stay with them, but her radio squawked out another medical emergency, and she rushed off.

Waiting for Doctor Ramanathan, Abby and Jordan were alone in the office with nothing but their thoughts.

"We're buried in her subconscious," Jordan scoffed. "I wonder if she dreams about us."

"She'll remember us," Abby said. "Maybe not right away, but after a few minutes, she will."

"How could she forget Timmy and Danny?" Jordan asked. "They were friends for life."

"We're taking her with us no matter what she remembers," Abby said.

"Definitely," Jordan replied.

She and Jordan made a pact with their eyes to go along with their strong, verbal agreement.

Doctor Ramanathan entered the room and introduced herself. "Please, call me Chandra."

Appearing as tired as the rest of the adults, the scientist wore a white coat and was tiny. The top of her head only came up to Abby's nose. She had black hair that was tied up in a bun.

Abby decided she would call her Doctor Ramanathan. How could she be on friendly terms with anyone who had done that to Touk?

"I can see the resemblance," Doctor Ramanathan said. "Lisette will be right out. I asked her to wash her face and hands. I'm responsible for the girls in Unit 2A. When Lisette left Medical Clinic 3, she moved straight into my unit."

"Doctor Ramanathan," Abby said. "We're leaving in a few days, and we're taking our sister with us."

"You can't stop us," Jordan added.

The scientist smiled, but her eyes looked sad. "We all understand that you are her family, and we will support whatever decision you make."

A moment later, the door opened and Toucan stepped out. Abby's insides froze, melted, refroze, and then turned to steam, all within half a second. Touk was beautiful, stunning in fact. Abby had expected to see a wild mop of red curls falling to her sister's shoulders and hiding half her face, but the stubble of red hair revealed the brightness of Touk's eyes. The last time Abby had seen her sister, she was weak and feverish, on a couch in a dusty building just outside Colony East. Now she was taller and stronger, and when she grinned, Abby saw she was missing a tooth.

"This is Abby and Jordan," Doctor Ramanathan said. "They want to talk to you."

"I know you!" Touk cried, looking straight at Abby. Abby felt as if she had turned into a million particles of powder and was floating above the table like a cloud. "You're the girl on the television. You're really pretty."

Jordan made a face. "You were on television?" he asked Abby.

"I'll tell you later," she replied. "Can we be alone with our sister, please?"

Doctor Ramanathan nodded. "I'll be in the next room. Just knock on the door if you need me."

"Bye, Mother," Touk said.

Abby spun her head toward Jordan as he did the same toward her, trading looks of shock.

"That's not your mother," Jordan said.

Touk grinned. "I'll bet you all the chocolate in the world that she is."

"Touk, do you know who I am?" Jordan asked.

"What's Touk mean?"

"It's short for Toucan," he said. "When you were born, you had a really big nose. Abby said you looked like a Toucan. Mom liked the name so much that she started calling you Toucan."

Touk's grin contracted. "Mother calls me Lisette."

"She's not your mother," Jordan said in a loud, insistent tone.

Abby saw a wave of confusion pass across her sister's face. Then the grin returned. "Chandra is my mother. I'll bet you five pieces of candy."

"I'm Jordan. I'm your brother. I'm Jordie."

Toucan giggled. "Jordie. That's a silly name."

Jordan pranced around the room. "I used to carry you on my shoulders. We'd go to the library on Castine Island. Our dad worked there."

Toucan's look of confusion returned, and then Abby noticed she had clenched her fists and was shaking uncontrollably. Jordan was frightening her.

Abby bit her lip hard. Maybe Sandy was right. Toucan really did not know them, at least not yet. Her memories would return, though, later today, or perhaps tomorrow. They had to take it slow with her.

Abby squeezed her brother's arm, and they made eye contact. He understood her message immediately. He should back off. He sighed, producing his own expression of confusion.

Abby walked up to her sister. "I like your hair. Can I touch it?"

Touk's eyes widened with fear, but her curiosity seemed to sweep that away, and she cheered up. "Yes, I want to touch your hair too."

Abby reached out and lightly dragged her fingertips across Touk's scalp. Heat flowed into her hand, up her arm, and straight to her heart. Abby felt the same radiant energy spreading through her head and down her neck and into her chest when Touk ran her fingers through her curls.

Abby kneeled so she was face to face with her sister.

"That is a pretty necklace," she said, pointing to the silver heart that dangled from a silver chain around Touk's neck.

"Sandy gave it to me. She said it came from the tooth fairy."

"You know what the tooth fairy used to give me?"

Touk shook her head.

"A dollar for my tooth," Abby said.

"What's a dollar?"

Abby swallowed the lump in her throat. "Just a piece of paper. Can I hold your hand?"

Toucan stuck out her hand. Abby gently took it in hers and closed her eyes, concentrating on the small slender fingers. Abby had often feared she would never again experience the sensation of holding her sister's hand.

"Tell us about your friends," Abby said and led Touk to the table. Abby sat cross-legged on top of it and Jordan did the same. They used to sit like this on a picnic table back on Castine Island, and Abby hoped small gestures would help trigger Touk's lost memories.

Toucan told them about some of the girls she lived with. Lydia was always serious. Molly had nice hair. Zoe, her best friend, was messy. Charlie, the only boy she mentioned, liked to trip them during recess.

"Hmm," Abby said. "I don't like boys who trip people."

"I tell him to stop it," Touk said.

Abby cocked her head. "Charlie listens to you?"

"I put my hands on my hips." Toucan demonstrated. "I look him in the eye and say, 'Charlie, would you like it if someone did that to you?'"

Abby burst out laughing, and Jordan rolled his eyes. He was soon doubled over laughing, and Abby was laughing so hard there were tears dripping off her cheeks. Touk first looked somewhat confused, but she got a mischievous gleam in her eyes, and then she started giggling. For a moment, all the sadness and horror in the world evaporated, and the magic of shared laughter brought the Leigh family closer together.

"What about Timmy and Danny?" Jordan asked, trying to catch his breath. "Are they still your friends?"

"Who are they?"

"They live on Castine Island. We'll take you there to see them. We're leaving in three days. You're coming with us. The first place we'll stop is Mystic, Connecticut."

Touk clenched her fists and gritted her teeth. Abby knew she was trying to act brave.

Jordan told her about the fun things she would do once they arrived at Mystic. "A few five and six year olds live near the clinic. You're going to love them."

Touk's lower lip trembled, and the pace of her breathing quickened. A wet sheen coated her eyes. Unable to stay brave any longer, the dam burst and tears poured from her eyes.

Jordan was trying too hard, pushing Touk to remember, and rushing her at a time when patience would yield the greatest results. He didn't realize he was threatening to take Touk from the woman she believed was her mother and from kids she thought were her best friends.

It happened fast. Before Abby could try to comfort her sister, Touk hopped off the table, ran to the door, and rushed into the next room.

Doctor Ramanathan emerged. "I suggest we give Lisette a chance to calm down."

"You are not her mother," Jordan snapped. "She's our sister. We want to spend more time with her."

"Lisette says she doesn't want to see either of you right now," Doctor Ramanathan said. "Should I bring her out?"

"Yes," Jordan said.

"No. We'll come back." Abby tugged her brother's arm. She was his big sister, so she could do things like that.

An hour later, they were back again, and the message from Doctor Ramanathan was the same. Abby smiled to hide the ache in her heart. "Thank you. We'll come back later."

They returned three more times, and each time learned that Toucan didn't want to see them.

"We'll see her in the morning," Abby told Doctor Ramanathan.

Jordan went to help package pills for the Grits to distribute, and Abby returned to her room, where she collapsed in her bed from sheer exhaustion and cried herself to sleep.

DAY 8
CDC BUNKER

Jordan had grown taller and stronger, and he had changed in more ways than Abby could imagine. Her brother had a huge heart, and he was in love with a girl who seemed to be just as much in love with him. Regardless of all those changes, Jordan still couldn't hide anything from Abby. The moment he stepped into her room, the look in his eyes told her there was something important on his mind.

"Hey, how's it going?" he asked.

Abby heard another topic rumbling behind the words.

"Spit it out," she said.

"There's a flight today going to the airport next to Colony East." Excitement spiked in his voice. "They're taking pills to Mark. They're setting up Wenlan's clinic as one of the main distribution centers. They need lots of help."

"You want to go?" she asked.

"If you want me to stay, I'll stay. I'll stay with you and Touk, and then we'll all take the truck to Mystic together. Abby, it's your call."

"Go."

His jaw dropped. "Don't you want me to stay?"

"I'll be fine. I promise."

"It's because I scared Touk, right?"

Abby sighed. "I wanted to say the same things you did. You just beat me to it." She shrugged. "We have to coax the memories out of Toucan."

"I'm sorry for the way I acted."

"By the time Touk and I get to Mystic, I bet she'll be remembering things left and right."

Jordan's brow pinched. "What if she doesn't remember anything at all?"

"She will," Abby assured him. "It might take a week or a month."

"What if she never remembers?" Jordan persisted.

Abby pushed that thought aside. "Is Toucan our sister?"

"Yes."

"Will she always be our sister?"

"Yeah."

"Well, that's the answer. She belongs with us."

"You'll get her to remember things, I know it." He threw his arms around her. "Be careful, okay? In the truck, don't let Touk sit too close to the back. You hit a pothole, and she'll fly out."

Abby nodded as Jordan dispensed other words of advice. They had reversed roles. Jordan had become the bossy big sister, and she was the twerpy little brother who didn't have a clue what to do. In truth, they had both grown and changed and taken on the best qualities of the other.

Jordan hugged her again, and before Abby knew it, her little brother was gone.

8.01
CDC BUNKER

Just before Abby rapped on Doctor Ramanathan's door, she took a deep breath and reminded herself to go easy on Touk. She viewed her sister's memories as frightened animals, hiding away in a cave. They would emerge when they felt safe, and the way to create a sense of safety was to make Touk happy.

Toucan clung to Doctor Ramanathan's leg.

"Where's Jordie?" she asked in a whisper.

"He's playing with someone else today," Abby said, trying hard to smile.

Touk immediately relaxed and let go of the scientist.

Abby had arranged for Toby to meet her and Touk in the cafeteria. Every familiar face might trigger a memory. She had instructed Toby to make no mention of anything outside Atlanta Colony.

When she and Touk first entered the cafeteria, Abby guided her to a bowl filled with butterscotch candies and chocolates.

Touk grabbed a large fistful.

Abby wagged a finger. "Only three, please."

"Five," Touk said, clutching her haul of candies.

Abby held up two fingers. "Two. That's it."

"Five," her sister repeated.

As Touk's grin widened, Abby flashed back to the hundreds of bargaining sessions she had previously conducted, Leigh versus Leigh, a battle of wills, seeing who was more clever, more stubborn. Negotiating had always been one of Abby's most advanced parenting skills.

"Fine," she said, her heart melting into a puddle at her feet. "Five."

Touk's satisfied smile and the flash of victory in her eyes was all too familiar.

They took a seat at a table and ate their candy.

Toby, per their agreement, waltzed into the cafeteria and acted like he was surprised to see Abby.

"What are you doing here?" he asked.

"Toby, this is my friend, Lisette. Lisette, this is Toby."

"Nice to meet you, Lisette," he said, extending his left hand to shake.

Abby glanced at her sister, looking for a sign that she recognized Toby. Touk's bright cheeks and high-wattage grin remained consistent.

Touk grabbed one of Toby's fingers and shook it. "What happened to your arm?"

"I had a little accident." His tone was serious. "Actually, it was a big accident."

"Abby knows how to fix arms," Touk cried.

Abby gulped. Was it possible her sister had just remembered she was the first medical responder on Castine Island?

"You really know how to fix arms?" Toby asked, maintaining his serious demeanor.

Abby's heart was hammering. "I have many talents," she said.

They waited for an eternity, staring at each other in silence, Abby praying Touk had a little more to say. But her sister said nothing more on the topic.

Later that day, in another prearranged meeting, Abby and Touk bumped into Spike. Abby wasn't sure Toucan would remember the boy who had driven them to Colony East from Portland, but Spike had a real soft spot for Toucan. Abby thought there was a small chance that Toucan, even though she had had a high fever at the time, might recall something about him — *anything*. A tiny strand of a memory could unravel more memories from which she could weave a tapestry of her life before Atlanta Colony.

"Spike, this is Lisette. Lisette, this is my friend, Spike."

Spike went down on his haunches, so he was at eye-level with Touk. "Lisette, I really like that name."

"Spike is a silly name," Touk chirped.

"Not as silly as Arthur," he said with a grin. "That's my real name. Spike is my nickname. Do you have a nickname?"

Abby wanted to punch Spike in the nose. She had told him not to try forcing her sister to remember anything.

"Yep," Touk said. Abby held her breath. "Lisette!"

Spike winked. "Nice nickname."

"I like your drawings." Toucan reached out and touched Spike's forearm, which had purple moon and comet tattoos from wrist to elbow.

"Purple is my favorite color," he said.

"Abby, what's your favorite color?" Touk asked.

"Not purple."

"I like green," Touk said. "When my EM Light is green, it means I'm happy. When everyone's EM light stays green, we get a longer recess time."

Abby remembered Sandy describing the spirit drill the Generation M kids participated in.

"Green is nice," Abby said, hearing the disappointment in her voice. Touk remembered absolutely nothing about Spike.

Spike excused himself, saying he had to help distribute pills.

"Want me to read a book to you?" Abby asked.

Touk's wide eyes gave the answer. Her sister voicing, "Yes, please," was mere formality.

Abby had heard there was a library somewhere. She loved libraries. They reminded her of her dad, who had worked at the Cambridge Public Library, and after that, at the Castine Island Library. As soon as Abby was old enough to sit still, he'd take her to the library on Saturday mornings and let her flip through the picture books. After the night of the purple moon, Abby had taken Toucan to the library on Castine Island, where she'd read to her by candlelight. She hoped reading stories to her now might stir some of those memories.

Abby asked directions, and soon, she and Toucan entered the library. It was empty, though judging from the pillow and dirty pair of socks on the floor, someone had slept here recently.

The CDC library was as Abby had expected it would be. There were more computers than books, and the books were on scientific topics. She never expected to find *Frog and Toad* or *Chicka Chicka Boom Boom*, but she had hoped there would be books that the scientists had read for pleasure, stories that could also be enjoyed by a precocious five-year-old. *Robinson Caruso* or *Twenty Thousand Leagues Under the Sea*.

With nothing like that on the shelves, Abby decided she would tell a story to Toucan. "What type of stories do you like?"

"Pirate stories," Touk said.

Abby's spirit soared. On Castine Island, that had been Toucan's number one request.

Abby picked up the pillow, fluffed it, and rested it against the wall, where she sat and invited Toucan to sit beside her. "I'll tell the story of Peter Pan."

As she proceeded, Abby took breaks to ask Touk how she liked the story, and if she had any questions. Her little sister loved the story and had plenty of questions. "Where is Neverland?" "How can Peter fly?" "How much does Tinkerbell weigh?"

Abby resisted the urge to ask Touk any questions that might trigger a memory, but then, out of frustration and impatience and anger at what the adults had done, she broke down. "Do you like underdoggies?"

A swing set constructed of heavy metal pipes, with three long pairs of chains connected to seats, was the highlight of the Castine Harbor playground. Every kid on the island, young and old, loved getting an underdoggie, where a pusher would run ahead and extend their arms straight to launch the swing on its highest arc while they ran under it. Jordan had specialized in giving underdoggies, and Touk had specialized in pleading with her brother to give them to her.

Toucan scrunched her eyes. "What's an underdoggie?"

Abby wanted to say, "You'll find out soon enough," but instead, she explained how you gave someone an underdoggie. Toucan lit up and said it sounded like fun.

"Have you ever owned a pet?" Abby asked.

A cat had followed Abby home the night of the purple moon. They had named it Cat, and Touk had loved to chase Cat.

Touk shook her head, saying she had never owned a pet.

"Do you like smoked fish?"

Touk used to hate smoked fish more than anything in the world, and when that was all they had, Abby typically bribed her to eat it by promising her a tiny piece of chocolate. "No fish, no chocolate," she'd say.

Touk said she liked fish.

Abby continued to prod, but Toucan eventually stopped speaking, replying only with expressions of confusion. Eventually, she looked for a way to escape the interrogation, the way she had when Jordan had asked the questions. She was frightened again, exactly what Abby had vowed she would not let happen.

"I want to see Mother," Touk pleaded.

Abby held her breath and tightened her stomach muscles to keep from crying out in anguish.

After dropping her sister off at the Generation M living quarters, she counted the day as a failure, but she was ready to work with Touk for as long as it took.

If necessary, Abby would take Toucan to Mystic, no matter how frightened her sister was. Touk would calm down as she remembered more, and one day, she would thank Abby for rescuing her from Atlanta Colony.

DAY 9
CDC BUNKER

Abby climbed out of bed in the morning when her internal alarm clock went off — a growling stomach. Her appetite had returned, and it thrilled her to think she could simply walk to the cafeteria and get something to eat. She thought about getting Touk first, but then decided she'd use breakfast to plan how they would spend the day together. In thirty hours, she, Touk, and Toby would board the truck heading to Mystic, and there was a lot to plan for.

Abby used the toilet, dressed, brushed her teeth with toothpaste — another small thrill — and opened her door.

A package, leaning against the door, tumbled inside. It had Abby's name on it, so she picked it up, sat on her bed, and opened it. Inside was a note from Doctor Ramanathan and some type of thick report with Touk's picture on the cover.

She read the note:

> Every member of Generation M has a profile. It includes information gleaned from databases that existed long before the first epidemic, test results, and observations recorded by the staff.

You might be shocked by the extent of the information we've collected. You have to remember that we wanted to build a society for the future, and the more we knew about each child and their family, the better we could meet their needs.

I do not know if Lisette will ever regain her memory, but maybe you will find something in here that might trigger a memory. I am wishing the best for you, your brother, and your sister.

Doctor Chandra Ramanathan

Clutching her sister's profile under her arm, Abby walked by the cafeteria and went straight to the CDC library. It was empty again, and she cleared a space on a table.

On the cover of the profile, beneath Toucan's picture, was the number 944. That was her sister's Atlanta Colony ID. Unsure of what she would find, but excited by the promise, Abby opened the cover.

The first twenty pages provided information on her sister's health, with charts and graphs of her temperature, oxygen saturation, blood pressure, white blood cell count, and more. None of it was helpful to Abby.

She turned a page and gulped at a photograph of Toucan taken when she had first arrived at Atlanta Colony. Touk, on the verge of death, was pale and thin and her curls hung limp, greasy, and caked with dirt.

Abby scanned the pages of test results, three types of IQ scores, and notes made by Touk's teachers. *"Shows curiosity," "Strong class participation," "Respectful of other students."* Doctor Martin, her History of Science teacher, wrote, *"Mind wanders easily. Spends much of class staring out the window."*

The next section took Abby's breath away. It reported on the Leigh family, listing, among other things, the places where both her mom and dad had worked, and precisely how much money they made. Abby's school grades were there and so were Jordan's. She found it very strange that she had grown up with Jordan and had gone to the same schools, but she had never seen his grades until now, sitting in an underground research library, a thousand miles from their home.

The next page showed a family tree that went back three generations. There was information on her grandparents and great-grandparents, all her relatives, with their ages at the times of their deaths, and what illnesses and diseases they'd had.

Abby spent little time on this section because it made her sad.

She read notes under the title "Field Observations."

"Intervened to settle a dispute."

"944 demonstrated strong leadership potential."

"Generation M members often seek her advice."

"944 doesn't back down if she believes she's right."

"Can be stubborn at times."

Abby realized she was smiling, proud of what others had seen in Touk.

The final section showed entries made by Doctor Ramanathan.

"Wants to call me Chandra, saying she already has a mother."

"Caring, friendly."

"Lisette can make the other girls laugh with ease."

Abby paused, thinking that so far, in the entire report, this was the first time that anyone had referred to Toucan as "Lisette," and not "944."

She continued skimming Doctor Ramanathan's notes.

Page after page, the comments were remarkably similar, and Abby learned as much about the scientist as she did Toucan. Doctor Ramanathan truly cared about her sister, in the way their real mom would have.

Abby's eyes widened as she read the next entry.

"Emotion Meter light registered yellow, then red. Lisette said she was waving the light around, and it reminded her of chasing fireflies with her brother and sister on Castine Island. Said it made her sad. She misses them very much. Evaluation with Doctor Perkins today. Must work with her to improve her emotional state."

Abby's blood chilled when she came to the end of the thick document, accepting there would be a long, rough transition period for her sister until her memories started bubbling up.

She raced back to her room and stuffed the profile into the bag she was packing for the trip to Mystic. The profile belonged to Toucan, not the adults who ran Atlanta Colony. When Touk was old enough to understand what the profile contained, Abby would give it to her and let her decide what she wanted to do with it.

She found Doctor Ramanathan alone in her office.

"Thank you for Touk's profile," Abby said.

"Was it helpful?"

"Yes, I'm keeping it."

"I hoped you would," Doctor Ramanathan said. "There's valuable medical information inside on your sister."

Abby had expected an argument from the scientist. "May I ask a question before you get Toucan?"

"Of course."

"Can you tell me more about the Emotion Meters?"

The scientist explained how Emotion Meters were used during spirit drills.

"Can I borrow two?" Abby asked.

Doctor Ramanathan gave her a quizzical look. "In the unit, the EMs connect wirelessly to a monitoring station. The station won't be operational."

"Will the lights work?" Abby asked.

"Yes," the scientist said. She went to a cupboard and got Abby two of the clip-on devices.

Touk stepped through the door, grinning. "Hi, Abby."

"Did you wash your hands?" Doctor Ramanathan asked.

"Yes," Touk chirped politely.

Abby took her sister's hands and inspected them close up. "Did you wash them well?"

Touk gave her a big nod.

"Want to see where I live?"

Touk immediately tensed her shoulders, and Abby quickly added, "It's only around the corner."

Her sister's face brightened. "What unit?"

"The wildflower unit," Abby replied.

Doctor Ramanathan smiled, but her eyes were looking sadder and sadder.

As they headed to her room, Abby was glad she was holding Touk's hand, because of the incredibly warm feeling it gave her inside, but also because it helped her walk in a straight line. Abby's heart was pounding because she hoped Toucan was about to remember she had a sister and brother who both loved her more than anything in the world.

When they entered the room, Abby pointed to the poster. "See, wildflowers."

"Where do your friends sleep?" Touk asked.

"It's just me here. It's too small for anyone else to stay."

Touk pouted. "Where does Jordie live?"

Abby thought fast. "He lives in the Mystic unit."

"Do you get lonely without friends?"

Abby shrugged. "Sometimes."

Touk's face lit up. "Want to be my best friend?"

"What about Molly and Zoe and Lexi?"

"They're my best friends too."

"Lisette, I'd love to be your best friend."

Touk held out her baby finger. "Pinky swear."

Abby had to sit as she locked pinkies with her sister. She, Touk, and Jordan had lived by the pinky swear code. It was the most important promise you could ever make. If you broke your promise, rumor had it your baby finger fell off. Abby was quite certain that the CDC scientists had not introduced the concept of a pinky swear into the Generation M curriculum. Maybe not all of Toucan's past had been erased.

Abby took the Emotion Meter devices from her pocket and gave one to Toucan. Touk clipped it onto her index finger without a word, and Abby did the same. The tiny lights on each meter were glowing green.

Just then, Abby's blinked yellow.

"Are you sad?" Touk asked.

"I'm a little nervous," Abby replied. "I've never used an EM before."

"Watch this!" Toucan closed her eyes, and soon her light had turned red. She held her finger out. "I thought about Charlie. He pulled Molly's hair the other day."

"My turn," Abby said and closed her eyes, picturing the cabin on the lake in Maine. Some ducks flew through the trees and splashed down close to the dock where she, Jordan, and Touk were sitting cross-legged. The Leigh family was finally together again.

"It's green," Touk squealed. "What did you think about?"

Abby opened her eyes. "A make-believe place. Have you ever squiggled your EM in the dark?"

Touk grinned. "Turn out the big light."

Abby flicked out the light, and Touk waved her arm, making figure 8's and random squiggles of green in the darkness.

"Does it remind you of anything?" Abby asked, barely hearing her voice above the blood pounding in her ears.

"A star!" Touk held her arm straight up.

Abby's EM light flashed yellow. "Anything else?"

She felt the weight of silence crushing her. Then her light turned red.

"Are you mad at me?" her sister asked.

Abby heard the quaver in Touk's voice, and she turned on the overhead light. "No."

"Are you still my friend?" Touk asked.

Abby felt a hitch in her chest. "Yes."

Soon, her EM light was green again.

"Friends forever," Toucan said with a grin that kept spreading wider.

Abby unclipped the device from her. "Yes, forever."

Doctor Ramanathan looked surprised to see they had returned so soon.

"Lisette, I need to talk to Chandra for a minute," Abby said.

Touk skipped into the Generation M living quarters.

"My friend Toby and I are leaving tomorrow." Abby paused and swallowed hard. "Please have Toucan ready to leave with me in the morning."

The scientist nodded. Her smile was gone, and the sadness had drained from her eyes. Her eyes held only emptiness, a feeling Abby knew too well.

DAY 10
CDC BUNKER

Abby crawled out of bed at six a.m. A day like no other, she was about to take the first step toward piecing her family back together.

She played out the upcoming events in her mind. She'd get Touk at nine o'clock, and the two of them would meet up with Toby in the staging area. They would board the pill convoy headed for Boston, scheduled to leave at noon, and sometime tomorrow morning, after traveling through the night, the driver would drop them off in Mystic, where they'd move into the clinic with Jordan, Wenlan, and Cee Cee.

In the shower, Abby shampooed twice and stood in the warm water for a long time, thinking it might be her last hot shower for a long time.

In the cafeteria, she poured a bowl of cereal, added soymilk, and took a seat. She pushed the cereal bowl away after taking three bites, her stomach in knots.

Something nagged her. She had so much to be thankful for, but she couldn't ignore the feeling that something wasn't quite right.

Abby had ninety long minutes to wait before she could get her sister. She tried to kill time by watching adults drag themselves in and out of the cafeteria. Staring at the clock on the wall, she watched as the seconds turned into minutes, and the minutes piled up.

She got up at 8:50 and washed her bowl and spoon in the sink. She selected from the bowl of sweets two butterscotch candies and three chocolates and put them all in her pocket. With her heart racing, she left the cafeteria.

If only the three-minute walk to Doctor Ramanathan's office took three hours. Better yet, she wished for thirty miles of hallways that would require three days to walk. Abby couldn't understand how a moment of joy had turned into a moment of such dread.

She knocked on Doctor Ramanathan's door, and when the scientist opened it, Abby took a step back, startled to see she had let her hair down. The long black hair fell elegantly below her waist. Her puffy, red-rimmed eyes revealed that Doctor Ramanathan had been crying.

Abby's throat pinched. What she gained by Touk joining her and Toby, Doctor Ramanathan lost.

"Lisette wanted me to let my hair down," Doctor Ramanathan said. "She loves to run her fingers through it."

Abby stepped into the office and saw Touk's pack on the floor. On the pack was a crumpled piece of paper.

"I'll get your sister now," Doctor Ramanathan said and exited through a side door.

Abby sat in a chair but popped up immediately to pace, brewing with fear, excitement, and doubt. What was best for her sister?

She uncrumpled a wad of paper on Touk's pack, thinking it might be a note, some message that would tell her the right thing to do. Seeing it was just a sheet of paper with a stick figure drawing of a duck, she crumpled it up again and tossed it into the wastebasket.

Doctor Ramanathan returned with Touk and said in a shaky voice, "She's ready for her big adventure."

Touk didn't look ready for an adventure. Instead, she looked ready to run and hide. Her lower lip trembled, and from the way she was scrunched up her eyes, Abby could tell she was fighting back tears.

"Where's my duck?" Touk cried.

Doctor Ramanathan scanned the area and removed the crinkled paper from the wastebasket. She handed it over to Touk.

"They play a game called Duck," the scientist said to Abby. "It's really a silly game, but Lisette's friends wanted to give her something as a goodbye present, so they gave her the duck."

Touk squeezed the paper in one hand and wrapped her other arm around Doctor Ramanathan's leg.

"Lisette, you are going to be fine, I promise," the scientist said.

"Touk, we have to go now," Abby said. "Do you want some candy?"

"No," she said.

Doctor Ramanathan sniffled. "You have to go with your sister."

"She's not my sister," Touk cried and threw her arms around the scientist's waist, her head disappearing behind a curtain of Doctor Ramanathan's long, silky, black hair.

"Lisette, stop that." Doctor Ramanathan's tone was gentle, but firm.

Touk let go and lowered her eyes. "I'm sorry."

"Listen to Abby," she said and then looked up at Abby.

Whatever words she was going to voice, Doctor Ramanathan caught herself and said nothing. For a moment, Abby thought the scientist would burst into tears, but she managed to hold them back. She gave her the saddest smile Abby had ever seen and then left the room.

Abby approached Touk and held out her hand. "Can I see the duck please?"

It seemed to take forever for Touk to give her the crumpled paper.

"Do you ever win the duck game?" Abby asked.

Touk nodded.

"I knew it. Leigh's have always been very good duck game players."

Touk crinkled her nose, a sign she was curious and wanted to know more. The normal Toucan would have blurted out a question or five by now. Abby, more than anything, wanted to see the normal Toucan again.

Abby sat cross-legged on the floor and looked up at Lisette. "My family is the most important thing in the world to me. Sometimes we argue and fight about silly things. Sometimes we go our separate ways. But we always love each other very much."

Abby took Lisette's hand and pressed her palm against her chest and held it there. "Can you feel my heart beating?"

Touk nodded, her nose still crinkled.

"Every member of my family lives in my heart. Mom and Dad. Babka and Babki." Abby smiled through tears as she listed the adults who had died on the night of the purple moon. "Everyone is there, especially my brother and sister."

Abby pressed her palm against Lisette's chest. "Lisette, your family is in your heart, too. Will you give me a hug?"

Lisette stood before her with her shoulders slumping, the life draining from her face.

"Please," Abby said.

Slowly, her sister inched forward and rested her cheek on Abby's shoulder. Abby gently encircled her with her arms, as if she was embracing something fragile that could shatter at any second.

Abby recalled one time when the family had been together. It was on Castine Island, in their kitchen, during a weekend when her mom had come to visit. Toucan was two years old, sitting in her highchair, eating Cheerios. Giggling, Touk started throwing Cheerios on the floor and shouting, "Cheeries, cheeries."

Dad was washing dishes while Mom was cooking something, and Jordan was sulking, likely because Abby had beaten him to the bathroom to take a shower first. At the time, Abby wanted to get as far away from her family as possible and go visit her friends in Cambridge. But now, looking back, she came to view those times in the kitchen as some of the happiest moments of her life.

She pulled Touk closer until she felt their hearts beating together as one.

Abby leaned back. "Your mother loves you, and you have so many good friends. This is where you belong."

Lisette's eyes widened with hope. "So, I can stay here?"

Abby nodded.

She gave one of the biggest grins Abby had ever seen and threw her arms around Abby's neck.

A small smile played on Abby's lips. She may not have gotten quite what she'd dreamed of, but at least one of her wishes had come true — to see the normal Touk just once more.

Abby stood and opened the side door. Doctor Ramanathan was staring out the window.

"Lisette belongs here," she said.

When Doctor Ramanathan hugged her, Abby knew she had better leave or her legs would buckle.

She headed for the door that led to the hallway a thousand miles away.

"Abby!"

Abby froze. Her heart stopped. Hoping for the impossible, she swallowed hard and turned.

"Can I have the candy?" Lisette's eyes gleamed.

"Three pieces," Abby said in a shaky voice.

"Five," her sister shouted loudly.

Her eyes blurring with tears, Abby grabbed the candy and gave it to her sister. She left without uttering another word.

10.01
CDC BUNKER

Abby fractured into tiny parts and floated toward the staging area like a cloud of bees, her body disconnected from gravity, thoughts disconnected from her mind.

The din of voices, rumbling truck, motorcycle engines, and blaring horns grew louder as she approached the area.

She stopped before the organized chaos and frenzied effort to save as many lives as possible.

Pills arrived from the Alpharetta plant by the truckload. Here, at the staging area, the pills were packaged into smaller containers and then shipped to various destinations across the country.

Toby appeared out of the crowd, wearing a big grin and dark circles under his eyes from days on end with little sleep. "Where's Touk?"

"She's staying here."

He turned red with anger. "Just when I thought I could trust adults!"

"I want her to stay. The adults will take good care of her. Chandra loves her. Touk's safe here, and she'll get the best education ever. My sister will grow up to be a leader."

Toby persisted. "We love her more. Abby, we'll be her teachers. We'll keep her safe."

Abby's brain was as conflicted as ever, but deep in her heart, she felt she had never been more right about anything. "If we took her to the lake in Maine, I'd be doing it for me. Leaving Touk here, I'm doing it for her."

"So we'll stay here," he said. "You can be around her."

Abby lowered her eyes. "I thought about that, but it might confuse Touk, and it would definitely confuse me. I have to go."

Toby put his arms around her, and as Abby pressed her cheek against his shoulder, she gazed at people helping people and felt something inside of her awaken.

She gently pushed back, keeping her hands on Toby's shoulders. "I don't want to go to the cabin in Maine."

He narrowed his eyes. "First, you're leaving Touk. Now you don't want to go to the place you've been telling me about for days. I'm worried about you, Abby."

"I don't want to go to Mystic, either," she said. "At least not right away."

Toby's jaw dropped. "Abby?"

"Jordan and Wenlan will be there to help the kids in Mystic. Kids are dying and frightened in other cities and towns. We know what they're going through. They need our help. I have to try to do something."

Toby took a deep breath and finally gave a nod. "That sounds like someone I used to know on Castine Island."

"I knew that person, too," she said with a little grin. "Does that mean you'll join me?"

Toby gave her a long kiss that she interpreted as a resounding yes. The boy had stolen her heart. He was the one; she was certain of that.

They split up and spoke to convoy drivers, asking them their destinations and exactly when they planned to leave. Every driver Abby spoke to had room for more passengers. When Abby and Toby met up, Toby reported hearing the same thing. The need for extra drivers and help once a convoy reached its destination was a constant. They narrowed their choices to one of two convoys. Every destination needed help, but these two were leaving within minutes.

"St. Louis or Cleveland?" Abby asked. "You choose."

Toby raised his eyebrows. "I've always wanted to see the Mississippi River."

An hour later, she and Toby were passengers in a truck that brought up the rear of a convoy headed for St. Louis, a city in the middle of the country. They sat in the far back, facing the shrinking Atlanta skyline, and then the buildings finally faded from view as the truck rumbled northwest. Bounced and jostled by potholes, they held hands to maintain balance and support. The convoy sped up, and the ride got smoother.

Abby saw a tiny bulge in her front pocket and knew from the shape that it was the last butterscotch candy. Touk had only received four candies. In their final bargaining session, Abby had firmly held the line.

She reached into her pocket and took out the candy. Using one hand, she carefully unpeeled the plastic wrapper and bit the candy in half. The two pieces were close in size, but she offered the slightly bigger piece to Toby.

He was sound asleep.

She set her piece in her lap and wrapped his half in plastic, which she placed in her pocket, and then held up her piece.

They would arrive in a city that had yet to receive any pills and where many of the survivors had probably never heard of AHA-B bacteria. Even the existence of the colonies might be news to many of them. They would arrive tomorrow, still many hours away.

Today, this minute, this second, Touk and Jordan were safe, and Abby was alive and holding the hand of the boy she loved and who loved her.

She placed the candy on the center of her tongue. As the bumpy ride jostled her side to side and the tornado of life swirled all around her, sweetness spread out.

ONE YEAR LATER
EMORY CAMPUS

Lisette adjusted her headphones for the daily spirit drill. They were comfortable and fit so snugly that she hardly felt them on her head.

"I will study hard." The woman's voice was soft and soothing.

"I will study hard," Lisette repeated.

Filled with excitement, she twisted and twirled pieces of her hair, hoping it would soon be long enough for her to use a hairband. Today was special, and Lisette couldn't wait for the spirit drill to end. The six and seven-year-old students were taking a field trip to the ocean. They were going to get to ride in a blue CDC bus.

It would be her first time seeing the ocean while awake. She dreamed about the ocean a lot. Ever since her biology teacher, Mr. Taber, had started the unit on marine life, she'd been having vivid dreams about the ocean. Sometimes, the water was purple, and when the big waves crashed on the rocks, a spray of purple droplets shot up.

Sometimes, she'd wake up in the middle of the night, smelling salty air. She wondered how the ocean really smelled.

"I will share the knowledge that I learn."

Lisette sat up in bed and placed her feet on the floor. "I will share the knowledge that I learn."

In the glow of the nightlight, she could see her roommate, Zoe, lying on her side in bed and pretending to write on the wall with her fingertip. The green dot of the Emotion Meter light made it easy for Lisette to make out the letters that Zoe was tracing: H-A-R.

She guessed immediately what Zoe was writing: CHARLIE. Charlie, who was six and half years old, lived one floor below them in Unit 4R. Over the past week, Charlie had lost three teeth. He had let Zoe wiggle all three. She was the only girl he let wiggle any of them. Lisette smiled fondly, wondering if Charlie ever traced the letters Z-O-E on his wall with his EM light.

"It is important to be kind."

"It is important to be kind," Lisette said as her impatience to leave Atlanta Colony on the bumpy bus grew.

"I believe in myself."

"I believe in myself," she said with a sigh, scuffing her feet back and forth, anxious to start the day. The friction warmed the soles of her feet.

The woman continued to say phrases, but Lisette ignored her, thinking about the ocean instead. Mr. Taber had said they might see all sorts of sea life on the beach.

"If we're lucky, we'll even find starfish," he had said. "They crawl around the bottom of the ocean, and sometimes the strong currents push them on shore. If they're alive, we'll throw them back in. If they are dead, then they will make a nice meal for the seagulls."

Lisette hoped they'd find starfish that were still alive.

Finished tracing CHARLIE on the wall, Zoe turned and removed her headphones. She signaled for Lisette to do the same.

"Will you sit next to me on the bus please?" Zoe asked.

A rush of warm tingles in her chest brought a smile. "Sure," Lisette said.

Having made a bargain of friendship, both girls put their headphones back on.

"I am strong, and I believe in myself." The woman raised her voice a bit, though she still sounded quite friendly.

"I am strong." Lisette lifted her arm high and pretended the green EM light was a fish swimming toward her.

Mr. Taber had said that some fish live at the bottom of the ocean where it is dark all the time. "They have parts of them that glow. It's like these fish are swimming around with their own little flashlights."

"I believe in myself," Lisette said, flopping back on the bed.

She stretched her arms and legs wide, imagining she was now a starfish, and she brought her finger within an inch of her nose. With a green spray of light in her eyes, she was face to face with a flashlight fish at the bottom of the ocean.

She jolted as sharp images of a girl and boy appeared in her mind. She recognized them immediately. The girl was Abby, the boy Jordan. The last time she saw and spoke to them seemed like a long time ago.

The scene she pictured felt so real. It was nighttime, and the air smelled salty. That meant the ocean must be nearby. Lisette held a glass jar in her hand. The three of them wereoutside in tall grass. The grass was dry and crunchy on her bare feet, and hundreds of blinking lights surrounded them. She caught one of the lights in a jar. It was a little bug. The light kept blinking on and off.

"Abby, look at this," she cried out.

Abby ran over. "That's cool, Touk, but you should let it go."

"Touk," Lisette said to herself, though she didn't know why she said it or what it meant.

Just then, Jordan slid in the grass beside them and lay on his back, looking up at the stars.

"Let her keep it," he said.

"The firefly wants to be free," Abby whispered in her ear. "Let it go, and I'll give you a piece of chocolate."

"Two pieces," she said defiantly.

The hair stood on the back of Lisette's neck as she remembered that she, Abby, and Jordan had gone outside to catch fireflies. Her brother and sister had let her stay up way past her bedtime. Lisette's heart raced, and she trembled all over. Abby was her sister. Jordan was her brother.

Lisette pulled off her headphones and drew her knees to her chest, afraid and excited at the exact same time.

The door to the unit opened, and Mother entered. Lisette noticed her EM light was flashing red.

Unhurried, Mother walked over to Lisette. She unclipped the Emotion Meter from Lisette's finger and sat beside her on the bed. She put her arm around her shoulder and pulled her in close. "What's wrong?"

Lisette sank into the spill of long, soft hair as if it were a warm pillow, and pressed her cheek against Mother's chest.

When Lisette breathed in, the smell of the ocean, raw and salty, swept away the sweet scent of Mother's shampoo. Memories rose from the depths of her mind in a stream of bubbles. When they popped, she saw new faces and heard voices. They were her friends on Castine Island. She knew Timmy and Danny. That was her home. The tide was low, and the rich scent of seaweed and clams uncovered by the water began to rise up.

Lisette pressed her ear flat and tried to count the beats of Mother's heart. The loud, rapid beats of her own heart made that impossible. Then she heard Abby's voice. "Your family will always live in your heart."

"I'm Touk," she whispered. Then louder, with a proud smile, "I am Toucan."

Made in the USA
Middletown, DE
12 November 2014